RAHAB LINK

J. ALEXANDER McKENZIE

Bethany Fellowship INC.
MINNEAPOLIS, MINNESOTA 55438

For Dora Ann Bradshaw,
fallen asleep.

The Rahab Link
J. Alexander McKenzie

Library of Congress Catalog Card Number 79-55750

ISBN 0-87123-492-0

Copyright © 1980
J. Alexander McKenzie
All Rights Reserved

Published by Bethany Fellowship, Inc.
6820 Auto Club Road, Minneapolis, Minnesota 55438

Printed in the United States of America

Acknowledgment

This book could not have been written without my having known two men:

Ted Harrison, unselfish and generous in life because it's just the way he is.

And Bob Levy, gone now, who gave to me the typewriter on which the manuscript was prepared.

I owe a debt to both . . .

J. Alexander McKenzie

The Canaan Trilogy

The Omega Document
The Rahab Link
The Jordan Intercept (Fall, 1980)

When God created man He foresaw that life on earth would need an ingredient to give it flavor.

So God said,
Let there be irony...

Anonymous

Prologue

The clock on the instrument panel told Ben Caplan that twenty-five minutes had passed since they had taken off from San Diego's Lindbergh Field. With their ETA less than five minutes away, he hoped they were now over the Coachella Valley, the area of their destination. Strapped in his seat next to the pilot, he swallowed hard as the light plane began to lurch violently.

"It's just the pesky thermals!" the pilot was yelling at him.

Somewhat reassured, Ben looked over his shoulder to check on the only other passenger besides himself. But Professor Wolf Shertok seemed as unperturbed as the pilot, as if riding a bucking roller coaster was a normal enough exercise on an early Sunday morning. The raw, early sunlight lent an even more striking quality to the already impressive visage of Wolf Shertok. The elderly professor was a page out of ancient Jewish history, like pre-Talmudic. The heavily lined and rawboned face was that of an aged farmer, a combination of two opposites, of implacable stubbornness and a kind of divine resignation, topped off by an unruly mass of coarse, wavy hair, which for some time now had seemed inclined to turn respectably gray, dissuaded, perhaps, by the will of its master.

The plane's left wing dropped abruptly, and they started a long, slow turn to the west. A few seconds later the engine lost more power. By now they were surprisingly close to the ground, and Ben briefly caught sight of a cluster of buildings in the otherwise desolate high desert rushing away under them. They should now be over the ranch called Canaan, owned and operated by Joshua Bain and Alan Hunt, a pair of enterprising young men who had gambled everything on this isolated piece of real estate and had just about pulled it off. Working together for over a year, the two men were affectionately referred to by their friends as the Canaan team.

The plane banked in over the short landing strip. A butler-type hangar stood next to the tarmac, and Ben noticed that the wind sleeve on the roof was hanging limp. He stiffened in his bucket seat as the pilot began his one-eighty. Although they needed Joshua Bain and Alan Hunt, he figured that the need was mutual. Rancho Canaan was not on the verge of bankruptcy, but it was having its financial difficulties, perhaps not an unusual circumstance for a business at the end of its first year. In its new format, the former dude ranch catered to the tournament crowds following the winter golf and tennis circuits who flocked annually into the Palm Springs-La Quinta wonderland. As of the first of June, yesterday, Rancho Canaan was formally shut down for the summer. For the Canaan team, it was now a time for reflection, a brief time of rest, perhaps, before turning to future plans. A time, too, for making ledger entries, of figuring profit and loss, of counting dollars.

The roar of the plane's engine brought Joshua Bain out of the open door of the hangar, the shady lee facing southwest. A pilot himself, he watched with interest as the single-engined aircraft turned in from its southerly heading. The right wing went up smoothly, then the nose down. Too tight, Joshua thought, seeing the plane was dropping in too close, off to the right of the center axis of the narrow strip. Then, almost as if by remote control he had made the delicate adjustment himself, the plane lost power slightly, correcting its angle of approach by allowing its own inertia to slew it sideways.

Nodding his approval, Joshua leaned back against the warm metal wall of the hangar. Standing an even six feet tall, he slouched forward in his natural tendency to crouch. He was a few pounds lighter now, after the past few weeks' outdoor work around the ranch, scaling in at an even one eighty-five. And, except for the distraction of his blue-gray eyes, he was the product of the desert he loved. Dressed only in frayed Bermuda shorts and weathered deck shoes, he was burned mahogany brown from top to bottom, so that there was little distinction between the rest of him and the dark brown of his curly, rebellious hair. At age thirty-three, Joshua Bain was capable of showing many moods. Now he was relaxed, looking perhaps a little confident. He was content, and he showed it in his easy motion, the continual hint of a smile around his eyes.

The plane had touched down on the tarmac and was now abreast of the hangar. Joshua lifted his arms and signalled the pilot to park in the early-morning shade off to his right. For a few moments, he watched closely as the passengers began to emerge from the plane.

Ben Caplan climbed out first. About Joshua's height, he was more slender and a bit nervous in his movements. He was also younger, about twenty-eight by Joshua's estimate. A special agent in the FBI's Special Litigation Section, Benjamin Caplan had been the intermediary between the Canaan team and the U.S. Attorney General, a past encounter growing out of their role in helping to frustrate a local conspiracy.* Joshua liked Ben Caplan, especially his brashness without being overly impulsive, tempered by a tendency to attend to small details and procedure. Ben Caplan had always managed to keep them, generally, honest.

The other passenger climbed awkwardly out of the plane, so that as he dismounted, the aircraft shifted in response to the loss of his weight. Clear of the wing, the older man straightened up, dwarfing Ben Caplan by two or three inches. He looked around him appraisingly, surveying in one sweeping glance the hangar and the surrounding terrain. In his left hand he carried a thin-line briefcase.

Joshua stepped forward wordlessly to warmly embrace Ben Caplan. He pushed him away after a moment, holding him by his shoulders while he briefly studied his face. "You look a little pale, my friend," he said good-naturedly. He was aware that Ben Caplan hated flying.

"God made him to be a shepherd," the older man suggested, his voice rumbling into the new desert morning, "so that he does not understand the way of the eagle."

Obviously embarrassed, Ben Caplan turned quickly to introduce Professor Wolf Shertok.

"An honor, sir," Joshua said as he took the extended hand. As expected, the grip was sure and strong. Joshua's first impression was that Wolf Shertok up close was a formidable man, one who could obviously inspire awe in his zealous support for the cause of his people, Israel.

With Joshua leading, they moved into the hangar, passing by an empty office on the left and pulling up next to a long workbench which ran for about twenty feet along the inner wall. Beyond the workbench, there was a second room opening into the hangar, the spare-parts and tool crib. The door to the wire-enclosed crib was closed and locked. A white pickup truck was parked about ten feet away from the workbench, and lashed down to the truck's flatbed was a pair of off-road dirt bikes.

---

*The Omega Document, Bethany Fellowship, Inc., 1979.

"You said you wanted in and out in a hurry with minimum exposure," Joshua offered, "so we can conduct our business right here." He had arranged three metal folding chairs in a semicircle on the bare cement floor between the bench and the truck. Across from them, beyond the truck, a DeHavilland Otter was parked tail inboard, and Joshua noticed out of the corner of his eye that Ben Caplan was staring quizzically at the twin-engined Otter.

"We sold the 690 two weeks ago," Joshua told him, refering to the Commander 690 he had legally inherited when he and Alan received a clear title to Rancho Canaan. He was smiling a little then, knowing that Ben Caplan's dossier on the ranch had not yet recorded the sale of the 690, which after deducting the cost of the used Otter, had left them with enough cash to make it into the next season. What Ben Caplan also didn't know, however, was that Rancho Canaan was in the process of contracting to develop a nine-hole practice golf course on the premises.

Wolf Shertok took the metal chair nearest to the bench, where he put down his briefcase. As he settled himself heavily into the chair, he glanced sideways at the sticker affixed to the truck's rear bumper, which read in bold letters, "I FOUND IT."

"A novel and meaningful expression," Shertok said, pointing to the sticker.

"My partner would be pleased to hear you say that," Joshua said. "He is proud of his conversion, likes to share it—"

"You mean he believes in Jesus Christ?"

"Yes, sir."

"Then why didn't you say so?"

Joshua shrugged once after a moment, not knowing what to say.

"I have a sticker on my bumper also," said Shertok soberly, "which says, *We Never Lost It*," and he looked squarely at Joshua, the hint of a smile under his heavily shrouded eyes.

"A novel and meaningful expression," said Joshua warily. He was curious why the older man appeared to be making an issue out of the bumper sticker.

"I think so," agreed Wolf Shertok.

"But it denotes a new kind of tactic," Joshua offered.

"Oh?" questioned Shertok.

"Yes, sir," said Joshua respectfully. "I think the word is proselytize."

Wolf Shertok drew his great brow together and cocked his head sideways before admitting, "Your interpretation is probably correct."

"Times do change," Joshua suggested pleasantly.

"Yes," Shertok agreed. "Even doctors and lawyers are doing it now."

Ben Caplan cleared his throat, breaking the following silence. "We are short on time, sir," he said to the older man, "and we have much to cover."

"Of course," Shertok said cordially. "Please get on with it."

Joshua gratefully relaxed, leaning back against the fender of the truck.

"As you may recall, Joshua," Ben started in a low monotone, "about a month ago, eighteen kilograms of plutonium were reported missing from a San Diego-based production facility, a company called Armatrex, Incorporated. The MUF, which stands for Material Unaccounted For, was thoroughly checked out by the FBI and the Nuclear Regulatory Commission."

Joshua was nodding affirmatively, for he did recall the news reports on the incident. It was also in the back of his mind that Israel and China had been somehow or other involved in the reports.

"Both the FBI and the NRC jointly agreed," Ben went on, "that there was a chance, but only a chance, mind you, that a foreign government might have been involved. Of course, the unofficial word that leaked out was that Israel had engineered the diversion."

"Nothing but lies!" Wolf Shertok insisted heatedly.

"All right, sir," Ben said placatingly. "You agreed to let me be the spokesman."

Wolf Shertok did not retreat, but he did manage to convey his silent consent to let Ben continue.

"The fact of the matter is that the Government could not produce hard evidence one way or the other. At best, what they have is circumstantial."

"What do they have?" Joshua asked.

"A QC inspector at the plant disappeared at the same time the MUF occurred. The FBI was able to trace him out of the country to Mexico City. His name is, or was, Stanley Fielding, a Jew. A native-born citizen with a gold-plate record."

"So what does that mean?" Shertok interjected again, and this time he had a look of contempt on his rugged face. "So every time a Jew anywhere commits a crime, does that mean the State of Israel is automatically at fault!"

Ben Caplan looked resignedly down to the concrete deck.

In sympathy with his friend and feeling his own impatience, Joshua was compelled to say, "Have we gone to all this trouble just to discuss unfair indictments—"

"I'm sorry," Wolf Shertok offered quickly, shaking his head stubbornly. "But you must understand how frustrating this all is." He held up his right hand in a gesture of conciliation. "I agree not to say a word unless I'm asked to."

"Another item working against Fielding," Ben continued, "was that he had a younger brother who immigrated to Israel several years ago. Fielding was also active in soliciting funds for Israeli causes, though on a very low-key basis. Also, the morning after Fielding arrived in Mexico City, the Mexican authorities verified that a man matching Fielding's description boarded a flight for New York City on a British passport bearing an alias. This man then transferred to an overseas flight to Tel Aviv."

Joshua simply shook his head once.

"Yeah," Ben commented, as if reading Joshua's mind. "A nice pat getaway, leaving a trail even I could follow."

"And, of course," Joshua noted then, "his brother hasn't seen him—"

"Naturally," Ben confirmed.

"So why doesn't the NRC simply clarify the situation, clear the air?"

"The NRC is bound by a National Security Council edict not to officially or otherwise release any information relating to weapon's grade nuclear material that turns up missing."

"It wouldn't matter that much, anyway, now," Wolf Shertok offered passively.

"That's true," Ben agreed. "The damage has been done; there are enough anti-Israel people in the Government and the U.N. to keep twisting it around, no matter what the truth is."

So the Jews were hurting, Joshua thought. Trumped up or not, the suspicion existed, unfortunately, at a time when Israel desperately needed all the support and confidence she could get from the United States. A suspected thief was on limited options at the door of the house he supposedly had just pilfered. "You must have something," he said. "It seems likely that Fielding was killed by the actual thieves, which means the man traced to Tel Aviv was an imposter."

"There's no question about that," Ben agreed. "After Fielding was traced to Mexico City, it was discovered shortly thereafter that an American matching his description was accidentally burned to death in an auto accident just outside Mexico City. Using the ID found in a briefcase in the car's trunk, the Mexican authorities routinely notified the next of kin through the American Consulate. The address was listed in Los Angeles. A brother showed up the next day to claim the body. Within two days the remains had been cremated and the brother returned home."

"So you've got his address," said Joshua, "from the Consulate."

"Yeah. An empty office on the west side."

Joshua raised an appreciative eyebrow. "Scratch one Stanley Fielding."

"But all is not lost," Ben went on, "which is why we're here." He got up from his chair to take the thin-line briefcase from Wolf Shertok. "About three months ago, Israeli intelligence in Beirut received a tip that a top Arab agent was leaving Lebanon for an unknown overseas destination. The only info available on the man was that he would be travelling under a known alias and that he had in his possession a letter of credit drawn against a Damascus bank. Well, after a week of close surveillance, which included stopovers in Zurich and Tokyo, he managed to elude his tail at Los Angeles International Airport. Even though he was heavily disguised, Tel Aviv went routinely to work trying to identify him. A couple of possibilities emerged. One, the right one it turns out, was that our travelling Arab was none other than one Fawd Al-Shaer." Ben pulled an 8x10 photograph out of the briefcase and handed it to Joshua. "This is the only picture we were able to get of him while he was en route."

"We?" repeated Joshua curiously. It was about time to start finding out some things about his guests. Waiting for Ben to answer, he studied the picture, a grainy, overexposed print of a man wearing a hat, dark glasses, and a heavy beard. For purposes of identification, the picture was worthless.

"Yes, we," Ben finally said.

"Ha Mossad?" asked Joshua.

"I don't know why that is necessary," said Ben defensively.

"Why don't we wait until we close the agreement?" Wolf Shertok suggested.

Joshua nodded his approval.

"The only ID details," Ben went on, "that Tel Aviv had on Fawd at the time was a sketch provided from the memory of a sole survivor of an El Fatah raid commanded by Fawd."

"So what's with this Fawd character?" Joshua asked as he handed Ben the photograph.

Ben grunted once, shook his head. "It's difficult to describe the man—"

"He's a ruthless killer!" exclaimed Shertok. "A mad dog, a beast diseased with hate."

Ben ignored the interruption. "Fawd is a kind of legend among his own people. Non-aligned and uncommitted to any one group, he is still a fierce and rabid supporter of Palestinian independence at any cost, especially at the cost of dismantling Israel."

"Okay," said Joshua, "so you lost him at LAX."

Ben nodded once. "He simply disappeared. About a month later, Professor Shertok came to me for help to track down Fawd. And, that's when I went on leave of absence from the Bureau. Tel Aviv had finally uncovered the letter of credit. It had been issued in the name of an export company here in Los Angeles, an Aerotec, Limited, which specializes in providing spares and other support material to Middle-East based airlines. Since it was my only lead, I started with Aerotec. I first made a covert entry, photocopying most of their files. I also staked out the office, and, working alone, it took me nearly two weeks to hit pay dirt."

"Fawd?" Joshua asked.

"In the flesh. One of the Aerotec outside salesmen resembled the sketch provided by Tel Aviv. So I followed him to one of his accounts, Lockheed in Burbank, and picked up his name off the salesman register in the purchasing lobby. A Paul Jaylis. I took his picture the next day, gave it to Professor Shertok. Within twenty-four hours, Anne Delemar positively identified Paul Jaylis as Fawd Al-Shaer."

"I presume this Anne Delemar," said Joshua, "is the sole survivor—"

"Yes. She was sent from Israel to identify Fawd if and when we found him."

"She is working with you then."

"Yes," Ben confirmed. "The next day we received orders from Tel Aviv to take Fawd as soon as possible. The basic plan was to kidnap him, take him across the Mexican border and deliver him to a transfer team who would ultimately get him to Israel for trial." Ben hesitated for a moment, reaching up wearily to rub his forehead. "Two days later, before we could grab him, the Armatrex MUF took place . . . It was like Fawd was one step ahead of us all the way."

"So you had a whole new ball game," Joshua observed.

"Yeah," said Ben. "So, for the past thirty days we've been backtracking Fawd to the time he entered the country. And, we are now absolutely convinced that he was involved in the MUF. He was, for example, in San Diego three times in the two weeks immediately before the diversion. During the same time frame, he exhausted an entire credit line of three quarters of a million dollars."

Joshua heard himself whistling under his breath. He could not conceive of a man spending such a huge sum of money without attracting attention unless he was a very clever man, a very clever man indeed.

"And there's no evidence," Ben said, "that any of the money went into Aerotec."

"Okay," said Joshua as he pushed away from the truck's fender to stretch his tiring back muscles. "So you've taken on the task of having to prove Israel's innocence, and the only way obviously is to expose the real thieves. And, you are convinced that this Paul Jaylis, alias Fawd Al-Shaer, masterminded the plot."

"He's capable of it," Shertok assured him. "And, it's in his style."

"Why is he still in the country?" Joshua asked then. "I mean, like, if he's done his thing."

"That's another added question we'd like to answer," Ben said, "beyond exposing him for stealing the plutonium."

"Well, then," Joshua said matter-of-factly, "expose him."

"We've gone as far as we dare go," said Shertok, "on our own, that is."

"You can understand, Joshua," said Ben, "that at the moment Israel cannot afford to be caught engaging in covert intelligence operations in the United States."

"You mean like a Jewish spy under every bed," Joshua said evenly.

"Something like that," Ben answered. "We're desperately trying for peace, Joshua, and we especially need credibility now."

Wolf Shertok grunted derisively as he stared out the open

front of the hangar into the distance. "Why is it," he said slowly, reflectively, "that we have to earn international respectability, while every other nation in the world is assumed to already possess it . . . "

Like, guilty until proven innocent, Joshua was thinking as he observed the bitterness in the older man's voice and demeanor. "So then," he said, "you want me and my partner—"

"Exactly," Ben confirmed quickly. "We need proof, absolute and without doubt. And we need a field team to put it together—and quickly. I can handle the inside, but we need a hard-nosed outside team."

Joshua addressed himself to Wolf Shertok, "You are aware, sir, that we are not professionals in this kind of business."

"Which is one of the prime reasons why you were selected," Shertok assured him. "If the operation blows up on us, the Canaan team will be much easier to explain than a pair of known or identifiable agents. Besides, Ben has persuaded me that you both are quite competent to carry out the assignment. And, more importantly, is the fact that you apparently can be trusted."

"All right, then," said Joshua, "how much are you willing to pay and when?"

"Twenty-five thousand now, in cash," Ben said, "and another twenty-five when it's finished."

Joshua shook his head. "Fifty thousand now," he said firmly, "and another fifty in thirty days, regardless of whether it's over or not."

Ben Caplan sighed heavily. He then looked apologetically at Wolf Shertok, speaking briefly to the older man in Hebrew, the words flowing rapidly, low and deep in his throat. Ben looked away, then, out the open front of the hangar.

"What was that all about?" Joshua asked.

Wolf Shertok shrugged his great shoulders indifferently. "He says I should try to understand that you are an assimilationist, that you've probably lost your Jewishness . . . "

There was less of a smile around Joshua's eyes now. "Is it also part of your strategy, Wolf Shertok," he said evenly, "that we now lapse into a discussion of who is more a Jew or who is less a Jew—"

"No," Shertok said. "But I will not deny him an opinion."

Joshua smiled thinly. "So that now, in your old age, you no longer find it better to dwell in the corner of the housetop."

Wolf Shertok roared at once, slapping his right knee, his brief explosion of laughter rattling the walls of the hangar. "Ah, Joshua," he said after a moment, "you are a hard man." He chuckled then, shaking his head wonderingly. "Would you settle for fifty thousand now, with twenty-five payable at the end of the operation, provided you produce?"

"Plus expenses?"

"Agreed."

Joshua thought for a moment before saying to Ben, "We're in as long as Alan goes along; if not, you'll know before the day's out." He turned to Shertok, "Would you mind, sir, if I had a private word with Ben?"

"Not at all," Wolf Shertok said quickly, and he stood up to face Joshua squarely. "By the way, do not be offended by my inquiry regarding the bumper sticker, whose message, you will have to admit, shows considerable influence from your partner," and he paused for a moment as if to allow the remark to register. "And, as you may now also be aware, all of our loyalties may very well be put to the test in the near future."

So that had been his motive, Joshua was thinking blankly.

"I'm sure," Ben interjected, "that Joshua's sympathies—"

"Don't misunderstand," Shertok said; "it is not my intent to expose sympathies, or, especially, to seek them. I simply want it on the record that on this morning we have contracted at least a friendly and reliable ally, which I am fully satisfied we have." He extended his right hand. "May God be with you, Joshua Bain."

Joshua watched the older man thoughtfully as he moved out of the hangar toward the waiting airplane. "He sure covers all the bases," he mused quietly, more to himself. Then it occurred to him that Shertok had made it clear that their relationship was a contractual one, a business enterprise, which appeared to leave both him and Alan off the hook in the event a test might require an expression of loyalty. He forced himself back to the present, turning to face Ben Caplan, who now was avoiding his eyes. "Okay, my friend, start giving with the answers. For example, what's the connection between all of you and Tel Aviv?"

Ben Caplan delayed before answering, "I am truly sorry, Joshua, for what I said—"

"Forget it, my friend. A man ought not to be sorry for saying what he believes. Besides, it is better that things between us be fully in the open."

Ben turned to the workbench and snapped the briefcase closed. "You're right," he admitted. "As you've already guessed, the Israeli Secret Service started the investigation, which they coded Operation Rahab. Wolf Shertok is a kind of quasi official resident for Ha Mossad, the Israeli equivalent to our CIA." He checked his watch. "We've got to get moving. Shertok has a dinner speech tonight in L.A., and he starts getting nervous if he thinks he might be late." He picked up the briefcase. "This is yours. I've detailed out all I can give you to date. Go over it and then burn what I've marked to be destroyed. I'm assuming Alan will go along." He was smiling as he handed Joshua the case. "There's also fifty thousand dollars in cash in here."

Taking the case, Joshua sensed an even higher appreciation for the prowess and wisdom of one Wolf Shertok. "I expect you're right about Alan," he said amiably, "and I'll probably be calling you tomorrow morning. We can make arrangements for a rendezvous near LAX. In the meantime, ask Shertok to get me a complete dossier on this Anne Delemar. Also, an action profile on Paul Jaylis."

"That'll have to come from Tel Aviv."

"I should hope so. And on Aerotec, too. And, at least one company which could or is doing business with Aerotec, a local company we can infiltrate and use."

"No problem. Shertok can probably arrange that in five minutes."

Grinning himself, Joshua fully appreciated Ben's overstatement.

Alan Hunt remained still until he heard the plane take off. He then took the headset off and shut the tape recorder down before turning to the door of the tool crib. A few seconds later, Joshua walked up to the wire-screen door to unlock it.

"Get it all?" Joshua asked thoughtfully.

"Every word," Alan said. He reached up to smooth down his long black hair rumpled by the headset. Shorter than Joshua by only an inch, Alan Hunt also weighed less at his normal one hundred and sixty-five pounds, so that his build was more slender, like that of a swimmer. He, too, was dressed only in a pair of well-worn Bermuda shorts, preferring soft leather moccasins. "Ben got to you, didn't he?" said Alan.

Joshua shook his head once. "What would you do if someone accused you of losing your . . . shall we say, your Americanness?"

The question caused Alan to chuckle knowingly. It was his claim, when he was questioned on the subject, that his nationality was the more provincial Californian, in lieu of the expected "American," since he was native born to the state and not at all sure of his mixed origins. It was Joshua's opinion that his partner's seemingly never-ending vigor was the consequence of his hybrid ancestry. "The question is not the same for me, is it?" Alan proposed. "I mean, if you really think about it, to ask *you* the question sounds and seems reasonable, as if the answer is important."

"Perhaps," said Joshua offhandedly.

"Kind of tells you something."

Joshua promptly changed the subject. "So what do you think? Do we go?"

"Why not?"

Joshua stared out the open front of the hangar, out across the high desert of Rancho Canaan. It was getting on toward midmorning, and the first wind was kicking up, bringing with it the need for decisions and planning. "Yeah," he said evenly. "Why not."

"The Lord has provided an answer to our prayers," Alan suggested.

Joshua nodded once, indicating at least passive agreement. "Yes, perhaps He has, but I have the suspicion that He's laid it out so that we're going to earn every penny."

"A fair proposition," Alan suggested as he moved to the rear of the truck. "In the meantime," he added as he dropped the tailgate, "we've got a fence to repair," and he vaulted to the truck's bed to start breaking the two motorcycles loose from their moorings.

*Hear, O Israel: The Lord our
God is one Lord:
And thou shalt love the Lord thy
God with all thine heart, and with all
thy soul, and with all thy might.
And these words, which I command
thee this day, shall be in thine
heart:
And thou shalt teach them diligently
unto thy children, and shalt
talk of them when thou sittest in thine
house, and when thou walkest by the
way, and when thou liest down, and
when thou risest up.
And thou shalt bind them for a
sign upon thine hand, and they shall
be as frontlets between thine eyes.
And thou shalt write them upon
the posts of thy house, and on thy gates.*

*— part of the inscription on a small parchment scroll,
called a MEZUZAH, placed in a case fixed to the door-
post of some Jewish families as a sign and a reminder of
their faith. Some believers, too, wear the MEZUZAH on
their person as an expression of their faith.*

Chapter one

According to Joshua's mileage estimate, the San Diego suburb of Del Cerro was only about a twenty-minute drive from Lindbergh Field. Coming onto the outbound Mission Valley Freeway, he checked his watch to see if he was right on schedule. Conscious now of the need for precise timing, he carefully steered the rental car into the right-hand center lane, holding the Cougar on fifty-five miles per hour because he had no inclination to tangle with the highway patrol over a speeding ticket. He used the few moments of free time to assess the past week's developments:

Item. Ben Caplan had spent most of the week profiling Aerotec, Ltd., running quarterly comparisons back for one year. A product-mix analysis on material purchased by Aerotec during the same period revealed that during the past two quarters ninety percent of the company's purchases of machined parts had been made from an organization bearing the strange name, Society for the Brotherhood of Man, a kind of commune operation located in the coastal community of San Eliso. According to Anne Delemar, who had been at the SBM commune for the past two weeks, the commune was self-supporting, drawing on several small in-house manufacturing operations, including leathercraft, back-packing equipment, and a machine shop.

Item. That Aerotec should be purchasing short-run machined parts was normal enough, since much of the aircraft spares export business included hardware, the nuts and bolts variety. However, the added shipping costs from San Eliso to Los Angeles plus the extended freight time would make the SBM commune noncompetitive with the hundreds of machine shops already in Los Angeles.

Item. Alan Hunt, posing as a close friend of Anne Delemar, had spent the past two days and nights as a guest of the Society for the Brotherhood of Man. Alan would meet Joshua at Lindbergh Field at 1:30 p.m., at which time they would drive back together to Los Angeles for a late-afternoon meeting with Ben Caplan and Wolf Shertok. The content of Alan's report would determine if he were to stay on at the San Eliso commune.

Item. With Wolf Shertok's approval, Joshua on Monday

had taken field command of Operation Rahab. By Wednesday night, he had in his possession Tel Aviv's best available report on Fawd Al-Shaer and a dossier on Sheila Vardi, alias Anne Delemar. On Thursday morning, with Alan Hunt en route to San Eliso, Joshua had assumed his cover role as a buyer for the West L.A. manufacturing company, also selected by Ben Caplan to provide their command center.

Joshua noticed on the next offramp directory that he had only a half mile to go. He flipped the turn indicator before starting to edge slowly into the right lane. His stomach turned over, a reaction to the upcoming fact that he might be about to make a most critical rendezvous.

A few minutes later he was cruising slowly past the Del Cerro synagogue. The building was windowless from the street, a stark granite structure reminding Joshua of a bunker. He spotted two unoccupied cars in the parking lot, so he turned the block to park on the adjacent side street. Before leaving the car, he once again checked the tape recorder hanging beneath his jacket and under his left arm. As he got out to walk slowly toward the synagogue, he continued to inspect the neighborhood, on the lookout for occupied parked vehicles which might hide a stakeout. He was feeling a little paranoid as he rounded the back corner of the synagogue to pull up in front of an unmarked service door. He knocked on the door hard.

A few seconds later the heavy metal door swung open. Joshua introduced himself to Rabbi Joel Meyers, who looked to be about fifty or fifty-five years old, and who upon taking his hand literally pulled him inside the building. The door closed behind them with a slam. Joshua realized he was in a darkened hallway and had to grope for a few steps while his eyes adjusted. He had the feeling that he had just been yanked bodily into some sort of fortified position on the Golan Heights.

"You're early," Rabbi Meyers said to him over his shoulder.

For good reason, Joshua thought without answering, while also wondering why Solomon in his wisdom hadn't added to his classic "there is a time to love, a time to hate," the further observation that there "is a time to be early, a time to be late."

"In here, please," the Rabbi told him severely, opening a door to a side room.

Joshua stepped in obediently to find himself in a small office. There was a desk and a couple of chairs to his left. An old but spotlessly clean mimeograph machine was at the other end of the room between ceiling-high shelves holding reams of packaged paper. He was turning to thank the Rabbi when he heard the door shut behind him. He again checked the tape recorder, making certain it didn't show. Satisfied, he flipped the rocker switch. The voice-activated unit began to record as he reported, "Saturday, June 8. Location is Del Cerro. Time is approximately 11:30 a.m. Subject is Mrs. Stanley Fielding."

The date imprinted under the porcelain tank cover in the bathroom read "APR 5 1932." It occurred to Alan Hunt that the house was old enough to be his father's. The old decaying house, apparently a Victorian variation at the time of its construction, still stood solidly enough, a tribute to the materials and workmanship of a more concerned and conscientious bygone era. Picking up his Bible and shaving kit, Alan left the bathroom to move along the second-floor hallway toward the stairway. Above him, the spacious attic had been converted to more living quarters, housing the commune's male singles, where he had spent the last two nights. This floor, apparently a buffer zone, accommodated the few married couples, while below, the first floor provided dorm space for the single girls. He dropped down the curved stairway, moved across the tiled foyer to the doors opening into the recreation room. The doors were open, as usual, another feature of the philosophical expression of the Society for the Brotherhood of Man, so that one could wander at will, without challenge, through the thirty-some-odd rooms of the enormous mansion. He gingerly walked through the open doors.

His objective was the so-called office, which took up a small part of the original living room, now converted to a library and a kind of after-hours recreational room. Both the wall across from him and to his left were covered from floor to the high ceiling with packed bookshelves. There were at least twenty chairs spread around the room, of various sizes and shapes, with several small tables. A single desk stood directly in front of the large bay window on his right. The floor space immediately around the desk was respected as the "Office." The only occupant of the room was sitting behind the desk, and he looked up as Alan tapped on one of the doors.

"Come in, brother," the man said congenially as he stood up.

Smiling in return, Alan walked across the room to take the hand of the man known only as Kabir. The commune's founder and senior elder, Kabir gestured for him to sit down. Taking his chair, Alan had already filed away everything in his mind he had been able to learn about the man before him. Age difficult to guess, probably thirty-five to thirty-nine. Height close to 5'6", slender build. Thin face, slightly receding chin. Long black hair, straight. Alert black eyes. Delicate features, especially his hands. His slender fingers were almost those of a child, and they caught the eye because they never bent at the first knuckle. His dark skin and facial features suggested that he might be from the Far East, maybe Iran, perhaps India.

"Anne tells me you may be leaving us for the weekend," Kabir was saying. His voice was well modulated, deliberate, at a lower octave than his size suggested. There was a slight accent, but Alan couldn't pin it down. One thing was for sure, Kabir was a well-educated man.

"Yes," Alan told him. "You see, I'm still undecided about whether to stay on." He looked away then, as if he might be embarrassed.

"I take it," Kabir suggested amiably, "that Anne Delemar is the foremost reason why you're here." He had been shuffling a few papers around in front of him while he talked. "Although I admit it is none of my business."

"She is a good part of it," Alan admitted, "but I'm at a kind of critical stage right now, trying to decide what to do with my life." He sensed at that moment that the words were not coming easy to him, that he was involved in a pretense which he could only justify on the grounds that it seemed to be something he had to do.

Kabir had looked down to the Bible in Alan's lap. "I understand that you are a Christian."

The statement seemed appropriate for the moment, and Alan was at once relieved that he had the chance to speak the whole truth. "I believe in Jesus Christ, and I have accepted Him," he said straight-forwardly.

Kabir nodded slowly, understandingly, as he said, "So you are waiting for the voice now to tell you to turn either to the left or to the right."

Alan realized he was staring now, slightly befuddled at the scriptural allusion. "Yes," he finally admitted. "Something like that."

"The will of God is often difficult to perceive."

"Amen," Alan confirmed.

Kabir abruptly straightened up. "You are welcome back if you choose to stay," he said evenly. "Mind you, though, if the voice tells you to be an evangelist, so that you are compelled to save the soul of every sinner you encounter," and he turned up his delicately boned hands, "we would prefer you seek other more fertile fields. Of course, we have no desire to demean your faith."

Alan was also smiling. "Of course," he said.

"You know the rules," Kabir went on. "So long as you and Miss Delemar are not married, you must reside in the separate dorm areas."

"I understand that, but I'm not sure about the money."

"If you can afford it, we ask three dollars a day, principally to cover the cost of your food. After you are employed in one of our vocational shops, there is no charge. Why don't you pray about it, then decide."

Alan nodded appreciatively. Seeing that the meeting was over, he stood up. He then reached into the back pocket of his slacks and pulled out his billfold. "May I please pay you for the time—"

"Absolutely not," Kabir insisted as he stood up.

After saying good-bye to Kabir, Alan moved out of the huge house. He estimated that the old estate grounds took up about six to eight acres of prime seaside property. The setting was like Southern California idyllic. The beach terrain in the area moved up sharply in a kind of escarpment about ten feet higher than the high tide line, and the rear of the main house sat back from where the high ground began at a distance of about fifty feet. The landscaping included a dozen varieties of trees, ranging from pine and fir to dense-trunked palms, all in an advanced stage of growth and together numbering in the hundreds. There were two major gardens, one directly behind the house and the other to the front. A hundred yards or so away from the house on either side were two separate cultivated areas where vegetables were grown.

Alan turned the corner of the house facing south, looking for Anne Delemar. It was Saturday, the day when all the commune members shared in the chores organized for the one day. As he crossed over the cement driveway leading alongside the house, he glanced curiously at the sunken loading dock used by trucks servicing the machine shop located in the basement. He was reminded again that the only door in the entire house having a lock was the one located on the west wall of the basement machine shop.

He found Anne Delemar, along with several other commune members, hoeing weeds. Her back was turned to him, and Alan was content to wait at the near edge of the cultivated field. It was getting warmer now as the day began to turn to its best time. The early morning haze was starting to burn off, and in another hour the sun would be fully out for the rest of the day. Later on, the afternoon ocean breeze would kick up for a few hours, bringing with it the aroma of plankton and seaweed filtering through the trees and shrubs, and the day would finally cycle down to a pleasant evening of subtly declining temperatures. He looked up then to see that Anne Delemar was walking toward him, picking her way carefully along the narrow furrow between the new corn. So far as he could tell, the only clothing she had on was a weathered pair of Levis, a loose cotton man's shirt, its tail out and hanging down over her slim hips. Like most of the others, she was barefoot. While working, she had pulled her long black hair around into a loose knot behind her neck.

Watching her come closer, Alan swallowed once, perhaps a little uneasily. It was important to their cover roles that they put on a show of affection toward one another, and, so far, he figured they had pulled it off convincingly enough. Now, however, it was good-bye time, and he was not so sure what he should do, especially with the others looking on. He was wishing for more time to think it over, but she kept on coming and then she was there, standing in front of him, and he was no closer to an answer than he had been before.

"Hi," she said a little breathlessly, her face slightly flushed from the work. She reached around behind her neck to break the knot to let her hair fall down around her shoulders. She shook her head once before reaching out with her free hand.

Taking her hand, Alan shifted once, glancing apprehensively over his shoulder. Without shoes she was still only an inch or two shorter than he was. "I've got to get going," he finally said.

She stepped in a little closer to him then, tipped up her head, and for the first time he noticed that her incredibly brown eyes were enclosed by a fine black line.

"Why don't we go down to the beach," she suggested.

"Yes," he said gratefully, and he quickly turned in that direction, along the provided way of escape. She dropped her hoe, deftly catching up as he strode out purposefully. A few seconds later, he helped her down the incline backing up the sandy beach. Even there, they could still be seen from the house, so as they began to walk slowly along the beach she moved in close to his left hip, her arm around his waist. Alan nervously checked his watch. He still had an hour before meeting Joshua at Lindbergh Field.

"You're pretty good with a hoe," Alan observed. The tide was out now, and the beach was quieter than usual. Ahead of them, about a quarter of a mile away, a group of board surfers bobbed about in the languid surf line as they waited for a set to build.

"I should be," she was saying. "In Israel, we also raise most of our food."

Of course, Alan thought. She would be right at home in the commune, and he glanced aside to look at her profile. Anne Delemar was not a beautiful woman, by some standards, he supposed. When she smiled, which was not very often, she showed her even teeth in a most disarming way. No matter how her face brightened, however, there was still in the depth of her dark eyes an implacable kind of suspicious hardness. Like she was pretending the mood she appeared to be in, and the pretense was difficult, so that when the brief mood passed the attending strain was also relieved. It was then that he noticed for the first time the thread-like scar coming down from the corner of her right eyebrow. He looked away and down as she glanced up.

"You have an unfair advantage," she said.

"How is that?"

"You know much about me, but I know nothing about you. Kabir says you are different, perhaps a bit of a mystery."

He laughed self-consciously. "I'm the least of any mystery."

"He says you are a Christian. I mean, a more serious one than usual."

"I don't know what that means," he said truthfully. "Maybe it's because I haven't known the Lord for too long a time. I don't try to be different, though I know I have changed. Why, does it bother you?"

She shook her head quickly. "Of course not. It's just that I'm curious, trying to find out more about you."

He stopped moving then, holding them both in the warm sand as he dropped his eyes to look down at her. "My grandfather on my mother's side was a Cahuilla Indian who in his later years managed a turkey farm near the reservation where he was born, which by the way, is not far from here. He married a Mexican immigrant, a migratory field worker, and, from what she told me before she died, my mother was born in a dried-out irrigation ditch." He hesitated, staring out to the open sea, before adding, "The timing of the birth was apparently awkward, since it was a few days before Thanksgiving, and my grandfather was busy butchering the turkeys. My grandmother died in the same ditch, unattended and alone, unable to get help." He looked down again to see that she was studying him. "I'm sorry—"

"There's no reason to be sorry," she assured him. "It is not necessarily so tragic a thing, since, after all, had it not happened you would not be here today."

Alan looked away again to the open sea, thinking that her logic was more utilitarian than most, that the suffering of his grandmother had been both right and useful in that it had produced him, ultimately. "So we are to accept," he said inquiringly, "that the means are justified by the end?"

It was her turn to look away, following his line of sight, before she answered, "That concept does not really apply, since its application involves a certain expectation and foreknowledge of the end."

She's no dummy, he was thinking to himself. Or, perhaps she had gone over this same ground before.

"Regardless," she was saying, "you've made it to this point."

He nodded his head in agreement. "I was born on the same reservation as my father."

"And your parents?"

"My father was a lusty hard-living rascal who loved his family, treated us all well." Alan realized he was smiling then. "It was kind of inevitable, I guess, that he didn't last too long. He was killed in an automobile accident when I was eight years old."

"And your mother?"

"She passed away several years ago. I have an older sister left, who is married, living in San Francisco. My mother tried her best to raise me, but I guess I had some of my father's gypsy tendencies. I left home early, spent most of my youth in and around San Bernardino and Riverside, where I became heavily involved in the local gang activity. I was arrested many times, escaping only because a lenient judge allowed me to join the service as an alternative to going to prison. I was farmed out of the Marines because of repeated offenses, mostly AWOL. I didn't take too well to the discipline. I've spent a lot of time on the beach, worked in Las Vegas in a martial-arts act for a while, and ran with whoever would have me, including one of the most noteworthy motorcycle gangs on the coast. You might say I don't come too highly recommended."

She was studying him closely now, and he looked away, feeling embarrassed at his outburst. "I'm sorry," he said again, "but you wanted to know."

"For my part," she was saying gently, "you come highly recommended. But, what really interests me is the way you are now. You've obviously undergone a heavy change. I mean, like, are you really a professional in this kind of work?"

Alan heard himself chuckle softly. "Hardly, an amateur at best. Joshua and I are involved because of our friendship with Ben Caplan, nothing more. You already know most of the rest, the ranch, and why we're here." He checked his watch. "I must be going," he added abruptly.

"I guess what I'm trying to ask," she said huskily, "is whether you will be back?"

"It will depend on the outcome of today's meeting. We'll have to go over the film first."

"What about the locked door in the basement?"

"We'll ignore it for the time being," he told her. "If there is something important behind it, then it's probably rigged to sound an alarm." They turned away from the tide line to start back up toward the main house. "If it's necessary, we'll come up with some sort of plan." They were both quiet for the time it took them to reach the south side of the house.

"What should I do?" she asked then.

"Just play it cool, like no change."

They walked on past the center front garden, to pull up at the edge of the gravel-covered parking lot. It was now absolutely time to say good-bye, Alan thought awkwardly. As if she were waiting, Anne Delemar leaned back against the front fender of the Jaguar.

"So there's the chance you might not be back," she observed, her voice low and throaty. Facing the direction of the surf line, she tossed her head once, letting the wind clear the hair away from her face.

"From what I can put together," he said finally, "I expect I'll be back."

She turned to look at him, the first part of a smile on her

face, and Alan Hunt didn't know what to make of the gesture.

"I hope so," she said softly.

He nodded once, started into the car.

"They might be watching," she suggested as she moved next to him.

He straightened up, and in his nervousness he almost glanced over his shoulder toward the house. He realized then that her arms were around his neck, pulling his head down. Their lips touched so briefly there was no time for response, and several seconds passed before he finally realized he had been left alone.

Joshua Bain knew he was impatient to the point of carelessness in dealing with the fine details of any endeavor. The thunder of the commercial jet passing directly overhead distracted him now, and he paused in his note-making to look up at the huge aircraft climbing out and away from the nearby runway. He was smiling then, grateful for the interruption, finding himself wishing that he were at the controls. Leaning against the trunk of the Cougar he had just turned in, he glanced once around the car rental lot, wondering now where Alan Hunt might be. His partner was his opposite in such matters, normally always prompt, very detail conscious, and immeasurably much more patient. Sighing once, he put the small notebook away in his jacket inside pocket.

The meeting with one Martha Fielding had been at best dull, tempered without any doubt by the surprise presence of Edwin Fielding, her father-in-law, who obviously had showed up to protect the best interests of his deceased son's wife. Martha Fielding's responses had been vague, even evasive, her demeanor close to one of depression. Joshua was nonetheless content with his impressions, the more reliable gut variety. Significantly, the most worthwhile outcome had developed at the very end, when Joshua discovered that Mrs. Stanley Fielding was being followed. The tail was very discreet, very professional, and made Joshua wonder why, after all the time since the MUF, the Government was still interested enough to budget such close surveillance.

The dark green XK-120, vintage year 1952, pulled up beside him, bringing him out of his thoughts. He surveyed the drophead coupe briefly before climbing in. Alan had nicely camouflaged the outside to make it look rundown, befitting a man of his alleged unemployed status. The engine, too, hidden under the strapped-down hood, loped and rolled now at idle, suggesting it was radically out of tune and in need of repair; when in fact the Detroit-bred V8 was at the peak of its full-house capacity, capable of delivering some four-hundred-plus raw horses to the rear wheels.

Folding himself into the passenger bucket seat, Joshua noticed that Alan Hunt was smiling broadly. "I'm glad to see," Joshua said, "that you've got something to feel pleased about."

Alan punched the transmission into low gear and started out of the lot. "It's good to be back on the beach," he said. "Although the San Eliso slope is a bit too shallow for the best surfing." Out of the lot, he followed the sign directing them to Highway 5, the coast freeway to take them to Los Angeles. "There's a storm between here and Hawaii," he went on, "so we should have stronger wave action by tomorrow night."

"So you figure on going back," said Joshua.

"At least for a while longer," Alan said. "We can take a look at what we've got, decide later on. But, there's something going on. It's weird, but mighty interesting," and he looked aside to Joshua. "How did it go with you this morning?"

"Likewise weird, and interesting," said Joshua. "First, it's inconceivable that Stanley Fielding would've willingly gone along with an anti-Israeli plot of any kind, especially if he actually knew, or even suspected, that he was working with an Arab agent."

"You say willingly," noted Alan. "You mean they forced him maybe?"

"Doesn't figure. It took weeks, maybe months, for them to cook up that diversion scheme. Unless Fawd had another inside contact, which the record disputes and which I doubt also, then he had to rely entirely on Fielding to give him the details on the plant layout, schedules, plans, procedures. Once Fielding gave him the info, Fawd then had to lay out the plan. Rework it, iron it out. Deliver it to Fielding. Set the date. Maybe even a dummy run. Transport had to be arranged." Joshua stared out the side window, pulling on his lower lip. "Had to take at least a month, even on a crash basis. Time, my friend . . . Time . . . "

"They still could've forced him," Alan said, "by threatening his family."

"Uh-uh," Joshua disagreed. "Time, remember. Sure, you can force a man to do about anything as long as he's present, standing right there, while you're holding a gun on his wife and boy. But for several weeks Fielding was out and about, and he's thinking all the time. Remember, he was dedicated to the Israeli cause. His kid brother is a pilot in the Israeli Air Force." Joshua shook his head. "And all he's got to do is walk to the nearest phone and call the FBI. And, more importantly, just the *chance* that he would do that has to make it too risky for an operator like Fawd. You see, we've got to go on the assumption that Fawd wanted the plutonium bad enough to have a more foolproof plan."

"So he bought him off," said Alan. "It's been done before."

"No chance," Joshua offered absently. "But I'm reasonably sure I know how Fawd could have pulled it off." He was quiet for a few seconds before adding, "All he had to do was to pose as an Israeli agent. I mean, like knowing as little as I do about Fielding suggests to me that Fawd must've had the battle half won before he even opened his mouth. There's no doubt that he conned Fielding, probably sold him a bill of goods about the survival of the State of Israel, how the material was probably going to be used for experimental purposes only, or whatever. But, that Israel *had* to have it, at any cost, in order to survive." He waved his hand. "Plus a whole bunch of other similar incentives that a clever man like Fawd could cook up."

Alan chuckled ironically. "It's astounding, sometimes, to realize how small the world really is. That Fawd, for example, even made the Fielding connection."

"Not at all," Joshua commented idly. "Further confirmation of the theory, in fact, like credibility. The younger brother, now an Israeli citizen, is proud of his brother and his work, especially his access to nuclear material which was never a classified matter. Assume that Arab intelligence was only reasonably efficient. Fawd might've even fronted himself in with Stanley, using his brother's name."

Alan stared thoughtfully down the freeway ahead of them for a few more seconds before answering, "So it's a workable idea. But, then, like you said, Fielding still had the time to think it over. Remember, Ben said that Fielding had a gold-plate record as an American citizen too. It must not have been easy for him."

"Yeah," mused Joshua after a thoughtful moment. "A dandy point. Fawd probably had him on a time-release program, like jacking him up at regular intervals. Besides, Fawd had to know better than I do that Stanley Fielding would never have turned in an Israeli agent to the FBI."

"So how does this theory help us?"

Joshua settled himself deeper into the comfortable bucket seat, so that his eyes were level with the top of the walnut-finished dash. "It's like when you start out on a deal like this," he said conversationally, "you actually start in the middle." He leaned his head back into the black leather seat and closed his eyes. "Something has happened beforehand, the start of it all. And, hopefully, something more will follow. Right now I'm trying to get the front end cleaned up."

"Is it cleaned up?"

"Not yet," Joshua said quickly. "This Fielding situation is far from being settled."

"It's too bad he's dead."

"That's the understatement of the year."

Chapter two

The street, Pepper Tree Lane . . .

It derived its name from the trees during the middle twenties, when several of its original occupants jointly agreed that the then popular Colorado palms were really a nonfunctional fad, so they planted the utilitarian pepper trees along the easement of their new street. Duly approved and recorded by the Los Angeles County road department, the new street in the beginning was a deadend, only two blocks long, zoned for private residences only. As time passed, the pepper trees flourished, their squat and dense trunks forming a seemingly permanent and impregnable picket line, a kind of comfort and reassurance to the home owners.

As time passed, too, change came inevitably to Pepper Tree Lane. Entry to the short deadend street was off Sunset Boulevard, which during the next ten years became a major east-west thoroughfare. And during the same time frame, the automobile came into its own, especially in sprawling Los Angeles, bringing with it the need for new and extended roadways. Because of its position, Pepper Tree Lane was turned into a minor link between Sunset Boulevard and a newly developed route between downtown and the San Fernando Valley, via the Cahuenga Pass.

In time, its geography made Pepper Tree Lane further unique, since it turned out to be at the center of the square mile deemed to be the hub of the county's population, an accidental demographic fact of little normal interest.

Pepper Tree Lane, however, was destined for a disabling encounter with fate before it took a more final place in history.

The cover company selected by Wolf Shertok was located in a Culver City industrial complex not far from the Santa Monica Freeway. Occupying ten-thousand square feet of production and office space, Visualon, Incorporated, was a company engaged in the design and manufacture of lighted panel systems for use in both commercial and military applications. The panel systems included LED matrix, edge-lighted units, as well as custom lighted displays, with heavy design emphasis on and preference for use in aircraft. Of interest to Joshua Bain and the Rahab team was the fact that the panels typically used mounting hardware of the type brokered by Aerotec, Ltd.

"I hope I can pull it off," Joshua said soberly, referring to the cover role he had to play as a buyer for the company.

Alan Hunt set the handbrake on the Jaguar and shut down the engine. They had just parked in the employee lot adjacent to the Visualon building. He glanced sideways at Joshua. "Shouldn't be a problem," he assured his partner. "After all, you've spent half your life in and around airplanes."

Joshua didn't answer as he climbed out of the car, putting the matter away until later. Alan joined him as he started toward the employee entrance.

"Let's keep it to ourselves," suggested Joshua, "about my suspicions concerning Stanley Fielding."

Alan grunted once. "Time to compartmentalize."

Joshua was chuckling under his breath as they pushed through the heavy metal door. Alan's use of the term "compartmentalize" was so out of character as to be comical. Neither of them was a professional in the field of covert investigation, having previously been involved in such activity as an accidental consequence of circumstances beyond their control. They'd been lucky, very lucky.

According to Alan Hunt, luck was the will of God.

A few seconds later they entered the Rahab command

center, a 9x12 cubicle, a compact space borrowed and partitioned off from the room used to store and repair the company's test equipment. Access during normal working hours was through the main lobby. Seated at one of the two small desks, Ben Caplan was on the telephone. He lifted his left hand in a gesture of greeting and continued talking. Wolf Shertok came up from behind the other desk. Like Ben, he too was in his shirtsleeves.

"Welcome to the tomb," he said disdainfully.

Joshua closed the door carefully. "Yeah," he agreed, surveying the room once again. Tight quarters, but functional. One did not loiter in this room; you either worked or got out. Ben hung up the phone as Joshua sat down on the corner of his desk. Alan Hunt slipped into one of the two chairs placed between the two desks.

"This is the ID on the Fielding tail," Ben told Joshua, turning up a piece of scratch paper.

Joshua ran over the name and address. "La Jolla," he said to himself. He had called in the license plate number to Ben before leaving Lindbergh Field. That Ben already had the registry indicated his contacts were both available and responsive.

"Tells us nothing," Wolf Shertok growled.

"For the time being," Ben agreed, "but it might eventually."

"What if he's underground for the Bureau?" Joshua asked.

"Will take some time to turn him," Ben admitted.

Sensitive area, Joshua thought, not wanting to put more pressure on Ben Caplan, whose limited sphere of influence may or may not include the right to nose around in the business of the Special Litigation Section.

"So let's get to the agenda," Shertok said impatiently as he turned up his watch to check the time.

Smiling at Joshua, Ben got up to face the blackboard hung next to his desk. "Start it off," he said to Joshua as he cleaned off the board.

"We've got to assume our first objective," Joshua began; "the reason why Fawd is still—"

"Refer to him as Paul Jaylis," Ben cut in.

"I mean why Paul Jaylis," Joshua went on, "is still in the country. The simplest logic translates this to mean that he has not yet finished his assignment, and it's on this assumption that we will proceed."

Wolf Shertok nodded slowly. "But we've got to hurry."

"Yes," Ben agreed, "but we will establish deadlines, acceptable and reasonable objectives. If we crash in helter-skelter we'll blow ourselves out." He turned to the blackboard and wrote after the numeral one the phrase, "Jaylis assignment?"

"We go after him in two ways," Joshua continued. "First, I try to get in his socks while posing as a buyer here at the plant, which should lead to the second area, the full penetration of the San Eliso commune."

"Why the commune?" Shertok asked.

"Tell 'em," Joshua said to Alan Hunt.

"They have a small machine shop in the basement," Alan reported. "Two of the four machine lathes are Swiss made, and both are nearly brand new. They have a large library in the house, and I checked the brand name out in the Thomas Register. Extremely tight-tolerance stuff, and, very expensive. They could turn out wristwatches in that shop.

"Is the shop busy?" Ben asked under his breath.

"Eight hours a day," Alan answered. "Plus, the whole place is super sloppy in security terms. It's part of their thing, mutual trust, their openness. Yet, there is one room in the basement which is kept locked constantly. It's like a vault door."

"What kind of lock?" Ben asked.

"Combination of some sort. At least three or four dial."

"You think it's possible the plutonium is there?" Shertok asked Ben.

Ben shook his head no.

"Not likely," Joshua agreed.

"But it could be," Shertok insisted.

"That's what we intend to find out," said Joshua, and he noticed that Ben had made two more entries on the blackboard: under the letter "A" the phrase, "Make contact with Jaylis," and under the letter "B" the phrase, "Penetrate SBM commune."

Alan removed a small, paper-wrapped package out of his shirt and handed it to Ben. "Here's the film and some notes. Get on this Kabir character. He runs the whole show by himself. He's got to be getting financial help from an outside source. They make some money off the shops, but not nearly enough to support the whole operation. If something's going down there, Kabir has got to be implicated."

"So you're going back," Joshua said to Alan, looking to Ben for confirmation.

Ben was rubbing his chin thoughtfully. "Did this Kabir invite you to stay on?"

"Yes," said Alan. "He asked me to return if I wanted to."

"Better to work there, right?"

Alan nodded in the affirmative. "It's their way—to work, to be involved."

"How about as a machinist," said Ben. "Not a journeyman, of course, but, say, as an apprentice?"

Joshua had picked up on Ben's apparent line of thinking. "Of course," he offered enthusiastically. "We've got a full day to put it together." Turning to Wolf Shertok he asked, "Can you get a man from the company here to put in some doubletime on Sunday?"

Wolf Shertok simply turned up his hands. "Why not?" He got up then, picked up the film cartridge from Ben's desk. "I'll get on it right now; might even be able to arrange a session for tonight. I'll get this film developed also." Without further word he picked up his jacket and left the office.

Taking advantage of the brief break, Joshua had removed from his coat pocket the tape of his meeting with Mrs. Stanley Fielding. He handed it to Ben Caplan. "When you get a chance, go over this tape carefully. Play it back a couple of times, then try to profile this woman's attitude. Like, does she act like a woman whose husband has been killed recently, especially under rather bizarre circumstances? Remember, they were married a long time, have a son, very devoted to each other."

"Anything more solid out of that meeting?" Ben asked.

"Negative," said Joshua after a moment. Still sensing he needed more time to think about it, he said no more about Stanley Fielding.

Alan Hunt addressed himself to Ben, "You mentioned at our last meeting that you would come up with some device for detecting radioactive material."

"Nearly forgot it," said Ben as he reached into a desk drawer to pull out a pair of wristwatches. He gave one each to Joshua and Alan. "Notice the calendar plate attached to the band."

Joshua inspected the watch briefly. It was a standard make, regular wind.

"The two lugs at the bottom of the plates are phoncy," Ben said. "Slip your fingernail under the plate at the bottom, then lift gently."

Joshua followed the instructions. The plate flipped up, pivoting on the two upper lugs.

"Notice the white plate under the calendar," Ben said. "It's sensitive to radioactivity and will turn to varying shades of gray to absolute black, depending upon the dose."

"You mean we've got only one shot?" said Alan.

"That's right," said Ben. "So check it regularly, three or four times a day. And, particularly, right before and after you go near a suspicious area."

"After all," reasoned Joshua, "we really need only one shot, right?"

"Let's hope so," said Ben, smiling thinly.

"So what's with Jaylis as of now?" asked Joshua as he strapped the watch on his left wrist.

"We're playing him loose for the moment," said Ben. "Putting a tight tail on him now might tip him off. We've got two men on stakeout, one across the street from Aerotec and one next door to his apartment, but both are on super low profile, just watching and reporting."

"So I meet with him when?"

Ben lifted his eyebrows questioningly. "With any luck, as early as Monday morning. Your secretary here in the PA's office called in the RFQ to the Aerotec general manager late yesterday, asking for a response not later than noon Monday. And, she requested the same outside man who worked with the Lockheed buyer, Struthers. Aerotec indicated that the outside man would be here between nine and ten on Monday to work out a quotation."

Joshua felt his stomach turn over. Playing the role of a buyer involved most of all learning the language of the trade: the esoteric jargon, the small talk, all the terms enabling purchasing agents and salesmen to communicate with each other. Once more he ran through his mind the list of terms provided by Wolf Shertok. PA was simple, Purchasing Agent. RFQ stalled him for a moment, then it came, Request for Quotation, meaning the company had put out a request for price and delivery on a specific item or items.

"Do you have your drop point designated?" Ben asked Alan.

"Yes," said Alan. "I'll use a small rock formation located on the beach near the south end of the commune property. It's shown in one of the photographs, designated with a red beach towel."

"We'll use the same color marker then," Ben said. "If you spot anything red there, then you check the DP immediately if possible. Look for a crumpled cigarette package."

"What about at night, say, after lights out?"

"If it's a real emergency," Ben told him, "then your sister will be calling you from San Francisco. Ignore any conversation but get to the drop point as soon as possible." He took a second to finish making a note to himself. "What do you think of Anne Delemar?" he asked then.

"A remarkable young woman," said Alan, and he looked aside, a gesture noticed by Joshua Bain.

"Her dossier suggests she has had a rough go of it," Joshua offered. "Do you think she can handle the heat—"

"Her head's on straight," Alan said quickly. "She's cool, very hip. In fact, she's even helped me settle down. And, she's a natural for that commune operation. She fits. Except for a slight accent, you'd never guess she's from out of the country."

Joshua remembered then that Alan hadn't seen the classified dossier on Shiela Vardi, alias Anne Delemar. "Her father was a petroleum engineer, educated in Germany," he explained to Alan. "He wisely got out of Europe before the war, apparently, along with his wife, and wound up working for the Americans in one of their overseas oil fields. Spent over twenty years in Saudi Arabia—"

"Nearly that long in Southern Iran also," Ben added.

"So Shiela Vardi was raised in an English-speaking school," Joshua went on, "provided by the oil company."

"Don't involve her anymore than you have to," Ben said to Alan. "She's here on a student's visa, and we're stretching things by allowing her to be away from school."

Not involving Anne Delemar might be more difficult than one might imagine, Joshua was thinking as he continued to study his friend, Alan Hunt.

"What's your gut analysis?" Ben asked Joshua.

Joshua turned back to the subject and the question. "There seems to be a scenario building," he said slowly. "But I can't put it together. One minute I feel like I've got a real handle on something, then, I've got nothing. It's like there's a giant credibility gap between my assumptions. I mean, from what Alan has come up with, I'd say that Jaylis is either manufacturing or securing the parts for some sophisticated device, which, for example, could very easily be an atomic weapon."

"So maybe that's his assignment," suggested Alan. "He's

secured the weapon's grade plutonium and shipped it to the Middle East. Now, he's going after the components."

Joshua was shaking his head. "Man, do you realize what you're saying? I mean, like this should all be laid in the lap of the authorities."

"Sure," said Ben. "Like, we go to the Bureau and advise them first off that there's a hippy joint down the coast cranking out atomic bombs for the Arabs."

Alan laughed under his breath.

"Okay, okay," Joshua said defensively. "So, provided it's true, we'll get the lousy evidence. But your statement points up the problem. If that's what is happening down there, then why are they so loose?"

"It could mean they're nearly finished," suggested Ben. "Like, they're getting careless, even a little cocky. Or, perhaps they consider the sheer improbability of it all their best possible cover."

Joshua rubbed his chin and then sighed heavily, realizing he was finally wearing down. "I need some sleep now," he said wearily. "Maybe tomorrow I can make better sense out of it," and he stood up, ready to leave.

"Get what you can on Kabir," Alan reminded them again as he also stood up. "He's got the potential to be a real heavy in a scene like this."

Joshua turned toward the door to follow behind Alan when Ben asked him to wait for a moment. Ben waited until Alan had left.

"It's important for you to know, Joshua, that we're grateful for your help." He leaned back in his chair and crossed his hands behind his head. "It's apparent you're the man of action this operation needs. Shertok made this point very clear to me this morning. And, I wanted you to know."

Joshua shifted uncomfortably from one foot to another. "We're just doing what you've paid us to do—"

"I doubt it can remain so simple a matter, Joshua. This operation is already showing signs of getting thick, outright dense, in fact."

"So?" Joshua was thinking impatiently.

Ben finally went on. "I wonder if you've really figured how important this may be to Israel, to us—"

"To us?"

"Yes; to all of us."

Joshua pondered the direction of Ben's point. "So we're on

the subject of loyalties and sympathies, like back at the ranch." He watched the muscles flex along Ben's jaw as his eyes narrowed.

"You're a Jew, Joshua."

The statement was direct but flat.

Joshua blinked once.

"I'm thinking about *you*," said Ben then. "It's not just the operation, or what Shertok thinks, or even what I think. It's you, Joshua."

"So you think I'm ducking it."

Ben allowed himself to lean forward over his desk. "Maybe it's even subconscious, I don't know. But in the last couple of days I've noticed you always seem tense and preoccupied, and you don't, to my knowledge, have reason to be so. Things are critical and sensitive, but we're making good progress."

Listening, Joshua had turned a quarter turn to his left to stare at the nearby wall. He was tempted for a passing moment to walk out, to return his share of the money, to just turn away from Operation Rahab. He realized then that Ben Caplan was taking a calculated risk. He had to admit that the stakes were obscure. "Two degrees to the front, sir," he commented under his breath. He briefly recalled another time, one of pain and trauma, and he quickly closed his eyes to shut off the recollection.

"What does that mean?" Ben asked.

Joshua turned back to face him. "It's called tunnel vision, where things are racing by you so quickly that you can no longer make them out, and, as the speed increases, your vision narrows to the front."

"You're exhausted," Ben suggested concernedly. "You've got to slow down."

"And confused, perhaps," Joshua admitted.

"There is learning in confusion."

Joshua laughed once under his breath, shaking his head.

"I'm sorry," said Ben. "But I was hoping you might want to talk about it."

"I might in time," Joshua admitted truthfully, and the stall was deliberate, because the subject had been on his mind often lately, not at all subconscious, as Ben had tactfully suggested, but Joshua was not ready to discuss it now.

The garage on Pepper Tree Lane . . .

After it had been opened for connecting traffic, Pepper

Tree Lane was rezoned to allow commercial building along the first one hundred feet from the center of Sunset Boulevard. In early 1934 a gasoline filling station opened up on the north west corner. By the end of the same year, an automobile repair shop was built across the street on the northeast corner. The garage was sturdily built. At five thousand square feet, the floor space was adequate at the time, when the automobile had a much shorter and narrower wheel base. Typical also were the two grease pits framed and poured into the concrete flooring, side by side, each extending down to a depth of six feet. Vehicles to be repaired were parked over these pits, wherein the mechanics could descend to work on the undercarriage or engine.

The intersection was a busy one, and the two businesses prospered over the next decade. Then, unexpectedly, the State of California decreed that the Hollywood Freeway would connect downtown Los Angeles with the Cahuenga Pass. Pepper Tree Lane fell victim to the right of eminent domain. It was wiped out, and all but two of its landmark trees were pulled out by their roots by D8 caterpillars. When the freeway was finished, Pepper Tree Lane had been reduced to a stub measuring less than one hundred feet. Only the garage and filling station were left, both trying unsuccessfully to remain open for business. The two remaining pepper trees were left opposite each other at the intersection of Sunset Boulevard.

Along with one of the two remaining trees, the filling station was ultimately removed and replaced with an asphalted parking lot for State highway vehicles.

The garage was finally abandoned but left standing.

Chapter three

Fawd Al-Shaer, alias Paul Jaylis, could not recall ever having been so far out in front. He rightly sensed his advantage. A compulsive gin-rummy player, he supposed he was on the verge of scoring a triple schneid. As he locked his apartment door behind him, he estimated they were in the third column now, with a spade up on the knock deck. He would know more about the lay of the hand presently being dealt as soon as he placed one more phone call.

Unhurried, finding it easy and natural to be casual, he dropped down the flight of stairs leading to the swimming pool. It was Sunday afternoon and warm, and the tenants were starting to move in around the huge kidney-shaped pool. The decor of the Tahitian Arms was tropical, lush, and so typically American, and he supposed that the apartment complex was in fact a test chamber where one could view just about all it took to illustrate the American Wasteland. The rigid sanitation control struck him as an obvious example, from the carefully scrubbed sidewalks right on down to the deodorized armpits of the tenants themselves, so that the matter of their basic survival had been reduced to dealing with the everyday germ. As he moved around the deep end of the pool, he caught the stares of several women who were prostrated in various poses under the afternoon sun. Exhibitionist females, he thought disgustedly, preoccupied with their fat thighs and imagined problems. Not one of them would last fifteen minutes on the Gaza.

He had a black rubber ball in his left hand, which he worked methodically, seeking to build his grip.

It was especially amusing to Fawd Al-Shaer that the apartment complex was within a block of the intersection of Beverly Boulevard and Fairfax Avenue, at the very center of the Jewish community, although the location had been originally selected to give him further credibility in dealing with Stanley Fielding. At home now in the camp of the enemy, he figured that if his neighbors knew his real identity, he probably wouldn't last the day out. The Jews, anywhere in the world, he had once proposed, had an inbred tendency to remember; they were the least able to forgive and forget, a characteristic akin to, and perhaps the result of, their innate stubbornness. It seemed a twist of historical irony, too, since the Jews themselves had been forgiven the most by their own God.

They would kill him without hesitation.

Shalom, only if it was expedient or profitable.

Vengeance used to be mine, saith the Lord God of Israel.

Exiting through the main foyer on his way to the nearby parking lot, Fawd strode out purposefully, crossing the clean concrete sidewalk. He checked his stride once, momentarily tempted to spit on the sidewalk, but moved on after remembering that such an action was illegal in this country. "There is a law to cover virtually every detail of one's going and coming," he thought. This explained why the country was ruled by attorneys, why the country's wealth was in the hands of attorneys, which explained, too, why every good Jewish boy thought first about entering law school.

He spat on the sidewalk, briefly infuriated.

Fifteen minutes later he was seated in a Wilshire bar just inside the Santa Monica city limits. He had not been followed, an important key to their present security plan. As he took the first sip of his iced Drambui, he began to relax again. Switching the rubber ball to his right hand, he worked it steadily, almost absently. Then he checked his watch. It was time. Walking over to the pay phone located next to the men's restroom, he punched a dime into the phone and dialed the operator. Using a credit card number, he asked for a 702 prefix number, which connected him to a motel in the most outlandish wasteland of all—Las Vegas, Nevada.

The motel operator transferred him to the requested room number.

Kabir came on the line with a forced "Hello."

"You sound jittery," Fawd suggested amiably.

"I'm sorry," Kabir apologized after a moment. "It's just that . . . " and he hesitated again.

So that was it, Fawd thought irritably, realizing that Kabir was obviously in the process of getting strung out. He drew a deep breath before saying, "I thought you had enough for at least another week," referring to Kabir's personal stock of cocaine.

"Normally," Kabir offered, "but you must understand that the past several days have been hectic, and, well, you can appreciate the strain on us all."

On us *all*, Fawd repeated to himself, sensing that Kabir was hinting. "I see," he finally observed, and he felt his stomach reacting. "So she's using it again," he added suspiciously.

"I didn't say that."

"Don't fence words with me," Fawd warned him, his voice turning hard. He struggled to maintain control, not wanting his emotions to interfere at this critical juncture. "When did she start?" he asked, still unable to dismiss the matter so abruptly.

"Just yesterday," Kabir answered reluctantly.

Familiar enough with cocaine users, Fawd wondered at the truth of Kabir's answer, since they all tended to hang together in a self-protecting society. It seemed to him the girl could be the one most likely to crack. She had been called upon to endure much in just a very short time, which was why he had programmed her in for only a low-key role in the operation. "She has no reason to be under strain," he heard himself commenting.

"She's very uptight," said Kabir. "The waiting is getting to her."

Probably so, Fawd agreed to himself, thinking then that she would come around when things began to break. "Are we on schedule?" he inquired, his voice back to normal.

"Exactly on schedule," Kabir assured him, as if he too was delighted with the shift in subject. "I leave for Los Angeles within the hour. I have a couple hours of work left on the pepper tree mechanism, then home."

The answer confirmed that the plan was set, that the high-risk portion was over. They could now even discuss the details on an open telephone line without concern. Nothing could stop them now; not chance, nor someone else's cleverness or design, not even all the cocaine available on all the streets of Southern California. And, it all had been so absurdly easy.

"The professor's people are getting close," Kabir stated, interrupting Fawd's train of thought.

Yes, Fawd told himself, noting that Kabir was careful in referring to Wolf Shertok. "That too is right on schedule," he said then.

"I expect one back this evening," Kabir added.

"Good," said Fawd. "And I have a meeting with one of their representatives tomorrow, probably the one called Joshua Bain. We can anticipate a more aggressive move out of them, probably and hopefully by the middle of the week." And that too was a part of it—the tendency of the Jews to keep pushing, even after the U.S. Government had all but quit.

"So we'll just stay with the plan," Kabir offered.

"Now especially," Fawd confirmed soberly. "And, unless you have something else," he added, knowing there was a last item for Kabir to deal with.

"Can you arrange a package?" said Kabir quickly, as if he was afraid Fawd might hang up on him.

"Yes, of course," said Fawd, tempted as he was to extend the man's misery, yet aware that for the moment Kabir needed the assurance to maintain his balance. "It'll be in the locker at the airport," he told Kabir. "I'll tape the key at the usual place."

"I'll need more now."

"I understand."

"Thank you, sir."

Fawd hung up the phone. He was smiling to himself as he walked out the front door.

So it was in the final column, he was thinking jubilantly, and a triple schneid was in the making. It had to be the last hand dealt, for he had just picked up a triple lay with a likely safe discard, one ideal for bait.

The opposition was down to the drop of one card.

The garage on Pepper Tree Lane . . .

The building was old, and in the attic the original building inspection tag was nailed to one of the joists supporting the decaying roof. The faded date on the tag showed that the roof system had been inspected in December, 1934. There was nothing left of the original structure now except for the basic framing, the roof supports, a part of the original stucco, and, the most significant, the original slab and foundation.

There was evidence of rejuvenation. A new six-foot chain-link fence surrounded the property, and the warning signs on the fence proclaimed it was protected by a security service. The roof had been hot-mopped. The walls had been replaced with vandal-proof lexan plates. Inside, the cement floor had been washed down with a strong solution of muriatic acid to remove the accumulation of grease and oil. A small room, measuring about nine feet square, had been partitioned off in the back right corner.

The new owner obviously did not intend to use the garage for automobile repair, because one of the grease pits had been filled with transit-mix, the new concrete finished off to match the existing floor level. The second pit was covered with a heavy steel-reinforced wooden cover, upon which were four recessed handles, indicating it was removable.

The last workman on the property had been a telephone company representative, who had installed three new telephones, each with its own separate number, in the small partitioned-off room, suggesting that the building would soon be open for some sort of business involving heavy telephone activity.

It was late afternoon, and their day of rest was winding down. Anne Delemar wished that the intolerably long Sunday would be over, and, too, that when the sun rose tomorrow it somehow could be Friday instead of Monday. For now, she sat nervously on the fringe of the discussion group, watching the rear door of the main house. There were about a dozen of the commune members spread loosely around the tiled garden patio, wasting time, by her estimate. A partially filled jug of red wine was moved to the feet of the young couple to her left, and Anne Delemar again glanced anxiously to the rear door. Kabir had arrived a few minutes earlier and was presently closeted in his private quarters.

It was her turn next to host the wine.

She couldn't have cared less.

The young man picked up the bottle, took a deep drink, returning it to the place near his bare feet.

"Two contradictory statements," he proposed thickly.

Anne glanced aside, studying the couple. She couldn't even remember their names, and she realized that they were all so alike—the long hair, cut and pulled over the head identically the same on both sexes, as if to minimize the outward differences between them, perhaps to support their tendency to be equal, to be the same, to look alike. It occurred to her that if the girls could grow beards they probably would.

"Having put your hand to the plow," the young man said, "and looking back, means you're not fit for the kingdom."

Most of the others nodded appreciatively.

"As opposed to the notion," he continued gravely, "that it is more difficult to stop pursuing a goal than it is to finish it."

In the following contemplative pause, Anne noticed that the stronger afternoon breeze was falling off, and she was picking up the aromatic odor of hash in the cooler air now settling around them.

"The latter is oriental in origin," one of the girls suggested.

"You're close, sister," said the young man appointed temporary proctor by virtue of fifty cents worth of red wine. "But it is a Hindu saying."

Anne pushed herself up and reached down automatically to dust off her jeans. This subject would take some time with this group. And, she had waited long enough for Kabir. She stepped around the randomly placed bodies to move into the house as unobtrusively as she could.

In the main hallway she stopped to knock tentatively on the scarred door to his private room.

Perhaps he was in the basement—

The door finally opened.

Kabir pulled her into the room.

"I was about to get you," he explained.

Anne simply nodded once before crossing the small bare room to sit down in the wooden chair next to Kabir's small night stand. There was an open magazine on the small table.

"How did it go?" she asked absently as Kabir sat down on the cot near his side of the night stand.

"Very routine," he told her as he picked up the magazine.

Anne remained expressionless as she took note of the revealed contents on the table top. She had obviously caught him working a new supply. The white powder was piled neatly at the center of a glass mirror measuring about ten inches square.

"How much?" she asked.

"Ten grams."

She watched without further comment as he used a playing card to divide the mound into several equal, smaller piles. Kabir worked the coke methodically and expertly, his slender fingers moving rhythmically, as if he were playing a musical instrument. Finished, he quickly transferred the bulk of the cocaine to four small glass vials, capping them off with black screw lids.

The taste in her mouth was metallic as she watched.

"One 'n one?" he suggested.

She had placed her right hand on the edge of the table, stroking the finished grain. "No," she said then. "I think I'll pass."

He grinned at her, obviously pleased. He had arranged the remaining powder into two slender lines. "Two for me," he said as he bent down. He had formed a new dollar bill into a tube. With one end of the makeshift tube in his right nostril, he placed the other end near the closer powder line. Closing off his other nostril, he sucked the line of powder up the tube. He immediately threw his head back, inhaling again. He clamped his eyes shut, grimacing.

Anne could appreciate the pained expression as the drug hit his nose membrane.

"When will we be finished?" she asked then, explaining the real reason why she now confronted him.

He hit the other line, again inhaling noisily through his nose, before answering, "It should be soon now, but there's no way to really tell." He rubbed his nose several times, shook his head, before settling down finally to stare distantly across the room. "You must be careful," he told her after a moment.

"What do you mean?" she asked defensively.

He closed his eyes, sat up more upright, assuming a meditative position. "It occurs to me," he said slowly, "that the prayers of a righteous man availeth much."

The oblique remark prompted Anne Delemar to realize how very little she knew about this man, the one they all knew only as Kabir. A strange and often distant one, he was given to many moods.

"That's in the book he carries with him," Kabir went on, "and he believes in it with all his heart and soul."

Anne understood he was talking about Alan Hunt, and she took an indifferent tack, unwilling to reveal her true feelings. "His religion is of no interest to me."

Kabir opened his eyes and was smiling as he said, "He will probably try to interest you, especially if he is attracted to you, which I suspect he is."

She laughed once, shaking her head.

"Don't take it too lightly," he cautioned her. "Remember, he thinks you are Jewish, and you could trip yourself up."

"I can handle myself when it comes to talking about religion."

Kabir smiled a little more thinly, and there was a hardness near his eyes, so that his face seemed divided against itself. "You ought to listen more and talk less. Right now, your present mistake is to accept that what Alan Hunt believes in is simply a religion."

She frowned then, saying defensively, "But you told me yourself, in fact you warned me, that he is a Christian."

"But he is not a religionist, in the traditional sense. There are Christians and there are Christians, like there are Muslims and there are Muslims. Alan Hunt is one of the sincere, truly affected ones, who relates to his God, a living creator to his mind. He accepts the Words as truth, lives it, via his whole inner being, instead of via church buildings and property, via bingo, via proclamations of dogma, which are a few of the parts of what you think as a religion."

"A semantic point," she observed.

"Much more so," he insisted. "You have already begun to detect it in his character in just the brief time you've known him. Alan Hunt has undergone a dramatic change, and it shows, clearly."

"I really couldn't care less."

"But you've found him kind and gentle."

"Yes," she had to admit. "You are very perceptive."

"That's why I warn you to be careful," he told her, and he stared at her intently. He reached up then to massage his lower forehead.

Anne watched, knowing the area under his fingers was by now nearly numb. Uncomfortable under his probing stare, she pushed herself up. "You ought to know me well enough," she proposed, "to realize your warning is unnecessary."

"Because I know you is why I warn you. Remember, we are aliens in this land. And if the whole truth were known, the good citizens of this country would be aghast, not merely offended, at our objectives. They would in fact have difficulty in even believing them. Which, in a way, is why we shall succeed. It's all simply too preposterous to conceive."

She was frowning then, until she realized that the drug was probably causing him to inflate the situation, to over-dramatize. "Our objectives are reasonable. Parity with the Jews—"

"Be careful!" he warned her, and he looked aside, avoiding her eyes.

"So what's the point?" she asked impatiently.

"That you can't indulge yourself in the normal; you're liable to start enjoying it."

"My personal objectives are still fixed."

"We all do what we have to do."

Indeed, Anne was thinking to herself, which was why she was here now, which, she supposed further, was also why Alan Hunt would be returning. She walked out of the room, resolved to end the matter in whatever way she could.

For Joshua Bain, his temporary west Los Angeles apartment was functionally located less than three blocks from their Visualon CP. However, the CP was closed down today on Ben's suggestion that they all needed the time off anyway. By the middle of the afternoon, Joshua was stalking back and forth between the small kitchen and the living room, trying to work off his restlessness. He was under orders to rest and relax, but the day had passed torturously slow, and he pulled up once more next to the service bar in the kitchen. His working notes and papers were spread out on the counter, and he tried again to arrange them in some semblance of order.

The Fielding subject still sat heavily in his mind, so he turned the pages of his notebook back to yesterday morning and the Del Cerro synagogue, back to his questions and the answers of Martha Fielding:

Question: According to the record, your relatives, from your side of the family, live in and around San Francisco.

Answer: That's correct.

Question: So that you're alone down here now, you and your son, except for your father-in-law, Edwin Fielding?

Answer: That's also correct.

Question: I have the impression, also from the record of your conversation with the Government investigators, that you don't particularly care for the San Diego area.

Answer: That is also correct. Although it is no great thing.

Question: Then you probably intend to return to San Francisco.

Answer: (After a long pause) Yes, in time . . .

Joshua remembered that his next question had been why, then, after over two months, had there been no apparent plans or evidence of her intended move to the San Francisco area. He figured that the house ought to be up for sale. Her son, Daniel, had even been enrolled in summer school.

Answer: There are still many things to settle first. Stanley's insurance, for example.

Joshua remembered dropping the subject at that point. He thumbed the notebook pages back to the beginning of their conversation:

Question: The evidence is overwhelming, Mrs. Fielding, that Stanley was heavily implicated in the MUF. Can you account for why he did it?

Answer: I have no idea, assuming it's true.

Question: You mean you think he didn't do it?

Answer: Stan is not a thief.

And therein was the basis for Joshua's concern, that Martha Fielding had referred to her husband in the present tense. Stan *is* not a thief. Ben Caplan would no doubt excuse the remark as a normal enough grammatical slip. Joshua

closed the notebook. Martha Fielding was not at all resigned
to her predicament.

On impulse, he moved to the far end of the counter, where
he opened the phone directory to the Los Angeles County
heading. He checked his watch before dialing the number for
the nearest county library. The woman answering the phone
informed him that the library would be open only until 5:00
p.m., which gave him over two hours. He elected to use what
little free time he had to do some digging—research time. He
stopped by the other end of the counter to rip a blank page out
of the notebook. Carefully, he arranged his thoughts before
starting the list, remembering that his time was limited. Priority items only. The first was "atomic weapons, construction,
theory." Next was "plutonium." He dawdled for a moment,
and then added, "Zion movement, esp' in U.S."

The room was quiet around him as he thoughtfully folded
the paper, placing it in his shirt pocket. Still preoccupied, he
moved to the front closet to get a jacket. He remembered then
that Ben had asked him to dinner at a La Cienega restaurant,
so he selected his best sport coat. Methodically he shut down
the apartment, turning out the lights and pulling the drapes
closed.

Ready to leave, he stopped at the front door, thinking that
he must add one more item to the library list, one which was
not really essential but worthy to be checked out if time permitted. Back at the counter, he unfolded the paper, delaying
several seconds before adding the subject, "Jewish history,
general."

It had been dark for nearly an hour by the time Alan Hunt
dropped down the freeway offramp. The exit off Highway 5
was one of two he could use to reach his San Eliso destination.
He had passed by the first, San Eliso Boulevard, the handier
and more accessible route, because he was stalling, reluctant to
move into the whole commune assignment without a full understanding of how he was to proceed.

His more official objectives seemed clear enough.

He had just finished a straight twelve-hour crash course in
basic machine shop work. He could read a blueprint, could use
basic measuring devices, such as calipers, various gauges,
could operate a drill press, use a grinder, the more basic machines, and, according to his instructor, he should be able to
set up and use a turret lathe for the more simple secondary
operations.

He carried a well-worn micrometer in his left hip pocket, supposedly a must for an itinerant machinist apprentice.

Driving the Jag slowly in third gear, he came to the intersection of Highway 101. He lingered at the stop sign, turning right only after seeing a car pull in behind him.

He finally had to admit that Anne Delemar was his problem.

Or, was it that *he* was his own problem?

Thinking about her took him from a high one moment to a sudden low the next. The clear, sharp image of her face passed through his mind once again.

A most profound complication.

Alan Hunt had been that route before, and knew the symptoms. His mind reacted first, then his whole being. He took a deep liberating breath, seeing the large house coming up on his left. Desperately seeking a handle, he sensed that perhaps he had to trust for the moment, to keep the faith, to believe that all things had to work to and for the good. As he pulled into the gravel driveway, the matter otherwise sat in his mind totally unresolved.

She had been watching for the Jaguar, and when she saw the car pull in to park, she went into the recreation room to wait. Kabir was at his desk, within the perimeter recognized as his unofficial office, and she nodded to him once before taking a chair across the room. There were several couples spread randomly about the large room. She avoided them all, preferring to be by herself. A few seconds later, Alan Hunt entered the room. He had his shaving kit and the ever-present Bible. Stepping tentatively inside the door, he looked about seriously, briefly scanning the room. Seeing her, he smiled after a moment, before turning toward Kabir's desk. She noticed again that his face changed dramatically when he smiled, making him look younger, even, perhaps, more innocent. She continued to watch him as he walked across the room. Alan Hunt moved like an animal, effortlessly and smoothly, not making a sound in his moccasins, yet suggesting he was ready to respond in an instant. He was quietly physical, very physical in fact, like, if he put his mind to it he could walk right on through the wall without breaking stride.

Anne Delemar felt her pulse working in her throat.

She waited several minutes before getting up, making sure that Alan noticed her as she left the room. She made her way slowly down the hallway and out the back door. The adjacent patio was now deserted, so she sat down on one of the red-wood benches. The evening air was chilly. Automatically she pulled her poncho closer around her body and, closing her eyes, began listening to the sound of the angry surf behind her, aware that the darkness seemed to heighten the effect of the night's sounds.

"Hello again."

Startled, she looked up to see Alan standing before her, silhouetted against the backdrop of the hallway light. He still had the Bible and kit in his hand, indicating he had come directly from seeing Kabir. She glanced aside quickly, making sure they were alone.

"I'm glad you came back," she said evenly as she stood up, realizing then that the moment for some reason was awkward for both of them. On impulse, she reached out to take his free hand. He put his Bible and kit on the bench nearest to her.

"Why don't we go down to the beach," she suggested, and, without waiting for an answer, she turned to move away from the house, pulling him along behind her, aware that she had decided to take the initiative, to lead the way to what she expected to follow. She was running by the time they reached the bottom of the slope.

The cool sand slowed them to a walk. A little breathless, she pulled up several yards short of the surf and dropped heavily. He sat down beside her, saying nothing, and in the pale gray light of the partial moon she thought he looked much too grim. Sobered a little herself, she thought that, after all, he had a right to be serious and preoccupied. Much more of a right than he could possibly imagine.

"How did you get mixed up in this?" she asked, again on impulse, hearing in her own voice a huskiness which ordinarily was a sign that her emotions were running higher than normal.

He had turned to look directly at her, taking his eyes away from the surf line.

"I mean," she added then, "you just don't seem the sort. It is not enough that you're a friend of Ben Caplan."

First smiling, he then looked back out to the darkness of the sea. "I suspect," he finally offered, "that may be true for both of us."

The answer was a disguised question, she surmised as she pushed her legs out toward the water, crossing them, working her heels into the yielding sand. She closed her eyes against the breeze sweeping in off the water.

"Did you talk to Kabir?" he was saying.

The more official question sat in her mind for a second or two. After Kabir had left for Las Vegas yesterday afternoon, Alan had called her to tell her that he might be coming back and that she should casually mention to Kabir that he had some experience in a machine shop, thus fronting him in for the work. She raced quickly back over the time spent with Kabir earlier in the evening, realizing that she had failed to bring it up. The omission on her part now upset her; she suspected she was on the verge of losing her usual concentration.

"Yes," she lied then, "a couple of hours ago. But he was busy, working on some kind of paperwork, and I doubt he even heard me." She opened her eyes, turning to look directly at him. "You still haven't answered my question. Like, what really brought you into this?" The countermove was direct and simple.

"Money," he told her after a moment, and the delay confused her estimate of whether he had fallen for the ploy.

"That's what seems to motivate most Americans," she proposed then, and she looked away once more to the open sea.

"That's what gets us started," he admitted, "but we usually manage to get more involved once we get into something."

She was aware of their closeness then, of their being alone on the deserted beach, and she decided that it was time to make her move. "Let's go for a swim," she suggested abruptly. Her plan, simple enough, was to precipitate an awkward enough scene to give her the escape the situation seemed to demand.

He was chuckling lightly. "I don't have a suit; it's in the car."

"Neither do I," she said as she jumped lightly to her feet. Facing the open sea, confronting the dark mass of water, she started to pull out of her poncho. Before pulling it over her head, she looked aside to see that he was simply sitting there, staring at the white water.

"You're certainly an odd one," she said after a moment, and she sat down again after letting the poncho drop back to her waist. She felt herself turning angry inside, realizing that she had just backed down from her carefully prepared plan.

"You're probably right," he was saying, as he turned to look at her. "And I don't know what to say. Perhaps I should apologize—"

"Don't bother," she offered, hearing the resignation in her

own voice. "I just hope you're not impotent, or something."

"Hardly," he assured her. "The only thing I can say is that you've become so important to me," and he hesitated before going on. "And I can't even figure it out myself, so how can I explain it?"

She had been studying him in the bad light, before telling him soberly, "Perhaps you'll have to forgive me. Because, you see, where I come from and live day by day, there isn't the time to play out romantic games. If it's right between two people, then we tend to share it while we can, without protocol or ceremony." She pushed herself up and took a step toward the house, figuring that it had all turned around backwards.

"Please don't go," he said as he stood up.

She sensed she was at a turning point at that exact moment, and she could feel the tug and pull within her, not unlike the ebb and flow of the water on the nearby tide line. She realized then that she had been holding her breath, and, as she let it go she heard the words slowly spoken out of her own mouth, "Can you believe that I'm tired, so very tired."

"Find rest then."

She was shaking her head. "I don't mean that kind of tired."

"Neither do I."

Kabir was right, she thought. Alan Hunt seemed to be possessed with a peculiar insight into things. "You're very perceptive," she said impulsively.

"Or, perhaps you're very open."

She laughed once, involuntarily.

"Let's go for a walk," he suggested.

She fell in stride beside him as he started slowly down the beach. There was only the sound of the surf. She was thinking that while she had not gained any ground, she had not lost any either. She was, in an expression favored by Kabir, simply back to baseline.

"In what way are you tired?" Alan was asking her.

She considered the question for a moment before answering candidly, "In just about every way possible."

"Maybe you're just down for the moment. We're all under pressure—"

"No, not really. It's just that when I was younger it all looked so exciting, and there was the sense of purpose, too."

"You mean like being on the front line?"

She glanced at him, curious at his exact meaning. "Yes,

you might say we're all living on the front line over there."

"And the newness has worn off—"

"Not so much that. Rather, it's like now I can't seem to see an end to it. It's like walking in endless quicksand."

"You seem to have grown much older than your age indicates," he offered after a moment. "It seems to me that cynicism is more characteristic of one's later years."

"One tends to be cynical," she reminded him, "when living in a twenty-four-hour-a-day war zone."

He nodded once appreciatively before suggesting, "A more precise logician might suggest we have little right to be cynical if we stubbornly resist solving the predicament."

They had slowly scaled a knoll overlooking the surf, and she stopped to look at him sharply. "That's both unfair and an over-simplification."

He shrugged as he pulled up to face her. "You know what they say about making beds and digging ditches."

She felt the quick warmth on her cheeks.

Alan Hunt sensed her anger, so he added gently, "But such well-worn observations do little to ease the burden of your fatigue." Feeling awkward himself, he looked down and away to what he could see of the white water and the open sea beyond. For that passing moment, he imagined he felt like the follower of Vishnu who at the end of his first pilgrimage finally topped the last hill to look down on the holy waters at Benares. Seeking inspiration, he was disappointed now, because the picture before him came into focus as an ominously dark seascape under the bleak, cloudless sky. A foreboding panorama. The Mother Ganges had gone dry. He then reminded himself that his hope was a living one.

"Why is it," he heard her asking him, as if she had just looked into his mind, "that you never mention anything to me about your religion? I mean, when I mentioned that I was tired, I figured you would toss God to me as the solution."

It was his turn to laugh once, and as he shook his head he was thinking about opportunity and how it seemed he didn't really know how to deal with it.

"What's so funny?"

"I'm laughing at myself, not you," he assured her.

"Something tells me I've touched on a sensitive point."

"Something is right."

"Why?"

"Can't you guess?"

"I'm tired, remember . . . " And there was silence between them, until after a moment, she finally ventured what sounded like a tentative question, "Do you mean because I'm Jewish?"

"Yes."

"That's interesting," she said reflectively.

"More than you can imagine," he said simply, before going on with a more resigned note in his voice, "Joshua is Jewish, as you may or may not know, and in two years of trying I've not been able to really find the right words with him either."

"Then I find it strange as well as interesting," she said, "since I understand that you and Joshua are the closest of friends."

"Yes," he seemed to admit, "there is perhaps a certain mystery about it all."

"That strikes me as an easy answer."

Alan took a deep breath, sighing heavily then as he realized that her probing was forcing him to face the issue himself, an issue which had been within him for a long time now, a nagging kind of persistent lump comprised of inquiry and doubt, of a crying out for resolution, so that he might somehow reach Joshua before it became too late. For a passing moment, he thought that it might be best to just start, somehow, and that the best place to begin would be with the record itself. "All I can do is to tell you what the Bible says," and he watched her carefully, but in the poor light he could not discern the expected expression of resistance.

"You should understand," she told him, "that I'm not a religious person. From what I can tell, most outsiders think Israel is some kind of religious state, but it's really no different from any other modern country. In fact, I can't remember the last time I was in a synagogue."

"You're a lot like Joshua, then."

"I hope that's in my favor," she said evenly.

Feeling himself momentarily encouraged, Alan began to explain, "The Bible says that we are all likened to be the branches of either the natural or of the wild olive tree. The natural olive tree is the more preferred, of course. And, the Jewish people, as God's chosen ones, make up the branches of the natural tree. Those Jewish branches which believe remain on as part of the natural tree. Those Jewish branches which reject the truth, however, are broken off. The rest of us, called the Gentiles, are looked upon as wild olive branches, and when we choose to believe, we understand that we are grafted onto the natural tree in the place of those broken off."

She reached out to take his hand, as if in his hesitation she sensed his difficulty in going on.

"We thus all owe an enormous debt to the Jewish people," he went on slowly, "and therein also lies what might be called a tragic irony. That in order for me to find the truth and to be accepted, a portion of God's most dearly beloved people had to first reject His program."

"Small wonder," she said after a thoughtful moment, "that you have a problem in talking to Joshua. After all, if God is all-knowing and always has been, wasn't it kind of dumb to select a people who He knew would reject His program?"

Alan nodded to himself understandingly. "That's not really true," he suggested gently, "because not all of the chosen ones rejected the truth. And in the future, not too long from now hopefully, all of Israel shall be saved. It's all in the same program, so to speak, and there's nothing we can do to change it."

"Sounds kind of fatalistic."

"For the game plan maybe," he seemed to agree, "but not for the individual players. We each, whether Jew or Gentile, have a clear opportunity to make a choice as to which side to play on. Each of us is given the grace to understand the truth. We have that choice now, and the same choice was available two thousand years ago. Your logic should also reveal to you that just because God *knew* something was going to happen doesn't automatically make Him *responsible*." She shivered in the cool night air, the tremor passing through her hand into his, causing him to suggest they return to the house. He helped her down the slope, walking close to her as they returned.

"You really have a problem with this," she suggested after they had taken several steps. "I mean, like you say 'the truth' and 'the program' when you really mean Jesus Christ."

He remembered Wolf Shertok making a similar statement to Joshua back at the ranch. Alan's thoughts tumbled briefly.

"Or should I say the Messiah," Anne was saying.

Alan cleared his throat. "Either is acceptable, but the Messiah is probably more appropriate for the moment."

They were abreast of the house again, and Alan was silent as he helped her up the sandy incline. On the patio she followed his lead to sit down on one of the redwood benches. "I don't know exactly how to explain it further," he finally offered. "I've even tried reading up on the subject, mostly because Joshua is Jewish, and though he's not exactly typical, you might say, I still want to answer his questions if and when they might come up."

"Since it's so difficult for you," she suggested, "hasn't it occurred to you that you may be wrong?"

"My own credibility is not the issue," he assured her. "Nor is the fact of the Messiah really in doubt. That part of the subject is especially credible for both of us."

She was frowning as she remarked, "Credible for you, maybe."

"For both of us, absolutely."

"Isn't that the center of the difference?"

"You mean the Messiah?"

"Yes."

"Not just Him, but the time of His coming."

She was nodding that she understood. "You say that He has already come, and we believe that He is yet to arrive."

"Something like that."

"It's hard for you," she said then, "to have to tell me that I'm wrong, or, at least, that you believe I'm wrong."

He glanced aside, before answering slowly, "We really shouldn't be at odds with each other. We run in circles when we debate with each other. The record is clear for anyone to review. Which brings me again to the point that God is in charge now and always has been. We can argue all we want and never change a thing. You see, your own prophets predicted the coming of the Messiah. The program was set in motion a long time ago, explained centuries before Christ was even born. The plan was literally set in concrete."

Anne realized she was frowning then. "If the record is so clear, then why, as you say, are we at such odds with each other?"

Alan Hunt bit briefly on his lower lip before answering, "There was a ruler of the Jews at the time of Christ, a leading Pharisee by the name of Nicodemus, who, for whatever reason, was inclined to accept Jesus as the true Messiah. The high priest who was instrumental in condemning Jesus was a man by the name of Caiaphas. Thus, at that time, these two men were at odds with each other over the validity of Jesus as the true Messiah. Both of these men were religious scholars and were well acquainted with the prophetic scriptures predicting the coming of the Messiah. Yet, they disagreed. And the record says that Nicodemus even defended Jesus before the Sanhedrin. Nicodemus, for example, must have pointed out that

Jesus had already fulfilled hundreds of prophecies of men like Isaiah and Ezekiel."

"Then how could the high priest dispute it?" she asked him.

"The same as current critics. He had elected not to believe and simply dismissed Jesus as an imposter. He believed that the fulfillment of the prophecies was the consequences of a clever plot, one devised probably after the birth of Jesus. Caiaphas would naturally have claimed that the miracles, too, and the escape from the tomb even afterwards, had all been fabricated by the conspirators."

Anne delayed for a moment before offering thoughtfully, "The theory of the high priest could be valid, you know."

"Oh, no doubt Caiaphas was convinced he was right. But, then, let's consider the logical response by Nicodemus, which I choose to call the magic question. If they were to reject all the evidence, how then would they ever know the true Messiah when He did come? Since, after all, they could with such ease dismiss all proofs on the grounds of a conspiracy."

Anne Delemar simply shook her head.

"Caiaphas' answer," he went on, "would have been that the true Messiah would restore the kingdom of David in all its glory and power, and so they would surely know Him. The true Messiah would be a king, a national leader."

She watched him as he looked down to the tile between his feet, shaking his head sadly. "It must have dawned on Nicodemus, the first evidence of the heavy and tragic irony of the moment—the high priest, caught in the irrefutable testimony of the prophets, yet still rejecting the apparent Messiah, looking instead to the future, to the expected arrival of one yet to come. So we have the Caiaphas error, one of double function, because in addition to his unbelief of the moment there was yet a second function to fulfill."

"Why is it so tragic," she asked then, "that we should still be looking for our Messiah?"

"Because," he said gravely, "there is in fact another one yet to come, one also predicted by the prophets. So the followers of Caiaphas to this day are still paving the way for his arrival. And that is the tragedy, because when he does come, they will accept him, perhaps eagerly, because he will appear to restore the kingdom of David in all its power and glory. He will be a king, a national leader of the first order, which is the second function of the Caiaphas error."

"That's kind of heavy," she suggested as she stood up beside him. "I mean, if what you say is true, then the Caiaphas error is a running one which has been with us for two thousand years."

"You said it; I didn't."

She didn't answer right away, moving instead to the rear door of the house, where she turned to face him. "Have you talked to Joshua about this same thing?"

"Yes, to an even greater extent."

"What did he say?"

"He had about the same comments as you."

"So you really haven't had much luck with him."

Alan reached down to pick up his Bible. The storm surf was starting to peak, producing a fine mist, which now was moving in across the escarpment, reaching them on the wind in damp waves of its own. "Perhaps not," he seemed to admit, "but Joshua is more interested now, which is a good sign."

"It seems enough to excite one's interest," she said quietly. "But, like I said, I'm not a religious person. So I'm not equipped to debate with you. However, I do know that the religious Jews in Israel are strong in their beliefs. Mostly, as you should be aware, because they feel those beliefs and the heritage it produced were what sustained them as a people. For centuries it carried them through the pogroms, the holocaust, or whatever. And, to believe in your Jesus Christ would break that unity down. They would feel they'd lose their Jewishness, their identity. Don't you understand?"

He pondered both the statement and her intensity before replying, "Then we now have what we might call the Anne Delemar error," and he held up his hand in a placating gesture. "Because to accept Jesus as the Messiah is to solidly reinforce that very same faith. He came not to reject or to destroy the religion of His own people, the natural branches, and He said so repeatedly. Rather, He came to fulfill. Any Jew, anywhere in the world, who would read his own prophets and then decide to believe would then become much more a Jew, not less. Don't forget, Christianity was originally a Jewish religion." He shrugged once, then shook his head, emphasizing his frustration. "It's your turn to try to understand. Those Jews who have chosen to believe are living testimony to the sheer truth of the situation. They are truly the natural branches—"

"Why are there so few of them then?"

He shook his head once again.

"You don't really know why," she added soberly.

"We both believe there is only one God," he said carefully. "And it all kind of got started when God made His first deal with Abraham, whose descendants were to convey the message. Things apparently didn't work out so well, however, so that in time God sent His own Son, the Messiah, not only to straighten things out but also to make sure we all would be able to share in the program. After all, God is now one-to-one to each of us. You don't have to be a member of a certain race or group to qualify—"

"You're beginning to sound discouraged," she interjected.

"You're probably right," he said evenly. "It's like when I'm around Joshua on the same subject, I wind up being on the defensive, as if I have to justify, or prove something."

"Then why bring it up?"

He looked away briefly, before replying, "I guess it's because I love him, and I desperately want him to be saved, not lost."

She fidgeted in the doorway in the following few seconds of silence before finally turning into the house to start down the long center hallway.

Alan watched her until she turned to disappear up the stairway leading to her second-floor dormitory. He sensed once again that he had bungled an opportunity. He sat down heavily on the nearest redwood bench, holding his Bible in his lap, and as he started to arrange his thoughts for prayer, he found himself beginning to understand why he was trying so earnestly to reach Anne Delemar with the truth.

Chapter four

By early Monday morning, Joshua was confident of only the fact that Operation Rahab was in motion on all fronts. It was his opinion, otherwise, that their production of hard evidence had been practically zero. Closeted alone with Ben Caplan in the Visualon CP, he felt it was time to voice his suspicions concerning Stanley Fielding, the missing and presumed dead QC inspector.

"The tail on Martha Fielding," Joshua insisted, "can give us some answers."

Ben Caplan leaned back in his chair, crossing his hands behind his head. The desk before him was covered with neatly arranged material, marking him as an orderly and well-organized man. "Like I suggested to you last night, you're too impatient," Ben said after a moment. "At best, that tail is no more than a flunky following someone's orders. And, assuming he's a pro, he's not about to give us even the time of day."

"So we'll pass on the flunky for the moment," said Joshua, who then resolved to give Ben just twenty-four more hours to solve the question of the Martha Fielding tail. "What is your estimate of how Jaylis was able to control Fielding during the time frame prior to the MUF, which I figure had to be at least a month, or more?"

Ben Caplan leaned forward, making an appreciative sound in his throat. "So you picked up on that too. The question, of course, was never in the official record, since the authorities were not aware of Paul Jaylis. However, I've thought about it on and off myself."

"Well?"

Ben Caplan sighed heavily. "I don't know, and I doubt anyone does, except Jaylis himself. He was the maestro—"

"Then at least make a guess!"

"Money perhaps, the man's idealism, maybe a combination of the two."

A combination of the two, Joshua thought appraisingly, an option he hadn't yet considered.

"You should read up on some of the profiles," Ben was saying, "of what we might call a typical operator, the type who offers his services to the CIA, for example. You would be amazed, perhaps even amused, to find out what motivates some people."

"No thanks," said Joshua tiredly.

"All we can say for certain is that it happened."

Joshua stalked back and forth in the small room. He again checked his watch; it was less than ten minutes until he met with their number-one suspect, Paul Jaylis. He knew he was not nearly so impatient as he was nervous; there was a small fluttery storm building in his gut. "Hasn't it occurred to you," he said then, "that Fielding might've double-crossed Jaylis? Or, that at the last minute he chickened out? And, with either option, that he has the plutonium stashed someplace?" He pulled up before Ben's desk. "Such a possibility would account for the tail, and, also would give Jaylis the reason to be still around." He turned away from the desk and began pacing to and fro again, realizing that he had broached his suspicion that Fielding might even still be alive.

"Those options have been carefully considered," Ben told him. "But the Mexico City exchange really happened, Joshua," he explained patiently. "We have eyeball witnesses from start to finish, from the moment he took the cab to LAX, at the airport itself, on the airplane," and he ticked off each point with a pencil, tapping the desk top. "Another solid witness at Mexican customs, plus coroner ID on the body before it was cremated, plus ID papers, plus, plus, plus."

"Fielding could've set it up," Joshua said, but with less conviction.

"Uh-uh," Ben disagreed. "Such a complex con would have been well beyond his means." He paused for a moment before going on, "Jaylis set him up, Joshua, and the operation was a minor one for a man of his capabilities. He simply used Fielding, and when he was finished with him, he disposed of him."

Joshua pulled up once more to the desk. "How do you translate Martha Fielding's attitude? Wouldn't you say that generally her answers were both defensive and conditional, as if she could still be thinking of her late husband in the present tense—"

"That's not so unusual for someone who's recently lost a loved one. She's simply refusing to accept that he's gone. Besides, she's a proud woman, Joshua, and she's lost her husband under rather rotten circumstances. She's bearing a heavy burden of having Stanley accused of being a thief, and by some, of even being a traitor. Shertok told me last week that she's even asked him to try to get her son transferred to another school."

Joshua reached up to pull thoughtfully on his lower lip. *Isn't that interesting,* he thought. *So she's trying to relocate the boy in the San Diego area.*

"I promise you," Ben was saying, "that we'll have an answer on the tail by noon," and he held up his hand in a conciliatory gesture. "I have contacts in both Washington and San Diego working on it right now."

Joshua nodded his approval.

"We trust your instincts, Joshua," Ben went on. "Which is one of the main reasons you're with us," he said, smiling as he checked his watch.

Taking the cue, Joshua reached up to straighten his tie, and the feeling in his belly started up again. Ben got up, crossed the small room to sit down before the electronic equipment jammed into the corner opposite his desk. The purchasing office to be used by Joshua was fully monitored at the CP, and the meeting with Paul Jaylis would be video and audio taped.

"You better get going," Ben told him. "Shertok is due here in a couple of minutes to watch the show."

Swallowing once, Joshua turned toward the door, thinking that it was now a little like countdown to kick-off.

"Oh, yes," Ben said over his shoulder. "We made a covert entry into the Aerotec warehouse Saturday night, a kind of follow-up and more thorough visit, and we found two hot items."

"Radioactive?"

"Yeah, only mildly so, but still contaminated," Ben said idly as he began to adjust the various dials on the TV monitor. "The front end of a fork lift and a crowbar."

So it appeared that Paul Jaylis had the plutonium, after all, Joshua admitted to himself.

"It's not decisive," Ben went on, as if reading Joshua's thoughts. "But it takes all kinds of special permits to handle and transport radioactive material, especially via airfreight, and Aerotec has no record of ever applying for such permission."

Which suggested, as Joshua had to further admit to himself, that any nuclear material on the Aerotec premises had been there illegally. As he pushed out the door he filed the matter away for the moment, figuring that on a scale of one to ten, the probability of Stanley Fielding being alive had slipped from about five down to a low of around one or two.

The garage on Pepper Tree Lane . . .

The door markings on the white sedan identified it as one belonging to the security agency contracted to protect the premises. The sedan had pulled in to park next to the huge pepper tree, as if to take advantage of the early morning shade. Its driver, a patrolman in the employ of the security agency, moved out of the car to the chain-link gate, where he unlocked the heavy padlock. The old garage was on his hot sheet, which meant that it had to be inspected in detail at least once on a random basis every eight hours. Following procedure, he slowly circled the now heavily secured building. Satisfied, he next opened the control box to the alarm system, verifying that all circuits were operational and that the back-up power system was charged. At the rear of the building, he peered curiously through a lexan window, and from what he could tell, the building was still empty. Perhaps, he thought as he moved on, the owners soon would be moving in something of value. Until then, he figured the property would be bypassed by thieves or vandals, who would likely not be willing to waste their time and risk arrest by breaking into a building which they could easily see was vacant.

He checked his watch, logging the time on his route sheet. It was exactly 8:45 a.m. Finished and satisfied that the premises were secure, he left the property a few minutes later, locking the gate behind him.

Inside the building, there was no sound except for the steady and insistent roar of the rush-hour traffic from the nearby Hollywood Freeway. The only recent change in the interior had gone unnoticed by the security patrolman: the addition of a two-inch metal conduit running from the grease pit under the heavy wooden cover to the small partitioned office. Inside the closed and windowless room, the three telephones had been removed from their connecting lines, placed neatly on the floor opposite from the even more recently installed item, a metal-covered console resembling a refrigerator. The conduit entered the console at its lower left side. Above the conduit connector, the three telephone power lines entered the console, protected and insulated away from the heavy metal wall by nylon grommets.

Inside the dark interior of the console there was only one item which was presently moving, the circular face of an electric timer, winding and indicating that the time remaining on the clock was forty-seven hours and thirty-five minutes.

The wall clock in his office read one minute to nine as Joshua slipped in behind his desk in the Visualon purchasing office. Conscious of his nervousness, he punched Ben Caplan's station on the intercom. Ben responded immediately from his nearby CP position.

"How do we look?" Joshua asked him, referring to the monitoring equipment. The TV unit was placed far back inside the ventilator shaft above and behind him. He knew there were several audio transmitters hidden about the room.

"Pull the chair in about a foot," Ben told him, "and turn it slightly more to the right."

Joshua got up, made the change.

His own intercom buzzed, startling him.

The lobby receptionist informed him that a Mr. Jaylis, from Aerotec, was waiting to see him. Plant security required that all visitors be escorted, so, following normal procedure, Joshua tried to compose himself as he moved down the connecting hallway and finally into the main lobby.

Paul Jaylis was at the receptionist's window, his back to Joshua, dutifully logging himself in. The lobby was otherwise empty since this was an early hour, even for most salesmen. Joshua moved quietly across the carpeted floor, thinking irrelevantly that on this their first meeting perhaps he had the advantage in approaching his antagonist from his blind and more vulnerable side. All he could tell at this point was that Paul Jaylis was two or three inches taller than he expected, that he was more on the slender side.

Joshua cleared his throat, feeling his advantage slip away as he briefly reminded himself that the action profile on this Monday-morning salesman reported that he was a ruthless and calculating killer and if he was at all vulnerable for the moment, it was because it was to his advantage and not Joshua's.

"Mr. Jaylis," Joshua inquired warily, now playing the role of the overworked and harassed hardware buyer, typically a junior on the purchasing totem pole.

Paul Jaylis turned to face him.

Joshua's first impression was that the man's edge was in his dark, probing eyes. His face was gaunt, angular, yet really not at all striking, neutralized obviously by the prominence of his eye line, itself slightly recessed under his black, dense eyebrows. Joshua realized he had taken a half step backwards, as if he needed more room between him and the hard, appraising look of Paul Jaylis.

"Yes, sir," Jaylis was saying as he extended his right hand. "I'm with Aerotec." His face broke slightly as he spoke, his voice well modulated, low in timbre, traced slightly with a British accent.

Joshua shook his hand, noting the moderate grip. Like his clothes, Paul Jaylis thus far was playing it right down the middle. Nodding in the affirmative, Joshua turned to lead his visitor back to his office. En route, he introduced himself as Joe Bates, a buyer in need of prompt help.

As he took his appointed chair in front of Joshua's desk, Jaylis asked how Visualon came to find out about Aerotec.

"We don't usually sell to local OEM's," he added, as if justifying the inquiry.

Joshua had to think for a second, trying to remember what OEM meant, and he felt the sweat trickling down his sides, knowing that Ben Caplan and Wolf Shertok were watching his every move. He felt his rising panic beginning to subside as he remembered that OEM was the industry abbreviation for Original Equipment Manufacturer. "We picked up your name from Struthers at Lockheed," he told Jaylis, and he shuffled through some papers on his cluttered desk. "Let's see," he went on, "about four months ago Aerotec supplied a short run of a couple hundred quarter-turns. You bailed Struthers out on a Palmdale shortage."

"Ah, yes," Jaylis responded, nodding his head. "I recall now. Are you after the same—"

"Negative," said Joshua, and he handed him a small folded-up blueprint. Watching him break open the drawing, Joshua knew they now had him thoroughly photographed, voice printed, and now, hopefully, fully fingerprinted. Ha Mossad no longer was without complete ID details on one Fawd Al-Shaer.

"We're after a similar quarter turn," Joshua went on. "But this is for the P6V program, and we require one complete shipset within four days."

Paul Jaylis looked up from the print. "Very exotic," he commented slowly. "The bar stock alone will take a special order; it's a special anti-magnetic copper blend."

"We have it in inventory."

Jaylis nodded approvingly. "What's the priority?"

"DX."

Jaylis offered an affirmative whistle under his breath, obviously recognizing the top military priority designation.

"What's your tooling time?" Joshua asked him.

"At least two days."

"The run will take only a few hours," Joshua suggested.

"That's true," Jaylis agreed, "but you've got to have GSI."

Joshua was ready for the abbreviation, meaning Government Source Inspection, because that was an integral part of their plan. "It can be arranged," Joshua assured him. "According to Struthers, your job shop complies with their QC standards."

"I see," said Jaylis. "It would save considerable time if we used the same job shop, since the QC inspection report is already on file at Lockheed."

"Exactly," Joshua confirmed, hardly able to conceal his pleasure that Jaylis himself had just cleared their major hurdle, to lock the fastener run into the San Eliso source.

Paul Jaylis straightened up in his chair, crossing his long legs, and Joshua was once again aware that he was being appraised. "We can deliver your fasteners," Jaylis said after a moment. "I estimate five hundred for set-up costs, which includes tooling."

"You're too high," Joshua snapped back.

"But the tooling is yours—"

"You mean Lockheed's," Joshua said, and they both smiled.

"Whatever," offered Jaylis.

"Fold the costs in," Joshua told him, "and bill us on a unit-cost basis." In his several days of schooling on the subject, Joshua had been repeatedly told that in order to appear normal in this business one had to be suitably devious.

"I'm curious," Jaylis was saying; "why don't you obtain parts from your regular supplier?"

Joshua grunted disdainfully. "The shop's doors were nailed shut last Thursday, by court order."

"Belly up," Jaylis commented.

"That's about the size of it," Joshua told him, feeling relieved that the meeting was drawing to an end. "As you're aware, Lockheed is on an extended-pay program with its contract suppliers."

"You mean it takes six months to collect."

"If you're lucky," Joshua said. "Their payables are under the control of a computer having sadistic tendencies."

"How do you pay?"

Joshua offered a small grin. "On this job, two percent ten days, net thirty; which are the terms we prefer. Also, we're A-one in D&B, which I presume you've already checked."

Smiling thinly and apparently assured, Jaylis then asked if he could keep the copy of the drawing.

"That's my office copy," Joshua told him as he reached to take it back. "I'll give you a confirmation copy of the purchase order before you leave, and I'll have a copy attached," and he turned to his intercom to call the purchasing secretary. Waiting for an answer, he asked Jaylis one last significant question, "I'll need the name and address of your shop for the Government Inspector."

"It's in San Eliso," Jaylis told him matter-of-factly as he opened his thin-line briefcase. "And, it'll be no trouble to find."

"I expect so," said Joshua to himself.

For Ben Caplan, locked in the cramped CP, the rest of the day twisted and turned on several developments:

Prior to his leaving the building, Paul Jaylis had invited Joshua to accompany him back to Aerotec for a plant tour, a normal enough gesture for a new supplier out to solicit additional business. Watching the exchange on the TV monitor, Ben felt that Joshua had acted correctly in finally accepting after several polite attempts to put Jaylis off. Wolf Shertok had been noncommittal, beyond the comment that fifty-thousand dollars disqualified Joshua as an amateur and that he could at least earn his way by spending a few hours with a devil like Fawd Al-Shaer. Perhaps, Wolf Shertok had suggested as he left the office, they could learn something worthwhile from each other.

Shortly before noon, Ben's San Diego contact had called in to report that the tail working Mrs. Fielding was in fact a private investigator operating on his own in the hope that Stanley Fielding was not dead after all. The investigator's name was Morton Campbell, and his motivation was the simple and straightforward matter of a twenty-five thousand dollar fee he might earn, since Stanley Fielding, at the time of his death, had been covered with a quarter-of-a-million dollar insurance policy. Because the identification and cremation of the remains took place in a foreign country under questionable circumstances, the insurance company was understandably balking at making payment.

Small wonder that Martha Fielding was uptight.

Ben was concerned with the report only to the extent it might demoralize Joshua.

Shortly before noon, Anne Delemar had called in to transmit a brief message from Alan Hunt, "From white to gray in machine shop, west wall." Apparently using one of the commune phones, Anne had been hushed and did not use any more time than was necessary, hanging up immediately. The message was complete anyway. Alan Hunt had uncovered low-level radiation in the machine shop. Using the diagram put together of the commune building, drawn from Alan's careful description, plus his several photographs, Ben identified the "west wall" as that wall in the basement supporting the only locked door in the building.

At 12:30 p.m., Joshua had called in to report that he was having lunch with Paul Jaylis at a nearby restaurant popular for its luncheon bill of fare. Ben had briefly reported Alan's findings, but did not mention the Fielding development for fear he might distract Joshua at a critical time in his dealing with Jaylis. Ben had suggested that Joshua order the liver and onions with a rasher of bacon.

Joshua had hung up on him.

Shortly after one o'clock, Wolf Shertok had stopped by long enough to drop off a courier packet from Tel Aviv containing the background report on the man known as Kabir. Real name, Keshab Henderson, AKA Spenta Mainyu, AKA Kabir Ali Mazda. Age probably thirty-eight years, based on data obtained from enrollment records at Cambridge University. Father's name, Orville Henderson, a British subject who had served in India for eleven years as a technical advisor. Mother's name unknown, presumed deceased and known only to be an Indian national. Subject employed civil service Indian government for six years following doctorate and research work at University of California at Berkeley. Record under AKA reports eighteen months residence Cairo, Egypt, also unknown period in Damascus, Syria.

Major while at Cambridge: Physics, mathematics.

Research work at Berkeley: Nuclear physics, both theoretical and practical applications.

Work performed for Indian Civil Service: Assistant project manager, Tarapur facility, India's first atomic power plant. Also temporary assistant PM for unidentified department R&D group terminated just before India detonation underground nuclear explosion, Pajasthan desert area.

The report ended with the statement that a supplementary report would be forthcoming as soon as contact could be made with Kabir's father, who was known to be alive and living near London, England.

It occurred to Ben Caplan that Kabir was yet another by-product of British colonialism, which in its more bizarre form often cropped up to haunt the Israelis.

He closed the cover of the report slowly, noting that there was nothing to tie Kabir in with any terrorist activity. His thoughts tumbled as he placed the folder in the center drawer of his desk. He tried to think logically, closing his eyes against the harsh light of the cramped office. His experience in law and with the Bureau restrained him from jumping to conclusions; the most likely error now would be to deduce without further evidence that Kabir was performing in the area of his qualifications. A nuclear physicist could pump gas for a living. But, on the other hand, fish tended to swim. His thoughts were suddenly interrupted by the insistent ringing of the door buzzer. He reached under the lip of his desk to punch the release button.

Joshua closed the door behind him.

Ben noticed that Joshua looked flushed.

"Tough morning," Ben observed as his friend fell into the chair opposite him. He reached to the tape recorder on the corner of the desk and turned it on.

"Not really," Joshua was saying as he pulled a small notebook out of his jacket pocket. He then released his tie, unbuttoning the top button on his shirt. "And to top it off," he added wearily, "I'm about half smashed," and he shook his head once. "Don't ever try to drink that guy under the table. He shoots whiskey doubles, no ice, straight up."

"The British influence," Ben said dryly. Another habit, he thought to himself. "So let's get your impressions while they're still fresh. We've got a lot of ground to cover."

Joshua sighed once before starting to thumb down through his notebook. "Personality first," he began after composing himself. "He's arrogant, supremely self-confident. Very much in control of himself. Deliberate. Seems to function thoughtfully. He can be polite or rude, from one moment to the next. He over-tipped our waiter, praised him for his service. Yet, a few minutes earlier, he ripped a waitress unmercifully because she was slow in bringing me coffee."

So, Ben thought, perhaps their Arab adversary was a chauvinist; perhaps yet another habit, a more old-world variety. "Would you say he angers quickly?"

"Yes."

"Would you qualify him as a cobra or a mongoose?"

"Definitely cobra," Joshua answered quickly. "Very slick, eyes are almost hypnotic. And, he's no dummy; very intelligent and informed. He would tend to finesse before using force. Unless, maybe, if he's angry."

"Would he be better at offense or defense?"

Joshua delayed before answering, "I'm sure he would prefer to be on the offense; but to be better at one or the other,

I can't say," and with that comment he tossed the notebook onto Ben's desk. "Additional comments are there, nervous habits, repetitive speech patterns. He carries a black rubber ball around with him, which he uses to exercise his hands, for what reason he never mentioned. Maybe he's an exercise freak."

Ben nodded as he put the book aside for the time being. "Any general impressions?" he asked idly.

"The man could blow your brains out without batting an eye."

Ben smiled appreciatively. "It's interesting," he said then, "that between the cobra and the mongoose, the snake usually loses."

Joshua merely shrugged once. "So, steer clear of mongooses."

Ben was smiling as he squared up a stack of papers on his desk. "I'm sorry to report some negative news," he said carefully, changing the subject. "The tail on Martha Fielding is a private type chasing a possible insurance reward."

"Oh, wow!" exclaimed Joshua.

"Stanley Fielding was covered with a quarter-million policy, and the wife's having trouble collecting. Like, you know, Fielding's death wasn't exactly normal."

"So it's like in the past tense, after all," Joshua observed wryly, not trying to hide his disappointment. "He was the perfect link."

Moving on rapidly, Ben recapped the Kabir background report.

"So," said Joshua after Ben had finished, "we lose one and we win one."

"Let's say we've got a possible," Ben said cautiously, confirming again that he was a careful man who went strictly by the book.

Joshua had turned in his chair, looking at him sideways.

"It's admittedly an awfully good possible," Ben conceded in response to the obvious skeptical stare.

"And Alan says the west wall of the machine shop is hot," Joshua said carefully as he looked down to stare at the floor. "It's getting near to decision-making time," he suggested after a moment.

"We don't have nearly enough evidence."

"Not for a court, maybe. I respect, and certainly understand, that you and Shertok, and the Ha Mossad, and especially Anne Delemar, are all involved in this operation on an additional level than Alan and, to a lesser extent, myself. You want this clown so badly you have a continually running ache in your belly just thinking about it. However, as somewhat of an outsider looking in, I've got to tell you this situation is getting spooky, to say the least."

"You don't think we can handle it?"

"What's to handle?" Joshua fired back. "Earlier this morning I had some doubt. But, suddenly it's like we're turning over rocks, finding goodies. I have the feeling that if we turned this investigation over to the Government, maybe they'd have Jaylis and his crew indicted within twenty-four hours," and he turned aside now to stare at the wall. "After I left him this afternoon," he added slowly, "I had the distinct feeling that he was laughing at me behind my back."

"You want to report what we've got?" Ben asked evenly.

Joshua shook his head no.

"Well, what then?"

"Why not set a reasonable time, some deadline we can shoot for," Joshua recommended, "that we agree to turn it over."

Ben pondered the suggestion briefly. "Let's call a team meeting to discuss it," he said then.

"Tonight?"

"Nine o'clock?"

"What about Alan and Anne; do they have time?"

"No problem," Ben assured him, reaching for a phone. "I can have a message at the drop point within thirty minutes. They can break out under the pretext of going to a movie in San Diego. Let's meet at your apartment."

"Good," said Joshua as he pushed himself up out of his chair. "I'm heading there now to take a nap, try to think all this out."

"Today was a productive one," Ben said, trying to sound encouraging. "We have enough ID details on Jaylis now to peg him no matter how he tries to hide himself."

"Let's hope so," said Joshua, once again shaking his head. "If Jaylis is a typical example of what you guys are up against, then I don't envy you one bit."

Benjamin Caplan took his hand off the phone, stroked his chin several times before replying, "This is just another tactical situation, Joshua. We're at war, literally so, as you know—"

"What a waste," Joshua said wearily as he turned now

toward the door. "What an incredible waste of talent, of man-power, of money."

"Please understand, my friend," Ben said, delaying the re-lease of the door latch, "that we're not involved in simply win-ning or losing; we're involved in the struggle for survival."

Joshua had turned to study him, saying nothing, his hand placed lightly on the door.

"What's on your mind?" said Ben, uncomfortable under the stare.

"You should've been named David," Joshua finally an-swered.

Ben shrugged once. "My father is a practical man, who felt at my birth that he might have produced a strong right hand."

Joshua nodded, saying, "There is one other important mat-ter."

"What is it?"

"Would you kindly push that button so this half-stoned as-similationist can go get some rest?"

Ben felt his face turning up in a grin as he pushed the but-ton.

Alone in his apartment, Joshua left his clothes in a trail on his way to the bedroom. Stopping next to his bed, he paused to contemplate the stack of books on the night stand. Along about three o'clock that morning, he had articulated to himself the wish that someone ought to come up with a simplified and abbreviated volume on Jewish history. After six or seven hours of cramming, his clearest conclusion was that his ancestors had consistently abandoned the theme to concentrate on the variations. He pushed the matter out of his mind as he turned toward the bathroom.

Stripped to his shorts, he went directly to the toilet and lifted the lid from the tank. On the underside of the lid he pulled away the heavy overlay of waterproof tape to reveal a small oilskin package. Back in the kitchen, he dropped the packet on the service counter before going to the sink, where he mixed himself a bromo, downing the foaming mixture in a single gulp. Feeling a little better, he sat down on one of the bar stools facing the counter to unwrap the packet. A few sec-onds later he turned the pistol in his hand, weighing it care-fully.

A memento from a time past.

He never guessed that he'd have need for the Viper again.

The memories pulsed in and out of his tired mind—a woman's face, briefly held, then gone . . .

He had fired the small automatic only twice. Once to test its action, finding it without recoil or sound, practically smokeless. The Viper was one of a kind, developed initially as an assassination weapon, a prototype whose design had been abandoned in favor of a heavier, bigger-bored version.

Its special 22-caliber cartridge didn't depend upon energy to kill.

The pure crystalline cyanide formed into the slug did the job.

Its moving parts were all teflon coated for silent action. Its titanium barrel had its own fluted, built-in silencer.

The second, and last time, he had fired the Viper he had missed, for which he was later thankful, because he was trying to hit a man, someone who had shortly thereafter perished as a victim of his own doing.

The Viper was carried in a special thigh holster, on the inside of his leg just below his crotch, where it would be difficult to locate during a more routine search.

He turned the weapon once more in his hand, bringing his thoughts back to the present. He had resurrected the Viper because he finally sensed that he might need it.

Operation Rahab was not only getting spooky; it was also, as he suspected, getting dangerous as well.

Ben Caplan arrived first, at a little after eight-thirty. Working together, he and Joshua methodically worked down the material gathered to date. Wolf Shertok entered the small apartment at five minutes before nine. He only had a chance to get a cup of coffee and sit down when Alan Hunt and Anne Delemar arrived. Having allotted only thirty minutes for the meeting, Ben Caplan immediately called them to order. Using the dinette table as a makeshift dias, he began with the reason for the meeting, that Joshua had asked to establish a deadline by which time they would agree to turn over all the evidence obtained to the appropriate U.S. Government agency.

"That was not the original agreement," Wolf Shertok growled. "You are in our employ. We obtained private investigator's licenses for you, at great expense and for a reason. You legally have the right of confidentiality. We are your clients. The information is privileged," and he looked to Ben for confirmation.

"Skip the legalisms," Joshua said brusquely. "You don't have to lean on us to protect your interests. What I'm talking about is the direct knowledge or evidence relating to the commission of a felony," and he raised his hand in a pointed gesture, "and in particular the commission of an act threatening the security of the country." He too then looked to Ben Caplan. "It is the simple matter of being an accessory, right?"

Ben held up his hands in a calming gesture. "Let's run over what we've got, then come back to this subject."

Both Joshua and Shertok nodded their approval.

Alan Hunt listened carefully as Ben systematically reported their findings to date. For some reason, the Kabir report did not surprise him. He looked at Joshua when the Fielding development was briefly mentioned; his friend's face remained expressionless. Ben finished his report with the comment that except for the radiation readings uncovered at Aerotec and the commune, their evidence was entirely circumstantial.

"What kind of case do we actually have?" Joshua asked Ben.

"Paul Jaylis certainly has the motive," Ben said. "Plus ample opportunity. He's now in the country illegally. Kabir's credentials qualify him to oversee a production operation involving advanced weapons components, plus he has the equipment enabling him to produce the parts. Aerotec's shipping manifests report many recurring shipments of such heavy, bulky items as complete jet and piston-driven aircraft engines, each weighing several thousand pounds, to critical Middle-East destinations. The plutonium, either in one shipment or broken up into small lots, could easily have been shielded off and smuggled out inside such crates. As for Kabir's production items," and he shook his head, "they would be duck soup to hide, considering the amount of freight Aerotec routes out of the country each month."

Alan Hunt began to respect the enormity of their problem.

Ben Caplan unexpectedly slammed his fist down on the small table, startling them all. "What we've got to have is physical evidence!"

"What kind of evidence?" Anne Delemar asked quietly.

"That shop is our best bet," Ben answered, pointing to Alan. "Any production procedure, especially with a lot of single piece items, involves at least three, possibly four, items. First, the blueprints, even if they are hand drawn. Second, the tooling, and third, the first articles. The fourth item might be special test equipment—go and no-go gauges, for example."

"They could all be destroyed," Joshua suggested.

"Not likely all," said Ben. "We've agreed that the reason Jaylis is still here is because his assignment is still not finished. Assuming atomic weapons construction is his objective, we can logically expect that they still have more of the components yet to produce."

"If we close hard right now," Joshua asked, "what are our prospects?"

"Two limited options," Ben replied gravely. "First, if we publicly expose him, then he'll simply disappear, or he'll be taken into custody for deportation. Maybe, and it's a weak chance, maybe we can present enough circumstantial evidence to convince public opinion that Israel was not involved in the MUF."

"No, no," Wolf Shertok insisted. "Our critics will simply argue that we fabricated the evidence. The gesture would probably hurt more than help."

"The second option," Ben went on, "is to revert back to our original plan: to kidnap him and transfer him back to Israel for trial on his past crimes."

"Don't you see," Shertok said quietly yet insistently, "we simply need more time."

Alan looked again to his friend and partner. The only evidence of Joshua's inner thoughts was the muscle drawn up along his jaw line.

"How much time?" Alan asked, probing now for some basis for agreement.

"On a crash basis," said Ben, "we must have a minimum of thirty-six hours."

Shertok grunted disgustedly. "What could be more reasonable. I should think three or four days would be perfectly acceptable."

"I'll be at the commune tomorrow morning," Ben went on, "posing as the government inspector, at which time I can thoroughly case the basement. Between then and midnight we'll have ample time to form an entry plan. We'll hit whatever's behind the door sometime after midnight tomorrow night. By sunrise, we'll either be in or out."

Alan checked his watch. He turned to look at Anne, who was relaxed back into the sofa, staring at the ceiling. Her dark hair was in close to the soft and delicate line of her throat.

"How's the machinist doing?" Joshua asked Alan, bringing his thoughts back to the room.

"Not bad," Alan told him. "Spent most of the day operating an automatic tapper, running in secondary threads on finished machine parts. Kabir says I might get to work on a turret lathe in a few days." He stood up, reached down to help Anne to her feet. "We must leave now," he said quietly.

"Stay away from the west wall," Ben warned him. "While the level isn't dangerous, it's wise not to take any chances."

"No problem," said Alan as he reached out to shake hands with Ben Caplan. He then turned to Wolf Shertok, who ignored him by staring adamantly at the floor between his feet. With Anne out the door before him, he stopped outside the door, waiting in the hallway. A few seconds later, Joshua came out of the apartment to move in beside him. He handed Alan a small paper bag.

"It's a thirty-eight special," Joshua told him. "I got it from Ben tonight."

"You really think I need it?"

"Hide it in the Jag for the time being."

Alan looked aside to see that Anne had moved down the hallway, leaving them alone. "You're in for a fight with the old man," Alan told him.

"No doubt, but the fee gives him the right." He glanced down the hallway toward Anne Delemar. "How's she doing?" he asked.

Alan placed the heavy bag under his left arm. "She is something else, my friend," he answered, and he realized that Joshua was now studying him closely.

"I suspect you're getting involved," said Joshua.

"You could be right," Alan said truthfully.

"Be careful, Alan Hunt."

"Yeah," said Alan, thinking that right now he'd rather be battling an angry storm surf, a much less complicated kind of basic confrontation.

"And good luck," Joshua added, a final kind of knowing glance passing between them as he turned back toward the apartment.

It was exactly three minutes before midnight when Kabir entered the Lindbergh Field passenger terminal. He walked hurriedly to the ticket counter holding his reservation, where he waited impatiently behind several people in line ahead of him. Nervously checking his watch once again, he realized that he was on time and had no need to be upset. The overhead TV monitor reported that his flight to New York City was on schedule.

The wall clock ticked off midnight, exactly.

They were all on schedule now.

He reached the counter, gave the girl the name, "Frank Desmond."

The girl went through her ritual. Her orderliness and efficiency settled him down. After giving her the money for the roundtrip ticket, he reached involuntarily to his chest, checking again that the heavy manila envelope was still secure under his shirt.

He carried no luggage, had no metal objects on his person, thereby assuring a clean run through the X-ray equipment.

With his ticket finally in hand, he turned toward the designated boarding area, thinking that he had ample time to visit the restroom, moving at a leisurely pace now, forcing himself to relax, to appreciate that it was all in motion now, nonreversible, and it mattered not how he, or any of them, felt about it.

Still, the decision to implement had come sooner than he had expected.

It was now Tuesday, and on the eastern seaboard, the area of his destination, it was already past three o'clock in the morning.

Either here or there, it was going to be a day to remember . . .

Chapter five

1:00 p.m., Tuesday, Eastern time.

Jerome Mason sensed he was on a fool's mission. At least, there was no middle ground, for either the Attorney General had been victimized by a truly warped crank, which was Mason's suspicion, or there was in fact one very large flap about to take place. He glanced aside to his driver, who was preoccupied with the rain-drenched and unusually nasty Washington traffic, before he tentatively lowered his window. It was still misting, the last of the brief summer deluge, and he was comforted a little to find the outside air cool, even a little fresh. The rain, he noted with approval, had at least temporarily cleaned up Washington.

The official Bureau car turned slowly onto Pennsylvania Avenue as he caught sight of the early afternoon sun, which for the moment was little more than a neon glow trapped in the squall line falling back toward Chesapeake Bay. Shifting his attaché case on his lap, he stared forward over the dash, chartreuse-colored telephone at the middle of the table. The rhythm lending cadence to his thoughts.

The briefcase contained the Bureau package on one of his best men, Benjamin Caplan.

The official sedan lurched to a halt, stopped by a red light, and the driver mumbled a definite expletive under his breath. Waiting for the light to turn green, Jerome Mason watched impatiently while the flow of traffic moved sluggishly across the intersection. A vintage VW van crowded through on the yellow light, and he thought once again that the traffic light was one of the purest forms of democracy, where one waited his turn, regardless of position or influence.

The driver punched the gas pedal then, and before Jerome Mason could sort out his thoughts, there it was, the familiar hulk of the White House. He straightened up, reaching for his ID, though it really wasn't necessary since the security staff would probably pass him through on his American Express card. Jerome Mason, the Director of the Federal Bureau of Investigation, was an easily recognizable figure of a man, who was often in the news. A few minutes later he was passed through the West Executive entrance.

Taken in tow by a staff member, he was escorted by a circuitous route to the President's own miniature war room, located several floors under the Executive Mansion. He was whisked through the main operations room, where he had only time to notice two persons on duty, an imposing bank of busy teletype machines, three or four massive TV monitors, and a raft of telephones—all secure. Seconds later he was left in an adjacent conference room.

Leslie Stalmeyer, the Attorney General, was on a phone at the head of the long table dominating the room. There were two men to Stalmeyer's right. The first, who simply nodded as he looked up at Mason, was Bill Morrison, head of the CIA. Mason did not recognize the other man. His first impression was that they all looked the same, very grim. Sobered himself, he took Stalmeyer's cue to move in to the seat directly to his superior's left, across from Bill Morrison. He then noticed a chartreuse colored telephone at the middle of the table. The phone was dial-less with the brass nameplate: "Private Line— President."

Mason put his briefcase down carefully on the table before taking his seat.

Stalmeyer cradled his phone noisily.

"I'm almost afraid to ask," Mason said evenly.

Bill Morrison, known for his self-control, was shaking his head gravely.

"It's for real," his boss snapped, and he reached down to the table and pushed a sheet of paper to Mason. "Read it once; then we'll get started."

The first item Mason noticed was that the letter was a copy, not an original. The next item was the thin blue line bordering the paper, typifying that the document had the highest possible security classification. The typed letter was without heading, starting out addressed to the President of the United States, followed by the opening salutation:

Mr. President:

You are hereby instructed to immediately formulate the necessary planning to implement the following:

A. The United States Government will at once commence action on all fronts to require the illegal State of Israel to remove all her settlements from the occupied west bank of the Jordan River. Assuming negative reaction from the Israelis, you are instructed to concurrently commence the reduction of economic and military aid to that Government to whatever extent necessary to obtain their cooperation. The deadline for Israeli compliance is exactly thirty days from today.

B. The United States will also at once establish the official and diplomatic recognition of the Palestine Liberation Organization. Your public announcement, prescribed below, will be firm and without reservation on this matter, especially the term, which will be indefinite.

C. Further, you will publicly admit your obedience and agreement to this order before the open forum of the General Assembly of the United Nations not later than this Thursday noon, Eastern time.

To insure your compliance, you are advised that a nuclear explosive device, capable of delivering a minimum 20-kiloton yield, has been placed in or near Los Angeles, California. The device is so situated to remain hidden and fully armed for whatever time you may require to comply with our demands, indefinitely, if necessary.

Please note the enclosed drawings and specifications. The source of our warhead nuclear material is the plutonium obtained from Armatrex, the San Diego processing plant, on April 25, this year.

To further demonstrate our capability, we will detonate a demonstration device today on the Yucca Flats test site at exactly 1200 hours, your time. This device will produce 3 kilotons.

You may further verify by interviewing one of your own FBI agents, Benjamin Caplan, who is presently on leave of absence from the Bureau in the Los Angeles area.

You will acknowledge receipt of this message by transmitting your agreement to cooperate over the Los Angeles radio station KOPE at their evening weather broadcast, between 2000 and 2005 hours. You may also pass messages at the 0600 weather broadcast, same station.

In all communications, refer to the code name, RAHAB.

You are to know that the undersigned carries on his person at all times the means to immediately, repeat, immediately detonate the Rahab device. You are cautioned to respect this foolproof protective mechanism.

We are resolute in our determination and will to succeed.

We will not tolerate any deviation from the above stated demands; they will be met to the letter. There will be no negotiation.

The letter was signed, "FAWD AL-SHAER."

"For *indefinitely*," said Jerome Mason, hearing the disbelief in his own voice, and he looked up to Les Stalmeyer. "You mean the Yucca Flats thing went off?"

"Right on schedule," Bill Morrison told him.

Already accustomed to terrorist sponsored crises, Jerome Mason still could not help but exclaim, "My God!" And he shook his head before adding, "So they're going for the jackpot this time."

"We shouldn't be surprised," Bill Morrison said, not trying to hide the bitterness in his voice.

As he handed the letter back to Stalmeyer, Mason realized now why he had the package on Benjamin Caplan. The only other information he had been given earlier by his boss was a telephone call telling him that the State Department had received a threatening letter and that Ben Caplan was involved.

The code name Rahab meant nothing to him.

He was trying to digest and interpret the general gist of the ultimatum when he realized he was being introduced to the man sitting quietly to the right of Bill Morrison.

"Doctor Ewing Melbourne," Stalmeyer was saying.

Still stunned, his mind tumbling, Mason had to catch up, playing back the pertinent details of the introduction that Melbourne was a wheel out of the Nuclear Regulatory Agency, having spent ten years as an advanced weapons designer, at the Sandia Laboratory, Los Alamos. He focused in on the man finally. Melbourne appeared to be an unimposing sort, probably laboratory oriented, who apparently helped keep his nerves under control by sucking on an unlit pipe. Doctor Melbourne's image suggested he should be puttering with orchids in an atrium instead of designing atomic bombs.

"The purpose of this meeting," Stalmeyer was saying, "is singlefold: to determine if there is in fact a legitimate threat present," and he held up the blue-bordered letter copy. "That's all," and he dropped the paper. "If it is for real, as it appears to be, then the President will be notified immediately." He sat down then. "Let's take the letter in sequence. First, the demand bit is irrelevant. Next is the demo shot."

"It went off," Mason said matter-of-factly.

"And we had nearly two hours," Bill Morrison added, "to get our monitor group out there alerted." He turned to Melbourne. "What kind of time schedule before they report their final numbers?"

Melbourne finally took his pipe out of his mouth. "Doesn't really matter," he offered after clearing his throat. "That baby went off, and there's no doubt it was nuclear. It was also underground, for which we can be thankful, and it still broke three on the Richter at Vegas." He went back to his pipe. Comment finished.

Bill Morrison began to jot down notes.

Jerome Mason pulled a pad out of his jacket pocket, opened a blank page. "How could they've pulled it off? Right on our own test range—"

"Simple enough," Melbourne offered. "Our security on the Flats is at a minimum. There are a number of deep probe shafts which could be breached by anyone able to break through a few feet of concrete."

"Next is the routine about the bomb placed in Los Angeles," said Stalmeyer, shaking his head gravely.

"Has no bearing," Morrison said resignedly.

Noticing Morrison's almost discouraging tone, Mason remembered then that the head of the CIA had family in the Los Angeles area.

"All right," said Stalmeyer, "that brings us to the drawings and specifications," and he looked to Melbourne, who once again removed his pipe; only this time he put it down on the table.

"We'll know more about it in a few hours," said Melbourne cautiously, "but at this point we can certainly say that the design is sound, very basic, in fact," and he reached up to scratch his forehead thoughtfully. "The schematics are highly original."

"On a scale of one to ten," said Morrison interestedly, "what's the chance of it working?"

Melbourne nodded slowly in the affirmative. "That's one of the peculiarities of the design; they've really over-engineered in assuring detonation. For the tamper volume they report, they've programmed in at least twenty percent more cap points than the design really needs. I would say in the ideal, with all support conditions favorable, the chances of it working would be at nine plus on your scale."

"Can you predict its yield?" Mason asked him.

"Later," Stalmeyer interjected. "Let's move on to the next item, the matter of the demo shot."

"What can we add at this time," said Melbourne. "Some nut has set off an atomic bomb in our own backyard."

"Can you believe it!" Morrison exclaimed.

Ignoring the comment, Stalmeyer went on, "So there's the matter of your agent, Jerry."

Jerome Mason sensed the overwhelming weight of the evidence; the sheer enormity of the situation caused his thoughts to break once again. He clamped his eyes closed, trying to find a handle, where to begin—

"—about this Benjamin Caplan," Stalmeyer was saying, his voice insistent.

"One of our best men," Mason finally offered. "For the past two years, he's been working in the Special Litigation Section."

"Have you contacted him yet?"

"No; like the letter says, he's on leave of absence."

"Who's in charge of your L.A. office?" Stalmeyer asked irritably.

"Burt Ingstrom."

"As soon as we break," Stalmeyer said, "you get Ingstrom on the horn and tell him to get out an APB on Caplan. That's first. Next, have him obtain an adequate building to use as an operations center—"

"I know what to do," Mason assured him. "Shall we use the same code, Rahab?"

"Definitely," said Stalmeyer, looking to Bill Morrison for confirmation. "They're familiar with the term, and using it will avoid confusion."

"Don't forget," Melbourne pointed out, "this Fawd character says he can trigger the device from his own person, which suggests he has some sort of trigger control mechanism with him."

"Could be a bluff," Morrison proposed.

"Can't take the chance," Stalmeyer said evenly. "We must inform all field personnel that if they come in contact with this man, unless specific orders are issued to the contrary, that they will not take any action to injure or disable him, nor will any threats be made against him." He looked to Jerome Mason. "That's your area of responsibility."

Making a note on his pad, Mason acknowledged the order with a terse, "Yes, sir," adding then, "Have you noticed that he does not identify himself with any group or organization?"

"He's with somebody," Melbourne suggested, "because it took a whole pack of people to put this package together."

"Doesn't matter," Stalmeyer said. "The important thing for the moment is that we all agree that there is a legitimate threat present, and that I will so inform the President."

Each of the other men present somberly indicated they agreed.

"What about the acknowledgment?" Bill Morrison asked.

"Have Ingstrom arrange to report receipt of the demand letter tonight," said Stalmeyer. "We don't want these guys getting nervous."

Jerome Mason pushed himself away from the table.

"Where're you going?" asked Stalmeyer.

"My office first, then home to pack. I'll try to get an early evening flight—"

"Negative," Stalmeyer told him abruptly. "Forget the office and home. You and Doctor Melbourne will leave immediately for Los Angeles. You've got a twenty-four-hour time limit to nail these clowns!"

"We've got to be careful," Bill Morrison pointed out. "If

this leaks, we can have a full-scale panic on our hands."

"You better believe it," Stalmeyer confirmed. "This goes top priority, total secrecy all the way on a strictest need-to-know basis."

"It's incredible!" Morrison exclaimed heatedly. "So here we go with the Arabs and Jews again. Why is it they can be so disruptive—"

"Stow it, Bill," Stalmeyer snapped. "Put your energy to work solving the problem."

Bill Morrison sighed heavily. "Sir, I'm going to have to tell you how it is first. You know how long I've been with the Agency—"

"Going on twenty years, I would guess."

"Closer to thirty years," Morrison said evenly. "And, it has been during that period that I can tell you without any doubt that both the Arabs and the Israelis have become the worst kind of international prima donnas. The two factions have become like two spoiled brats. And we've encouraged them, even aided and abetted them . . . " and he shook his head wearily. "The Arabs, I guess, mostly because of their oil, the refugee problem. And the Jews for a number of reasons, the most legitimate because of the holocaust. But sooner or later the world community has got to put its foot down. Don't you see," and he pointed to the ultimatum letter, "this is just another expression of their childish arrogance. So that, finally, because of our own indulgence, we've got them playing their games right here, as Doctor Melbourne put it, right in our own backyard. I tell you like it is; their collective butts should've been paddled ten years ago—"

Jerome Mason noticed that Doctor Melbourne looked shaken at hearing the head of the CIA describe the Israelis and Arabs as international prima donnas in need of butt paddling, a quote which would easily make the front page of the *Washington Post*.

"Are you finished?" Les Stalmeyer asked.

"Yes, sir, I am."

"Then we all know what we have to do."

Bill Morrison and the Attorney General left the room together.

As he came out of his chair, Jerome Mason was thinking that Les Stalmeyer was going to be the bearer of some very unhappy news when he reported to the President of the United States. He could only guess at the response of this upper and more clinical end. As the Attorney General correctly understood, time itself was now the important influence. If the investigative resources of the Government could wrap it up in a hurry, say in less than twenty-four hours, then the matter would pass as hardly a ripple across the Washington scene. As he turned to reach for the nearest outside phone to call Burt Ingstrom, Jerome Mason abandoned speculation on the broader implications, should the matter drag out.

He noticed then that Doctor Melbourne was still seated, staring vacantly at the papers before him.

"Forget what Bill said," Mason told him.

The Doctor looked up. "There's a certain truth in what he proposed."

"Forget it," Mason repeated. "He's upset because he has family in Los Angeles. His oldest son and wife, with two children. A grandfather, you know, tends to be overly protective."

"And he can't warn them?"

"No way."

"That's terrible," Melbourne suggested.

Jerome Mason paused before dialing the Los Angeles number. "It's just as terrible, sir, that you should suggest he might warn them. Or, didn't you hear the security classification assigned to this investigation?"

Doctor Melbourne reached up to rub his forehead. "You're right. It's just that I'm having trouble coming to grips with the situation. It's all so grotesque—"

"Come to grips with it," Mason advised him sternly, "and the sooner the better. You see, you might be just the one to solve it for us."

Chapter six

5:30 p.m., Tuesday, Pacific Time.

Burt Ingstrom slammed his phone down. Alone in his headquarters office, he leaned forward over his desk to jab the intercom switch for his secretary, who finally answered after what seemed an interminably long delay.

"The Director will be here in fifteen minutes," he snapped at her. "Give me the word the instant the helicopter hits the roof!"

He stood up then, sighing once, thinking that he had to get control of himself. Burt Ingstrom was a bull of a man from the waist up, broad-shouldered and barrel-chested, who when erect stood just short of five feet six inches, helped along to that height when wearing his usual two-inch elevator shoes. A reserve Marine colonel about whom it had once been remarked that he should sue the Government for building the parade ground too close to his fanny. He strode militarily toward the closed door leading to the adjacent office.

Joshua Bain opened his eyes as Ingstrom entered the room, and he was not at all encouraged or comforted to notice that Ingstrom appeared to look even angrier now than he had when he left the room a few minutes earlier.

"That was the Director," Ingstrom told them, emphasizing the word "Director" as if to accent the imminent probability of the official judgment about to befall them all.

Ben Caplan, seated to his right, simply groaned.

Wolf Shertok, seated farther across the room to his right, remained immobile.

Burt Ingstrom did not return to the desk in front of the opposite window, choosing rather to begin stalking back and forth in front of them. "He will be here in a few minutes," he added cryptically.

"Did he mention anymore—" Ben said curiously.

"No, nothing."

So, Joshua thought, all that Ingstrom apparently knew was that they had been assembled to account for what they knew about the name Fawd Al-Shaer and the code word, Rahab. In the thirty minutes prior to the Director's phone call, the three of them had as best they could reported all they did know, and truthfully so, upon the advice of Ben Caplan.

"I honestly don't know where to begin," said Ingstrom. "From what you've told me so far, I'd say it'll take a grand jury a month just to sort out the charges. Like, a half dozen counts each on accessory after the fact, withholding evidence, illegal entry, forging false documents, conspiracy," and he stopped before Ben to look down at him contemptuously. "And you are guilty of the worst kind of misconduct—abusing your office. One of your operators could probably be classified as an illegal alien!"

"The arrogance of the man," Wolf Shertok growled. "Using our own code name," and he shook his head disgustedly.

"We've got a hole in the organization," Joshua added, "big enough to drop an elephant through."

"He played us like a fiddle," said Ben.

Burt Ingstrom stared at the three men, his expression turning bewildered under the arch of his sandy, straw-like hair. "I get the feeling," he finally said, "that what I'm saying is going right over your heads."

"We're very aware of what you're saying," Ben assured him. "It's just that, well . . . that what we're up against is about five times more than double the trouble."

"How about to the tenth power," suggested Joshua ruefully.

"Okay," said Ingstrom as he turned back to the desk, dropping heavily into the chair behind it. "So we'll wait for the old man."

Joshua took note of the threat in the man's voice.

"You are finished!" Wolf Shertok was saying.

Joshua realized the older man was talking directly to him, and he shook his head understandingly. "Your investment will be returned."

"That's totally unfair," said Ben emotionally. "I was responsible for security."

Joshua noticed that Ingstrom's nordic expression had softened into the hint of a smile. "That brings us to a certain question," Ingstrom said. "Like, who is behind your little scheme?"

"We operate independently," said Wolf Shertok quickly, and he looked out the open window behind the desk, an almost casual display of indifference. "We are in fact entirely on our own," he added then.

"Come on," said Ingstrom. "You're trying to tell me you've done all this without any outside help. You're insulting my intelligence. Why, your expenses alone have been enormous, at least into six figures."

"We have the support of sympathetic people," Shertok insisted. "Some very wealthy people in fact."

Looking aside to Ben Caplan, Joshua understood that Ingstrom's intelligence was beyond being insulted; it was now being tested, the usual position of anyone daring to take on Wolf Shertok.

"What are their names?" Ingstrom demanded.

"A confidential matter," said Shertok.

The intercom buzzer interrupted the confrontation.

Ending round one, which Joshua scored easily to Shertok.

Ingstrom answered the phone, hung it up almost immediately. He pushed himself up from behind the desk to start toward the door. "The old man is due on the roof any minute now." Then turning in the doorway he commanded, "Don't leave this office, you understand?"

"Are we under arrest?" Shertok asked him bluntly.

"You will be," Ingstrom warned him, "if you take one step out of this room."

The statement and its qualifier seemed clear enough to Joshua, who settled himself deeper into his chair. All they could do now was wait, and he was wishing that Alan Hunt were here to lend his support, for his friend had a novel way of dealing with such crises: he simply left it all up to his Lord.

7:30 p.m.

With Les Stalmeyer on the line at the Washington end, Jerome Mason began his status report by reporting that Burt Ingstrom was en route to the broadcasting offices of radio station KOPE to supervise the acknowledgment statement. "It figures why they're using that station," Mason added, "because they transmit at fifty thousand watts from Catalina Island. A receiver can pick up the KOPE signal, especially if it's on high ground, from practically anywhere in the state."

"Where are you?" Stalmeyer asked him.

"I'm alone in Ingstrom's office. We've got a building picked out on the west end, at the airport, but it won't be operational for another hour."

"I've got clearance from the other agencies," said Stalmeyer, "and you've got carte blanche to use any agent or employee assigned to the area. Now, what's with your agent, what's his name, mentioned in the letter?"

Jerome Mason paused for a moment, arranging both the notes before him and his thoughts. The Ben Caplan trip was delicate at best. "Briefly it boils down to a private investigation," he began carefully, "involving several people working with Ben Caplan in an effort to clear Israel of suspicion in the diversion of the Armatrex plutonium."

"The same plutonium mentioned in the letter?"

"That's right," Mason confirmed. "Their investigation suggests strongly that an Arab agent actually engineered the MUF."

"By the name of Fawd Al-Shaer."

"Exactly."

There was a following pause.

"What's with this private investigation routine?" Stalmeyer asked.

"It's going to be tricky to unravel that," Mason admitted. "The group is headed up by Professor Wolf Shertok."

"The Zionist lecturer?"

"The same."

"Sounds kind of heavy."

"Plus," Mason went on, "there is a Joshua Bain and Alan Hunt also involved, a couple of free agents who worked with us in breaking the ETC case last year. Apparently they were hired by Shertok." He allowed his superior a second or two to digest the details before going on. "I have to go along with Burt in suspecting that the Israeli Secret Service is heavily involved, unofficially, we'll probably discover. Shertok has been well supported, even to the point of using an Israeli citizen operating here under a student's visa."

"So what do they have that can help?" said Stalmeyer resignedly.

And that was the difference, thought Mason, between a man like Stalmeyer and Burt Ingstrom. While Ingstrom was running around trying to find ways to lock up Shertok and his people, Stalmeyer more wisely asked for their help, at least for the time being.

"They have plenty," Mason said energetically. "Caplan has a fully equipped CP, which we're right now in the process of shifting to our own operations office. While they don't know where Fawd is, they've directed us to a location down the coast which has turned all the evidence we need to verify that the letter is definitely legitimate. Melbourne is there right now, and he called a few minutes ago to report that he's up to his ears in the most fully equipped, garage-type laboratory he has ever seen, even including a computer."

There was another pause.

"What's really with this Shertok bunch?" Stalmeyer finally demanded, the first note of skepticism in his voice.

"They're as much on the level as they could be," Mason assured him. "They were scheduled to hit the laboratory today, but Fawd and one of his key men disappeared on them early this morning, which threw them into a panic. Ben Caplan, with Joshua Bain pushing him, was within an hour of calling us in anyway."

"I don't know, Jerry," Stalmeyer said hesitatingly. "These

two free agents, what're their names?"

"Joshua Bain and Alan Hunt."

"They sound like a couple of amateurs—"

"Let me decide, please, Les. They're already in motion; let me get caught up."

"Okay; so what do we do with them?"

"I don't know for sure," Mason admitted. "I've assigned Caplan and Bain to my personal staff, to keep them out of Ingstrom's hair. By the way, they were not aware of the Rahab device itself."

"Have you told Caplan everything?"

"Yes, and Joshua Bain."

"Okay, Jerry," said Stalmeyer, "keep it contained, and you will continue to report on the hour, if possible."

"What's from your end?" Mason asked him.

"Not much," Stalmeyer answered slowly. "The President has given us our twenty-four hours. After which, if necessary, he intends to appoint some kind of committee of his own. Of course, as he rather tactlessly pointed out, he would rather not have to go through that kind of exercise."

Understandably so, thought Jerome Mason, aware that the Attorney General had just in no uncertain terms told him to get busy and solve the problem. "Is Bill Morrison there?" Mason asked him. "I want to open up communications with Israeli intelligence."

"I'll pass the message," said Stalmeyer. "By the way, tell Melbourne to call his Yucca Flats people. The demo shot apparently turned out less yield than the letter said it would."

Mason turned the report in his mind. "Maybe we should let them know, along with the acknowledgment, that their prize baby was a fizzle. Might shake them up, bring on a mistake, or something." He checked his watch and saw that it was four minutes to eight. "Can't make it tonight; how about tomorrow morning at six?"

"Consult with Melbourne first," Stalmeyer told him. "The significance of the lower yield might reveal something which may affect our strategy. At least, let's kick it around before leaking it to anybody."

Mason silently respected the wisdom of his superior's reasoning.

"So you actually have nothing hard," Stalmeyer stated.

"Not yet. We're hoping the San Eliso laboratory will produce something."

"Go get 'em, Jerry," he said, and he hung up.

Jerome Mason waited patiently for Bill Morrison to call. He hoped for results out of the San Eliso laboratory, but he had his doubts. After an intensive hour with Ben Caplan and Joshua Bain, it was obvious that their adversary gave them nothing but the bluest of blue sky, and he now suspected that the trend would continue. No doubt the lab would probably turn into just another carefully staged contribution in the Fawd Al-Shaer overall stroke job.

The breach in Ben Caplan's security suggested a more productive prospect.

The subject took him to the amateur, Joshua Bain. No chance for a leak there, at least not deliberately. And it occurred to him that Joshua might in this instance be more than just passively involved, since he, too, was a Jew, one whose mother and father had perished in a concentration camp. Joshua Bain had proved his loyalty to his country last year, dramatically so, and it was possible that now he was being tested on a more personal and more difficult level.

8:30 p.m.

The basement machine shop was still crowded, as Alan Hunt observed with a rising sense of indifference. Handcuffed to the spindle of an automatic screw machine, he shifted his weight once more to his left foot, looking down at the still form of Anne Delemar, who seemed finally to have gone to sleep. The man assigned to guard them had mercifully released her from her shackles a few minutes before, along with the somber warning that he would blow her brains out if she made a move to escape.

To escape from the commune now would be tantamount to a miracle.

The first of the Government agents had arrived by car nearly two hours ago. Then the helicopters came in on the beach. Alan Hunt figured the rest of the state was defenseless, or at least vulnerable, since he estimated that the greater majority of federal law enforcement officers were presently on the commune premises. He guessed at least fifty of them, all in civilian clothes.

He counted eight spotlights placed around the shop.

He wondered once more what it could be that would produce this kind of over-kill.

The mysterious door on the west wall had been opened,

and, based on the foot traffic in and out, the room behind it was obviously the center of attraction.

His nose itched, and he leaned over to scratch it.

"Watch it," the guard said nervously, waving his handgun, a 9mm automatic.

Alan stopped midway, debating whether to scratch his nose and chance getting shot or to back off and endure the itch. He laughed amusingly, confronted with the absurd choice.

The guard glared at him menacingly, his jaw muscles working slowly. The 9mm began to shake.

"I have to go to the bathroom," said Alan.

"Do it in your pants."

Alan Hunt patiently contemplated the man who now had become his adversary. Then asked him quietly, "Why are you so angry with us?"

The guard's eyes narrowed suspiciously.

"I get the feeling," Alan went on, "that you would really enjoy blowing out our brains."

The guard continued to stare at him, his face slack, expressionless, until after a few seconds Alan looked aside, not wishing to antagonize the man. Perhaps, he thought, the guard was uptight because he too was as much in the dark as he himself was. Movement on the staircase caught Alan's eye, and he turned slowly to see that Ben Caplan was entering the shop.

Joshua Bain followed close behind. This was his first time in the basement shop, but he immediately recognized the layout, having familiarized himself with the photographs and drawings provided by Alan Hunt. Having been accepted by Jerome Mason, he and Ben had driven directly to the commune, where they intended to do what they could to help in the investigation. Ben Caplan flashed his ID for the third time since they had entered the commune grounds; this time to the agent stationed at the foot of the stairs.

"Where's Ingstrom?" Ben asked quickly.

"In there," the agent told him, pointing toward the open doorway on the west wall.

Joshua was several steps into the shop before he saw Alan. His friend's arms were elevated and it took a passing second for Joshua to comprehend that Alan was handcuffed to one of the machines. Perplexed, he weaved his way across the room.

"What's going on here?" he asked as he pulled up to face Alan's guard. He noticed then that Anne Delemar was slumped on the floor.

"Who are you?" the guard demanded.

"Is she hurt?" Joshua asked, ignoring the question as he turned to Alan.

"She's all right," Alan told him.

Anne Delemar looked up then, blinking against the harsh light of the floodlamps.

"What's going on here?" Joshua demanded, a cutting edge evident in his voice.

"These people are under arrest," the guard told him, and he stood immobile, his weapon leveled directly at Alan's stomach.

As if anticipating Joshua, Alan said quickly, "Play it cool, old friend. Like, you've got to take it up with a guy called Ingstrom."

Joshua hesitated for a moment. "Are you both all right?" he asked quietly.

"We're just fine," Alan told him, trying his best to sound convincing.

"I'll be right back," Joshua promised as he turned to stalk back across the shop. He cleared the doorway, entering the room which for all of them had been mysterious because until now it had been totally inaccessible. In the wake of his rising anger and frustration, Joshua was oblivious to its equipment and furnishings, realizing only vaguely that it was more spacious than he had expected. He glanced around the room once, sorting out the several persons present until he picked out the man in charge, Burt Ingstrom, whose back was to him and who was engaged in conversation with Ben Caplan and a man Joshua didn't recognize. Joshua walked directly to Ingstrom's side. He put his left hand on Ingstrom's upper arm and whirled the stocky agent around to face him.

It took the startled Ingstrom a moment to recognize Joshua.

"Turn 'em loose," Joshua said to him.

Flushing noticeably, Ingstrom studied Joshua briefly before replying, addressing himself to Ben Caplan. "You best remind him what's going on down here."

"I said turn 'em loose," Joshua repeated, and this time he didn't bother to hide his own feelings; the statement was an easily defined threat.

"What's going on?" Ben asked.

"The hippy and his girlfriend," Ingstrom said, and he took a step away from Joshua. "I was told to take them into custody."

Joshua felt his hands clenching up. "He's got Alan cuffed
paused for a moment to stare down at the light-sprinkled basin
"With some clown holding a weapon on him."

"For God's sake, Ingstrom," said Ben. "Your orders were
to hold them until we got here and to turn them over to *our*
custody."

"All right, all right," Ingstrom snapped defensively. "So
you go release them. I'll be delighted to be rid of the creeps."

Ben headed for the door.

Joshua stood still for a moment, debating with himself,
weighing the probable consequences, until Burt Ingstrom himself made the final decision for him.

"I remember working with you last year, Bain," Ingstrom
said, watching over his shoulder as Ben left the room. "And I
don't understand how this time you let yourself get mixed up
with this bunch of Jews—"

Joshua took the closing step between them, at the same instant dropping his right shoulder slightly, just enough so that
the one blow came from the floor. The blood pounded behind
his eyeballs, cresting on his rage, causing him to miscalculate
enough so that his clenched fist missed the chin, catching instead the left cheekbone.

Burt Ingstrom folded like a struck tent.

9:30 p.m.

Kabir finished his system check about an hour behind
schedule. Shutting down the computer, he moved away from
the center console to enter the second-floor connecting hallway. The computer room had been sealed off from the rest of
the house, made dust free and airtight to protect its sensitive
equipment. Now Kabir elected to get a breath of fresh air before returning downstairs. Moving along the hallway to cross
through the den and emerging onto a flying redwood deck, he
paused for a moment to stare down at the light sprinkled basin
of Los Angeles, California. Breathing deeply of the cool
mountain air, he had to admit that the safe house selected by
Fawd was altogether perfect to suit their needs and purposes.
With three thousand square feet of floor space, the mountain
home was located on a three-acre estate site less than a mile
from the Mount Wilson Observatory. Completely surrounded
by heavy timber, the isolated two-story house was the product
of a Hollywood big spender gone bankrupt, a white elephant
which had sat on the open market for several years before be-

ing quietly acquired by its new owner, an absentee corporation shown on the title papers to be based in Las Vegas, Nevada.

He estimated that the cantilevered redwood deck was about thirteen miles on a direct line from the Los Angeles civic center.

On that same line, at a known distance of exactly twelve-point-two miles, was ground zero, the garage on Pepper Tree Lane . . .

The skin on the back of his neck started to react, and he involuntarily reached up to massage the affected area, looking up and to his right, out toward the Pacific Ocean.

At the forward rail of the deck was a sixty-power telescope. Even on a typical, hazy day, he could easily pick out Catalina Island. Now, he could even read the red lights on the KOPE transmitting tower.

Another important plus for the house was the buried telephone cable installed when the house had been originally built over thirty years ago. Abandoned several years ago in favor of the present overhead line which serviced the house phones, the buried cable was integral to their control of the Rahab trigger.

As Fawd had appropriately suggested, they had the finest box seat in the house from which to view the drama unfolding below them.

In his present state of cocaine-induced euphoria, Kabir took another moment to savor the sense of power delivered into their hands.

Los Angeles belonged to them now.

The accomplishment seemed profound, and he shook his head, still astonished that they had pulled it off. And now for the first time, it came to him that ultimately it would have to end. They could not stay on this mountain forever. Which was Fawd's problem, he resolved dreamily.

He turned away from the redwood deck, pulling the sliding door closed behind him. In the hallway, he remembered with a start that he had neglected to check the remote signal booster and reset the trigger timer. Back in the computer room, he moved hurriedly to the far end of the console, where he opened an inspection panel. Then stooping down to depress the first button on the small white actuator box he waited three seconds and then hit the button again until it lit up, indicating reset. Downstairs, Fawd had an exact duplicate of the actuator box, about the size of a pack of cigarettes, attached to a belt around his waist.

Fawd could trigger Rahab by manipulating the two buttons on the actuator box. As a safety precaution, it was necessary to complete three separate circuits before the bomb was triggered. The first circuit was made by pressing and releasing the first button. The second circuit was completed upon depressing the second button. The third and critical circuit was made when the second button was *released*. Thus, if Fawd was under threat of personal attack, he still could retain positive control over the ultimate trigger, guaranteeing his safety at the same time. Knowing this, a potential attacker would certainly back off, for once the second button was depressed it had to be held down to prevent detonation. The procedure was an absolute insurance policy for Fawd's protection. Which was why he had been building up his hand grip for the past several weeks, since he might be called upon to hold the critical second button down for hours, perhaps even days.

The white box was a remote controller, whose signals were picked up by the computer booster and transferred by a buried cable to three automatic telephone dialers installed a hundred yards north of the estate on the original buried cable.

Once the booster took over, the trigger system functioned at the speed of light.

The actual bomb trigger, which was at the bomb site, was activated by the bell circuit of the third telephone dialed. The bomb trigger was designed so that it would not activate unless all three numbers had been dialed, in the proper sequence, with the first two numbers dialed within five seconds of the other, a procedural precaution eliminating accidental detonation as the result of random wrong-number dialing.

As a safeguard against power failure of the telephone system at either end, the trigger on the bomb was on continuous countdown, under the separate control of an attached 48-hour timer, which was manually reset back to zero twice daily by depressing the first actuator button twice in succession. Thus, if the telephone power was lost for any reason, they had at least the better part of two days to reach the bomb and reset it at the site itself.

Fawd's insurance policy was thus doubly indemnified.

Rahab was secure; only the two of them knew its location.

The trigger was foolproof.

Kabir closed the inspection panel. He straightened up and then headed for the downstairs living room.

Fawd was waiting for him, standing impatiently before the

fireplace. It was cool at night at the high altitude, and Fawd was straddle-legged in his terry cloth robe, warming his backside against the wood fire. As Kabir entered the room, Fawd slipped the actuator box back into the clip attached to the belt wrapped around his bare waist. In addition to its portable belt connection, the box was more permanently secured to a connecting chain, of the type used to restrain dogs, which was looped around Fawd's neck. He could thus handle the actuator box without danger of losing it.

"It's your draw," Fawd told him as they both took their chairs at one end of the wood table fronting the huge bay window opposite the fireplace. The main living room was the centerpiece of the house. The twenty-foot high ceiling was laced with heavy wooden beams.

Kabir picked up his cards and fanned them out. His hand was decent. He passed on the upturned card, drawing from the deck instead, picking an unneeded queen of spades. He looked over the discards, noticing the queen of hearts already down, so he dropped the queen, presuming it to be safe.

He winced inside as Fawd picked up the queen.

"Gin," said Fawd, the familiar note of triumph in his voice as he dropped his hand.

Kabir noticed that the queen filled out a run from the ten to the king. As he laid his hand down to be counted, he remarked, "The gut pull was a lucky one."

"Not lucky at all," Fawd said. "You were baited."

"Even so," Kabir argued, "it was a gamble that you don't usually take. After all, you were sitting on a deficit of thirty points without that queen."

"True enough," Fawd agreed as he wrote down the score. "But I'm so far ahead, with two schneids working, that the gamble was worth it."

Kabir pondered the explanation, seeing in it an analogy. "Is that why you've left her in the enemy camp?"

Fawd was smiling as he shuffled the deck of cards. "It is not the same, really," he said lightly. "There is technically no gamble involved in leaving her there."

"She can be made to talk. They have drugs, you know. And, in a situation as serious as this, they're going to use anything and everything—"

"She knows nothing, at least critical to the operation," said Fawd confidently as he began to deal a new hand.

Kabir arranged his cards. "They will discover her quickly.

Maybe they already have."

"Of course they will."

"So, what's the advantage?"

"Twofold," Fawd explained. "First, it's another blind alley they can chase around in and waste their time. Also, if they play it the way I'm sure they will, she might even be of further help."

"How should they play it?"

"You'll see," Fawd assured him. "Turn the knock card."

There's more to it than that, Kabir thought as he reached for the knock deck. Another facet in the arrogance of Fawd Al-Shaer: to throw it up to Wolf Shertok and his people, to show them who was the more clever. He turned the knock card and was not surprised to see the ace of spades. The Fawd luck was holding.

"How'd the system check go?" Fawd asked him.

"Routine. I reset the trigger timer."

"So I noticed," Fawd observed caustically, obviously having seen the light on his actuator button. "You were over an hour late."

"I was busy," Kabir explained. "You asked me to set up the plastic in the basement. And, I was more than an hour late in getting in from the airport."

"A schedule is a schedule," Fawd told him. "We go from eight-thirty to eight-thirty on the reset. No deviations, you understand. If things get hectic around here, I've got to know exactly how much time is available. An hour could kill us, literally. If you have to, put yourself on an alarm system."

Kabir endured the lecture silently. He played a card then, before changing the subject. "I raised the temperature in the basement by another five degrees. The central heating ducts are less efficient down there." He noticed that Fawd showed no interest in the report, and he didn't bother explaining further that the wet cells stored in the basement were sensitive to cold. He was not so sure he cared either, since the storage batteries were the third back-up system down, and since he could not imagine the circumstances that could possibly ever require their use.

The house was virtually a fortress already.

"Did you prime the plastic?" Fawd asked brusquely.

His mood is terrible, Kabir noted to himself. "Yes, sir," he answered. "I'll install the connecting wires tomorrow morning." Another Fawd toy. The explosive, twenty pounds of it, was left over from the bomb detonator. "Where do you want it?"

"Put the timer over there," Fawd told him, pointing to the staircase. "I found a hidden panel there this morning."

So that was it, Kabir thought as he looked over his shoulder to the base of the staircase. He's found a hidden panel. Historical intrigue. Perhaps the house at an earlier time had been a hideout for a different set of occupants. And Fawd Al-Shaer, with his seemingly limitless imagination, had come up with yet another device to blow something to kingdom come. We are all, Kabir thought cryptically, becoming demolition engineers of the first order. If you can't cure the world, blow it up. The boom gap. And he had to swallow hard to keep from smiling.

Chapter seven

Trying to think back to the early afternoon meeting at the White House, Jerome Mason imagined that several days could easily have passed in between. He had paused briefly to recall how many hours he had left of the allotted twenty-four.

Less than eleven to go.

He knew he would never make it without sleep, for he was already running out of steam.

Around him now, the operations center was starting to shape up. The Bureau had commandeered the small vacant hangar, located on the south side of Los Angeles International Airport, about six hours ago, as best as he could recollect. Presently seated behind the desk in his selected office, the largest of four located at the west end of the hangar, he assessed the logistics thus far accomplished. A teletype machine was in and working. Secure phones, with scramblers, were linked directly to Les Stalmeyer's office, the Bureau headquarters in Washington, and the Chief of the Los Angeles Police Department. The three other offices were in the process of being converted to field labs of various capabilities, with priority assigned to sort out and interpret the evidence obtained from Wolf Shertok's group and the San Eliso commune. There were ten agents assigned to the center for the moment, with no telling how many more were out digging right now. Fawd Al-Shaer's apartment, including his office at Aerotec, had been stripped to the bone. Several vehicles, used by Fawd and his known associates, were parked in the hangar and in the process of being dismantled.

Finishing off a tepid cup of coffee, he once again lifted the telephone to his ear, punching the button to automatically get Bill Morrison at his CIA office. Waiting for Morrison to come on the line, Mason ran his free hand through his mane of graying hair, scratching his scalp, thinking that he was about to gag on the lousy taste in his mouth. Morrison answered, sounding like he, too, was on the verge of collapse. Mason simply identified himself, hearing in his voice the lagging sound of his fatigue.

"Cheer up," Morrison told him. "Tel Aviv has just come through with the opinion that Shiela Vardi is an imposter."

"The opinion," Mason repeated dully.

"They're not positive yet. She is supposed to be the only child of a couple slain by Arab commandos during an El Fatah raid on their kibbutz. According to the way it was supposed to've happened, the girl Shiela was kidnapped by the commandos and held captive for a couple of days, during which time she was raped repeatedly and savagely beaten. In fact, when she was finally released, her face was so badly mangled it took a team of medical people six weeks just to get her face back together again. By her account, Fawd Al-Shaer intervened on her behalf, saving her life. She thus became the only living Israeli who could identify Fawd."

"So," Mason said, "is she or is she not the real Shiela Vardi?"

"Tel Aviv won't commit until we forward her prints."

"But they think she's a phoney."

"Ninety percent sure," said Morrison, "after they started following up today. There is too much evidence that she very well might be a double agent. The Vardis had no other relatives in Israel, having immigrated less than a year before from Iran, so there was no one around, friends or relatives, who could possibly peg her as an imposter after she was released from medical treatment. But the clincher is that because of our inquiry, they pulled her application for a student's visa, which Israeli intelligence arranged for, and found that her signature is a forgery."

"Kind of embarrassing," Mason mused aloud, thinking

that the Israelis had been duped in arranging for one of Shertok's operatives.

"Not really," Morrison said. "It was a clean setup, and she was badly needed, so much so that they probably would've sent her even if they knew she was a double."

"I'll call Ben Caplan," Mason said, "and have him pick up her prints tonight."

"Aren't you going to pick her up?"

Mason rubbed his hand wearily through his hair before answering, "Don't know for sure yet—"

"You've got to," Morrison insisted. "She might even know where the device is hidden."

Mason chuckled cynically. "Believe me, Bill, from what I've learned about this Fawd character I can guarantee you that if Shiela Vardi is his agent, then she is still around because it best suits his purpose."

"You don't think she knows something?"

"Forget it," Mason told him abruptly. "Ben is due in here at midnight for a strategy meeting, and I'll discuss it with him then."

"I thought it was important," said Morrison after a moment.

Jerome Mason sighed heavily. "It's like everything we're running up against," he finally tried to explain. "The evidence is overwhelming. I've got a whole hangar full of it. But, would you believe, we really don't have a single clue as to the location either of him or the device. Nothing. Zero. Like zip."

"Stalmeyer reminded me," Bill Morrison said, "that this Fawd has handed us the ball; like, we're on the offensive."

"There's only one problem with that," Mason retorted witheringly, "we've got the ball on our own one-yard line. Ask any offensive ballplayer who has been in that kind of field position, and he'll tell you that you're still on the defensive—"

"Okay," Morrison said, "but ten hours isn't much time."

"Tell me about it. I've got the entire Special Litigation team in. Two psychiatrists are due in here in less than an hour to start profiling Fawd. Melbourne tells me he could stop right now and guarantee that in x-number of seconds Los Angeles could be a wasteland uninhabitable for two hundred and fifty thousand years." Remembering that Morrison's son and his family were still in the area, he regretted making the last statement.

"Who's on the shrink team?"

"Don't know their names; Ingstrom is bringing them in."

"Get Katherine Felton," Morrison told him. "She's in San Francisco, I think."

"Kate Felton?"

"Yeah. She's the one who worked on the Hanafi thing. And that last hijack, Delta in Miami. She's unreal—"

"Get her for me, and quick."

"Consider it done," Morrison said. "What else can I do to help?"

"My next call is to Les Stalmeyer. And, right now, all of you start using your influence to reach the Arab fat cats, or, in your view, the prima donnas, who are probably behind this scheme. Believe me, it took a ton of money, literally, to put this together. Several million at least. And Fawd didn't get those kinds of bucks robbing Israeli banks. It's got to be petro-dollars, and I mean heavy."

"We're already working on it, Jerry."

Jerome Mason slammed the phone down angrily. Give anybody enough money or power and eventually they'll find a way to abuse it. The story was as old as mankind itself, easily predating the Torah, the Koran, or whatever. He grabbed the phone again, punching the Les Stalmeyer button, thinking it was good that he was upset, that the amenities be damned, that it was time he started acting the role popularized in the media, that on occasion Jerome Mason fancied himself a latter-day General Patton.

It was an easy matter for Ben Caplan to obtain Anne Dele-mar's prints. With the help of one of Ingstrom's men, he lifted the latents from the water glass she had used while she was in temporary custody in the basement machine shop. With the evidence in his inside jacket pocket, he came back up to the first floor of the now nearly deserted mansion, looking for Alan Hunt. Anne Delemar was asleep in her dorm quarters. The rest of the commune inhabitants had finally gone, the majority having left the moment Ingstrom passed the word to let them go. Two media reporters had showed up during the night, and both had been rather curtly informed that the operation was a routine one, with drugs involved. A narc bust. Ben wondered how long the lie would hold.

He passively checked his watch, seeing that it was a little past eleven o'clock.

He had accepted without question that Anne Delemar was

a double agent in the employ of Fawd Al-Shaer. No other connection could have accounted for the massive leakage in their
security system, and he was only surprised that he had not suspected her earlier. He agreed totally with Jerome Mason that
she would likely be of little use to them, beyond the remote
hope that maybe Fawd in this instance might have made a mistake. Somewhere, somehow, Fawd had made a mistake, perhaps even several, for he too was a mortal, flawed maybe in his
own unique way, but still flawed.

Ben found Alan Hunt alone in the recreation room. The
only light in the room came from the small desk lamp on the
desk used by Kabir.

Jerome Mason's instructions regarding the status of Anne
Delemar was that the matter was to be strictly contained. Alan
Hunt, especially, was not to be told. Ben had mixed feelings
over his inability to tell Alan Hunt, for he, like Joshua, suspected that the two team members had become romantically
involved with each other, although Ben could not diagnose to
what degree. As he walked up to face Alan now, he wondered
if there were such a thing as a degree factor in the matter of the
heart; one was either in love or not in love.

"I've got to leave with Ingstrom in a few minutes," he told
Alan, who was pacing to and fro in front of Kabir's desk. "We
have a meeting with the boss at midnight in L.A."

Alan stopped and turned to face him. "What about Anne
and me?" he asked quietly.

"You're both in my custody until this thing is cleared up."

"Are we still working?"

"I hope so," said Ben as he turned the corner of the desk to
flop heavily into the chair behind it. "I want to keep the team
intact, even though we're working for a different employer, the
U.S. Government."

"What about Shertok?"

"He's pretty well out of it, by mutual agreement, though I
can consult him as an advisor. He can still open a lot of doors
for us, quickly, if needed."

"So the Ha Mossad thing has turned sticky."

"It'll blow over," Ben said. "For the moment, it's a point
far down on our scale of priorities."

"You still can't tell me—"

"Not yet, my friend; only that we must locate Fawd Al-
Shaer—and quickly."

Alan settled himself on the corner of the desk, which had

been swept clean by Ingstrom's men. He looked out the bay window, over Ben's shoulder, his face shadowed in the glow reflected from the desk lamp. Despite the poor light, Ben noticed the strain showing in Alan's face, and he supposed that Alan Hunt, like the rest of them, was showing signs of exhaustion. He absently checked his watch again, knowing that if he didn't get to his feet, he would fall asleep in a few minutes.

"Did Joshua tell you where he was going?" Alan asked him.

"No; only that he was going to San Diego."

"Probably the Fielding thing," Alan suggested hoarsely, clearing his throat.

"I'm glad you both decided to stay on."

"We discussed it before he left, and he said he would stay with it, regardless of the money." Alan looked aside then. "So I guess it's important. We've both got our reasons, more so now, I suppose."

You are much too honest, Ben thought, to be in this sort of business. While he was reasonably sure why Alan Hunt was still hanging in, he wondered what motivated Joshua Bain.

"Will you stick close to Anne, please?" Ben said then.

"Fine with me."

"It's turned bad for all of us, especially for her and Shertok."

"I understand."

No you don't, my friend, Ben thought dejectedly, finding it difficult to face Alan now. No matter how many years one carried on in this stinking business, the deception bit still went down hard. He resisted the temptation to look into the future, sensing the outcome of it all, knowing that Alan Hunt was in the process of being thoroughly ripped off.

"I wish I could understand it," Ben heard himself saying.

Alan nodded slowly while he reached up to pull the hair away from the side of his face. "Why not take a minute or two tonight," he suggested carefully, "and ask for some help."

Ben drew a reflective breath before responding, "You mean like praying?"

"Something like that."

Pushing himself out of the chair, Ben stood in the same place, his hands jammed into his pockets. It was starting to turn cold in the unheated house, and shivering from the chill he suddenly realized that it was his turn to say something. His first impulse was simply to put Alan off because of the personal nature of the subject, because so few people could understand, or even care. But he figured that he owed Alan Hunt an answer, a decent and reasonable one. "You have an understanding way about you, Alan," he began slowly and carefully, "so I assume you can grasp what little I have to say." He paused for a passing moment.

"I'll try my best," Alan assured him.

"For thousands of years," Ben went on, "my ancestors prayed for deliverance, and you know as well as anyone what it got them." He pulled his service revolver out of its belt holster and laid it on the desk under the lamp. "About thirty years ago we picked up one of these and started shooting back. You also know what that has finally gotten us."

Alan picked up the revolver and turned it once in his hand. "So this is your salvation."

"Amen, brother."

Alan was about to speak but they were both distracted by the sound of footsteps from the direction of the hallway. The stocky form of Burt Ingstrom appeared in the doorway. Alan handed the revolver to Ben, who then turned the corner of the desk.

"Have Joshua call me," Ben said as he started toward the door.

"Good luck," Alan called after him.

Clearing the doorway to follow after Ingstrom, Ben Caplan chuckled once to himself, realizing that Alan Hunt had gotten in the final word in more ways than one, for he recalled that Joshua Bain had once remarked that it was the convicted opinion of Alan Hunt that luck was the will of God.

The neighborhood was older, twenty years or so, by Joshua's estimate. As he cruised slowly down the darkened street, he could see clearly enough to notice that the lawns were well kept and the homes appeared to be in a state of good repair. Middle class to upper middle class, he guessed. An area of little pretense, a more practical slice of living space, one where he expected to find the likes of Edwin Fielding, sole surviving parent. The house numbers stenciled on the curb showed in his headlights, but he pushed the Jag on past the number and pulled into the curb at the next intersection. Satisfied that the street was clean, he U-turned, working his way slowly back down the street. Then he pulled into the curb, parking several houses away. Before getting out of the car, he checked to confirm that the Viper was secure in its holster.

The elder Fielding answered the doorbell promptly.

"I'm sorry to bother you this late," Joshua told him, repeating the same opening remark he had used when he called forty-five minutes earlier.

"It's no bother," Fielding said, leading him into the house.

Joshua took note of the neatly kept furnishings, which matched the exterior, provincial, expected. They were in the dining room, and Fielding gestured for Joshua to sit down at the table.

"I've been alone for six years," Fielding went on, "since my wife passed away." He smiled as he moved along the table toward the bar counter between them and the kitchen. "And believe me, I'm happy for the company."

"It's important," Joshua said. "Otherwise we could put it off."

Edwin Fielding had moved to the kitchen side of the narrow counter, and now faced Joshua. Joshua guessed that he was about seventy years old. There was a healthy translucence in the old man's face, which was not at all weathered or beaten; only a slightly darkened swelling under the eyes indicated he might be tired.

"To procrastinate is to mortgage the future," Fielding said as he wagged a stubby forefinger at Joshua. "When you get as old as I am, you'll come to see that time itself assumes a more valuable role, and you'll be opposed to hanging a lousy second trust deed on it, too." He had pulled a bottle out from under the counter. "How about a drink, sir?"

Feeling his own face turn into a smile, Joshua nodded yes, thinking that he had about an hour left before he collapsed. Watching the old man fuss around in the small kitchen, Joshua was pleased that Edwin Fielding seemed perceptive and alert, even cooperative, even though he didn't have any idea how that might help.

The wall clock in the kitchen reminded him once more that they were all in the final, eleventh hour.

He tried to straighten up in his chair as Fielding took the seat opposite him. Two ice-filled glasses were on the tray next to a fifth of sour mash whiskey. Fielding poured them both a solid three fingers.

"To the future," said Fielding, lifting his glass.

"Mortgage free," responded Joshua.

Joshua downed the whiskey. The scalding sensation produced an involuntary cough.

"What do you want?" Fielding asked abruptly.

Joshua toyed briefly with his half-filled glass before answering, "I'm not so sure exactly what I want," he remarked, remembering back to the synagogue meeting with Martha Fielding and this same man. At that time Edwin Fielding had not been so responsive. "Except that I'd like to talk to you about your son."

"You mean Stan, of course."

"Yes, sir."

Fielding took another drink, pursing his lips thoughtfully as he placed his glass down on the table. "What do you want to know?"

"Would you think it strange for me to suggest that he might still be alive?"

Fielding stared at him, his eyes clear and unblinking behind his gold-rimmed glasses. "Forgive me for being suspicious of your motives," he said evenly. "But I suspect it's the case of you and those around you *wanting* him to be alive."

Joshua tipped his head once, saluting the man's candor and wisdom.

"Are you working for the insurance company?" Fielding asked him bluntly.

"Absolutely not," Joshua assured him. "Please recall that our initial contact was on the recommendation of Professor Shertok."

"I remember," said Fielding, "but it seems strange to me that you should be so persistent, particularly in view of the circumstances. You know, it is not good for a father to survive his son. It's almost unnatural. The burden of grief is entirely a special one—one which can never be resolved. Every day, for the rest of your life, you think about it, you remember vividly each day as he was growing up, from the day he was born. And there is no remedy to ease the pain." He turned the glass contemplatively in his hand. "I think you are a wise enough person to realize how upsetting this kind of thing—"

"I'm well aware of it, sir. And please understand that the last thing in the world I want to do is to get your hopes up." Joshua shook his head in a gesture denoting his concern and understanding.

"Tell me about yourself," the old man said abruptly. "You strike me as being honest and sincere. But, then, maybe you're just a clever man."

The whiskey in Joshua's stomach gave him a warm sensation. "What do you want to know?" he asked, respecting the old man's right to his curiosity.

"You're Jewish, aren't you?"

"Yes."

"And your parents, where do they—"

"They're dead."

"I see," Fielding said solemnly. "I was wondering about your last name."

"It's not Jewish," said Joshua. "I was adopted shortly after the war."

"So you weren't raised a Jew."

"No," said Joshua, turning his glass thoughtfully in his hand. "My adoptive parents travelled a lot. I guess you might say I was finally raised a Californian."

"Not a bad way to go," suggested Fielding. "I raised my family here too," and he paused before adding, "Please forgive me for prying, but I've always felt you can find out a lot about a man by what he has to say about himself, especially about his personal side."

"It's all right," Joshua said. He was thinking that trade-about was fair play anyway. "But there isn't much more to talk about. I grew up very typically, went off to war, in Vietnam, where on my second tour I was shot down and captured."

"You were a POW," said Fielding. "That is something to talk about."

"It, too, is something to forget," Joshua suggested soberly.

"I suppose so," Fielding said sympathetically. "So you forget such things by working, getting involved in investigations like you are now?"

"To an extent, by working mostly. What I'm doing now is only temporary."

"Must be hard on your family, perhaps your wife."

Joshua didn't respond right away, choosing instead to push his empty glass across the table. The old man's last remark had triggered the release of the most personal of memories, those which he not only could not share but also those he could not enjoy or tolerate now, especially in his weakened condition. "I have no family," he said haltingly, trying to control the break in his voice. "I was married once, for just a little while, but she is gone . . . dead."

Fielding had filled both the glasses again, and Joshua picked his up, emptying it in one gulp.

"I am truly sorry," Fielding said. "It appears you have

lived with death more than most at your age. Such experience, I suspect, should tend to make one more fully appreciate life—"

"Or," said Joshua thickly, "it will tend to make one bitter, even cynical."

Fielding nodded his head slowly. "Interesting that we each react differently to the same cause . . . All right, so what is it you want from me?"

Joshua leaned forward to steady himself on the table. "The first thing is to keep this to yourself. Discuss it with no one, especially with Martha."

Fielding filled the two glasses, saying nothing.

"Has Stanley ever spent any time in Mexico?" Joshua asked slowly.

Fielding smiled briefly. "He's spent half his life below the border. He and Dave, his younger brother, were in Baja every chance they got while they were growing up." He was sipping the whiskey now, and Joshua followed suit while he waited. "Dave was a motorcycle nut, the motorcross routine. But Stan loved to fish. I guess his mother and I got him started when he was very young." He leaned back in his chair now, his eyes closed. "My God," he went on, his voice turning melancholy, "it's like a hundred years ago. We used to always go to Ensenada over the holidays, like Labor Day, the Fourth of July. Stayed in a little motel north of Hussongs. I remember that for Labor Day we'd have to make our reservations in May. There was an old pier next to a fish cannery, with a village wrapped around it. You could catch halibut the size of this table right off the pier."

Joshua said nothing, reaching slowly up to his right cheek to find the skin numb under his eye.

"We used to bargain for lobster in the village," Fielding went on, his voice a monotone. "Two-bits apiece in a wet gunny sack. And the shacks were made out of cardboard and corrigated tin with dirt floors, and they smelled of old grease and chicken fat. And you had to squat down in the greasy dirt and hassle with the men. By the time he was ten or eleven, Stan could argue with them in their own language." He reached for his glass and drained it for the third time.

We are both getting a little drunk, Joshua thought absently.

"Those were wonderful times," Fielding continued, his voice turning a little more slowly. "After fishing all day, we'd settle down around an open fire right on the beach. The Mexican beer in brown bottles, in a tub of ice, and their labels coming off after a while in the water. And you'd go to sleep just lolling around. It was altogether the most restful place. The tide.line down there is covered with fist-sized rocks, and when the waves rolled in the stones would tumble over each other, a kind of backdrop for the Mexicans and their language, the sound of it musical and soothing."

Joshua looked up to see that the old man was crying, the tears running out from under his glasses, down his translucent cheeks.

"Stan loved it down there," Fielding said, and he pulled a handkerchief out of his back pocket.

Joshua made a mental note to himself, with a certain sense of loss. It was inconceivable that this man could knowingly be involved in any scheme involving his son.

"But Martha didn't like it," the old man added sadly. "She said it was dirty, not good for the boy. And what Martha wanted, with Stan, Martha got."

Joshua felt himself slipping into sleep. He sat up once more, working his eyelids, feeling their weight. "At least she'll be taken care of with the insurance," he heard himself saying.

The old man allowed a small ironic turn around his mouth. "That twenty-five thousand won't take her far. Even if she invests—"

"Twenty-five thousand," Joshua said dully.

Fielding had placed his glasses back on his nose. "That's right, twenty-five thousand." He shrugged once. "And thank God for that. Stan originally was going to sign for fifteen, but I talked him into another ten. I know for sure, because I wound up paying the first six months' premiums."

Joshua was suddenly wide awake, and he lurched to his feet. "Can I use your phone to make a collect call?"

Fielding gestured indifferently toward the phone, wall-mounted above the kitchen counter. "Direct dial it," he told Joshua.

Ben Caplan took the call from one of the battery of phones on Jerome Mason's desk. The conversation was all one way, from the other end, and he hung up the receiver after no more than eight to ten seconds.

Jerome Mason checked his watch to find that they were already one minute into Wednesday.

"That was Joshua Bain," he heard Ben saying. "I've got to meet him tomorrow morning in San Diego."

"What's he got?"

"He wouldn't tell me, but he claims it's super hot."

Mason drew a deep, angry breath. "By all rights, I should veto the meeting," and he pointed to the nearest phone. "Get him back on the line, right now!"

"But I don't know where he was calling from."

"What the devil does he think is going on here?" Mason demanded. "You know I could have him picked up on an APB. If you remember, he pulled the same stunt on us on the ETC investigation."

"And he cracked it wide open," Ben reminded him. "Besides, he can't stand Burt, and he's wary of sharing anything with him right now."

A personality problem, Mason thought disgustedly, and he glanced across his crowded office to Burt Ingstrom, who was engaged in conversation with one of his men. The left side of Ingstrom's face was swollen purple, attesting to the severity of the punch that had put him on the floor. It had been Mason's decision to excuse the incident, after hearing Doctor Melbourne's testimony that Ingstrom had triggered Joshua with an unwarranted racial slur. He pushed the matter out of his mind as he came up out of his chair. The strategy meeting was scheduled for midnight exactly, and they were already several minutes late. "In view of this Bain development," he told Ben, "you head for San Diego right now. Check into a motel near the airport and get some sleep."

"You don't want me in on the meeting?"

"Negative; it'll drag on for a couple hours. Remember, your primary responsibility is to contain and come up with a way to use Anne Delemar. She's yours. Use what men you need from the pool. And I want a detailed plan, with an alternative, as to how we might capitalize on the Delemar situation, as soon as you can come up with it. Talk it over with Joshua. But don't let Alan Hunt in on it. If he's as emotionally involved as you suspect, they could rabbit on us together."

Aware of his superior's mood, Ben did not bother to defend Alan Hunt. Joshua's partner and Anne Delemar were still together at the commune, technically still under his custody, under the strictest surveillance, and Ben knew of no way they could presently escape.

He turned away from the desk without further word, heading for his car. As he passed out of the office to thread his way across the hangar area, he was conscious of the enormous burden now resting heavily on the shoulders of Jerome Mason.

From what he could tell, they still had nothing to lead them to the whereabouts of Fawd Al-Shaer or his bomb.

One of the hundreds of potential leads came to his mind as he walked down a line of small trucks and vans.

By Melbourne's estimate, the weight and size of the bomb was formidable.

Had it been moved from the commune intact or in parts?

Melbourne guessed it was moved in one piece, possibly in two or no more than three increments. So, locate the transport, the trucks, then tear them to pieces, bolt by bolt, seeking clues of any sort.

Locate them—if they could.

The fleet of Aerotec delivery trucks were prime suspects, since just two weeks ago they had all been put through a thorough cleaning process, even down to steam cleaning the engines and running gear; a procedure explained away by the Aerotec general manager as a routine matter of vehicle maintenance, though he could not produce evidence of ever ordering the work done before.

Perhaps another Fawd diversion.

Fawd Al-Shaer had shown himself to be a virtual genius at his trade.

Fawd still had to rely upon others.

Statistically, no matter how thorough and expert the plan and its execution, there still had to be x-number of mistakes made.

However, not one had been turned yet.

Their twenty-four hours were running out.

Chapter eight

It fell to Alan Hunt to do the dishes, which he did leisurely, taking his time because it appeared that time was all they had. Anne Delemar was standing at the nearby counter, drying each plate as he finished. It was nearing eight o'clock, and they had just finished breakfast, voluntarily prepared by Anne. The last of the four agents assigned to the commune house had just left to take up his post. Alan picked up the last plate, dunked it in the sink, swishing the dishwater into a turmoil as he watched through the window over the sink. The agent seemed to move listlessly across the nearby patio, almost aimlessly, as if he weren't sure where he was to go or what he was to do.

"I don't envy him," Alan said, more to himself than to anyone else.

Anne took the plate and began turning it slowly in her towel. "You sound uptight," she said after a moment. Her voice moved softly in the cavernous kitchen. She handed him the towel then, watching as he dried his hands.

"This is turning into a king-sized drag," he suggested somberly.

"So maybe it's my company," she said, a mock petulance in her voice.

He laughed lightly, reaching out to take her hand. Together, they moved out the side door into the new day. It was still hushed and cool around them as they strolled slowly across the garden. Alan was conscious of her presence next to him, her arm around his waist. It was with some difficulty that he brought his mind to bear on the fact that the two of them had obviously been left out of the action. He tried to remember the day of the week. It was Wednesday, he decided after a moment.

"So what's wrong?" she asked him.

"We've been abandoned."

"Fantastic," she said. "So we should enjoy it."

"No," he insisted then. "There's something wrong. When I talked to Joshua on the phone this morning, he was evasive, and, believe me, Joshua isn't usually that way. You see, there's a kind of thing between us; we always level with each other."

They turned the garden once more, pulling up to sit down at a redwood patio table.

"What did he say?" she finally asked.

"He couldn't say much on the phone," Alan admitted. "But it appears that Paul Jaylis, or Fawd, is still at large. He suggested that the Stanley Fielding situation might develop into something around noon." He checked his watch. "So we've got four hours to wait." He drummed the fingers of his right hand on the table. "I'm positive there's more going on than we've been told."

"Of course there is," she offered, taking his hand under

hers. "This is a heavy security scene, remember. Joshua probably doesn't know any more than we do. He's busy, so is Ben, which simply means they've been assigned. You know they'll call us when they need us. I mean, like it could happen at any time," and she moved closer to him, dropping her left hand to his thigh. "The surf's quiet," she said suggestively. "Why don't we go for a swim?"

He pushed up and away from the table. "No; there's something really wrong—"

Anne Delemar was on her feet in a moment, anger crossing her face. "You're what's wrong," she said heatedly.

Confused and frustrated, Alan reached up, almost defensively, to pull the hair away from his face, thinking irrelevantly that he needed a haircut. She was moving away then, toward the house. As he pushed out his hand in a helpless sort of gesture, he became vaguely aware that she was mumbling something. He pursued her several short steps, finally yelling after her that he couldn't hear what she was saying.

Stopping at the head of the path, she turned to face him. "I was saying you should go out and . . . and hand out some tracts!" With that she whirled and ran toward the kitchen door, pulling it open angrily.

Watching the door slam behind her, Alan came to the conclusion that she was even more uptight than he. It came to him then that she had travelled half way around the world, volunteering to do her share in this the more bizarre of imaginable exercises, and, despite her own frustration, she had tried to ease his burden, willing to carry, in effect, a double load.

Oh, Lord, he thought, I'm becoming the most miserable of men.

He shook his arms, slack at his side, as if he were psyching himself up for a ten-meter dive. Moving toward the kitchen door after his moment of preparation, he tried to remember where he had left his bathing suit.

By eleven minutes to ten, Joshua Bain was starting to fret, worrying that Ben Caplan would not show by the exact deadline. The timing was critical. Confined in the small synagogue mimeograph room, he paced to and fro before the wooden desk, checking his watch every thirty seconds. Having spent the remainder of the night at Edwin Fielding's house, he at least had the advantage of a hot shower and a decent breakfast, though he was still in the same clothes he had put on over twenty-four hours before. He was about to head for the side entrance to the synagogue when the door to the small room opened. Ben Caplan entered the room, looking haggard and beat, just like Joshua felt.

"You cut it a little close," Joshua told him.

"Not later than ten minutes to ten," Ben chided him good-naturedly.

Joshua sat down on the corner of the desk. "We don't have much time before they get here," be began. "The reason they're coming is because we've got to put the heat on Martha Fielding, and I mean heavy heat, to get her to tell us about her husband."

"You still think he's alive?"

"More now than ever," Joshua said. "Your private dick tailing her—"

"Campbell?"

"Yeah, well the insurance policy is for only *twenty-five* thousand. And, for the going market reward percentage, the best he can hope for is a paltry two grand or so."

Ben frowned thoughtfully.

"I spent the night with Edwin Fielding," Joshua went on hurriedly, "and on my way there, before midnight, I cruised by Martha's house. The place was being watched all right, but a different guy in a different car. Figuring a minimum thirty-day surveillance, Campbell has got to be already in the hole, if," and he repeated again, "if the reward money is really what he's after." He paused for a moment before going on, "How did you get the info that the policy was for a quarter of a million?"

Ben Caplan had moved behind the desk to sit down. He reached up to his forehead, rubbing his hairline. "My San Eliso operative got it from Campbell himself," he said after a moment. "When you made the inquiry, I called him up and sent him down to check it out. He posed as a rep' from the State Attorney General's office, supposedly conducting a routine check on local private investigators. It's a common practice. He simply asked Campbell what he was up to, and Campbell told him."

"And your man didn't follow up, didn't check it out with the insurance company?"

"I guess not," Ben admitted, "but he had to get back to the commune, and the answer made sense, was logical."

Joshua shook his head, realizing that at the time Ben's operator had been strung out, trying to hold down too many assignments at once, and, the answer was indeed both logical and reasonable.

"He could still be after the reward money," Ben proposed, but there was a lack of conviction in his tone.

The following moment of silence was interrupted as the door swung open to admit Martha Fielding. Edwin Fielding followed her, closing the door carefully behind him.

Joshua introduced Ben Caplan, who came up from behind the desk, offering the chair to Martha Fielding.

"You're right on time," Joshua said politely, addressing himself to Edwin Fielding.

Martha Fielding took the chair offered by Ben Caplan and thanked him in a subdued, barely audible voice.

Joshua leaned against the nearby wall, folding his arms across his chest. He looked directly at Martha Fielding. "We appreciate your coming," he said gravely, "and I must tell you both that the reason we're here is of the utmost importance, even more serious than we are allowed—"

"Never mind," Edwin Fielding said, interrupting him. "Martha and I had a long talk in the car, and she has something she wants to tell you of her own free will."

Joshua looked at the old man. He was smiling in a knowing kind of way.

"Stanley is alive!" Joshua said.

Edwin Fielding nodded his head slowly, and both Ben and Joshua looked expectantly at Martha Fielding.

"How do you know?" Ben asked.

"Tell them, Martha," urged Edwin Fielding.

Martha Fielding was a small woman with narrow, thin shoulders, and, as before, she was dressed in a plain dress of a single dark brown color, matching her eyes. Her hair was stylishly done, cut back away from her face, and she wore very little make-up. She now avoided their look, preferring to stare down at her hands before her on the wooden desk top. She had her car keys in her hand, turning them nervously.

"Please tell them," said Edwin Fielding again.

Martha Fielding bit once on her lower lip before saying, "I received a letter from Stan—"

"When?" Ben interrupted quickly.

"About two weeks ago."

"Where is it?" asked Joshua, feeling a new sense of hope shoot through his body.

"I burned it," she said quietly, "because he told me to."

"Are you sure," Ben probed gravely, "that it was from Stanley?"

"Oh, yes," she answered; "it was in his handwriting."

"How did you get the letter?" Joshua asked. "Was it postmarked?" He reached under his arm, inside his jacket, to make sure the recorder was turned on and operating.

"Our son," Martha said, "his name is Daniel, after his maternal grandfather, brought the letter from school. It was in a plain envelope with my name on it, and it had been given to Dan's teacher by a stranger."

"How do you know this?" asked Ben.

"I stopped by the school several days later and talked to Dan's teacher. He told me that a man simply stopped by his classroom during recess and gave him the letter."

"Any description?" Joshua asked her.

"Only that he was a Mexican-American."

"What did the letter say?" Edwin Fielding said then, encouraging her.

Martha Fielding closed her eyes. "It was very short. Four things. It said that he was alive and that I shouldn't worry. And, that he would be contacting me when it was safe to do so," and she hesitated.

"The fourth thing?" said Joshua.

"At the beginning and at the end," she answered, "he said I was not to tell anyone, even his father, and that I was to immediately burn the letter, which I did."

Joshua looked across the small room to Ben Caplan, who gestured for him to move outside the room.

In the hallway, Joshua pulled the door closed behind him and turned to face Ben Caplan. "What do you think?" he asked, enthusiasm evident in his voice.

Ben pulled on his lower lip. "Let's get Campbell cleared up first," he suggested.

"How?"

"To start with, we'll run a check on Martha Fielding's house to see if it's bugged, and, if so, how elaborately. I'd like to see how much money Campbell is really spending."

Joshua considered the suggestion. "That'll be easy. All we have to do is to keep her away from the house for an hour, or whatever."

"Not that easy," Ben countered. "If we assume the worst, that Fawd is after Fielding because he knows he is alive and can hurt him, then he'll have double coverage on the house."

"Oh, man," said Joshua wearily.

"Doesn't it seem strange to you," Ben pointed out, "that the Fielding angle is the one item that Fawd has really worked hard to keep us away from. I mean, like he practically laid out in writing all the rest of his plans . . . "

"Why?" asked Joshua after a moment.

"Who knows," Ben offered. "It could be that Fielding knows something, maybe he isn't even aware of it, that could lead us to Fawd or the bomb."

Joshua sighed heavily.

"It could even be that Campbell is simply carrying out a contract," Ben said, "and Fawd couldn't care less."

"It's still my hunch," said Joshua, "that Stanley Fielding is our link."

"So let's find out."

The two men returned to the small mimeograph room, where Ben quickly issued his instructions to Martha Fielding.

"Go home directly from here," he told her. "When you get there, both of you act like you smell gas in the house. Talk it up normal. Call the gas company and tell them that you smell gas leaking into, say, your kitchen. They will tell you to shut off the gas at the meter. Advise them that you have small children and that you want it investigated at once."

"I don't understand," said Martha Fielding.

"These men will pose as the inspectors," Edwin Fielding suggested.

"Wait a minute," said Joshua as he closed his eyes and hammered his forehead with the palm of his left hand. Then signalling for Ben to follow him, Joshua walked out of the room once again. In the darkened hallway, Joshua pulled the door closed behind him.

"We're being too cautious, too clinical," he insisted vehemently. "Did you notice what Martha Fielding was fiddling with?"

"Yes; her car keys, so—"

"So let's assume the worst. You can go through all the routine charades you want to, but I can tell you right now, her house is bugged. And, unless I miss my guess, her car is too."

Ben raised an appreciative eyebrow.

"Yeah," said Joshua, "so the tail who followed them here now knows that Fielding is in fact alive and that we probably know it as well. Unless he's some kind of super dummy."

"What difference does it make?" Ben asked. "The most

likely explanation for the heavy surveillance is that Fawd already knows that Stanley Fielding is alive."

"I agree," said Joshua. "But this morning marks the first major change in the scenario. Now, *we* know."

"Uh-huh," said Ben thoughtfully. "And, with us now in on the hunt, what has Fawd got left which he can use to smoke Fielding out?"

"His family."

"Oh, boy!" exclaimed Ben. "Their son, Dan," and he checked his watch. "He's still in class at school."

"Use your own people down here," Joshua cautioned him. "Like plainclothes."

Ben started for the nearby door.

Joshua grabbed his arm. "Take it easy; don't spook her and the old man. Just get the name of the school. Then find the Rabbi and use another office phone."

With Ben gone, Joshua leaned back against the hallway wall, trying to sort it all out. He was confident they would reach the boy in time, since Campbell and his people had had only about fifteen to twenty minutes to respond. Obviously, with the authorities convinced that Fielding was dead, Fawd had elected to leave the family alone, hoping that Fielding would eventually contact them. So long as only he knew the truth, Fawd had the advantage.

Yet, knowing that Stanley Fielding was most vulnerable when it came to his family, why hadn't they already kidnapped one or all of his family and thereby easily forced him to come out of hiding?

Joshua turned the obvious question in his mind for several minutes until he produced the most reasonable explanation. Because Fawd wanted Fielding's actual status kept a secret.

The answer simply led to another question.

Why?

Probably because Fielding knew something very important, something so critical that Fawd couldn't afford to let the authorities get to him first.

Another answer, another question.

Like, what did Fielding know?

Possibly the location of the bomb and/or Fawd himself? Yet this more obvious observation didn't fit into the Fawd pattern—the man's enormous flexibility, his careful planning and execution. Joshua shook his head, doubting that Fawd could have goofed so badly, that the entire program could be wrecked by the testimony of an underling like Stanley Fielding.

It was quite possible, he thought dejectedly, that the Fielding exercise was nothing more than a capricious antic devised by their adversary.

Joshua Bain took a deep, reflective breath. The only certain point he could deduce was that Ben was right: one Fawd Al-Shaer, for whatever reason, had gone to a lot of trouble to keep them away from Stanley Fielding.

So, what now?

Make a public appeal for Fielding to come forth?

Pick up Campbell and his group?

Or, drive back to San Eliso, pick up Alan Hunt, and head for Rancho Canaan, where the weeds needed chopping, the walls needed painting—

Ben Caplan appeared at his side.

"It's all right," he told Joshua, breathing rapidly. "I got to the principal, and he's pulling Dan into his office. A car will be there in a few minutes."

"Why don't you tell her," Joshua suggested, "and keep your eye on both of them."

"Why, where're you going?"

"I don't know for sure," Joshua answered honestly. "First, I'm going to take a stroll out front to verify that the street is finally clean."

"You're probably right," said Ben quietly. "I also put out an APB on your private eye, Campbell."

"We're about half an hour late," Joshua suggested. "Your only shot might be the school, but I doubt it." He reached under his left arm to release the small reel of tape and handed it to Ben. "How much time does your boss have on his twenty-four hours?"

"It expired about fifteen minutes ago."

"So we concede another round to Fawd Al-Shaer."

"Whatever," said Ben laconically, as if he had gone through such deadlines before.

"Wait a minute!" said Joshua suddenly. "Get the old man, and call the school to set up an appointment with Dan's teacher. There's the chance Edwin Fielding can identify the courier who delivered the note."

"I've already made the arrangements at the school," said Ben. "A police artist is going to meet us there in thirty minutes."

Joshua chuckled approvingly, having to admit to himself that there was merit in every system, whether in his own more gut level way of doing things or in Ben's systematic and methodical procedure. He reached up impulsively to put his arm around Ben's shoulders. "So let's get on with the program, my perfectionist friend," he said affectionately.

Outside in the parking lot, Joshua quickly surveyed the street to verify that the tail on Martha Fielding was no longer present. As he slipped in behind the steering wheel of his car, he realized that he would have to reassess the whole Fielding situation. For some reason, the candid remark of Edwin Fielding jumped into his mind: *I suspect it's the case of you and those around you wanting Stanley to be alive.*

And the old man had been correct, for he rightly understood that life was divided up between its reality and how people both interpreted and wanted it to be.

Joshua now appreciated and understood Alan Hunt's frustration as he had tried to explain the error of the high priest, Caiaphas.

Small wonder, he thought then, that the world was in such turmoil.

How easily the truth could be made a lie. If someone *wanted* to believe something strongly enough, he could even be compelled to believe by circumstances, or perhaps in the shadows of an unsolved mystery, by the lack of light, a kind of blindness, sometimes self-imposed, perhaps even asked for.

Joshua Bain had the sinking feeling that they were being set up.

So, he told himself determinedly, find the light.

It occurred to him then that he first had to locate the switch.

The twenty-four-hour deadline had passed at 10:00, Pacific Time. Jerome Mason recalled, when he had climbed out of his motel bed nearly two hours ago, after four hours of fitful sleep, that he had known then they would never make it. Now, he wondered if another day would allow them enough time. Leslie Stalmeyer was trying hard to be understanding. Bill Morrison was heavily sympathetic.

There was the defined hint of faint praise in their reactions.

Jerome Mason was ready to admit he couldn't pull it off alone. Looking numbly up from his desk, he glanced to the status board, a 4x12 strip of blackboard covering the wall to his right. He counted six Bureau teams logged in beside the name of each agent in charge. Plus, there were, at last count, twenty-three individual agents out pounding the pavement. Then, there was Doctor Melbourne's group, the psychiatrists, the Rahab team. And, on the average of about one every thirty minutes, the need to add another agent because of a newly developed lead.

He reached up to his incoming basket and picked up the top piece of paper. It was a copy of a lengthy telegram from the computer manufacturer who had supplied the San Eliso unit. The first paragraph verified that two complete systems had been purchased and delivered on the same date to the Aerotec address. *Two systems*, he thought. So, where was the second one? He punched the wire into the slot marked "Dr. Melbourne."

He figured he had to make a decision every three to five minutes.

Fighting his sense of negativism, he pushed up out of his chair.

The odds were getting astronomical. They had to score somehow, someplace.

He now wanted to talk to Kate Felton, the senior psychiatrist assigned to the team, but he saw that she was on the phone at her assigned desk.

He moved instead to the open hangar, where he approached Jeff Bingham, the agent in charge of the team tearing into the Aerotec vehicles, which had been totally dismantled after being vacuumed and thoroughly inspected for everything from soil samples to any other possible contamination. Seated at his portable field desk, Jeff Bingham looked up as his superior drew near.

"Anything new on number six?" Mason asked him. The vehicle tagged with number six was a two-year-old van with a long bed. In the dismantling process it had been discovered to have been recently equipped with both oversized shocks and heavy-duty springs.

Bingham shook his head. "Not yet. We've picked it clean; it's up to the lab now."

Mason scanned the papers spread over the cluttered desk. "Wasn't this fleet also serviced around the same time as the steam-cleaning job?"

"Yes, sir," Bingham answered. "Over a period of several days."

"Before or after?"

"After the cleaning."

Mason grimaced disappointedly. "Okay," he said then. "Get a couple of men over to the garage that did the tune-ups. You know what to look for, and don't forget the warrant." Turning away, he thought that only God knew what good a used spark plug might do them.

He sensed they were grasping at straws.

The psychological profile on Fawd Al-Shaer suggested the man had tendencies toward megalomania. How had Kate Felton put it? *Infantile feelings of personal omnipotence and grandeur.*

The grandiose performance.

Fawd Al-Shaer was going to make up for thirty years of humiliating defeat in one grand swoop.

Back in his office, Mason saw that Kate Felton was off her phone. As he walked over to her desk, he couldn't help but smile to himself. Doctor Katherine Felton looked like she should be tending a San Pedro bar. He guessed she was about five feet tall, figuring she must weigh at least a hundred and seventy-five pounds. Kate Felton was short and fat, a fact she was proud of, along with her flaming red hair, cut short and in a constant state of disarray. As he reached her desk, she looked up at him over the rims of her half-sized reading glasses. There were two ashtrays on the desk. Both were full of cigarillo butts, the black and loathsome-smelling remnants of her chain-smoking habit.

"You look terrible," she told him, her voice husky like a man's. There was a long ash on the cigarillo she had in her right hand. No one knew for sure, but the best guess was that she was in her middle forties. Another familiar Felton trademark was that she wore house slippers instead of shoes, wherever she went, claiming shoes were both unnatural and always ill-fitting.

"You'll look the same way," he assured her, "about this time tomorrow," and he flopped down in the chair next to her desk. "So you've got this Fawd character pretty well diagnosed," he said in a more official tone.

She pulled her glasses off, and with the gesture the long ash on her cigarillo fell on the desk top. She simply brushed the ash onto the floor. "As best as we can," she answered thoughtfully. "We've gone over his dossier, the tapes, both audio and video, supplied by Ben Caplan. The Rahab team notes, too, plus the ultimatum letter."

Mason nodded and listened. Kate Felton was the ninth person, so far, officially informed of all the facts, including the existence of one atomic bomb located somewhere in or around Los Angeles, California. "A question," he said then. "Would we expect to find our subject with the device?"

"Negative."

"So," reasoned Mason, "we wouldn't identify him as suicidal?"

"That's not the point. He could be suicidal, though I'm reasonably sure he isn't. Among his other peculiarities, Fawd is a paradox within himself. This is the man they call the Father of the Holy War. His record indicates he has almost a supernatural ability to persuade and inspire his commando followers to donate their lives to the cause. Yet the forays he has been known to lead have always been the hit-and-run variety, with a way of escape, as opposed to the outright suicide missions."

"You mean he's a coward."

"No, no, not at all. I doubt that the man even concerns himself with his personal safety. On the other hand and in this specific instance, it's a necessary part of his delusion that he not only succeed but also be around to witness his success."

"You mean," said Mason, "that if he feels he must execute that he *probably* programmed himself to survive?"

"I'd bet on it."

"You sound so positive."

There was a following pause before Kate went on. "Do you remember the movies of a triumphant Adolph Hitler after the fall of France, trooping and stomping around the little railroad car—"

"Okay, okay; I get the picture. Have you an opinion yet on how to handle the message regarding the Yucca Flats thing?"

"Very definitely," said Kate. "We've been going over Kabir and his background very thoroughly. He's your weak link, and no question about it. He's a heavy coke user, and he needs it for several reasons. So, for starters, get Fawd down on Kabir, the heavier the better."

"So you figure to get them fighting between themselves—"

"Not necessarily. Kabir is not the type to fight back, at least not until he is forced into a corner. You should tell Fawd that his demo shot was a fizzle, and, do it in an insulting way. Belittle him if you can. You know, like cut him down."

Mason grunted appreciatively. "And Fawd takes it out on Kabir."

"If he doesn't he'll be totally out of character."

"If the heat gets on, will Kabir tend to fold first?"

"Absolutely. He's not the gut idealist that Fawd imagines himself to be. Kabir is both practical and a technician, and a good one apparently, and his reward is the satisfaction of seeing his design work well. Attack his work, and you attack him; it's one way to reach him."

"Can he be bought out?"

There was a pause as Kate apparently went over the question. "With money I'm not so sure. He can be bought, perhaps with immunity, that he can be guaranteed sanctuary in a foreign country, and you should know why that is an answer."

"The cocaine."

"Of course; the mere threat of jail would drive him to almost any other alternative." She shuffled through the papers on her desk then. "I've got a supplementary report on Kabir from Tel Aviv here someplace. It seems his mother was a Jainist."

"What's that?"

"A religious bunch in India. Real ascetics. It's a cardinal sin to just step on an ant. During the late forties, when Kabir was still a youngster, his mother got herself involved with a radical sect, calling themselves Moksha, which in their religious jargon means liberation, or, to be liberated. Anyway, India was in turmoil at the time, and Kabir's mother was killed in a street demonstration. According to Kabir's father, the boy witnessed his mother's death. A rather ugly affair."

"Tough experience for the kid," Mason observed.

"More than you realize," Kate confirmed. "His father is still alive, retired and living in England. The Israelis located him a couple of days ago. The father also claims that Kabir was pretty much raised a mamma's boy, was strongly influenced by his mother until she was killed. The father tried to help by sending Kabir back to England, where he spent the rest of his youth banging around in private schools."

"Apparently it didn't help."

"Too little, too late," said Kate cryptically. "From his history since his mother's death, he appears to have forgotten the incident. However, I've been going over his notes collected at the San Eliso commune, and the word Moksha has turned up on several of his doodle sheets."

"Guilt feelings?" mused Mason.

"Something like that," Kate seemed to agree, and she stared distantly out across the office.

"What about the Anne Delemar thing?"

"That's more difficult to analyze," admitted Kate Felton tiredly. "Lacking any other tactical reason, aside from Fawd's mania, it suggests that maybe this woman is the way to reach him. Like, Fawd demands recognition. Hiding like he is now, he's underground, out of the limelight. So he's boxed himself into a conflict situation. The plan requires, rationally, that he not be discovered. Yet, here he is pulling off the grandest of plans, and he's cooped up in some lonely hideout, perhaps climbing the walls by now, because he doesn't have an outside soul, let alone an audience, to show the appreciation he figures he deserves."

"You mean he wants to be found?" Mason asked skeptically.

"He demands recognition. Why do you think he ordered the concession speech to be made before the General Assembly of the U.N.?"

"It still doesn't make sense," Mason insisted.

"Stop trying to make sense with this man. Remember, he considers himself invincible, and this reasoning has been reinforced through his successes up until this time."

"All right," said Mason. "I'll keep it in mind. Do you have anything else before I hit the phones again?"

"One more point, which I classify on the encouraging side—"

"Finally," Mason said to himself.

"Like any smart terrorist," Kate went on, "Fawd has developed a plan, and he naturally has programmed the odds to be in his favor, overwhelmingly so, since it appears he is more clever than most. And he's had the backing of both time and money to put it together. Things have gone well for him to this point simply because he is on schedule—per his plan, that is. And, you're not going to get a break, really, until you somehow manage to alter the plan, to introduce a disruptive factor, a catalyst, anything, which will force him into impromptu decisions. I call it the extemporaneous factor."

"A plausible theory," Mason supposed. "But in a situation such as this, it seems an over-simplification to—"

"It works," Kate told him. "We've applied it effectively in each terrorist case for the past two years. Granted, we're in a more complex format, but I can guarantee you that once you either force or lure Fawd Al-Shaer into heavy improvisation, you'll take him, hands down. A part of it is because then he'll be reduced to his basic character, as vulnerable as the rest of us but in his own unique ways."

Mason was still shaking his head doubtfully. "It's hard to imagine the man is vulnerable in any way."

"Baloney. Don't forget, you haven't been up against him personally; you've been bucking the plan itself, which took months, maybe even years, to develop. Believe me, sooner or later that carefully prepared string will run out if you can weather it. Then you'll be standing eyeball to eyeball."

"What about Ben Caplan's exercise for tonight?" Mason asked. "I told him to clear it with you before he left."

She nodded once. "He didn't tell me much, but I can guess enough to suggest that it's what I call a third-party entry. I'm starting to dig into this Fielding situation now, but I doubt seriously that Fawd will expose himself at this time."

"It could produce a deviation—"

"But it's third party. We're not dealing with Fawd directly, but rather through an intermediary. So, he has ample time to counsel the situation. Based on his performance to date, Fawd should have the Fielding option already programmed in any way. At best, it's a super long shot. The safe bet is that Fawd will not be required to make a single impromptu decision in dealing with Ben Caplan tonight."

"Should I cancel the exercise?"

"No; let them go through with it. Like Ben pointed out to me, it's really all they've got to go on right now."

Jerome Mason sighed heavily. "Okay," he said finally, "so what's your best recommendation as of right now?"

"Find him. That's all. Just find Fawd Al-Shaer. Until then you're going to keep getting crunched, because you're just going along with his ball game."

"Sure," Mason muttered under his breath. "All we have to do is find him." He glanced over his shoulder to see that his aide was holding up two fingers, indicating that he now had two calls holding. He turned back to see that Kate Felton was studying him.

"Would you like some personal advice," she said, "from an old warhorse who's been this route before?"

"Anytime."

"Get yourself some help, and, the sooner the better."

Jerome Mason closed his eyes, absorbing the suggestion, thinking that Kate Felton's intuition was most remarkable. "I've already made the arrangements. Bill Morrison is already en route; should be here in a couple of hours."

The police helicopter veered sharply into a ninety-degree turn as it came abreast of the commune manor house. Ben Caplan swallowed hard, watching the water zip by no more than ten feet below them. Without warning them, the pilot kicked the bird around to drop to the beach. All flyers were the same, Ben thought, looking aside to see that the pilot was smiling. With the chopper on the sand, he gratefully climbed out of the small hatch without looking back. Stooped over and with his briefcase clasped to his chest, he trudged heavily across the dry sand toward the embankment, holding his breath and squinting against the swirling dirt and sand.

At the top of the knoll, he turned to watch the helicopter spin gracefully up and away from the beach, out then across the water, gaining altitude on an even angle, on its way back to Los Angeles.

Jerome Mason had given them six hours to use Anne Delemar.

They were going to need at least nine hours to make it really work.

Joshua suggested to go ahead and take the six, while they could, and then try for the extra three later on.

As he turned toward the house, he found Alan Hunt standing by his elbow.

"Everybody here?" Ben said hoarsely.

Alan nodded once. "Joshua just arrived."

"Let's get on with it," said Ben curtly, starting toward the house, not wanting to dawdle with Alan Hunt, who must continue to be kept in the dark—even more so now.

Ben reassured himself that it was integral to the plan, especially now, that only he and Joshua knew the truth.

Joshua Bain was on the phone at Kabir's desk when they entered the recreation room. Anne Delemar was seated nearby. Leaning forward, she reached out to take Alan's hand, saying something to him in a low whisper. Ben discreetly took note of the look that passed between them. He dropped his briefcase on the nearby desk as Joshua hung up.

"It's set with Breck," Joshua told him, loudly enough for all of them to hear.

"What about Mario?" Ben asked, knowing that as of this moment the plan was in motion.

"He left Fielding's house at the same time I did."

"What's happening?" Alan asked as he sat down next to Anne.

Ben sat down on the corner of the desk, folding his arms across his chest before answering, "Stanley Fielding is alive."

Alan lifted an appreciative eyebrow as he smiled at Joshua. Anne remained immobile, showing little reaction beyond pursing her lips thoughtfully.

Ben then recapped their morning meeting with Martha and Edwin Fielding. "Joshua and Stan's father went immediately to the school and obtained a complete description of the man who delivered the note to Dan's teacher," he added.

"And we got our first break," said Joshua. "Because old man Fielding recognized enough about the description to point us in the direction of one Mario Sanchez, a long-time friend of the family and a very close personal friend of the two Fielding boys."

"Does he know where Fielding is?" asked Anne.

"Negative," answered Joshua. "Or at least he claims he doesn't know."

"How'd he get the note?" Alan asked.

"Through a relative in Ensenada," said Ben.

"That's great," exclaimed Alan. "Mario Sanchez has probably got five hundred relatives south of the border."

"Hey, man," said Joshua. "It's a contact, and he's helping us right now."

"All right," said Alan, "so how's he helping us?"

"He's already across the border," said Ben, turning up his watch, "and should be in Ensenada right now. And he has in his possession a personal note written by Stanley's father, a strong note I might add, urging Stanley to at least make contact with us tonight."

"Bear in mind," Joshua added, "that Stanley Fielding has shown he trusts Mario Sanchez and the Ensenada contact, so we can figure a reliable connection."

Good credibility, Ben thought to himself.

"What about Mrs. Fielding and her boy?" asked Anne.

Ben casually looked aside to Joshua, who too obviously appreciated both the question and its source.

"They're safe," said Joshua. "Wolf Shertok agreed to let them stay at his place in Del Mar."

"Stanley's father is with them too," said Ben. "The Professor's home is on a private estate bordering the cliffs near the beach. We have several agents on twenty-four-hour security. Believe me, there's no way they can be harmed now."

"So like I said," Alan repeated, "what's happening now?"

"With Shertok's help," Joshua explained, "we've made arrangements for a safe place to meet Fielding tonight."

Alan Hunt whistled under his breath and shook his head. "Man, like that's kind of soon—"

"Oh ye of little faith," said Joshua.

Alan smiled. "Good point, brother."

"The meet will take place," Joshua went on, and he gestured at Ben Caplan, who on the cue opened his briefcase, "at nine o'clock tonight at a retail sales store on Mission Hill Road in National City."

Ben had unfolded a map of the area and laid it out on the desk. Both Alan and Anne came forward to lean over the map. "As you can see," said Ben, "National City is just above the border, which reduces Fielding's exposure on this side, assuming he's now in Mexico."

"The address is 906," said Joshua, "and you can't miss it. It's an outlet for the sale of fiberglass spas for residential installation. The site is both very public and open, plus very easy to find as you drive down that particular street. Shertok agrees with us that Fielding is going to be very wary, obviously, in view of his conduct to date. So, we want him to come in seeing that the coast is generally clear as best as he will be able to tell. I drove by the store on my way here, and it's set back from the street behind a large front parking lot. The owner, Jonathan Breck, has been instructed to have all vehicles and employees clear of the area from seven-thirty on, tonight."

"This could break it," suggested Alan thoughtfully as he returned to his chair. "Assuming that Fielding is going to be jumpy, we'd best not have an army of agents camped around the store."

"Exactly," agreed Ben Caplan. "Just the three of us will be at the site. Joshua will cover the inside, the only one there, hopefully to make face-to-face contact. Alan, you and I will split up—you in front, me at the back, and completely out of sight."

"We'll case the location again this afternoon," said Joshua, "and we'll be on site from eight o'clock on in case he shows early."

"There's no way I can help?" said Anne.

Oh, baby, thought Ben, we're counting on you—

"No need," Joshua told her. "We can handle it. A fourth person would just be in the way."

"What if he doesn't show?" Alan asked conversationally.

"He's got an option," said Joshua. "The letter from his father insists that he at least send us a report on what it is he might have on Fawd."

Alan nodded approvingly. "So we've covered the bases; it'll either be him in person or a messenger. What are the odds, one way or the other?"

"It's a break-out," Joshua suggested. "Now that he knows his family is safe, he ought to be willing to risk himself. The old man's letter is pretty strong." He shrugged once. "I would say that we can at least bank on a message."

Ben Caplan snapped his briefcase closed. "Between the two, either him or a message, I'd say we're working on an easy eighty-twenty chance."

Outside the house, Alan headed for the Jaguar after saying good-bye to Anne. He would follow behind the other two men, who were riding together and now waiting for him in Ben's car. As Joshua settled himself in the passenger seat, he glanced over his shoulder toward the house.

"So now it's up to her," he said passively. Only he and Ben knew the truth; that neither Stanley Fielding nor his messenger would be showing up at the spa store tonight. The plan was entirely a fabrication, a simple ruse, to bait Anne Delemar into contacting Fawd Al-Shaer, with the hope that they could force something to happen. "What's the chance of Fawd showing?" he asked as Ben turned the car onto the highway leading south.

"Hardly any at all," Ben suggested. "The best we can hope for is that Kabir might be there. Remember, Campbell and his people are on the run. So, unless Fawd has other operatives in reserve, which is unlikely . . . "

"Hah," grunted Joshua. "Don't sell him short."

"You think she went for it?"

"Should have," Joshua said after a moment. "The story is certainly plausible enough, and, considering the time and effort he's put into chasing Fielding, I'd say Fawd would have to follow up. If I were in his shoes, I would. Besides, Jerome Mason obviously went for it. So did Shertok. So, it should almost be a certainty that she'll buy it." He turned aside then to look directly at his friend, Benjamin Caplan. "While we're at it," he said gravely, "how come you elected yourself to be the one to pose as Fielding?"

"I'm the same size, remember. It'll be dark enough to keep them guessing, whether it's Fielding or a messenger. Got to be to our advantage—"

"I suppose you're right," Joshua conceded reluctantly, settling back into the seat again and closing his eyes as he ran over the plan once again. It was Ben's thesis, agreed to by Jerome Mason and his experts, that Anne Delemar had been left behind by Fawd for some purpose, most likely to communicate. At least she had the capability of reaching Fawd in an emergency situation. Tonight's exercise, by Joshua's guess, would verify that she could reach Fawd, plus, as a hoped-for bonus, would produce a body or two, someone they could pick up and interrogate, or, perhaps even follow if the plan came off as hoped.

There was no Mario Sanchez, although Edwin Fielding did come up with a probable on the Mexican messenger, an Ensenada friend of Stanley's who owned a charter sportfishing boat, the *Errante*, which at the moment was supposed to be nearly a hundred miles at sea chasing albacore. Both the U.S. Navy and the Mexican Coast Guard were out after the boat right now. Joshua figured production on the lead by midnight, or, at the latest, by tomorrow morning.

Regardless, Stanley Fielding was still the link, not Anne Delemar and the fact that she could reach Fawd, or then again, how she might do it.

To guarantee the maximum results, the operation was absolutely airtight, not so much as a matter of good procedure, as Ben early pointed out, but because Joshua knew they were all a little paranoid over Fawd's uncanny ability to have always been ahead of them. Tonight would be different. At Ben's insistence, not even Jerome Mason knew the truth. Not that the Director himself, nor even someone as reliable as Wolf Shertok, couldn't be trusted; rather, it was those near them, their phones, the very walls around them, which could relay a message, innocently, indirectly, or whatever.

If Mission Hill Road was to fail, it wouldn't be because of a leak.

Then, thinking about Alan Hunt, he opened his eyes. "I'm going to have to break it to Alan tonight," he said after a moment.

"Yeah," said Ben. "Mason wants her bad."

"She won't do him any good," Joshua suggested. "Fawd couldn't be that stupid."

"Maybe. But there's a heavy team working on it now; maybe they can come up with something to make her pay off."

"You mean like Fawd isn't perfect."

"That plus time."

Yeah, thought Joshua, time right now was the enemy of them all. Or, conversely, it might be said that time was at the same moment their friend as well. Feeling himself getting jammed, he reached up to flip on the car radio, looking for a music station.

It was the first time she had been really alone in several days, and Anne Delemar didn't know exactly what to do with herself. The great house was empty now, except for the four agents still patrolling the premises, who from time to time came into the house to use the bathroom or the telephone. The afternoon TV bill of fare was atrocious, and she gave it up after less than fifteen minutes. Feeling restless, she made her way out of the house, turning finally to the south vegetable garden. It saddened her that the food would probably go to waste. Another two weeks and the weeds would triumph.

Perhaps there was a lesson in the victory of the weed.

What did Alan call them . . . the tares.

Anne turned toward the ocean, thinking she might look for seashells to add to the collection started by Alan. His face came into focus in her mind, and she wondered again if he might be in danger tonight.

She had given herself until two o'clock to decide what to do about the Fielding development. Her instructions were precise and limiting: she was to break silence only under the most *extreme* circumstances. For she had only one shot. And, the contact procedure was complex, requiring perhaps more time than she had available. She checked her watch and noticed she had about ten minutes to decide.

Anne sauntered off toward the tool shed, feeling the afternoon sun warm across her shoulders, thinking that she would cut down at least some of the weeds, which stole the water and food from the soil, producing nothing in return.

Special agent Jeff Bingham got up from his desk as the half-ton pickup truck began to back into the hangar. Briefly surveying his assigned area, he moved a few steps off to his right, lifted his hands to begin directing the driver in toward the space where he figured to store the truck's load. The sign painted on the truck's side panel identified it as one from the garage which recently had overhauled the Aerotec delivery fleet. A few seconds later he waved for the driver to shut it down.

One of his men got out of the passenger side of the pickup. Bingham dropped the tailgate.

"This is it?" he questioned. The only item on the bed was a single fifty-five gallon metal drum.

"We're lucky we got this much," his man answered, and Bingham noticed in his voice the same tone of weariness, bordering on discouragement, which seemed to have overtaken them all.

They wrestled the heavy drum down the sloped tailgate to set it a few feet from the truck.

"Give him a receipt," said Bingham huskily. Breathing heavily, he leaned over the drum to briefly inspect its contents: a menagerie of dirty, used auto parts, some loose, others in marked plastic bags. This assortment of junk kind of marks the end of the line, he thought.

He turned to face the opposite end of the hangar. The old man had wisely set up a portable field lab on the premises, thus saving them the downtime of transporting back and forth to the LAPD headquarters downtown. The partitioned-off lab was about fifty feet away, and he decided he was too tired to walk it both ways. Returning to the desk he lifted the phone and punched an intercom button.

Seated next to Jerome Mason's desk, Bill Morrison sat patiently waiting for the Bureau Director to get off the phone. Having just arrived by commercial jet, he once more reached for his left ear, probing it with his little finger, trying to relieve the pressure still lingering on the eardrum. From what he could tell regarding Mason's telephone conversation, the person on the other end was Doctor Melbourne, who at last report was huddled with his colleagues at the Sandia Laboratory. Mason hung up then and told his aide to hold all his calls.

"That was Melbourne," he confirmed. "He's got a theory, but he won't talk about it until he has a chance to meet with the people at Armatrex in San Diego."

"If he's got something, Jerry—"

"You know Melbourne better than I do. He's an empiricist. Has to try something a dozen different ways first." Mason held up his hand in a helpless gesture. "He refuses to talk about it until he has further verification."

"Hustle him to San Diego then."

"I'll set it up for early tomorrow morning. And if Joshua Bain is available, I'll have him escort Melbourne to Armatrex."

"Why Bain?"

"First, because he's already down there and knows the area. And, because Bain is the type to put pressure on the good Doctor. The two of them are about as opposite as they can get." Mason made a half turn to his left and pointed over Morrison's shoulder. "There's your private desk, and I'm sure glad you're here."

"I'm not so sure I am," said Morrison truthfully.

"Does your son know you're here?"

Morrison shook his head negatively.

Mason dropped the subject, knowing that Bill Morrison had his own special fire built under him. "Les tells me you located Fawd's backers."

"It wasn't difficult," admitted Morrison. "The original plot apparently started several years ago, between at least three conspirators, and possibly as many as five. The chief hancho is the Libyan Finance Minister—"

"Oil money," said Mason, shaking his head.

"The plot is fairly provincial. Israel has atomic weapons; therefore it's only fair and just that the Arabs should too. Balance of power, and so on."

"And I suppose," said Mason, "they know nothing about this Rahab scheme."

"Absolutely not. In fact, they've volunteered to help in any way—unofficially, of course."

"On the assumption," Mason said bitterly, "that if Los Angeles goes up in smoke, it won't exactly help their cause."

Morrison simply grunted once and shook his head.

Mason slammed his fist angrily on the desk top, startling Morrison.

"You tell me, Mister CIA," Mason growled, "why is it that Tel Aviv knew all about Fawd Al-Shaer entering this country, perhaps even being able to find out why he was sent here, without *our* knowing about it?"

Bill Morrison reached up, rubbed his forehead, and then

answered carefully, "Ha Mossad's answer to that question is the same as you'll get from any of our friendly overseas agencies. Like, why should they provide us with sensitive data when the chances are that such data will wind up in the papers within a couple of weeks anyway?"

Jerome Mason slumped forward over his desk. "So help me," he said heatedly, "if and when this is all over, I'm going to make every last detail public; the people of this country are going to know—"

Bill Morrison chuckled sympathetically. "Don't waste your reputation," he advised sincerely. "Within a couple of years, there'll be half a dozen congressional committees organized and twice as many books published to prove the whole Rahab bit was a fabrication. The most likely scapegoat will be the U.S. oil industry, perhaps Israel as well. Or, more sensationally, an elite wealthy group, probably right-wing . . ." He shrugged.

Jerome Mason stared at him, his great mane of disheveled hair framing a look of total incredibility.

"Think of the movie rights," Morrison added flippantly.

Jerome Mason leaned back in his chair and began to laugh, a subdued kind of chuckle which turned into an uproar.

The best Morrison could come up with was an understanding grin.

Jerome Mason finally came forward in his chair, wiping his eyes with the back of his hand. "You know what?" he said after clearing his throat. "I'm going to plant some clues along that line, really screw 'em up."

Morrison was glad to see the man's good humor. "What's with Anne Delemar?" he asked abruptly.

"Ah, yes!" exclaimed Mason, sighing heavily as he organized his thoughts. "Ben Caplan has a ploy to use her right now. I've given him until six o'clock tonight." He then briefly explained the Fielding development. "We're arranging for appeals in the Mexican media, radio, newspapers, and TV, to get Fielding to come in on his own if he doesn't show tonight."

Morrison noticed that Mason's aide was holding up four fingers, obviously reporting the number of calls holding. He got up and stretched. "You have someone to brief me?"

"Burt Ingstrom will fill you in and give you the cook's tour," Mason told him as he reached for the phone. "The first thing you can do to really help, however, is to work out a story for the reporters."

"Les is taking care of it," Morrison told him. "We're supposed to be involved in a confidential exercise involving internal security, which should buy us at least forty-eight hours."

"And the U.N. announcement?"

"Eleven o'clock tomorrow morning, unless we break things."

Mason shook his head negatively as he put the receiver to his ear.

Chapter nine

At precisely eight o'clock, Kabir turned on the radio receiver which was wall-mounted next to the fireplace in the living room. The KOPE announcer reported the station's call letters, followed by the time, and as he began his weather report Kabir made his final tune adjustments. He then checked the tape recorder. Behind him, Fawd Al-Shaer was still stalking to and fro across the gigantic room, as he had been for most of the day. The ever-present rubber ball was in his hand, and he was working it now even more furiously than usual. Kabir sniffled once and rubbed his nose, thinking that a two 'n two hit would settle Fawd down.

"It's nearly time," he said, his voice losing itself in the huge room.

"For what?" Fawd demanded gruffly without breaking stride.

Kabir didn't answer. Leaning his head back indifferently, he waited until the announcer finished his weather report. The man's dull, flat monotone changed as he reported the key word, Rahab. "You are advised," the announcer went on, "that your Yucca Flats pop was no more than a fizzle . . ."

Kabir straightened up, at the same time noticing that Fawd had come to a halt.

" . . . less than ten percent of your estimated yield," the announcer was saying, "which allows you a ninety-percent error factor, also giving you the benefit of the doubt. While we are willing to negotiate, please know that your poor record of performance suggests that we are dealing with an amateur who is perhaps more of a danger to himself. Please review your capa-

bility, intelligently this time, and reconsider your position."
There was a following pause, then music.

Fawd stood stock still in the middle of the room. His eyes
narrowing to slits, he stared at Kabir, waiting.

"It's a bluff," Kabir blurted out.

Still wordless, Fawd advanced threateningly across the
space between them.

"It's not true!" Kabir insisted, as he cowered against the
flagstone wall.

Fawd stood menacingly before him. Reaching out then, he
grabbed Kabir by his arms, lifting him bodily up the flagstone.
Kabir winced as the rough stone cut into his back. "They're
trying to psych us," pleaded Kabir, squirming helplessly in his
grasp.

"You will go to your computer," hissed Fawd, "and you
will prepare a tape of your procedure, which you will immediately transmit to Zurich."

"We've already done that," said Kabir. "It checks out—"

"You will do it again," interrupted Fawd, and he released
Kabir, telling him, "And I will personally break your neck
with these two hands if the Americans are right. Do you understand?"

Kabir nodded weakly.

"Get moving!" Fawd ordered harshly.

Kabir jerked obediently into motion, stumbling once as he
headed for the stairway leading to his computer.

Jerome Mason gestured for his aide to turn off the radio.

"What's that supposed to do for us?" questioned Bill
Morrison. Like the rest of them, he had stripped down to his
shirtsleeves.

Mason pondered the question as he stared at the remnants
of his dinner, cold french fries and half a hamburger. He
reached for his coffee, hoping to wash away the greasy taste in
his mouth. Swallowing once, he decided it was a trade-off, and
he wondered again if and when it was all going to end.

"It's Kate's idea," he said after another moment. "We're
trying to reach Kabir through Fawd. The physicist apparently
can't take a whole lot of pressure."

"Strictly a long shot," Morrison proposed, half aloud.
"We'll have better luck with Anne Delemar."

Mason didn't reply to the remark, aware that Bill Morrison had been against giving Ben Caplan an additional three
hours' extension on bringing in the Delemar woman. He

checked the wall clock curiously. The Rahab team was forty minutes away from their gig, which also meant that Burt Ingstrom was already on his way to the San Eliso commune to pick up Anne Delemar. He noticed then that one of the lab technicians was standing in his office doorway. Mason waved him in.

Bill Morrison came forward in his chair as the technician stood in front of Mason's desk.

"What have you got?" Mason asked dryly.

"An interesting item," the technician told him, and he put what appeared to be a round filter of some kind on the corner of Mason's desk. He held up a small plastic bag in his other hand. "This is a carburetor filter from one of the Aerotec vehicles," the technician explained; "and these," he added, holding up the plastic bag, "are specimens of microspores, or pollen, with petal and pistil fragments, from a plant in the genus arctosyaphylos." He smiled slightly. "You might know the plant by the name manzanita."

"The stuff came out of the filter," Mason guessed aloud.

"Yes, it did," the technician confirmed. "And it's not too old either, no more than a few weeks. Quite extensive concentration too, I might add. I would say the vehicle bearing this filter probably came into contact with the plant, or plants, rubbing up against them maybe. This genus has many varieties, and during the bloom stage the small heath-like flowers cluster together—"

"So," said Mason tiredly, and he thought that all lab techs were the same, like Doctor Melbourne, given to lengthy explanations as if to justify the few seconds' audience they were afforded after hours of work in their laboratories.

"So I just checked with a local botanical expert," the technician went on, "who helped me identify it, and he confirmed that this particular variety of manzanita is rather unique, since it is typically found in this coastal area only at elevations of four thousand feet and higher." The technician casually dropped the plastic envelope into the open center of the carburetor filter. Then, turning again, quite casually, he headed back toward the door.

It took a second or two for the impact of the statement to register on Jerome Mason's tired mind. Suddenly he bolted out of his chair. "Wait a minute!" he yelled.

The technician stopped and turned slowly. The hint of a smile was on his face.

Mason first turned to his aide. "Get Bingham in here, and

fast." Next he addressed the lab technician. "Tell me more, like, what are the chances we can guarantee that this filter was at a given altitude, say, could it've picked the stuff up at three thousand feet?"

"Not possible. The concentration of this sample is extremely heavy. Like I said before, the vehicle had to be right there."

"It could've been in a caravan," Morrison said, "following behind another vehicle which could've brushed against the plants."

The technician nodded once. "Very close behind, like bumper to bumper."

"Get on it, Bill," Mason said energetically. He was thinking about Kate Felton's contention that Fawd Al-Shaer's mania would prompt him to be able to view the outcome of his grand plan. "Of course," he exclaimed. "The fool has to have a grandstand seat," and he turned back to his aide. "Get area maps in here, across that wall," and he gestured to the partition behind Bill Morrison's desk, "so we can build an aerial view of all the mountain ranges around the Los Angeles basin." After turning to his desk, he took Bill Morrison by the shoulder. "Get a final report from the lab; get this altitude business nailed down. Then trace out an area on the maps, outlining all those potential zones falling—"

"I understand," Morrison assured him.

Special Agent Bingham appeared at the doorway.

"Take this filter," Mason told him, "and match it up with the vehicle it came from, and start with number six."

Bill Morrison stopped on his way out the door. "You realize," he said thoughtfully, "that all this does for the moment is to give us who knows how many hundreds of square miles—"

"Get with the botanist," Mason interrupted him. "Maybe he can narrow it down." Coming close to Morrison's elbow, he said, "I really wish you'd take charge of this." He reached up and pulled on his lower lip. "Your experience in field reconnaissance might produce a way we can locate the hideout." Morrison nodded his head understandingly. "You mean like overfly the area, thermal sensors, infrared—"

"Exactly," Mason said confidentially. "You've got to have in that CIA bag of tricks the means to locate a hot object in open terrain."

"You better believe it," Morrison said excitedly. Hurrying out of the room, he yelled back over his shoulder, "Get on the phone and line us up some help!"

Turning back to his desk, Mason felt a new surge of energy flowing through his body. Morrison's parting remark brought to his mind the sheer logistical needs of the probable means to nail down the location visited by the vehicle bearing the filter. Under normal circumstances, they would have to work their way painfully and slowly through no telling how many agencies just to get a single aircraft capable of overflying and photographing the region under suspicion. He lifted the receiver of his phone, punching the button for Les Stalmeyer, thinking gratefully that one of the advantages of being trapped in the Southern California area was that they were surrounded by nearby military aircraft bases.

Les Stalmeyer came on the line after one ring.

"I haven't got the time to explain," Mason told him, "but I want a direct line, on a secure phone, to the Chairman, the Joint Chiefs."

"You mean General Morgan himself?"

"In the flesh," said Mason, "and I want him informed by the Secretary of Defense, on direct orders from the President, that he is to proceed according to our needs and wishes, without need of verification from higher authority!"

There was a short pause before Stalmeyer answered, "You're coming on kind of strong, Jerry. I don't know . . . "

"What time is the announcement before the United Nations tomorrow?"

"You know the time," said Stalmeyer defensively. "Tell me one thing," he said then, "is Bill Morrison in on whatever this is—"

"He's in charge of it."

"All right. But it'll probably take the better part of an hour to work up and down the line, as you've specified."

"Thanks, Les," said Mason, hanging up. Pushing the consequences of his rather rash action out of his mind, he turned to punch the button for Kate Felton.

Bill Morrison stuck his head back through the door. "Remember your radio announcement about the fizzle?"

Mason frowned and nodded yes.

"It just came to me," Morrison went on, "that Fawd might try to get to the device, like, maybe to check it."

"Possible," Mason agreed.

"It would probably be the physicist, Kabir."

"Yeah. Or, it could be another accomplice. But if it's a technical problem with the device, then you're probably right. Why, what's your point?"

"If Kabir is with Fawd, as we suspect, then shouldn't we at least monitor the roads leaving the suspected area?"

A valid point, Mason conceded to himself. "Not only that," he said. "Ben Caplan figures that Kabir might even show there tonight. For that matter, he might've already come down." He turned to his aide. "You're from around here. What's the road situation in and out of the local higher mountains?"

"How high?"

"Four thousand plus."

"Only one range like that close by," his aide said. "The San Gabriels, right above us to the north. Two main locals going in, one above La Canada, leading up near Mount Wilson; a second, farther east, Highway 39, I think, going up out of the San Gabriel Valley."

Only two main roads, Mason thought.

"There's a jillion other smaller trails," his aide went on, "but I don't think any of them go through to that altitude."

Mason looked at Burt Ingstrom's desk, remembering then that Ingstrom was en route to pick up Anne Delemar. Looking up at his aide, he had to think for a moment to recall his name. "Agent Bradshaw, you've just been drafted. Get the Governor on the phone, and don't worry, he's already been briefed to expect to hear from us. Tell him I want two teams of highway patrolmen, in plainclothes, assigned to you immediately. Take pictures of our suspects with you. Keep out of sight, and just *watch*—nothing else."

Agent Bradshaw picked up his phone.

"Call LAPD too," Mason told him. "Arrange for a helicopter to be on standby at some middle-ground point. If you positively make a suspect, put him under aerial surveillance, but at high altitude."

"In the dark?" asked Bradshaw.

Mason sighed heavily, thinking that he had lost track of time. "Have the chopper on station before dawn," he said.

Bill Morrison appeared at his left elbow. Leaning down, he began to speak softly, only loud enough for Mason to hear. "Agent Bradshaw is no doubt qualified to do this," Morrison said gently. "But he is now one of twelve or thirteen who know about the bomb, the real reason why we're here. So now you're going to have to bring in another aide, tell him about it too, plus putting Bradshaw out on the streets."

Mason closed his eyes. "You're right," he admitted, and he

opened his eyes to look directly at Bill Morrison. "I'm starting to make mistakes."

"You're exhausted."

"I can still handle it," said Mason stubbornly. "All I have to do is to pace myself, take more time."

"You're going to bed, my good friend."

Realizing the truth of the matter and as it affected the situation, Jerome Mason allowed himself to chuckle knowingly. "You realize," he said then, "that the present attrition rate suggests we probably need a third hand in control here?"

"Why don't I place a call to Les Stalmeyer," Morrison suggested, "at your request, of course?"

"Good idea," Mason agreed, and he pushed himself up from his chair. "I'll stick around until Ben Caplan calls in. We should have some word in about thirty minutes. You know what we'll need, so you handle General Morgan when he calls."

"Fair enough," replied Morrison.

The drug bit into the tender membrane of his nose as Kabir sniffed several times in quick succession, exhaling in short bursts through his mouth. He used a tissue to clear the tears away from the corners of his eyes. Alone in the computer room, he was working slowly and methodically, which was his usual habit. The cocaine hammered into his system, and he began to feel more relaxed as he hid the small vial behind the CRT cabinet located at the left end of the massive computer console.

In a separate console left of the CRT cabinet, the magnetic tape reels were still spinning rapidly, their memory system in the process of being converted to the narrow tape now punching out directly below. It would take several more minutes for the transfer, and Kabir resumed his seat before the keyboard. As he leaned into the chair, the pain across his back made him flinch. Leaning forward, he reached around as best he could to check on how seriously the rough flagstone might have injured him. He found just a few superficial scratches.

Waiting now, he closed his eyes, and, once again, sensed that Fawd Al-Shaer was expecting, or demanding, too much of them all, including Rahab.

Reluctantly Kabir had to admit that his present position was one of his own making. No one had forced him. His original contract for one hundred thousand dollars had been only a part of his early motivation. The opportunity to design, to actually fabricate, the nuclear device, was alone enough to draw him into the plot, and his mind turned pleasantly over the memory of the early days, having started over three years ago. The surreptitious meetings in Cairo, where he had first met Fawd, followed by others in Tripoli and Benghazi. What excitement! And Zurich, their real home base, where the actual design and final bills of material had been laid out. All was under his supervision, including the two Germans contracted to help him. At first aloof and snickering about being under the control of such an unknown manager, they finally came to respect him as a talented authority.

Rahab, originally the hope of the Arab bloc.

Equity with the scheming Israelis.

Par, balance, even deterrent.

Altogether a reasonable objective, as Anne Delemar had put it, plus one hundred thousand dollars safely deposited in a Swiss bank.

Not until later had the mastermind, Fawd Al-Shaer, determined for Rahab a worthwhile side use—atomic blackmail—a spin-off profit.

As a result, Kabir had his share kicked to two hundred and fifty thousand to finance his cooperation and support.

"Not bad pay for a summer's work," he mused.

Then, realizing that the tape transfer was complete, he got up slowly and turned off the tape machine. Preoccupied with his reminiscing, he transferred the punched tape roll to its transmitter as a matter of habit. Then, activating the transmitter, he watched it briefly to ensure its proper operation, knowing that the formulae detail was simultaneously being transcribed at its downtown terminal, a cover export company, which in turn would pass the information to their Zurich terminal, where it would be analyzed and judgment passed on its validity. Turning away from the transmitter, Kabir was not the least concerned with the outcome.

Rahab was fully operational.

And that fact was starting to worry him, since Rahab originally was supposed to be secure for no more than forty-eight hours.

Noting the time, he moved to the opposite end of the computer console, where he routinely reset the trigger timer. Finished, he settled gingerly back into his chair.

Fawd's assurances had been specific from the start, that

they were only to force the United States to publicly admit its illegal intentions to appropriate OPEC oil properties on the Persian Gulf, thereby liberating the oil sheiks.

And then they were to simply wrap up Rahab and silently steal away.

Escape plan Alpha—via Canada.

Escape plan Bravo—via Mexico.

The original planning, indeed, had still been reasonable.

Then came the Camp David accords, the unilateral action by the Egyptians, and Fawd Al-Shaer had gone into a rage, an extended display of the worst sort Kabir had ever witnessed. And the terms of the ultimatum went from the relatively simple matter of OPEC intrigue to the present twofold object of PLO recognition and the removal of Occupied West Bank settlements.

And the new terms extended the time factor of their present holding pattern from the original two days to at least thirty, perhaps even more, depending upon Fawd Al-Shaer's whims.

Kabir considered the extension unacceptable.

After all, what was Rahab to Fawd Al-Shaer, a spin-off, merely an intermediate and passing advantage. Or, was Rahab to be the means to an end, the final consequence of the years of planning . . .

Kabir knew he could not question Fawd, who in his paranoia would automatically suspect his intention to want out, whether or not such intention was real. He got up then to check the transmitter, thinking about Anne Delemar. She could help clear the air if she were only here, though he suspected she was in the dark even more than he.

The U.N. announcement was due tomorrow morning.

Assuming the United States carried out its end, then he figured it would not be unreasonable at all to expect he should be either in Canada or Mexico by the weekend, or Monday at the latest.

That had been the original schedule, and Kabir intended to stick to it.

Anne Delemar paced nervously back and forth in front of Kabir's desk. It was beginning to get dark outside. Once again she checked the wall clock: 8:45.

She realized she was frustrated, in part, because for the first time in her adult life she had been forced to make decisions entirely on her own. Before, she had always had her comrades to advise her, to help her, even to justify her actions. Because of her isolation this day had dragged on interminably. She seemed to measure each minute, even each second, counting and waiting, listening all the while only to her own inner voice—her conscience maybe, which, according to Alan Hunt, just might be the still, small voice of God.

God, according to Fawd Al-Shaer, favored those who stood firmly on the side of what was right.

What was right, anymore? That her own people were outcasts in their own land?

She stopped pacing for a second, reached up to touch the fine scar line reaching from her left eye to her chin. This was the kind of sacrifice, Fawd had suggested, which would cause your people to remember you for a hundred years.

The second hand on the wall clock turned relentlessly.

How many seconds, she wondered idly, are there in a hundred years?

The image of Alan Hunt formed in her mind, and she felt her face under her hand turning into a smile. He was a gentle, kind man, who would possibly face death tonight because of what had started in an alien, foreign land thousands of years ago. Ironic, she thought, that the affairs of another world could so easily reach out to affect another, even unfairly perhaps.

And, that had been her decision.

A matter of simple priorities, as Kabir would put it.

A judgment call, as Alan would put it.

It was even better, she thought, that he would never know.

His Bible was open on the desk, and she finally stopped to bend down over the Book. She read, aided by the last light coming in through the window. Her attention was drawn to an underlined verse, "*For the grace of God that bringeth salvation hath appeared to all men.*" She closed the Book, thinking that he had left it there deliberately, and that he was the least subtle of all men, still trying to reach her even though he was many miles away.

The rolling, rhythmic sound of a helicopter brought her out of her thoughts.

It is possible they will try to use you.

She stood stock still, waiting. The minutes ticked by and she glanced once more at the clock.

Five minutes . . . to nothing.

The sound of heavy footsteps in the hallway.

Burt Ingstrom, the arrogant pig, came into her line of view.
"You are under arrest, Anne Delemar."

Don't resist them.

For a passing moment, she imagined the heavy, reassuring weight of an AK-47 in her hands. She held up her right hand then, forming her hand into the image of a make-believe pistol. She cocked her thumb back.

"Bang," she said softly.

Burt Ingstrom flinched.

His accomplice, standing behind him, laughed.

Anne Delemar extended both her arms, thinking that she was glad it was over; thinking, too, that she wished they had come at noon instead, so that she could've been spared the afternoon's trauma.

Chapter ten

The western sky turned from pale orange to red. Viewing the sunset from inside the store, Joshua supposed that now the failing light would be to no one's advantage. He checked his watch: five minutes to go. He walked to the front of the store, which was covered from ceiling to floor with plate glass windows. Mission Hill Road was a typical four-lane city street, with an extra lane on either side for curb parking. Directly across from the store was a split parking lot—one side for a bank, the other for a nearby two-story business building. Alan Hunt was to take up his position in the shrubbery line dividing the lot, with Ben Caplan's car next to his hiding place. Joshua opened the large swinging front door and then let it close. At the signal, Alan Hunt started the engine on Ben's car and raced it a couple of times before slipping out to enter the planter area.

Satisfied with his front, Joshua moved quickly back through the store to the side entrance. He checked the Jaguar, putting the starter key in its slot. They now had one car running and one ready to go. He pushed through the side door, back into the store, wondering where he should station himself. Set back from the street about thirty feet, the building was about fifty feet across, and the entire front area was given to the display of the various fiberglass spas sold by its owner, Jonathan Breck. Left of center, set back behind the great fiberglass tubs, some measuring eight feet across, a working spa was in at ground level. Its therapy jets were on, and the sound of moving water was a pleasant and relaxing one.

Joshua thought for a passing moment that they might try to work out a trade deal with Breck to install one of the spas at the ranch. He checked his watch then. Two minutes past nine. Three minutes to go. They had deliberately timed Ben to show five minutes late.

He reached around to his right hip, verifying again that the walkie-talkie was secure before stalking impatiently to the rear of the store to check on his back, his blind quarter; and in the foreboding silence of the room he sensed that they were too thin, perhaps close to helplessness. He tried to reassure himself on the high positive correlation proposed by Ben Caplan, that the higher the risk on their part the greater the chance for a score. It now occurred to him that Ben really hadn't specified which side was going to score. Minor tactics, he supposed, in this the strangest of life-and-death struggles, a war of sorts, wherein tonight the MLR had been drawn down Mission Hill Road. Standing near one of the rear windows, he slowly pulled aside one of the venetian slats.

By now, he thought as he scanned the nearby rooftops, Anne Delemar should be in custody, a fact which would ultimately have to be revealed to his friend, Alan Hunt.

"A lousy business," he grumbled to himself.

He moved back to the receptionist's desk, checked behind it to confirm the two weapons: a twelve-gauge pump shotgun next to a machine gun with a spare clip taped to its butt. He turned toward the front door in time to see the sedan pull into the parking lot. He braced, feeling his belly jump, noticing that the Ford had Mexican plates, the same plates on the cover vehicle to be used by Ben Caplan.

As arranged, Ben was supposed to pull in close to the front door, instead of parking in the slots provided closer to the sidewalk. The shorter distance from the car to the front door would not only give him better protection but also allow less time to study him, perhaps to turn him as an imposter. He now pulled in short of the front door, got out, and strolled casually across the intervening asphalt.

Joshua pushed the front door open and reached out to grab him.

"See anything?" asked Ben coolly. He had a wool fisherman's type cap on, pulled down low over his ears, as well as a pair of dark glasses.

"Nothing yet," said Joshua, as he pulled him into the foyer. Immediately placing himself between Ben and the street, he guided Ben into the private office opening up behind the desk.

"You're awfully protective," Ben told him.

"And you're a fool," Joshua replied. "You took too long to get from the car to the door."

Ben leaned against the wall of the small office. "If they're really out there, then let them get a good look. Besides, what difference does it make; it looks like a bust anyway."

"Not necessarily," said Joshua. "Let's assume they're a careful, shrewd bunch."

"You mean with the Fawd touch."

"Yeah, and I mean like we're very vulnerable." He moved carefully to the office door, where he glanced anxiously out through the front windows. "I'm beginning to think we should've taken Mason's advice to cover this neighborhood with a dozen men."

"The Fawd touch, remember," Ben reminded him. "A dozen men and we wind up with a guaranteed no show."

"Maybe," said Joshua doubtfully. "Like, how many misses do we need to score before we admit that we're just shooting in the dark? Our chances here are so low we couldn't even construct a probability curve—"

"You're on the wrong track," Ben corrected him gently. "We're not so much after success here as we are to disrupt their planning. At worst, we'll put a deviation, a squiggle, in their scheme. We're after a response, anything, which might lead to a mistake, give us an opening—"

"Okay. Like, how many minutes do we need to make it look like we're having a very meaningful and revealing discussion?"

"Maybe ten."

"That's all we give it then."

"How's Alan taking it?"

"Haven't told him yet," admitted Joshua.

"Oh, man! He deserves better."

Joshua nodded his agreement. "I'll break it to him as soon as we finish here. He's heavily involved, you know, and I was worried the news might mess up his concentration. He's our only outside cover, remember."

"Don't underestimate him," Ben suggested amiably, pausing a moment before adding, "Alan Hunt is on the verge of becoming my adopted second conscience—"

"Play it cool," said Joshua good-naturedly. "That man across the street is, shall we say, into a scene which can rather dramatically alter your outlook—"

"You sound experienced."

Joshua smiled. "I've been the route."

"So what's your opinion? I mean, about his Messiah?"

Joshua felt a small frown form on his forehead. "At this point, I'd say I believe a shade more than I disbelieve."

Ben nodded slowly, thoughtfully, and Joshua searched his face for a reaction.

"I kind of got that impression," Ben said after a moment. "And that reminds me, for some reason, have you been thinking about what we talked about back at the CP?"

"You mean about Israel?"

It was Ben's turn to smile knowingly.

"In a way," Joshua offered then, "you two are a lot alike. Alan is concerned about my soul, and you're worried about my Jewishness."

Ben nodded once more. "It's because we both love you, I suppose."

Joshua searched for the right words to respond, but he came up empty, watching instead as Ben checked his watch.

"It's strange they should be giving us the time," said Ben after a moment. "Like, you could be making a critical phone call."

Joshua snatched up the phone on the nearby desk, punched the lever several times. "It's dead!" he exclaimed, slamming the phone down. "I checked it about ten minutes before you came in, and it was all right then."

Ben pulled his dark glasses off. "They must've dropped the wires upstream."

Joshua tried to convey his sincerity as he suggested, "It's about time we both became the devoutest of cowards."

"Amen," said Ben.

Joshua reached around to his right hip to lift the walkie-talkie from his belt. Pushing the transmit button, he exclaimed into the mike, "Come in, Alan."

A few seconds later, Alan Hunt responded, "You're coming in loud and clear."

"Looks like we might have a go," Joshua told him. "The phones in here are dead. What's happening out there?"

"Clear so far," Alan told him.

"What about the roof behind us?"

"Still looks clear, and I can cover you from here."

"They might be waiting for us on the street," Ben suggested. "Either in a car, maybe that business building."

"Hang loose, partner," Joshua told Alan, and he replaced the transmitter on his belt.

"Let's go," said Ben. "I'd rather be a moving target than a sitting duck."

"Out the side door," Joshua told him. "You take the machine gun and I'll take the twelve-gauge. We'll split up and each take a corner at the back side of the building. We'll have cross cover that way."

They both made it to the receptionist's desk and snatched up the weapons. As they turned toward the side entrance, Joshua thought that the odds were definitely in their favor now.

He was on his second step away from the desk when the first burst of automatic fire ripped across the front of the store.

The fiberglass tubs exploded—

Joshua instinctively rolled to his left, changing his direction.

Alan Hunt came upright at the savage burst of gunfire.

The whole front of the store disintegrated!

The source of the firing seemed to be to his left, and he spun in that direction, bringing his weapon to bear. He saw the muzzle blast coming from a second story window on the business building. He realized then that another automatic weapon was operating from off to his right. Firing from the hip, he poured a full clip into the second story window in an effort to pin that assailant down. Fumbling to reload, he looked back to his right to see a red van lurch into the parking lot—

Momentarily blinded by the shower of fiberglass, Joshua came to a crouch, finally orienting himself to the front of the store. A flash of bright red crossed his vision. He began to fire the shotgun, pumping as fast as he could pull the trigger, seeing that Ben was still off to his right, down on one knee.

The muzzle blast of the twelve-gauge BAROOMED savagely.

Joshua assumed that Ben was also firing, but he could no longer hear, couldn't differentiate sound.

An object floated in from the front of the store, moving lazily in an easy arc—an olive-drab canvas bag.

Joshua screamed the warning, "Satchel charge!"

He rolled once more to his left. Expecting the hard resistance of the carpeted floor; instead, he felt himself falling, falling into an enveloping softness . . .

Alan Hunt drenched the red van with automatic fire, concentrating on the engine compartment and cab. As he reloaded for the third time, he glanced once more to his left. The second-story window was quiet. He started warily across the street, holding his fire now as he saw no movement coming from the van or store.

Traffic on Mission Hill Road was at a halt.

The explosion caught him at the curb line.

He saw it first, a pale orange ball of fire behind the silhouette of the van. The roof of the store came up in one piece, even and neat. He felt the air sucking out of his lungs. The shock wave hit him then, a giant fist slamming him backwards.

A white van had been standing by in the alley at the rear of the business building. The blue lettering on the two sides denoted that it belonged to a janitorial service with a local address. The driver behind the wheel was a young girl, early twenties, slender, with long dark hair falling in close to her face. Waiting now, she raced the accelerator again, her eyes locked expectantly on the service entrance. The alley was lighted briefly, and the following shock wave passed the far end of the building, to her front, drawing with it airborne dirt and debris.

Ten more seconds, she thought, and she started counting down.

She was relieved to see the door fly open. A man emerged, carrying a large metal tool kit. He raced to the passenger side of the van and climbed in hurriedly. He was about the same age as she.

"The door!" she exclaimed.

"It's self-locking," he said as he shoved the tool kit down between his feet.

She noticed the splotch of blood then, high on his left shoulder. "You're hurt—"

"Never mind; get moving."

She hit the gas. At the corner of the building she slowed, looking left down the parking lot. The spa building was aflame and a total wreck, and in front, the red van was on its side, burning furiously. "Oh, God!" she cried.

"Get moving!" the man snarled at her.

She punched the gas once more. At the street, she turned right, away from the scene. The approaching siren confused her, causing her to take her foot off the gas pedal.

"What's wrong with you?" he snapped.

The emergency vehicle crossed one street behind them, and she saw in the rear view mirror that it was one of the fire department paramedic trucks.

"They must've been standing by," he said, and turned back from the rear window. He picked once at his left shoulder; then, almost casually, he reached up to smooth down his hair.

She turned left at the next corner, then down the next alley. Per plan, she then pulled in behind a trash dumpster and shut down the engine. They both jumped out, after checking to see that the area was clear. Within seconds they both had entered a second vehicle, a pickup truck, parked on the other side of the dumpster.

"Check list," she said as she took her place behind the wheel.

He reached into his inside shirt pocket, through an opening in the coveralls, to pull out a piece of paper, which he handed to her.

"Key," she said, starting down the list.

"Check," he said, holding up the key he had used to enter the building.

She worked down the list quickly, verifying that he still had his ski mask, walkie-talkie, field glasses, his weapon, that his coveralls were still intact, that he hadn't been seriously injured, no witnesses. Finally, they both peeled the surgeon's gloves off their hands.

"So you say you're not seriously hurt," she questioned him.

"We'll report it as a minor scratch."

It took her less than ten minutes to pull into a gas station located nearly two miles away. Parking next to the pay phone, she killed the engine.

"He's dead, isn't he?" she asked quietly, referring to the third member of the team.

"Yes, he is."

"What happened?"

He shrugged once, grimacing painfully. "A couple of things. I'm sure the guy who showed up wasn't our target, so I had no choice but to commit the van." He reached out to slam the dash with his right fist. "I couldn't be certain soon enough in the bad light—"

She placed her hand on his left arm. "You did the right thing; remember, if there was any doubt we had to go the way we did."

"Plus, the one on my side of the street could handle his weapon; he nearly got me with his first burst." He reached up to his left shoulder. "If I hadn't pulled away when I did, I'd probably still be up there, with my brains all over the wall. He kept me down for the first two or three seconds after the van hit the lot. After that, it really didn't matter. The timing was too critical." He shook his head then. "The fuse on the satchel charge was too short."

"You're lucky you weren't killed."

"And they were shooting heavily from the inside. Sounded like a shotgun and a machine gun, plus the guy from across the street."

"That's odd," she said then. "We expected that one of them inside wouldn't give us any trouble."

"Never happen."

"All right," she said slowly. "I'll make the call and report we were successful."

"You saw for yourself."

"I'll have to report the casualty. What about you?"

"Report it all."

She put her hand on the door handle. "We can cover for him at the college. I can make up a story for the dean—"

"No you won't," he cautioned her. "Just get out and make your report."

Chapter eleven

It was still quiet in the airport operations center, as it had been for the past hour since the first report had come in from San Diego. Trying in some way to lift his own spirits, Bill Morrison came out of the office to walk to the open hangar door. He had once again fought down the temptation to pick up a phone to call his son, to tell him to pack up the family immediately and go anywhere—San Francisco maybe, Lake

Tahoe. Leaning against the metal jamb of the hangar door, he stared out across the darkened LAX landscape, thinking that he should take a long walk. Maybe get in his car and head for the nearby beach.

Benjamin Caplan was dead—fallen in the line of duty. Their first known casualty.

Joshua Bain was in a San Diego hospital, having miraculously survived, his prognosis uncertain.

Alan Hunt was up and around.

There had been at least two, possibly three, assailants in the ambush team. Professionals, tough and inventive, who got the job done. They, too, paid the price. At least one was known dead, whose destruction was so complete that identification was next to impossible.

Stanley Fielding was presumed to be still at large, and the price on his head had escalated by an amount now measured in more personal terms.

Anne Delemar, the responsible one, was safely in custody.

Jerome Mason was en route by helicopter to San Diego, even now more badly in need of sleep, yet operating on a revived supply of energy and will, along with his anger, perhaps even sheer guts.

Shivering in the cool, damp air, Morrison checked his watch, seeing that he had less than fifteen minutes before his briefing with the team from the Marine photographic squadron located at the nearby El Toro Marine Corps Air Station.

Rahab had turned into a nightmarish grind.

He moved listlessly across the concrete deck on his way to the makeshift interrogation room. The door to the field lab opened in front of him, and one of the technicians stepped out, nearly colliding with him. He had a clipboard in his hand, and he excused himself before asking if Jerome Mason was in his office.

"No," said Morrison. "What've you got? I'll give it to him."

"Looks like we're on a plant kick," the man told him, and he pulled a 4x6 card off his board. "Please give this to the old man."

Morrison took the card, a lab analysis report. The subject index reported it concerned spectographic and chemical analysis of an item bearing a Latin name he neither recognized nor could pronounce. "What does it mean?"

"It's item number 247 from the six van," the technician

told him. "Test specimens from both the inside bottom drain channel on the right door and from under the weather seal on the windshield. Berry and leaf fragments, all from the common pepper tree."

"Pepper tree," repeated Morrison tiredly. "And what does that do for us? Isn't this kind of tree fairly widespread?"

"Very much so," the technician confirmed. "Grows anywhere and everywhere out here on the coast. Originally from Peru, it favors a mild climate and is prolific—"

"Okay. I'll put it on Mason's desk." Morrison folded the card once and put it in his shirt pocket. For all the help it could give them, the fragments could just as well be crabgrass. He moved on to enter the interrogation room.

Anne Delemar and Kate Felton were still seated opposite each other across the small intervening table. The stench from Kate Felton's mini cigars almost gagged him as he gestured for Kate to come outside with him. He noticed that Anne Delemar still looked indifferent, even bored, and he felt his own anger building as he closed the door behind him.

"Anything new?" he asked.

Kate Felton shook her head. "I'm beginning to believe her, though," she said, and she looked down to the hangar deck, where she was tracing an imaginary circle with the slipper on her right foot. "Especially knowing what we do about Fawd. It appears she knew nothing about the bomb scheme, but she won't deny or admit anything."

"Why not put her under? We can use the facilities at the UCLA medical center."

Kate shook her head again, more emphatically. "She's our only connection, the only way we can hope to open up communication with Fawd. If we ever hope to negotiate with him," and she traced another circle, more slowly and deliberately this time. "My chubby belly tells me that he left her behind expressly for that purpose. Fawd Al-Shaer imagines himself totally in charge of this operation, as he virtually has been from the beginning. I can see his hand in and on this situation as well."

"That means we've got to get her to voluntarily cooperate."

"That's right. We've got to reach her, persuade her somehow."

"Stalmeyer says the Libyan Ambassador has volunteered to help."

Kate took a deep drag on her cigarillo, exhaling a billow of smoke across the hangar. "That could definitely help; but, it would be even better if it were someone closer to her level. Remember, she was probably a field soldier, no doubt spent most of her life in the camps, near or on the front lines. Such people tend to mistrust generals."

Conceding the point, Morrison thought that there might be someone closer by who could help. "Have you mentioned anything to her about the incident in San Diego?"

"No; I didn't want to upset her."

Morrison almost laughed bitterly, not really appreciating her concern. "Leave me alone with her for a moment," he said, pushing his way back into the small room. He had already decided what they must do to try to extract the cooperation of Anne Delemar, but for the moment he was tempted to try another, less subtle tack.

"You realize now," he said to her abruptly, "that you are an accomplice to first-degree murder," and he studied her face under the harsh light of the single overhead bulb, hoping for a reaction. She avoided his eyes, looking down at her hands clasped in her lap.

"It's obviously different where you come from," he went on bitterly, "where you can sneak down out of the hills at night and commit murder, excusing your actions in some sick, twisted way. In this country, when you commit murder, you are hunted down, tried in a court of law, and, if found guilty, you are punished!" He leaned forward to the table, glaring down at her. "There is a certainty of punishment."

"I do not understand," she said indifferently.

"You passed a message to Fawd this afternoon, which led directly to the death of one of your team members."

She frowned slightly, biting on her lower lip.

A reaction, finally, he thought hopefully.

"You have no feeling," he went on, "about having helped kill someone you know personally, someone who perhaps cared very much for you?"

"Who?" she asked then, so quietly that he had to strain to pick up the word.

"Does it matter?"

She looked aside then, before asking softly, "Do you know what grace is?"

His eyebrows dropped at the corners as he answered, "What was that?"

"Grace," she repeated. "It's appeared to you, or, perhaps it will—"

"What are you talking about?"

"Has something to do with love instead of hate—"

The sound of an approaching helicopter filled the room, and Bill Morrison stalked out, shaking his head.

"She's all yours," he said testily to Kate Felton as he started toward his office. He pulled up after a few steps, adding over his shoulder, "You should figure a way to plug this Alan Hunt into the situation."

Kate Felton nodded understandingly.

Back in his office, Morrison sat down behind Jerome Mason's desk, where he punched the phone button for Les Stalmeyer. The Attorney General came promptly on the line.

"When are you flying out?" Morrison asked without introduction.

"Tomorrow morning."

"Can you bring the Libyan Ambassador with you?"

"I expect so," said Stalmeyer after a moment. "You mean you've made contact with Fawd Al-Shaer?"

"No. But we need help with Anne Delemar. She isn't about to talk to us. Not only does she not trust us, she hates our guts, or, at least, that's the feeling I get. Kate Felton thinks she's telling the truth in that she wasn't aware that Fawd was planning this blackmail scheme. But she thinks we're lying, that we're making the story up just to get her to help nail Fawd."

"Didn't you show her a copy of Fawd's ultimatum letter?"

"Yeah, Mason finally did; but she dismissed it as a trick."

"Okay. I'll do what I can."

"Also, isn't there a PLO rep. at the current session of the United Nations?"

"There sure is," Stalmeyer said. "In fact, we're briefing the U.N. people tomorrow morning early, before the announcement. The PLO man is on the list."

"Get him out here too, if you can. Kate feels the Delemar woman might be more responsive."

"Yeah," Stalmeyer interjected. "Plus, if and when we start talking to Fawd himself."

"That's right. Two of his own people on the scene has got to help. And, don't forget, Kate Felton must review the U.N. announcement—"

"Check your teletype. I sent the draft to the comm' office a half hour ago. If Kate wants any changes, have them back here as quickly as possible."

Bill Morrison felt encouraged as he hung up. Movement from across the room caught his eye, and he turned to see that two uniformed Marine officers had appeared in the doorway.

No small wonder, he thought then, that Jerome Mason couldn't keep up with it all.

The ritual of his physical diagnosis seemed finished, and Joshua Bain already felt restless. By all rights, he should be sound asleep, but his eyes were locked open, an outlet for the thoughts milling about in his mind. Weary of staring at the ceiling of the small private room, he pushed himself into a sitting position at the head of the small hospital bed. There was still a residual buzzing in his right ear, a declining kind of signal, and in the brief exertion he felt light-headed, a passing dizziness.

The doctor told him he had a slight concussion.

The harsh smell of cordite lingered in his nostrils.

He tried once more to form the picture of the last moment he saw Ben Caplan, but the image of his friend refused to develop amid the vicious crescendo of noise . . . the remembered sounds of a fire fight . . . the bits and pieces he could not separate . . . then the metallic rattling of Ben's automatic weapon . . . the clatter of the bolt hammering each separate round into the chamber . . .

The door to his room had opened, and it took him a second to realize that Alan Hunt was standing at the foot of his bed. Thank God, he thought, and he allowed his eyes to close. The door closed itself with a minor hydraulic hiss; the following silence was at once unbearable to Joshua. He swallowed hard, trying to open his mouth. His lips were dry, the taste of old brass—

"So you made it," Alan said.

Joshua felt his head tip slightly, an affirmative nod.

"How is Ben?" he heard himself saying, his voice uncertain. He cleared his throat then, waiting once more in the heavy silence.

"I'm going to have to give you a mountain this time," Alan said softly and gently.

"No, no," Joshua said, aware he was shaking his head slowly. "How bad is it? I mean, is he here too?"

"I'm sorry," Alan said, "but Ben didn't make it."

"No!" Joshua insisted, and he hammered his right fist on the bed.

"It's done, Joshua," Alan said firmly, "and you must accept it."

The threat of the following silence began to diminish as Joshua Bain forced himself to understand, to comprehend that Benjamin Caplan was gone.

"I thought it was Fielding at first," Alan went on, "or one of his people, like it was supposed to be. But when we couldn't find Ben anywhere . . . " and he hesitated. "I had to make the identification. It was a bad shock, Joshua, and I had trouble believing it myself . . . "

Joshua drew a deep breath through his nose, trying to clear his mind, aware then of the question in Alan's voice.

"I had to report it to Mason," Alan told him.

"Why!" Joshua finally exclaimed. "Why, why . . . " and his voice trailed off with the comment, "and I come out of it without a scratch."

"You fell into the spa," Alan told him. "You were below floor level and under water when the explosion hit. Saved your life, according to the paramedic who helped me fish you out."

"How incredible," said Joshua as he buried his head in his pillow. Along with his anger and frustration he felt something welling up inside. He swallowed against his grief, hearing himself say in a breaking voice, "And how do you align this on your scale of justice?"

It took a moment for Alan to answer, "Ben saw himself as a soldier, Joshua, and you know yourself that there is no justice on a battlefield."

Joshua composed himself before he turned his head to look at Alan. "We can't allow it to be explained away so easily. My heart, my gut, everything about me, tells me that this is wrong, terribly wrong. Ben's life meant more, was worth much more, than just a . . . a lousy battlefield statistic!"

Alan simply shrugged once. "Ben was convinced he was doing right, and I don't feel we can take that away from him, especially now."

Joshua sensed the futility of the conversation, but he determined that the matter was far from finished, for he had too many questions requiring answers now.

"Can you please tell me," Alan asked, "exactly what's happening? I just called the commune, and the agent who answered the phone said that Anne was no longer there."

Joshua realized that they both must get on with it. "I guess I'm going to have to give you a mountain in return," and he paused briefly, wondering where to begin. "The rendezvous we set up tonight was a ruse, one that only Ben and I knew about. We couldn't tell you for a serious and justifiable reason. And, that part of it was strictly a judgment call; perhaps we should've told you."

"I don't understand."

"I'm not sure I do either," Joshua admitted candidly. "But what it boils down to is that Anne Delemar is under arrest and in custody."

Alan Hunt stood up slowly. "What are you talking about?"

"I'm sorry," said Joshua flatly, "but she is a double agent. It is an absolute fact, like it or not—"

"I don't believe it."

"It's your turn, my friend, to accept it," Joshua insisted. "She has been working for Fawd since the beginning. She was the leak. And we used her today . . . "

Alan had turned away from the bed to move to the window, staring out through the venetian blinds. "And you used me also," he said slowly under his breath.

"Would you really have rather known before?"

Alan did not answer.

"Regardless," Joshua went on. "Tonight's trip was thought to be a necessary one. A deviation, as Ben put it . . . to trigger Fawd into making a mistake."

"Where is she?"

"I suppose she's at the CP."

Alan started for the door. "Whom do I have to go through to see her?"

"Jerome Mason."

"I'll see him when he gets here then," Alan said. "When I called in my report, he said he'd be here within an hour."

"Fair enough," said Joshua understandingly.

Alan pushed the door open.

Watching his friend, Joshua sensed a response in his mind. "Wait a second," he said on impulse.

Alan hesitated in the open doorway.

"Perhaps we both can understand the high priest now," Joshua suggested.

"You mean Caiaphas?"

Joshua nodded.

"Maybe there is a parallel," Alan said after a thoughtful moment.

"Like you said, there is the image of things hoped for."

"More than likely," said Alan, "there is the viewing through a glass darkly. Like, there are things we're just not expected to understand."

And the door closed behind him.

Jerome Mason excused himself from his resident escort in the corridor outside Joshua's room. Alan Hunt was also behind him, waiting soberly in the main lobby, obviously on edge, like all of them now, apparently interested foremost in making the return trip back to Los Angeles. Kate Felton would know better how to deal with Alan Hunt, so he assumed as he pushed his way into Joshua's room. He was not surprised to see Joshua sitting up in bed, looking fit.

"You look twice as bad as I feel," Joshua chided him.

"I'll trade you the taste in my mouth," Mason retorted as he sat down in the only chair in the small room, "for all your hurts and pains."

Joshua pondered the offer before replying, "I'll settle for a change of clothes."

Mason nodded he understood, moving quickly past the small talk to business. "Just what were you two trying to pull? From what I can gather, you knew that Fielding wasn't going to show, so you apparently set Ben up to take his place—"

"It's all my fault," Joshua admitted. "It was my idea from the start, then Ben picked it up . . . "

"The idea was sound, Joshua, but you both underestimated the opposition."

Joshua could only shake his head. "It was so close. Another lousy five seconds and we'd have cleared the building."

Jerome Mason sighed, then continued. "There'll have to be a full report and investigation. You can give me a deposition later. For the time being, I'll assume the full responsibility, and, if you can pull your act together, I'll also log in the report that I was fully aware of all your plans."

"What do you mean, pull my act—"

"Start cooperating with us. You can yell security to me all day long, but I'm convinced you went along to keep this airtight just because you wanted to play it out yourself. It's a habit you've got. This lone-ranger kick will end right now, or I'll put you in protective custody—"

"Okay, so I'll cooperate, but I'm still going after Fielding."

"With my permission and in due time. First, as soon as you can get out of here, which your doctor says will be in about eight hours, you will meet Doctor Melbourne and escort him out to Armatrex."

"You've got other people."

"Ah, hah, my headstrong friend, cooperation, remember."

"Yes, sir."

"I've already appointed you as a Federal Marshall," Mason went on, and he reached inside his jacket pocket. "Here's your ID and a search warrant for Armatrex. You spike Melbourne into that company and watch him like a hawk. He's on to something, and I want him acting instead of meditating about it. You push him, do what you have to, and report directly to me every thirty minutes."

"So you think it's that important."

"Ben Caplan would do it."

"That wasn't necessary," said Joshua as he took the papers.

"I'm sorry," Mason said truthfully.

"Have his folks been notified?"

"Wolf Shertok met me at the airport; he's taking care of it."

"I will pay for whatever is involved," said Joshua. "There is a Rabbi Meyers at the synagogue in Del Cerro, and I'd like to meet with him after we finish at Armatrex tomorrow. If you can arrange it, please have Edwin Fielding meet me there also."

"Don't want to face the Rabbi alone, huh?"

"Something like that," Joshua seemed to admit, and he changed the subject. "How is Shertok taking it?"

"He's upset, and he's angry that you didn't tell him the whole truth in your plans either. Like me, he figures you were crazy not to have had a dozen men to help you. You were lucky that those paramedics were on standby."

"Ben arranged for that at the last minute; he was worried about Alan being so exposed."

"Have you told Alan Hunt about Anne Delemar?"

Joshua nodded yes. "He's upset," he said listlessly. "But he bailed out before I could tell him about the blackmail routine."

"He's going back with me to L.A.," Mason said. "I'll probably have to tell him then. Don't worry about him—or Shertok; they'll both survive."

"I suppose so," said Joshua, shifting his weight. "What did tonight get us?"

"Not much," said Mason. "One of the two known assailants got away clean. The other is unidentifiable for the moment; the van was a total burn and he was trapped inside. There's a team working on it right now. I expect the van was stolen."

"They were professionals."

"No question about it," Mason agreed. "They had the right weapons and explosives, an organized way about themselves. And, more significantly, they had little time to prepare."

"How did Anne Delemar get the message out?"

Mason shook his head. "We still don't know. We had the place under total electronic surveillance. At least four agents watching her every move. She was alone in the house for only about ten minutes. Used the bathroom once."

"Make any phone calls?"

"Negative. But, how she did it is not critical; it is obvious that at least that part of your plan worked."

"Still didn't get us much."

"For one thing, we know that Fawd certainly wants Fielding dead."

"Come on, Mister Director," said Joshua sarcastically, "that hardly even qualifies as frosting on the cake."

"It does for me, Joshua. The overkill in that hit was obvious."

"Yeah," Joshua agreed. "I understand the store was a total wreck."

"They could've just as easily picked Fielding off with a rifle or automatic weapon, but they picked the maximum route, certainly more risky for them. Strange, considering how short they were on time."

"So, they wanted to make sure."

"I expect," Mason said, "at some time or another that Ben Caplan told you there is always a reason for everything. The reason for the overkill was simple: they wanted it *all* destroyed. Especially a written note, in the event a messenger showed up instead of the real Mister Fielding."

It began to fall into place for Joshua then. "You've got to be right," he asserted. "Ben took a long time to get in the front door. The guy across the street probably had glasses on him and suspected he was a messenger—"

"So they went with option two—double whammo."

"They sure knew what they were doing," Joshua mused bitterly.

"And they wanted Fielding bad, or his message. Which is why the priority on Fielding has kicked up a few notches in the past couple of hours. In fact, as soon as you finish with Melbourne, I want you on Fielding full time. As of an hour ago, Les Stalmeyer has requested an all-out search by both the Navy and Coast Guard for that missing fishing boat. My local resident down here will front you into the Naval District headquarters here in San Diego as soon as you can get to it, hopefully by late afternoon. And, I'm holding you personally responsible for Fielding's safety once he's picked up. I wouldn't consider it overreacting if you surrounded him with a platoon of Marines."

"I get the point."

Jerome Mason pushed himself up from his chair, weaving unsteadily for a moment.

"You should be in this bed," Joshua suggested sympathetically.

"I'll find one back in L.A."

"What's our chances?"

Jerome Mason gave it his best educated guess, "Probably fifty-fifty, and getting better as each hour passes. We've worked our way into good field position."

"Thank God for time, then."

"Works against us, too," said Mason gruffly as he turned toward the bathroom. "Don't know how much longer we can keep it under wraps. The U.N. message goes out in the morning. It's got to leak sooner or later," and he closed the bathroom door behind him, unwilling for the moment to consider the consequences of it becoming public that an armed nuclear bomb was stored in or near Los Angeles, California.

The two Marine officers had quickly and efficiently converted the far end of the CP office to a photo-interpretation center. A new and more detailed set of maps provided by the Forest Service was posted behind a long table, which was positioned so that one could turn back and forth between the two without taking a step. The table was drafting-board high, upon which the two officers had laid out the tools of their trade: T-squares, straight edges, angles, two-dimensional magnifying glasses in their squat frames.

Seeing that they were nearly finished, Bill Morrison picked up a heavy manila envelope from his desk and moved on to continue his briefing. The older officer was a captain, the VMP

Operations Officer. His younger assistant was a first lieutenant, the squadron's Intelligence Officer.

Morrison shook his head approvingly as he pulled up next to the end of the table. He noticed that the maps were covered with clear mylar. Per their instructions, the forest service technicians had outlined and shaded in pale yellow those areas above four thousand feet elevation. He handed the manila envelope to the Captain.

"This is a duplicate set of maps," Morrison told him. "We'll both stick to the grid coordinates."

The Captain took the envelope. Like his companion, he was clean shaven and alert. Bill Morrison envied them for a passing moment.

"Is this some kind of practice exercise?" the Captain asked curiously. He was slender, his dark hair cropped militarily close, and he looked at Morrison now with unblinking, steady eyes, waiting, like his assistant, at ease and comfortable. Bill Morrison appreciated how much in the dark they had to be, along with all the rest of those being called upon now, without explanation, to perform without being told why.

He reached around to his hip and pulled out his billfold. He then held up his ID, slowly, allowing them both to inspect it thoroughly. He next pointed to the desk at the far end of the room. "That belongs to Jerome Mason, the Director of the FBI. In his upper right hand drawer there is a copy of a Top Secret teletype message from the Commandant of the Marine Corps to your wing commander at El Toro. Which is why you're here, gentlemen. Would you like to see it?"

The two officers had assumed a more noticeable position of attention.

"No, sir," the Captain said emphatically.

Morrison turned his attention to the Intelligence Officer. He moved his head slowly and deliberately, before asking, "And you?"

"Absolutely not, sir."

"And I presume, gentlemen," Morrison went on slowly, "that you have both been advised by your Commanding Officer that this operation is under the highest possible security classification and that you're not to discuss it with anyone except on the strictest need-to-know basis."

"Yes, sir," the two officers admitted in unison.

"Excellent," Morrison said pleasantly. "Now that you both understand that this is not a practice exercise, you will return to your base." He turned up his watch. "An Air Force transport will be touching down at El Toro in less than an hour. On it will be a team of technicians with certain night clarification gear, also highly classified. This equipment will be installed in the camera bays of three of your aircraft. The specs on this equipment have already been transmitted to your people; your aircraft should be ready and waiting. It is important you get airborne by, say, one o'clock."

"Our target area is the shaded portion on the map," said the Captain.

"Exactly, those zones over four thousand feet."

"What about flight altitude, number of passes, corridor widths?"

"We've made recommendations to your skipper," Morrison told him, and he pointed to Ingstrom's nearby desk. "You've got an open channel on that radio. Go over the details when you get back to your squadron. If you have any questions then, give me a direct call."

"We'll assemble the material here?" the younger officer asked him.

"Yes. Develop it in your lab, and when you send the first prints also send along two of your best interpreters. We'll use helicopters, on a priority basis, for all transport. I suggest you now get moving."

He was back at his desk when the two officers started out of the office. The younger officer detoured out of his way to pull up before him.

"I presume your gear is heat sensing, or at least uses energy of some sort—"

"Perhaps," Morrison said. "Why?"

"The Mount Wilson area," the officer pointed out, "is used by several TV stations to transmit their signals. That kind of energy is going to tear up your exposures." He turned his cap in his hands self-consciously. "Just thought I'd bring it up," he added, and he turned to leave.

"I'm glad you did," Morrison said to him gratefully.

With the two men gone, Bill Morrison closed his eyes, thinking that now he must get on the phone again. The local TV stations would have to be canvassed to determine which of them broadcasted from Mount Wilson, and, of those, which continued to do so past one o'clock in the morning. Those doing so, would, of course, have to shut down temporarily. He pulled a piece of paper in front of him, jotted down a note, aware that if he didn't get it into writing, he would probably forget it within thirty seconds.

Chapter twelve

8:00 a.m., Thursday morning, Pacific Time.

Joshua Bain turned up the volume on the car radio as the announcer reported that the U.S. Ambassador to the United Nations was about to begin a special report to the General Assembly. Ewing Melbourne, his unlit pipe clamped between his teeth, looked sideways at Joshua and raised his left eyebrow curiously. They had just pulled into the Armatrex parking lot, and Joshua slipped into one of the spaces marked for visitors. Shutting down the engine, he turned the ignition key so that the radio stayed on.

"Let's hear what he's got to say," Joshua suggested, knowing that Melbourne was anxious to get into the plant.

"Why not," Melbourne agreed. "But it seems a bad sign that it's gone this far. I get the feeling that we're about to go public."

Joshua didn't answer, listening instead to the Ambassador as he began in a sober monotone:

"Mister Secretary, I have been instructed by the President of the United States to deliver the following message to the General Assembly. It is part of the instructions that the message is to be given at this precise time and on this date. The President also wishes to advise the General Assembly that the nature of the subject is so sensitive at this time to preclude any public discussion by any official of the U.S. Government. We are all thus advised to avoid speculation on the subject and to especially be patient and tolerant in allowing our Government to resolve the situation. . ."

It occurred to Joshua that there were certain members of the General Assembly who were not inclined to be patient and tolerant with the U.S. Government.

"The message is in three parts," the Ambassador went on. "Part one is to confirm that the President's office has received a communication from a private source suggesting that our Government implement plans to formally recognize a designated organization whose title and principals at this time are deemed appropriate to remain confidential in the best interest of security and common propriety. This same source also suggests that our Government exercise its influence to alter a certain program established as official policy by a friendly foreign government. Part two is to report definitive action has been taken, and is continuing, to implement the prescribed recommendations and that evidence of such action is available for inspection by interested and qualified parties. Part three is to suggest that it is considered reasonable and desirable to obtain objectives through an acceptable funding program, mutually agreed to.

"The President wishes that this entire subject therefore be negotiated to a final close as quickly as possible. Authorized and already involved persons, both in and out of this Government, are urged to proceed accordingly . . ."

"Thank you, Mister Secretary . . ."

Joshua turned the ignition key to off. They couldn't afford the luxury of editorial post-mortems. He noticed that Melbourne obviously agreed, for the Doctor was already climbing out of the car.

The cramped interrogation room was quiet for a few moments after Kate Felton turned off the TV set. Alan Hunt looked sideways at Anne Delemar, who showed no sign of her reaction to the Ambassador's brief report.

"Don't you believe it now?" Alan said hopefully.

"I suppose I must," she finally offered, a note of resignation in her voice.

Alan turned to Kate Felton, who was across the table from them now, busily scratching notes on a yellow lined pad.

"How will Fawd take it?" Alan asked.

"He will be furious," Anne said quickly.

"Exactly," confirmed Kate, and she looked up, shaking her head approvingly.

"How furious?" questioned Alan, mindful of the fact that Kate Felton didn't seem at all concerned that ground zero could be just around the corner.

"Not that furious," Kate told him reassuringly, as if she might have read his thoughts. "Our antagonist is basic in this respect; he has not yet had his forum, as he anticipated. The U.N. message is right now serving its purpose as a kind of put-down. To a more normal person, the situation would be a disappointment, a passing kind of thing. However, the President did comply with Fawd's ultimatum; he has made the public announcement, at the prescribed time and place, with the statement, albeit indirect, that Fawd's demands are being complied with." She looked to Anne Delemar. "Don't you agree?"

"I don't know for sure," Anne said after a thoughtful moment, "but you are pushing him. This is the real Fawd Al-Shaer you're dealing with, one of the new breed. He's known among his people as the Father of the Holy War. I've watched him at work, and I've seen him take young people, frightened and unsure of themselves, and in a matter of a few weeks convert them into a dedicated and hardened commando team. And, all of them, quite willing to donate their lives on behalf of the cause—"

"Were you once frightened and unsure?" Kate asked gently.

"Very much so," she admitted candidly. "Which is why I can tell you that you're right now attacking his honor, even his very identity . . ."

"I have to agree," said Alan after a moment. "The man has gone to a lot of trouble to obtain his own satisfaction, on his own terms. I get the feeling that we've twisted it all around so that he feels frustrated, and I just wonder how far he will go before he does something erratic."

"Like pushing the button," Kate suggested.

"Yeah, that's exactly what I mean."

Kate put down her pencil and folded her hands before her on the table. "The fundamental thing you have to understand about Fawd Al-Shaer is that you must from the very beginning show no sign of weakness, of yielding. And that is not a matter of simple bravado; it is a sound, clinical move. Remember, we are not *treating* him right now, we are *dealing* with him. We are simply after time. . ."

It was deathly quiet in the massive living room, and Kabir imagined he could hear the sound of his own breath passing through his nose. Fawd Al-Shaer had turned away from the wall-mounted recorder to walk slowly and deliberately to the bay window overlooking the grounds. The content of the U.N. message ran through Kabir's mind while he waited and watched. Fawd's back was to him now, and he was thankful that Fawd's hands were still at his sides, hanging limply along the folds of his robe.

"Play it again," said Fawd, his voice flat, expressionless.

Kabir obediently pushed the replay button, starting the

tape over after it had rewound. The Ambassador's voice invaded the room for the brief few seconds it took to complete the report. Kabir watched Fawd intently, unaware that the tape was still running until Fawd turned to glare at him. Kabir abruptly reached up to shut off the machine once again.

"The pathetic fools," Fawd stormed as he turned back to stare out across the grounds.

"I don't understand," Kabir said, "the part-three business, an acceptable funding program—"

"Don't you understand English?" Fawd snapped at him. "It's an offer to buy us out."

Kabir found himself intrigued by the proposal.

"That's what they'd like us to think," Fawd said thoughtfully. "But what they're really trying to buy is time . . ."

"It seems they've done what you wanted," Kabir proposed. "At least, we have their word—"

"They've done nothing!" Fawd interrupted angrily, and he turned, moving his hands to his hips.

Kabir's stomach constricted, leaving him with a feeling of weightlessness. Frightened, he swallowed hard. His mind could think of only one thing: for the first time he understood that Fawd Al-Shaer was fully capable of pushing the Rahab button. The Zurich confirmation was in; Rahab was fully operational. He reached up to his throat in a defensive gesture, thinking desperately that there was nothing he could do, absolutely nothing, except, maybe, to run. The temptation was overwhelming, and he had to force himself to stand steady. Fawd would cut him down before he got ten feet away from the house.

Both Mexico and Canada had moved to another planet.

He noticed then that Fawd was studying him.

"You needn't be afraid," Fawd said, and there seemed to be a genuine sense of concern in his voice. "At least for the time being," he went on. "We've not spent so much time and money to just wipe a city off the face of the earth, now, have we?"

Kabir vigorously shook his head no, not caring that the relief must be showing in his face and in his manner.

"It's my fault," Fawd conceded, and he started purposefully across the room. "Get to the typewriter."

Kabir moved quickly to the desk to sit down before the portable typewriter. Fawd began to stalk back and forth behind him as he turned a single piece of paper into the platen.

"Address to Mister President," Fawd began. "Your response of this morning at the United Nations was both evasive and diversionary." He spoke slowly, allowing Kabir to stay with him on the machine. "You have deliberately avoided, arrogantly and without respect, to reveal the true facts. Accordingly, you will report to the world within forty-eight hours, not later than noon the day after tomorrow, that the United States will immediately cease all, repeat, all aid to the so-called State of Israel. This action is in addition to that prescribed in my initial letter and will be appended thereto as item D." Fawd paused then, breaking his stride, pulling on his lower lip while he stared down at the carpet near his feet, before continuing, "Your embargo will specifically and without exception include all military and economic support. Any transport en route will be recalled. And, I warn you at this time, that you will in this instance be specific in your response. All parties and plans will be clearly identified. There will be no tricks. Further, if receipt of this message is not confirmed by eight o'clock tomorrow night, Friday, then I guarantee you that the details of Operation Rahab will be released to the wire services within the hour. Do not mistake the intent and will of our determination." He stopped behind Kabir and placed his hand on his shoulder, causing Kabir to flinch.

"Sign it Fawd Al-Shaer."

It was eleven-thirty when Joshua Bain made what he figured was his eighth phone call to Jerome Mason. The report was the same: Doctor Melbourne is still working with the Armatrex staff and still has nothing of substance to report. This time Jerome Mason curtly advised Joshua that Doctor Melbourne had until noon, and not one minute later, to submit a resumé of his findings. Joshua shook his head as he hung up the phone. He was alone with Melbourne in the Armatrex QC office. The Doctor was seated at the Chief Inspector's desk, buried behind an array of papers, notes, company reports. As Joshua cradled the phone, Melbourne looked up to comment, "If you went to the bathroom as often as you make the same phone call, I'd say you had a serious bladder problem."

"Mason says you have thirty minutes to produce."

"So he's getting edgy too."

Joshua said nothing, knowing he had already indicated to Melbourne that time was critical, that he was impatient to get on with what he had to do. He respected that Mason's ultimatum was aimed to help him as well as the rest. He noticed then that Melbourne had dropped his pencil and was frowning.

"What is it?" Joshua asked.

"I suppose the time doesn't really matter," Melbourne admitted, and he let his slight frame slip back into the chair so that he was staring at the ceiling over Joshua's head. "Have you heard of Ockham's razor?"

Joshua shook his head no.

"It's a kind of philosophical axiom," Melbourne started to explain, "one which most scientists should respect but generally ignore. You see, Joshua, it's in most of our natures to seek the more complex answer; seems to satisfy our ego, perhaps, when more often than not the simplest solution is the answer. I recall a few years ago my car stalled on the freeway. I couldn't get it started. It took me twenty minutes to work my way through the electrical system, to verify it was intact. Then I moved to the carburetion, and, finally, strictly by accident, and after nearly an hour's intensive investigation—"

"You discovered you were out of gas."

Doctor Melbroune chuckled appreciatively, showing tobacco-stained teeth. "You're right! And, that demonstrates Ockham's razor."

"So what has Ockham told you now?"

"I got the details from our Yucca Flats site several days ago on the precise apportionment of the energy from the demo device. The readings didn't jibe with the designer's predicted yield. My response, and those of my associates helping me, was to try to find fault with the designer's computations, either in his basic design or in perhaps his detonation technique. I've got a half-dozen theories as to why it was a fizzle, but it wasn't until yesterday that the truth started to dawn on me." He leaned forward now to pick up his battered pipe. "You see, we were all working on the assumption that both the core and tamper material were the plutonium isotope, specifically two-thirty-nine, which was the metal stolen from here last April. Yesterday morning I even went to the more complex route of assuming that at least the tamper was a uranium isotope, perhaps two-thirty-eight, with a plutonium core. And, like when I ran out of gas on the freeway, it came to me, quite by accident, that the entire mass was in fact a uranium isotope, two-thirty-five, to be exact. The computations fit," and he picked up his slide rule and began to manipulate it absently.

Joshua Bain sat on the edge of the desk, transfixed at the revelation.

"It's so simple," Melbourne stated.

"Wait a second!" Joshua said incredulously. "You're telling me the bomb is made of uranium instead of plutonium—"

"No," Melbourne corrected him clinically. "I'm telling you that the Yucca Flats shot was uranium. At least, I'm convinced it was."

"Well, then. I mean, that's one and the same thing . . . like, it's highly probable."

"Pure conjecture, still."

Conjecture my foot, Joshua thought excitedly, and it began to come to him in bits and pieces. The Fielding ploy began to fall into place, yet he couldn't for the moment get it all to fit. Knowing he needed time to sort it out, he picked up the phone and direct dialed Jerome Mason, who came on the line after one ring.

"What I've got," Joshua told him flatly, "is too hot to discuss on an open line."

"Where are you?" Mason asked.

"We're still at Armatrex."

"Get out to the parking lot and wait. I'll have an escort pick you up within five to ten minutes. Get on the secure phone at the resident's office and call me immediately."

Joshua dropped the phone in its cradle. "Let's go," he said curtly. On his way to the door, he stopped suddenly, snapping over his shoulder, "Did the uranium come from here?"

Doctor Melbourne was out of his chair, picking up his jacket. "No doubt about it," he stated as he hurried to catch up with Joshua. As they entered the parking lot, Joshua slowed down, turning his head sideways as he listened to the closing sound of sirens, which he estimated were no more than a couple of blocks away. Jerome Mason had obviously programmed in the pick-up already.

"Wasn't the uranium MUF reported?" he asked curiously.

"It was, in a manner of speaking. In a processing plant of this size, they figure to lose as much as a hundred pounds of uranium per year. It winds up in air filters, burial pits, and general waste situations. It all has to be reported and accounted for on a quarterly basis, though. I've gone over their inventory records for the quarter just closed, and the average is over by about the amount we're looking for; however, you have to understand that under normal circumstances shortages of this nature take months to clear up. In fact, as their chief of security told me this morning, what's the big deal?"

"*What's the big deal?*" Joshua repeated dully to himself, still stunned at the irony of the development. A terrible irony, he thought then, which, while he still didn't understand how or why, probably had been responsible for the death of Ben Caplan. "Give me another educated guess. Would you say, based on your technical evidence, that Fawd *thought* he was using the plutonium?"

"I would have to say yes," says Melbourne carefully. "The technical evidence is pat. Also, remember that Fawd said in his letter that they were using the plutonium."

"Of course," said Joshua. "I forgot about the demand letter. That brings us to one last guess, then. Would you say that Fawd doesn't actually have the plutonium?"

Melbourne simply shrugged. "Now you're out on a speculative limb."

"Come on, Doctor," Joshua urged. "Take the plunge. You've sat in that San Eliso lab and gone over their abandoned notes, so you've got some feel . . ."

Doctor Melbourne clicked his pipe stem between his front teeth, a little more rapidly than usual, before he finally said guardedly, "The drift of the evidence would suggest they do not have the plutonium. But," and he pointed the pipe stem at Joshua, "don't quote me, because I'll deny I ever said it."

Fair enough, thought Joshua, and he looked around to see a black and white police car pulling into the far end of the lot.

Jerome Mason hung up his phone. His last order to Joshua Bain had been to find Stanley Fielding, at any cost, and as quickly as possible. Mason did not know what to make of the fact that the Yucca Flats shot had been uranium instead of the presumed plutonium, beyond the obvious possibility that Stanley Fielding saw and took the opportunity to con Fawd Al-Shaer, switching the plutonium for the lower grade uranium. Once Fawd discovered the switch, he had gone after Fielding, which explained the San Diego scenario to date. The objective, now, was to take Fielding into custody to find out what he really knew.

For the first time since the nightmare commenced, Jerome Mason sensed that the odds had tipped in their favor, that they may have finally crossed the fifty-yard line. Under the control of Bill Morrison, the overflight operation seemed about ready to produce. Last night's initial mission, a series of high-level flights, had turned twenty-six probables in the San Gabriels alone. Between nine and eleven this morning, then, the same flights flew exactly the same pattern, only this time taking high-resolution photographs. Now in process was the grinding task of comparing the results of the two separate flights, overlaying the black-and-white photographs with the plates exposed on the first run. He pushed up out of his chair to start across the office toward Burt Ingstrom, who, along with the two photo-interpreters assigned, was hunched over the long table provided for the exercise. Several blue flags were already pinned on the mylar-covered wall map. Mason was looking for one single red flag.

As he stopped before the map, Mason was aware that behind this very wall was the interrogation room, which was still occupied by Les Stalmeyer and his rather elite crew trying to persuade Anne Delemar to cooperate.

"How does it look?" he asked Burt Ingstrom, who straightened up, rubbing his eyes briefly. The swelling under his left eye had gone down, but the discoloration remained, now nearly black.

"I would say we've got it down to five," Ingstrom reported, and he turned to face the map. "We've got six men out running, posing as forest rangers, and in constant radio contact. Also two men each at the tax assessors office and at each of the utility companies. The plat maps are really doing it for us now. Also, fortunately enough, it's the season up there now, and our people can circulate around without arousing too much suspicion. With any luck, we could have a red flag up in less than an hour."

Mason nodded his approval. Ingstrom was going about the investigation in his usual thorough way. The first overflight had turned in exposures denoting hot spots in the open terrain, those sites whose energy and mass could reflect the aboveground location of such heavy energy producing items as the missing computer system purchased by Aerotec, along with probable support equipment, including even vehicles, the building protecting the material, other hardware, whatever. Each suspected site was first identified, then checked out for ownership, then a rundown was made on any unusual electrical or telephone service recently installed. "There's only one thing," Mason told him. "Get on the radio again and warn each of your field men that there is positively to be no contact—keep clear of the sites for at least a quarter mile. Their only function is to monitor in and out traffic, and only then if both you and I agree it warrants red identification."

Burt Ingstrom stepped out militarily toward the mobile transmitter on his desk.

The man's energy astounded Mason.

Bill Morrison had finally collapsed, asleep in his nearby motel room.

Mason made his way across the office, stopping in the doorway to survey the hangar. The Aerotec vehicles, including the now famous number six van, were lined up neatly, reflecting Burt Ingstrom's urge for orderliness. Mason supposed the place could pass locker inspection.

The door to the interrogation room opened, and he watched interestedly as Les Stalmeyer emerged, followed by the Libyan Ambassador and the second emissary, a short, slight man known only to Mason as someone having something to do with the PLO. It took only a few seconds for Stalmeyer to escort the two men to the Cadillac limousine waiting just outside the hangar door. A moment later, the limousine pulled away, followed by two other escort vehicles. Mason moved to meet his superior several feet away from the interrogation room.

"We nearly blew it," Stalmeyer exclaimed under his breath. "The Libyan got carried away near the end. Flatly said he'd been authorized to offer a flat million dollar reward for Fawd's capture. Plus, if Fawd ever set foot on Libyan soil he'd be shot on sight."

Mason shrugged. "Can't really blame him for being super defensive. After all, the plot originated in his own camp."

"Kate Felton saved it. She had the Arabs off balance, beautiful timing. And, the Delemar woman says she'll cooperate, so let's come up with a plan right now to use her."

"To contact Fawd?"

"You'd better believe it, and the sooner the better."

It was getting near sixty-forty when Mason turned to face Kate Felton as she left the interrogation room.

"Congratulations," said Kate huskily. She was smiling as she extended her hand to Les Stalmeyer.

"You deserve most of the credit," remarked Stalmeyer as he took her hand. "You were superb as the mediator in there," and he turned to Mason. "Are you ready?"

"Would you gentlemen excuse me," Kate said quickly. "I

think I'm going to my motel room and collapse."

"Of course," said Stalmeyer, "and, thanks again."

"Just be careful," Kate warned them as a parting comment. "Don't push her too hard. Remember, she's watched us use the tactic against Fawd," and she turned away toward the hangar door, shuffling in her house slippers.

Alan Hunt had been standing up since Kate Felton left a few minutes earlier, watching Anne Delemar the whole time, not knowing what to say. She looked up at him now, the hint of a smile around her mouth.

"So you're uncomfortable now," she said slowly, "being alone with me and knowing my real reason for being here."

"No," he said truthfully. "I was just thinking about another place. The ranch. It's high desert, the kind of place you'd probably like."

"Probably," she said thoughtfully.

"We'll go there, if you like, after this is over."

She laughed ruefully, reaching up self-consciously to cover her mouth.

"You don't want to go," he said.

"Of course I do," she countered. "But things are upside down now; there is no way I can hope for such a thing. Even if things go well, it may be years," and her voice trailed off.

Alan reached down to lightly touch the back of her hand.

He was aware then that Jerome Mason had entered the room, pulling the door shut behind him.

"Well, now," Mason said congenially, looking at Anne, "I understand that you have volunteered to help us," and he sat down across the table.

She nodded yes, looking up at Alan briefly before answering. "But there are two conditions," she proposed slowly. "First, that Alan be present at all times, as long as he agrees."

Mason simply lifted an eyebrow. "Is that okay with you?" he asked Alan.

"Yes."

"The second," Anne went on, "is that you must understand I will not betray Fawd. In other words, if you get him you'll have to do it without my help. You see, I agree now that what he is doing is wrong, and I'll do what I can to stop him, but I will not help you apprehend him. Am I clear?"

"Yes," said Mason, and he paused for a moment before going on. "Will you now answer some questions?"

"If I can."

Mason reached for a lined tablet on the table before him and folded over a fresh page. "First," he began, "do you know where Fawd is now?"

"No."

"Can you contact him directly?"

"No."

"Did you pass a message to him yesterday at the commune?"

"Do you mean about the Fielding meeting," she asked slowly, "the one where Ben Caplan was killed?"

"Yes," replied Mason. "And let me qualify the question to this extent. Did you contact anyone yesterday regarding that meeting?"

"I did not," she answered firmly.

Alan Hunt stared up at the ceiling of the small room, once again hearing the denial. Deep down he felt that she was telling the truth.

"Miss Delemar, believe me," said Mason sincerely, "I can understand your reluctance to—"

"You must believe me," Anne told him.

Mason held up his hand to stop her. "The fact is obvious, even to you, that Fawd had the information, the details of which were carefully contained. How in the world did he find out, and so quickly?"

"I've been thinking about that," Alan said. "Isn't it possible that he had the recreation room bugged."

Mason shook his head. "Ingstrom himself went over that room with a team the night before. They found nothing. In fact, the entire building was clean."

"So, they were using conventional detection equipment," Alan persisted. "With the money and contacts that Fawd obviously had, couldn't he have secured special and more sophisticated listening devices? I checked this with Bill Morrison, and he said that the East Germans have perfected—"

Mason had lifted his hand again. "Anything is possible, Alan. But we're forced now to deal with probabilities. Time is killing us right now, and we have to proceed, go forward, on certain assumptions."

"I did not do it," Anne told him again.

"So let's move on," Mason said easily. "What do you know about Stanley Fielding?"

"Nothing, beyond what I have learned from the Rahab team."

"Did Kabir ever mention to you anything about uranium,

or, the numbers two-thirty-five, or did he ever give you any indication that he suspected problems with the explosive material to be used in the bomb production."

"No," she said, shaking her head for emphasis. "In fact, Kabir was always very optimistic about how things were going. You see, I knew very little about what was taking place, beyond Fawd's initial explanation to me that we were finally going to have the same weapons possessed by Israel."

Jerome Mason dawdled momentarily with his ballpoint pen before asking, "If you don't know where Fawd is, have no way of contacting him, how is it then that you can help us?"

"I said there is no way for me to contact him now, *directly*," she explained patiently. "However, if he was forced to go underground, he arranged for a way of contact, and we went over the plan several times. He said that the authorities could get a message to him by radio and that the code word Suez should be used."

"Which means?" said Mason, prompting her.

"Within two hours after the radio signal, I am to follow a certain route to a designated point, where I'm to wait to be contacted."

"Here in the city?"

She paused for a moment. "Yes."

Mason leaned over his lined tablet and appeared to be making notes.

"Can we follow her?" Alan asked.

"I don't think so," Anne interjected.

"She's right," Mason agreed. "Our object is to open up communication with Fawd, and we must maintain the credibility of the contact. One of us along would probably scare him off."

"Do you think Fawd will really show?" Alan asked doubtfully.

The two men looked at Anne, who answered, "I would guess Kabir." She shrugged then. "There might be someone else."

"It doesn't matter," Mason pointed out. "We're not so much trying to take Fawd into custody right now as we are to find his lousy bomb and disarm it." Mason stood up. "And right there, Miss Delemar, is where we desperately need your help."

"I'll do what I can."

Mason gestured for Alan to follow him out of the room. At

the door, Mason turned back to Anne. "What is the name of the city where you're to make the rendezvous?"

"I'm not sure. I have the street address memorized, and I'm supposed to use a cab. All I remember is a race track."

"Santa Anita?"

"Yes, that's it," she confirmed. "It's near there."

Mason pushed the door closed behind them and turned to Alan Hunt. "We'll pass Suez along at the eight o'clock broadcast tonight, which means that she should be making contact around ten. Between now and then we'll come up with a message for Fawd and at least a basic plan on how to follow it up."

"What can I do?"

"Just stay with her, keep her cool. I'll have to put two men with you, within sight at all times. You've got a few hours, so head for the motel and try to relax. You'll use the room next to Bill Morrison. Try to reassure her that we're being honest and sincere with her, which we are, by the way."

"She's working herself into a tight spot," Alan suggested. "If Fawd is as unstable as Kate says, and if he picks up on her change of heart—"

"I wouldn't exactly say she has had a change of heart," Mason told him soberly. "But, go ahead and talk to her about how to take care of herself. However, don't scare her off. I'll arrange for Kate to talk to both of you before you leave."

Alan nodded approvingly. "By the way, Joshua asked me to have you find out from Tel Aviv how we can return some money to them."

Jerome Mason reached up to scratch his scalp. "You mean the funds you were paid to work in the operation? I don't understand."

"Don't try, please. Can you make the arrangements?"

"Why don't you go through Shertok?"

Alan shook his head negatively. "Joshua wants it this way, especially after yesterday, and I agree with him."

"Okay," said Mason wearily. "I'll have Morrison plug it in."

"Where is Joshua?"

"Right about now," Mason said as he started for his office, "he should be meeting with Edwin Fielding and a rabbi, making the arrangements for the remains of Ben Caplan. Shortly thereafter, he'll board a Navy ship on his way to someplace off the coast of Baja."

Alan Hunt smiled to himself, thinking that if Stanley Fielding had made only one mistake it was to get Joshua Bain on his tail. "You know, Joshua won't quit now."

Mason pulled up a few steps away, then turning, he faced Alan. "I know that Joshua has a one-track mind on this Fielding thing."

"He's after Ben's killer."

"Fielding didn't do it."

"He's the only lead Joshua has."

Mason pondered the statement. "It's strange how Joshua Bain consistently gets to me. I've given him official sanction, in fact, direct orders, to find Fielding. Yet, I've got the feeling that while the rest of us are beating our brains out trying to find Fawd and his bomb, Joshua is still on his own private little expedition."

"You have to understand," Alan said quietly. "Ben was not only like a brother to Joshua, but their relationship was also . . . how can I put it . . . " and he paused for a moment, knowing he was fumbling for the right words. "It's like Joshua still had something to prove, or settle, between them, and he never had the chance to see it finished. He feels he still owes Ben, perhaps now even more than we can imagine."

Jerome Mason simply shook his head, obviously not understanding, and he turned on his heel as if unwilling to pursue a matter whose priority was not worthy of his attention.

On this occasion, Joshua used the main entrance to the synagogue. Edwin Fielding met him in the foyer and greeted him warmly before leading him to the private office of Rabbi Joel Meyers. The two men sat down opposite the Rabbi, who promptly offered his condolences to Joshua over the death of his friend, Benjamin Caplan.

Joshua thanked him as he reached into his jacket pocket to pull out an envelope, which he handed to the Rabbi. "Here is my personal check. I left the amount blank. I just didn't know how much to make it out for."

The Rabbi opened the envelope and smoothed the check out before him on his desk. "Well, we can guess probably around fifteen hundred for the details in Kansas City. I talked to Ben's mother this morning, per your request, and she indicated no special provisions."

"He'll be flown back, right?" asked Joshua.

"Yes."

"Make it out for five thousand," Joshua told him. "If there

is any left, please ask them to keep it for their own use. Also, please keep the source anonymous."

"That's very generous," the Rabbi commented as he filled in the amount.

"Not really," Joshua said. "You can rightfully say that the State of Israel is making the payment. Of course, while I'm not informed on what the going rate is for one sound and loyal Israeli soldier, I consider five grand a bargain price."

Rabbi Joel Meyers glanced up, appraising Joshua briefly over the top of his horn-rimmed glasses. "That comment," he said softly, "is not only inappropriate and uncalled for, but callous, stupid, and a clear indication of a fully qualified fool." Putting his pen down, he folded his hands before going on, "And if that remark offends you, then I suggest you leave now, and you can take your check with you."

Edwin Fielding cleared his throat. "Please, Rabbi, Joshua is under a tremendous strain—"

Joshua waved him aside. He was in no mood either to walk out or to relent. "How do you assess, then, the sacrifice of Ben Caplan?"

Rabbi Meyers continued to study him for another passing moment. "I doubt if I can," he admitted, "at least to your satisfaction. He is dead, and that to you is virtually inexcusable. I expect that had he been killed in a pure and simple accident, you'd still be insisting on some kind of answer." He shook his head then and frowned. "To try to explain death under any circumstances is a hazardous occupation. The job description is not suited for mere mortals."

"You remind me of Alan Hunt, a Christian friend of mine, who always seems to find a way to bring God into his explanations."

"That would be fair enough in this instance," the Rabbi assured him, "since Ben Caplan had a deep belief in his God."

It was Joshua's turn to frown.

The Rabbi reached into his upper right desk drawer to pull out a small manila envelope. "That surprises you," he observed as he opened the flap on the envelope.

Joshua didn't answer.

The Rabbi handed him a small metal cylinder, about an inch long. Joshua turned it in his hand. The object appeared to have something engraved on it, but it was so badly disfigured, perhaps burned, that he couldn't recognize what it might be. "What is it?"

"It's called a mezuzah," explained Rabbi Meyers. "Historically, the more orthodox of our people posted the mezuzah at the entry to their homes. It is a scroll with twenty-two lines of sacred passages spoken by Moses. More recently, many Jews, orthodox or not, have taken to wearing the mezuzah on their person, usually on a chain around their necks, as a demonstration of their faith. It is significant to our conversation that on no less than two occasions the words on the mezuzah command the bearer to love the Lord thy God with all thine heart, and with all thy soul, and with all thy might."

Joshua said thoughtfully, "So this is Ben Caplan's."

"It was on him when he died. It is in fact the only item of personal effects that was recovered at the scene."

"How did you get it?" Joshua asked idly.

"I gave it to him," Edwin Fielding explained. "Wolf Shertok gave it to me this morning; he said you might like to have it."

Joshua nodded that he understood. Coming out of deeper thoughts, he realized that Edwin Fielding was here by special permission of Jerome Mason, and that the elder Fielding must still be under heavy guard, meaning there were agents on the premises, in the parking lot out front. He reached forward to put the mezuzah back on the Rabbi's desk. "Please forward this to Ben's mother; I already have enough to remember Ben Caplan."

The other two men came to their feet as Joshua stood up.

"I guess," Joshua said softly, "I didn't know as much about Ben as I thought I did."

"Nor perhaps about yourself," Rabbi Meyers suggested.

"You could be right."

"Mister Fielding has told me a good deal about your background," the Rabbi said to him.

Joshua noticed that Edwin Fielding had left the room.

"You mean that I'm a Jew," said Joshua flatly.

"That, among other things. You at times seem to be on a quest, Joshua, and, this might be as good a place as any to start. That is, if you're really serious. You might, in time, even discover your own answer to explain the sacrifice of Ben Caplan—"

Joshua checked his watch. "I've got less than thirty minutes to get aboard a U.S. Navy destroyer."

Rabbi Joel Meyers extended his right hand across the desk. "Go with God, then. But please for me, and your friends, a big favor . . . "

"If I can."

"Leave vengeance to the one who handles it the best."

Chapter thirteen

The day had passed by more slowly than usual, by Kabir's estimate, and then he realized that for the first time since their arrival, Fawd had not offered to play gin rummy. Listening to the last of the eight o'clock weather report, Kabir thought he would invite Fawd to play, to help pass the time and perhaps improve both their moods. The closing message on the radio got by Kabir before he could catch it. Fawd came out of the kitchen, a cup of black coffee in his hand.

"Did you hear that?" he said, his mood seemingly improved.

Kabir didn't answer, turning instead to crank up the recorder. A few seconds later the critical part of the newscast was isolated and he played it back: *Anne will cross Suez tonight with a message.*

"Aha!" Fawd said jubilantly, and he slapped his right knee. "It took them a day longer than I figured. She must've put up some fight." He had put his coffee down on a nearby table. The familiar rubber ball was in use again, and he began to pace the floor, working the ball methodically.

"Can it be a trick?" Kabir offered. "They've got to be hurting badly, you know."

"It'll be under control," Fawd assured him. "Besides, the letter has to be delivered tonight anyway."

"I'll meet her," Kabir offered, "and deliver the letter for you." He pushed away from the fireplace. "I'll change clothes and check out the motorcycle."

"No," said Fawd quickly. "You check out the motorcycle, and I'll change clothes."

Kabir felt his breath go out of his chest, and he coughed loudly, pretending to clear his throat, trying to cover the reaction which revealed his disappointment. Watching Fawd start up the stairway, he realized he was stuck here in the house. Anne Delemar was his best chance. Going over the development, he began to feel better, figuring that with Fawd gone he could still get away, with at least several hours' head start.

There was a twenty-six-foot power boat anchored in a private slip at the Oceanside marina, fully fueled and stocked with food. There were a hundred thousand dollars in American currency in a watertight can hidden in the bilge.

Optional plan Bravo—

Mexico in two hours.

He quickly moved out of the house to the converted wood shed now used to protect what he considered their most critical equipment: three motorcycles, all motocross equipped and perfectly in tune. First he checked the gas tanks, verifying that they were full. Then, mounting the one nearest the door, he cranked it up. The bike started immediately. As he pushed the idling machine out into the open, he cranked the throttle several more times. He was impressed with the special mufflers, especially the oversized twin baffle system designed so that the bike ran practically quiet at normal throttle. He knew that the muffler system would eventually burn the valves out, but it didn't matter for the brief time they would have to use the machines.

Fawd turned the corner of the shed, catching him by surprise.

"I should be back by midnight," Fawd told him.

By which time, Kabir thought, I'll be halfway to Mexico.

"Do you have the letter?" Kabir asked, pretending a concern he really didn't feel.

"Yes," said Fawd as he pulled on a pair of black leather gloves, which matched the rest of his clothes. There was the telltale bulge at the center of his stomach. The box went with him, even now, his own final insurance, a kind of warranty that Kabir did not envy.

Fawd straddled the idling machine. "Don't forget to reset the trigger," he said as he pushed off, heading south.

The sun was on the distant Pacific horizon as the motorcycle and its passenger silently disappeared into the undergrowth along the south edge of the estate. Kabir lingered for a few moments, following in his mind the route now being taken by Fawd. They'd both travelled the trail several times, practicing so that they could negotiate the way down the mountain, especially and necessarily in the dark. Kabir figured he would give Fawd a thirty-minute head start.

Back in the house, he moved purposefully to the computer room, where opposite the computer console he knelt down to confront the floor safe. Taking his time, he deftly worked the three-dial combination. He had enough cash in his billfold to take him to the boat, but there was enough cocaine in the floor safe to take him around the world several times. Fawd had been specific in his orders that the safe was not to be opened by anyone except him, unless an extraordinary circumstance should require otherwise. Lifting the heavy metal lid, Kabir assured himself that the present moment was indeed an extraordinary circumstance.

There was the immediate hiss of a hydraulic mechanism, a plaintive kind of sigh, and Kabir whirled on his heels to see that the only exit from the room was now sealed. He lurched to his feet and ran to the door, where he hammered futilely on the heavy steel plate, realizing finally that he couldn't beat down the door with his bare fists.

After a few passing moments, he moved back to the safe. Dropping to his knees, he inspected the seat area of the lid receptacle. He found the pin, perhaps twenty thousandths in diameter, protuding next to the lid hinge. Using his fingernail, he depressed the pin, itself a trigger held down by the closed lid, and waited. He was not surprised, however, that the steel door remained firmly closed.

He grunted disgustedly to himself, sitting back on his heels. Fawd always thought of everything, including defecting assistants. So now one Kabir had to come up with a story, a very convincing and believable story, by approximately midnight. He sniffled once and reached into the safe, thinking that a two 'n two would help. He found the slip of paper on top of the cache of cocaine.

"To my predictable friend," the note began. "There is enough air in this room to last you about four hours. Suggest you rest easy and try to sleep if you can, for then you will use less oxygen."

Kabir recognized Fawd's handwriting.

He dropped the note back into the safe and closed the metal lid. Becoming alert, he moved slowly and deliberately to the computer console, where he opened the panel to reset the trigger timer. He then sat down before the keyboard, thinking that he would take it easy while he spent the next several hours figuring out a way to alter the program, somehow, in some way, to his advantage.

The bomb was Fawd's basic lever.

If he could find a way to take control of the bomb, he would then control Fawd.

Just the thought of facing Fawd again made him

shiver. He knew he could never pull it off.

He felt his pulse quicken—a fact which meant his oxygen consumption was up.

Taking a deep breath and measuring its effect, he then forced himself to relax and to think of less exciting things, like an unhurried and uneventful boat trip to Mexico.

The bridge deck rolled gently under his feet. Joshua Bain was thankful to be out of the cramped and noisy confines of the helicopter. He figured his stomach was about back to normal as the destroyer's skipper pulled up next to his elbow. "You're sure we've got the right boat?" Joshua asked concernedly.

"Positive," the young Captain assured him. "The skipper of the Mexican cutter definitely identified her name on the fantail. It's the *Errante*."

"What's her position?"

The Captain led him to the nearby chart table, where he picked up a pencil. "Here," the Captain told him. "Roughly a hundred fifty miles due west of San Benito Island."

"And us?"

"We're here, the better part of two hundred miles north-north-east."

"They're running," Joshua commented idly.

"Very much so," the Captain agreed. "They are over a hundred miles farther south than we expected." He paused then, looking directly at Joshua. "The Mexican skipper is waiting for instructions."

"You say they've refused to heave to."

"That's right, and they also refuse to communicate."

"What's their course?"

"Due south."

Joshua drew a deep breath and rubbed his hand across his mouth, feeling his day-old growth of beard. Once again he was getting tired. He glanced up to the bulkhead clock behind the con: 2120 hours. Nine-thirty. "When's the earliest I can get to that ship?" He leaned over the chart, surveying the Mexican coastline below San Benito Island.

"The crew chief on our chopper says he's got to have at least two hours. That bird is very tired."

Joshua grinned. "Welcome to the club."

"We're overtaking them by about fifteen knots," the Captain said. "If all goes well, I would guess you could be there in four and a half to five hours, unless, of course, we request the cutter to force her to heave to."

Joshua shook his head in the negative. "No. Tell the cutter to take no action; just keep our little *Errante* in range and under close surveillance."

The Captain scratched the brief message on a clipboard and handed it to Joshua, who initialed it.

"Also," Joshua added, "have him report immediately any other vessels in the area or out-of-the-ordinary activity." The comment turned in his mind, prompting him to ask, "How many minutes away are the carrier aircraft?"

"The fighters?"

"Yes, the fighters."

"At full bore, maybe twelve, fifteen minutes," and the young Captain showed his discipline, though not entirely covering his curiosity.

"Put the fly boys on alert," said Joshua then. It had come to him that whoever was on the *Errante* ought to suspect that their time was now limited, that they might have a contingency plan or option. Being so close now, Joshua was not about to let the quarry escape. "The instant you receive a report of any deviation, even the least change, you will at once scramble a carrier flight, and make arrangements for me to talk to the flight leader. Also, keep an open channel with that cutter, with voice verification once every ten minutes."

The young Captain was writing furiously on his clipboard now. He hesitated, then looked at Joshua. The Captain was not tall, a little on the stocky side, and, without his uniform, he might have very well passed in civilian clothes as an insurance agent or bank teller, on his way up.

"You know how much all this is costing the United States taxpayers?" the young Captain asked him sincerely.

He would make a better accountant, Joshua was thinking. "I can guess," he answered evenly.

"That ship must be awfully important."

"She is, Captain, and I'm sorry that I can't explain why."

The Captain's discipline showed again as he returned to his clipboard.

"Can I get a coded message out?" Joshua asked then.

"Yes, sir; we have crypto gear on board."

Initialing off his orders with a borrowed pencil from the chart table, Joshua took a single sheet of paper and moved to the port side of the bridge to stare out across the placid darkened water. Conscious of the ship's swift movement, Joshua was still impatient, more now than ever before. Alan Hunt would have better appreciated the moment—the tranquillity of the passing sea, the apparent peace. Joshua sucked in a deep reflective breath as he felt a passing sense of guilt for overplaying the situation. Stanley Fielding was more likely an anticlimactic matter, so Joshua had come to suspect. Fielding could stay free and keep running for another six months and probably not affect the present crisis. But he was proof, Joshua hoped, so that justice was involved. Justice—the principle of the just dealing of men with each other, as Ben had once put it. Roughly adding up the cost, Joshua admitted to himself that Stanley Fielding, indeed, might just turn out to be one of the most expensive witnesses ever brought before an accused.

Convinced and full of resolve, Joshua turned back to the chart table, where he began writing the urgent and classified message which he addressed to Jerome Mason, Director, Federal Bureau of Investigation, care of the Los Angeles field office.

At a lower elevation now and entering more dangerous ground, Fawd throttled back, slowing to a crawl. There were no more fire trails this low, so he worked his way carefully along the more narrow hiker's path. He stopped at hundred-yard intervals, checking the terrain carefully under the soft light of a quarter moon. He knew he was almost invisible against the darkly mottled chaparral, so he pushed on confidently, entering the last of the foothills in a matter of minutes.

He checked his watch as he passed the final landmark, the Sierra Madre Reservoir. It was nine-thirty, and he was right on schedule.

He pulled off the black ski mask, slipping it into the pocket of his right thigh.

He entered the first paved street just south of the reservoir.

Two minutes later, he pulled into the driveway of the safe house, a small cabin-type bungalow fully hidden from the street. Parking before the garage, he ignored the house itself, seeing only that it was dark and apparently still secure. Using a small flashlight, he checked the crack running around the garage door, confirming that the black threads spaced across the opening were still intact. Using a master key, he unlocked the garage door. He then pushed the bike to the rear of the garage, moving around the dark blue van. With the bike secured, he moved to the van and lifted the front hood. It took only a few seconds to attach the two battery cables. Inside the van's cab, he started the engine, letting it idle as he moved into the van itself to start checking out its equipment.

He was humming to himself as he returned to the driver's seat and punched the van into reverse. Beside him, on the passenger seat, was the manila envelope marked with the single word, RAHAB. He double-checked his left thigh pocket, making certain he still had several dimes.

He took one deep breath, rolled his head back and relaxed his neck muscles. Find a mailbox first, make one phone call and then on to Suez and whatever that might bring.

At exactly five minutes before ten o'clock, Anne Delemar pushed out of the back seat of the sedan. Alan Hunt followed, turning to Jerome Mason, who remained seated behind the car's steering wheel.

"I'll go with her to the corner," Alan said as he started along the sidewalk, walking slowly. Anne matched him stride for stride, slipping her hand into his.

"You know what to do?" said Alan softly.

"It's not that much," she suggested. "I give him the note, and, otherwise, I just . . . how did Kate put it?"

"Just stay loose."

"A nice expression."

Alan felt his throat tightening up. "Remember, don't antagonize him, and especially don't try to persuade him one way or the other. If you do, he'll likely turn on you."

"I understand."

They were at the corner now, and stopped to face each other. She glanced down the street toward the car, putting her hand on his chest in a tentative, unsure gesture.

"We could just keep going, you know," she said quietly. "I know where there is a boat, and probably money too. There are places we could go to, right now, and never look back."

He chuckled once, pulled her close, feeling her against him from top to bottom. "Yes," he said then, "there is sometimes a way which seems right to a man. But it's like when you first leave a straight line, your distance is still close, so close to be even acceptable, but as your line of departure continues so does the distance between you and the original line. The angle is ever widening," and he pushed her away just enough so that he could look into her eyes.

"In my country," she told him, "you would be a teacher."

"Is that good?"

"It would be for my country."

He kissed her, only vaguely aware her arms were coiling around his neck, and for the first time he matched the eager hunger in her mouth, a twisting, painful encounter, and he felt compelled to totally envelope her, to draw her into his own being.

She pushed away from him after a moment, making a small whimpering sound, and before he could reach out for her again she was gone, hurrying down the darkened street.

"Good luck," Alan heard himself saying.

He stood still for a few seconds, hearing the diminishing sound of her footsteps complementing the pounding of his own heart. His mind whirled in confusion, and he shook his head to clear it, isolating the thought that the way of escape sometimes was a difficult one, albeit certain. He was aware then that a car had pulled up beside him.

"Are you all right?" Mason asked him.

Alan turned, commenting bitterly, "No, I'm not all right."

"You're too involved," Mason told him as he climbed into the car.

"That's correct," Alan confirmed. "And would you believe that is the only part of this whole mess that makes any sense." He sighed heavily. "She suggested we go away together, and I turned her down. Now, I'm not so sure—"

The buzzer on the car's mobile radio rang once, breaking his thoughts.

Mason snatched up the receiver and identified himself.

"Give me the location," he said after listening for a moment, and he pulled a pad and ballpoint pen out of his jacket pocket. "I'll handle it," he said, "and have a postal inspector meet me there, like now!" Hanging up, he pointed to the glove compartment. "There should be a map book in there. Get it out and look up the intersection of Second Street and Grandview Place."

Alan punched the release on the compartment door. "What's happening?" he asked as he pulled the thick book out of the compartment.

"They just got an anonymous call at Ingstrom's downtown office," Mason said, as he hit the ignition. "There's supposed to be a package in the mailbox at that location bearing the name Rahab." He flipped on the inside overhead light.

Alan found the two streets in the alphabetical listing first. "They're in Arcadia," he reported.

Jerome Mason hammered the steering wheel with his right hand. "The gall of the man," he said disbelievingly. "The Suez contact point is right here, too, right under the shadow of Mount Wilson. It's like he's thumbing his nose at us, daring us to find him."

"It's like Kate says," Alan suggested; "he thinks he is invincible."

"Yeah," Mason observed soberly then. "As long as he's got the handle on the bomb, he's about as invincible as one can get."

At the second intersection, Anne Delemar turned the corner back to her right. Dressed in blue jeans and a heavy cotton pullover, she slowed her walk to a more normal pace. The street was a minor business one, fronted by small shops, most of them having closed several hours earlier. Traffic was light. At the middle of the block, she dropped down the alley, moving quickly until she found the rear entrance to the TV repair shop. The door was open, as it should be, and she slipped inside, locking it behind her. She flattened herself against the inside wall, closing her eyes so they could adjust to the darkened interior.

The sound of a phone ringing startled her, causing her to jump. She turned to her left, and slipped into the small office. The phone was on the desk. She picked up the receiver, answering with a hushed hello.

"Suez?"

It was a question from the other end, and she recognized both it and the voice.

"Anne," she responded.

"Problems?"

"None."

"Excellent, my dear," Fawd said conversationally. "As of right now, you are on a strict time schedule. This is as far as you have gone before, remember?"

"Yes," she said, hearing the rapid sound of her own breath on the receiver. She did not expect Fawd—

"The rest is even easier," he assured her. "But you must do exactly as I say because I'm at a pay phone and you'll not be hearing from me again."

"I understand."

"Turn on the desk lamp and then check the time."

She followed the orders in sequence.

"From now on you just listen; remembering in order so that you can repeat it back," he told her slowly, spacing his words carefully. "First, walk across the hall to the opposite door. Enter the room. On your left are two power switches at waist level. Turn them both on. Both of them. Right below the two switches is a shelf with a flashlight. Take it. Cross the room to the second doorway, open it, go down the stairs. At the foot of the stairs in the basement will be a door on your right. Open it, and from there on you simply follow your nose until you reach the metal hatch which will open into an underground drainage tube. At that point, you turn right again. Follow the tube, which is large enough for you to walk in, until you reach the end, which will put you in an open culvert. Repeat it back."

She did, thinking she had done it perfectly.

"You forgot that the power switches are at *waist level*."

"Waist level," she repeated.

"Hang up and go."

She placed the phone down, moved out of the office. Inside the opposite door, she reached to her left, turned on both switches. The room lit up. She found the flashlight, moved on to the second door. It took her about eight minutes, by her estimate, to negotiate the designated route. As she emerged from the mouth of the culvert she breathed easier, thankful to be out of the dank confines of the drainage tube. A car horn sounded once, brief and partial, and she turned to see the van parked next to the guard rail above the culvert opening. She scrambled up the adjacent slope and entered the van on the passenger side.

"In the back," Fawd snapped at her as he hit the gas.

She obliged, moving awkwardly around the seat. The best she could tell in the poor light was that the van's interior was packed with what seemed to be electronic gear. She put the flashlight on the floor beside her.

"Undress," Fawd told her over his shoulder.

The van stopped, and she had to catch herself to keep from falling forward. Fawd came over his seat then, and she could hear that the engine was still running. There were no windows and she had no notion where they might be. At best, from the time passed, they were no more than a block or two away from the culvert. Fawd threw a switch to activate the inside lights.

"Undress, I said!" Fawd hissed.

She stared at the probe in his hand.

"Your electronic gear is strong enough to check me out with my clothes on." Her voice was even and cool, betraying no panic.

They stared at each other another long moment.

"I'm not bugged, you know," she spoke again.

"You might not even know it," he warned her. "Did they ever put you under with drugs?"

"No, never."

"They could've done it while you were asleep."

She controlled an impulse to laugh. "So check with your precious electronics." While he considered her thoughtfully, she noticed the TV screen mounted above the inside of the cab. It took a second or two for her to realize it was reporting the inside of the room opposite the office in the TV repair shop. He had been, in a way, right there in the room the whole time, watching and waiting to see if she was being followed. The TV transmitter explained the need for the second power switch.

Fawd, his face impassive, finally began going over her carefully, area by area, removing the only item she had brought with her, the white envelope bearing the Government's message. He made her turn around and scanned her thoroughly with the probe, not once, but at least three or four times. Finished, he turned back to the console to shut down the scanner.

"You're clean," he told her almost grudgingly, and turned back to face her, watching her for several seconds—in fact, studying her.

For the first time she realized that panic was almost ready to take over her senses.

"The engine is running," she reminded him. The catch in her voice gave her away, and he laughed. But he turned away without a further word and climbed over the seat. The van lurched forward. She grabbed the back of the seat for balance, then lost it again as the van stopped. This time Fawd turned off the engine. She could see enough through the front windshield to guess that they were in a garage. Fawd came back over his seat once again, squatting down at the rear of the van's interior. He watched the TV screen for a few seconds before reaching for a knob to shut it off.

"It's safe to say you weren't followed."

"They agreed not to follow me."

"Don't think I'm being too cautious; you should know me better than that. But," he went on to explain, flourishing with his hands, "I'm like a child when it comes to equipment like this. They are really toys, expensive ones, I might add . . . "

The Fawd bravado, she was thinking while she pretended to listen. He was unwilling to admit his dependence on the sophisticated and expensive equipment. He'd rather have her believe that it was his true style to face the enemy with his bare hands.

He had removed the envelope from his pocket and unfolded the single sheet of paper inside. Anne Delemar had been permitted to read the note, and she watched his face for a reaction. He simply frowned part way through. He folded the letter up then, staring in the direction of the front windshield.

"They blame me for Caplan's death," she said.

"How is that?"

"They say I contacted you to report the meeting where he was killed."

"What kind of meeting?"

"They supposedly were to meet Stanley Fielding. But, it was a fake, designed to lure you or one of your people in."

"Stanley Fielding is dead," Fawd said flatly. "His ashes are in a lock box in a Beverly Hills bank. That kind of bait wouldn't have lured me around the block," and he paused before going on. "It turned out well, though. Caplan was a Zionist pig, deserved to die. I'm sorry I can't take the credit."

"You can indirectly," she proposed.

He studied her briefly, before noting, "You've changed."

"We all do in time."

"And philosophy, too," he observed, and his manner was decidedly pleasant, putting her on guard. "I'm curious about its origin. Is it from yourself, or, perhaps from a newly found friend?" he added. The Fawd glint was in his eye now.

She took immediate note of the allusion to Alan Hunt, and again had to control her impulse to laugh. He actually was jealous. *Don't antagonize him.* "It's original Southern Californian," she said instead.

He laughed lightly.

"Isn't it dangerous for you," she said, not liking the lull between them, "to be here?"

He lifted the front of his wool pullover, exposing the small metal box clipped to his belt. "I can go up to a radius of several more miles and still level this city in a few seconds." He was grinning then. "I'm actually as safe here as any place."

"Was the note good news or bad news?"

"Perhaps a little of both," he admitted. "But we will have to study it."

"Why didn't you tell me about the bomb?" she asked abruptly.

He glanced away from her at the question. Then pushing himself forward, he crawled on his hands and knees to the side door. "Remember, it's a basic rule," he answered, at the same time unlatching the side door, "that you can't tell what you don't know." The door came open with a slipping metallic sound.

She was relieved to see that they were ready to start moving again.

Within seconds, Fawd was out of the van, his shoes grating on what sounded like a cement floor. "Come on," he said, motioning to her through the open door. "We're going for a motorcycle ride."

She was immensely relieved that he had not asked her for her opinion on the bomb, because she might have told him the truth—that she was tired, very tired, and perhaps she didn't belong in the movement anymore. She admitted she was confused. Without the last minute restraint of Alan Hunt, she might have kept right on walking tonight, right on past the TV repair shop. Crawling past the array of electronic equipment, she sensed that it was all somehow or other completely insane, a preposterous kind of delusion, one of their own making and responsibility, and it saddened her that they all had to ultimately share in the consequences.

Chapter fourteen

Following Joshua's instructions, the helicopter pilot pulled up and away from the cutter, veering due north to hover on station within one mile, where he was to wait for as long as his fuel would allow. Clear of the canvas drop harness, Joshua rearranged the windbreaker under his arms. The chopper had about thirty minutes of fuel left in its tanks. Time, as usual, was critical. Widening his stance on the rolling bow deck of the small cutter, he turned his attention to the nearest crewman, asking for the Captain. He had lost track of time, not really caring anymore, guessing now that so long as they were in the same time zone it must be nearing midnight. It was dark around them on the open sea, and his eyes began to adjust under the light of the partial overhead moon.

The crewman escorted him to admidships, aft of the cabin superstructure. Moving along the port rail, Joshua realized the ship was smaller and more lightly armed than he had expected. There was a small gun forward, looking no larger than a twenty millimeter, along with a deck-mounted machine gun farther aft. The Captain, portly in his badly fitting khaki uniform, greeted him in Spanish, smiling broadly and obviously pleased to have Joshua aboard.

Joshua smiled weakly, thinking that lately nothing seemed to go right, that ten of their thirty minutes would be consumed in trying to communicate—

"I am your interpreter, sir," one of the nearby crewmen said.

Thank God, Joshua intoned to himself. As best as he could tell in the poor light, the young seaman looked to be in his middle twenties. "Your name?" Joshua asked him politely.

"Jesus Prado, sir."

A good sign, Joshua admitted to himself, thinking that Alan Hunt might have had a hand in arranging the scene. He pointed toward the *Errante*, which was lying about a hundred yards off the port bow of the cutter. The sportfisher showed no lights, appearing to be dead in the water.

"Her engine stopped," Jesus reported, very officially. "They have used the starter many times."

Engine trouble, Joshua said to himself, and it figured, since the *Errante* had been pushing hard for many hours.

Jesus Prado spoke in Spanish to his Captain, apparently keeping him informed.

"Do you have a bull horn?" Joshua asked him, holding up his right hand in the gesture of a pistol grip near his mouth.

Jesus frowned once, then smiled. "Yes, sir." He repeated the question to the Captain, who turned to one of his men, speaking rapidly. The Captain took Jesus by the arm, speaking to him at some length. Jesus in turn addressed himself to Joshua, "The Captain wishes to welcome you on board. He has a direct order from the President himself to cooperate. We are all honored."

Joshua forced himself to smile broadly. "Tell the Captain I am the one who is honored. He has a fine ship, and he should be proud," and he glanced over his shoulder to the lights on the waiting helicopter, aware that the amenities had just consumed another three or four minutes worth of precious fuel. If the chopper had to return to the ship, he would be stuck here for several more hours. He looked anxiously to the *Errante*, hearing over the intervening water the sound of a starter grinding insistently.

One of the crewmen emerged from below deck carrying what looked like a bottle.

Where's the bull horn? Joshua wondered impatiently.

The Captain removed the cap from the bottle, which he handed to Joshua. In the line of duty, Joshua thought helplessly, and he tipped the bottle up. The tequila burned his throat. He gasped once, nodding vigorously as he handed it back to the Captain.

"Please move the ship closer," Joshua said hoarsely to the interpreter. If they didn't get moving they would all wind up stoned, a kind of appropriate finale to an otherwise uneventful exercise. He was relieved to see the Captain respond with a string of curt orders.

Within a few minutes the cutter was closer in to the *Errante*. Joshua came on deck with a bull horn, which he himself had located in a cabin locker stuffed full of fishing gear. He quietly issued the orders to show no arms and to leave the cutter's searchlight turned off. As he studied the darkened ship, his final objective, he felt his pulse quicken. In the language of Jerome Mason, he had now reached the one-yard line with a first down and goal to go.

The bull horn was raised to position. "This is Joshua Bain," he stated, hearing his own voice resonating across the open water. Behind them, the helicopter droned on as a constant reminder of how short his time really was. "This is Joshua Bain," he repeated, "and I'm coming aboard. I'm unarmed!" He gestured with his free hand to move the cutter in closer.

He felt the engine surge under his feet. The other ship remained dark as they pulled in closer. Still no sign of life. Joshua lifted the bull horn one more time. "I have an urgent message from Edwin Fielding for his son, Stanley." The two ships were only a few feet apart now, and even in the bad light Joshua could easily make out the other ship's trim. The *Errante* was a typical sportfishing boat with a full walkway running her entire rail. Easy to board from any point except over her higher bow line. The bridge was much higher than the cutter's. Following his orders, the helmsman was steering the cutter in on the other ship's aft quarter, giving him a good view of the bridge's hatch.

A distant horn blasted across the water. Startled, Joshua

jerked around to see the helicopter searchlight blink on and off, signalling that he had only a few minutes left.

The cutter bumped gently against the other ship, and Joshua quickly stepped across the lower rail and down to the deck of the *Errante*. He stood poised, his knees unlocked. The Viper was high on the inside of his thigh. Staring intently at the open bridge hatch, he blinked once, picking out the form of a man. The figure cleared the hatch, facing Joshua, who noticed that the man was armed with what appeared to be a carbine. The weapon was pointed at the deck.

"Get off my boat," the man warned him in a strong and heavily accented voice. "We are in international waters, and you have no right—"

Joshua Bain finally lost his patience. "International waters be damned!" he snapped angrily. "And I'm not going to debate with you. In fact, as of this moment, I've got two options for you. The first is that if I pull off this deck, then in about fifteen minutes this precious boat of yours is going to be blasted out of the water by a flight of U.S. Navy jets. Or, you can get Stanley Fielding up here and we can all get on with our business," and he felt his hands clench. "I've had it with you screwballs!"

He allowed the standoff to continue for ten more seconds. Then he began to count down slowly, ten, nine, eight—

A second form took shape behind the first man, followed by the sounds of an argument, the words low and quick. Abruptly then, one of the two forms disengaged to move along the opposite rail. Joshua saw that he was a man of slight build, stooped. Joshua braced as the form drew closer. Finally the man turned the bait tank and walked directly up to Joshua.

"I am Stanley Fielding," the man said simply.

Joshua stood perfectly still for a few moments, thinking that he ought to be grateful, or relieved, or something, but actually he didn't know what to say or do. Instead, he felt absolutely let down, like a hunter who after a long chase finally cornered his prey to then discover that somewhere along the way he had lost his urge to kill—

"I hope to God you're worth it," he remarked bitterly.

The meeting was scheduled for 4:00 a.m., and Alan Hunt entered Jerome Mason's office a few minutes early. Unable to sleep, he had spent the past several hours alone in his motel room, working his way through the Psalms, hoping that the triumph of David might improve his own outlook. This time he had come away from the Book with the impression that it perhaps was more a tribute to the triumph of the Lord, whose grace and mercy seemed to know no limit.

Mason's office was already filling up. Les Stalmeyer, Bill Morrison, Ewing Melbourne, and Mason were all bunched around the wall map at the other end of the room. Burt Ingstrom stood in the center of the group, a pointer in his hand, talking at his usual clip. Kate Felton was at a desk at the other end of the room, where Alan elected to try the psychiatrist for any new information she might have. He dropped into the chair next to Kate's desk.

"Any word about Anne?" he asked.

Kate looked up from the paper in front of her and shook her head no. "At least," she said, "I haven't heard."

"What's your opinion on her chances?"

Kate Felton didn't answer right away, choosing instead to dutch light another mini cigar. "You're in love with her, aren't you?" she finally said.

"What does that have to do with it?"

"Everything," Kate told him. "In your present state of mind, what you're asking me to say will only further aggravate you. And, believe me, I've got enough uptight people on my hands already."

"Try me."

Kate took a deep drag on her cigarillo. Exhaling, she broke into a spasm of coughing. Watching her, Alan was afraid she might choke, and he asked her if she would like some water. She waved him aside, seeming to settle down after a moment.

"I'm sorry," she said, still gasping.

"Why don't you quit?"

"Why don't you?" she snapped back.

Touché, he thought.

"She'll make it all right," Kate told him then. "This exercise is a lot less hazardous than some she's been involved in before."

"You're only guessing—"

"Come on, my young and innocent friend," she chided him. "I'm familiar with your record on faith and hope, but now you're pushing charity a little hard. This chick you've latched onto is at best an admitted terrorist. Besides, as cool as she is under fire tells me she is experienced. She's hard, and she's tough. And you're right in saying we're only guessing at her identity and past record. But, Fawd has always been a loner, in everything, never having carried on a known affair. Tel Aviv may never find out who she is. Her face is changed, and she'll never look the same as she once did. But, she's a part of the movement, I guarantee you."

"Yes," Alan admitted. "She told me that much herself."

"And what else?"

"Very little," said Alan. "She is afraid of reprisals against her family."

Kate Felton reached up to ruffle her short hair. "My professional opinion is that she'll be just fine. She's young, attractive. And, she'll come out of this with immunity, no doubt. I expect her will to survive will pull her through."

"Aren't you ever wrong?" he asked bluntly.

"Very seldom, my impetuous young friend," and she was smiling now. "Your hope is that she will change, perhaps already has. I can only wish you good luck in that regard."

It was Alan's turn to smile. "What else is happening?" he asked, hoping to change the subject. He liked the gruff and outspoken Kate Felton and had no wish to antagonize her.

"We'll know more in a minute," Kate said, looking toward the end of the room where the men were grouped together. "For one thing, Fawd has issued a second demand letter."

"So that's what was in the mailbox."

"Yes, and this time it's a lulu. He's escalated into the absurd."

"Does it buy us some time?" Alan asked hopefully.

"Just the opposite; he's given us a deadline this time of Saturday noon."

Tomorrow, Alan thought, reminding himself that it was now the early hours of Friday. He guessed that the new demand letter might be the reason for the meeting. "So what do we do now?"

Kate Felton looked into his eyes. "Pray, all you can," she suggested sincerely.

"I've been doing a lot of that already," Alan said soberly. "Why?" he asked. "Has it turned all that bad?"

"We might have to evacuate the city," she said simply.

Alan looked up to the distant ceiling. "Oh, wow!" was all he could say.

"The word's out that the President blew his stack when he was told about the second letter."

Alan tried to imagine evacuating Los Angeles, and all he could come up with was a montage of ultimate panic. The toll would be devastating, both in life and property. Martial law. It would take a dozen divisions of armed troops just to maintain any semblance of order. He looked toward the other end of the room and was relieved to see Jerome Mason motioning for both of them to join the group. They both got up quickly.

Les Stalmeyer addressed the group without delay, "It seems we've got our first major break," and he looked at Jerome Mason. "Jerry will explain."

"Gladly," said Mason, lifting his right hand to a series of three enlargements pinned on the wall map. "This is Fawd's hideout," he announced.

"You're absolutely certain," Kate Felton said skeptically.

"No doubt at all," Bill Morrison told her. "We almost had it narrowed down prior to midnight. The clincher came a few minutes before twelve when one of Ingstrom's men, watching the place from a safe distance, observed a motorcycle entering the grounds from the south, from the vicinity of Little Santa Anita Canyon. Using a night scope, he was able to identify the two riders. Our friend Fawd was at the controls with Anne Delemar behind him as a passenger."

Alan Hunt swallowed hard, not knowing what to think of the report. He supposed it was more good news than bad. At least Anne had still been alive at midnight.

"Our problem," Les Stalmeyer interjected, "is how to apprehend Fawd and at the same time prevent him from triggering the device. We've been discussing it at length, for the past three hours to be exact, and still haven't come up with a solution."

Doctor Melbourne continued, "We don't know how the trigger mechanism is activated. Based on the detail of the weapon itself, we have to assume a sophisticated and reasonably foolproof system, no doubt electronic."

"He can trigger it from where he is now," Kate Felton reminded them.

"So he claims," said Melbourne. "And, he can also have the device set on a timing mechanism. We're assuming, also, that the bomb itself is not at the mountain location."

Alan was beginning to appreciate their dilemma. Solving the one problem of Fawd's whereabouts only led to a more serious one. Until they resolved the trigger question, they obviously couldn't storm the hideout.

"We're going to move anyway," Bill Morrison was saying. "We'll take between now and, say, noon today to inspect the house and its immediate grounds as thoroughly as we can. Burt Ingstrom will leave immediately with three men whose only function is to scout the outer grounds and locate any surveillance system protecting the property. There's a large cabin about one mile northeast of the estate which we've already designated as our CP. Before first light, I, Jerry Mason, Alan Hunt, and a second crew of six men will occupy the CP and set it up. We will then approach the house as close as we can, based on Ingstrom's survey. We will spare no option in this phase of the investigation. I've already called on my people to deliver our most sophisticated listening and other type search devices."

"What happens," Alan asked then, "if we don't score by noon?"

"We'll still have about eight hours of light left," Mason proposed.

"I thought we had until tomorrow noon," said Kate.

"Don't bank on it," Stalmeyer warned. "While I can't tell you all of it, I can report that the President is seriously considering evacuating the city, and we need to give him as much time as possible to make that decision."

"Noon is a reasonable objective," Morrison said.

"Let's get to it," Stalmeyer told them.

As the group broke up, Alan spoke privately to Jerome Mason, "I'd like to go with Ingstrom's group; I can help out, work a radio—"

"I've got you scheduled to go with me," Mason told him, "in case we isolate or contact Anne Delemar," and he paused, pulling on his lower lip. "By the way," he said after a moment, "I've received a coded message from Joshua, which, shall we say, touches on a sensitive area."

"How's he making it?"

"You must keep it to yourself; like, absolutely no one else is to know," Mason warned him. "He picked up Fielding about an hour ago."

Alan was grinning from ear to ear.

"It isn't funny," Mason said sternly. "He managed to run a Navy helicopter out of gas over the open sea, and, according to a very angry and upset Commander of the Eleventh Naval District, the chopper pilot and Bain are presently involved in a drunken party aboard a Mexican Coast Guard cutter."

The report was too much, and Alan broke into laughter, opening a vent that had been closed for a long time.

Jerome Mason finally allowed the first wrinkle of a grin to cross his face.

Alan caught his breath. "What has Fielding got? I mean, what does he have to help us?"

Jerome Mason started to turn away. "I can't tell you anymore right now. You are aware, however, that the Bain luck is becoming a legend."

The remark sobered Alan Hunt, who merely stared at the retreating back of Jerome Mason. Praise the Lord, he exclaimed inside; thereby acknowledging the source of his friend's good fortune.

The silence in the huge room was overpowering, and Anne Delemar asked if she could turn on the radio. She had been in the same chair for the past two hours, bucking Fawd head to head at gin rummy. He now looked at her searchingly across the narrow table. It was his turn to deal, and he squared up the cards on the table between them.

"Be my guest," he said easily, "and please get me a fresh cup of coffee while you're at it."

She picked up his cup and moved directly to the kitchen, noting that this was the first time he had allowed her out of his sight, setting aside her one trip to the bathroom. She found the coffee maker on the counter next to the sink. It was still dark outside, about an hour before daybreak, she estimated, and she could not distinguish anything in particular through the windows facing the outside. She poured his coffee quickly, returning to the living room, where she detoured past the radio mounted next to the fireplace. She located a music station, turned the volume to a low point, just loud enough for her to hear from across the room. They were still up because Kabir was upstairs, someplace, trying to determine how the substitution of the lower grade uranium might affect the Rahab device.

"It's kind of romantic," Fawd suggested as he began to deal the cards.

Anne at once regretted turning on the radio. "It's relaxing," she countered coolly.

He grinned at her from over the top of his cards.

She dropped her discard, ignoring him.

"It occurs to me," he remarked casually, "that no matter how serious the situation, or how high the stakes involved, that we cannot eliminate the man-woman thing."

So now it's the sex gambit, she thought resignedly.

"You're being too hard on Kabir," she said, changing the subject.

His face hardened perceptively. "He was trying to get away."

"You're only guessing. He needs the cocaine; you know how he is about it, and you were deliberately baiting him, leaving it in the safe and knowing he had the combination."

"It's easy to see he wants out," said Fawd. "If we didn't need him, I'd let him go. Being around him now even makes *me* nervous."

"That's understandable," she said. "He feels he has carried out his end of the bargain."

"Not yet, he hasn't."

He played his discard, one needed by Anne to fill out a four-card run. She checked the knock card, laying down her hand with two points under the allowed number. The knock card was a spade.

"Pure blind luck," Fawd said as he exposed his hand, holding over thirty points.

"Skill," she chided him, knowing that if there was one way to get to Fawd Al-Shaer, it was for a woman to beat him at his own game.

"You realize," he told her seriously, "that you're the only one who gives me a run at this game. It's got to have something to do with sex."

"No; it's just because I know you better than most."

"Deal," he told her.

She picked up the cards and shuffled them expertly. It's time, she thought, and she began to deal slowly, not offering a cut.

"Why don't we leave," she offered after a moment.

"What do you mean?"

"Let's pack it up right now while we're still ahead."

He sighed once and picked up his cards, not answering her.

"Well?" she insisted.

"You're beginning to act like Kabir. We're not yet ahead, at least not far enough."

She tried to be as sincere as she could as she suggested, "If we keep on going, it's got to end badly. If that bomb should go off, it would hurt our people a thousand times more than it could help."

"There's no need, or plan, for it to go off," he replied intently. "So long as they do what I ask, and they will; they have no choice. Don't you see, *they have no choice*!"

His vehemence startled her into momentary silence. Then she realized the wisdom of Kate Felton's suggestion that she deal with him delicately. It must be the pressure making him so sensitive. "I suppose you're right," she admitted then.

"Trust me," he assured her. "Or have you forgotten that I promised over a year ago that we had to inform the world, dramatically, of the plight of our brothers and sisters—"

Yes, she thought, and we all made the promise, but not in this way.

"And we promised to intensify the campaign," he further reminded her. "And the Americans were warned, were told in advance, that their interests would suffer unless they opened their eyes to the truth." He threw his cards down on the table. "Don't you see, once this hits the media, the worldwide coverage, even the response, will be enormous. Two million Americans under siege. Why, we can hold them at bay for weeks, even months." He wagged his finger at her for emphasis. "We are about to play the major historical role in shifting world opinion to our side."

He really believes it, she thought incredulously, that holding a couple of million people captive was going to endear them to the rest of the world.

She suddenly felt helpless to reach him.

There was a buzz from the direction of the fireplace, a sound like that of an intercom ringing.

She followed behind as Fawd moved to the control panel located next to the recorder.

"What is it?" she asked curiously.

He reached up to push one button, then tripped a toggle switch. "It's Kabir," he explained. "He wants out of the computer room. The buzz was his signal. I cleared it with this button, then released the door with this switch."

"Sounds like a prison," she commented.

"Not really. Just sound security procedure," and he gestured to the rest of the panel. "The grounds are protected by a system also. There is an intercom system linking all the major rooms in the house." They both turned away from the panel as Kabir came down the stairway.

Anne returned to her chair, noticing that Kabir looked exhausted.

Kabir handed Fawd a long roll of computer tape.

"So what does this tell us?" Fawd asked as he scanned the tape, which obviously meant nothing to him.

"It will work," Kabir said flatly, and he fell onto the long couch, leaning his head back wearily.

"So they have the same figures," Fawd said. "So they know it will work also."

"They're just as aware as we are," said Kabir, apparently too tired to hide the sarcasm in his voice, a very out-of-character role, "that we can in a few seconds still convert Los Angeles into an uninhabitable wasteland."

Fawd walked slowly up to the couch and dropped the tape on Kabir's lap. Stroking his chin thoughtfully, he then moved back across the room to the fireplace. "Why, then," he asked, "did they bother to tell us about the uranium, going through the Suez exercise?" And he turned to face Anne. "It looks like they wanted you in here, wouldn't you say, my dear?"

He was totally paranoid, she thought, seeing the suspicion heavy on his face. Quickly she fell back to one of Kate Felton's alternatives. "I got the impression," she told him, "that they are more interested in where the plutonium is, which might be an even greater threat to them."

Fawd grunted approvingly, obviously taken in by the intrigue.

Diversion, she thought jubilantly, and if she ever got the chance she would hug Kate Felton's neck.

Fawd turned to Kabir. "You're positive you only worked with the uranium?"

Kabir tipped his head forward. "I'm positive that the material in Rahab is the same as that used in the test device."

"So where is the plutonium?" Fawd asked, more to himself than to the others. Walking over to the card table he picked up two rubber balls and began to stalk back and forth before the fireplace, working the balls in his hands. "So Stanley Fielding tricked me, somehow . . ."

Chapter fifteen

5:30 a.m., Friday morning, Pacific Time.

By first light, Bill Morrison had his team in position. With

Ingstrom's three men, he had nine agents spread around the mountain estate. Jerome Mason had stationed himself on the site providing the best view of the southern side of the large house. Alan Hunt had just returned from the cabin CP, and had squatted down next to Mason, reappraising their location in the steadily improving light. They were on the forward slope of a small rise running north and south. The house was about a hundred yards to their front, on a northwest angle. He spotted the chain-link fence circling away about fifty feet below them. The terrain was rough, densely covered with undergrowth and heavy timber. Their best cover between them and the house was a thick stand of manzanita falling away down the slope. He started to rise slowly, curious to see what he could of the house.

"Stay down!" Mason warned him.

Alan obliged, dropping to the ground. "Here's the coffee," he said, placing the quart thermos next to Mason. "And Ingstrom says that the SWAT team is holding at the observatory."

"Anything from Stalmeyer yet?"

They were on radio silence in the close vicinity of the house, except in case of an emergency, and Alan had volunteered to act as the runner, moving back and forth from Mason's position to the cabin CP. "Ingstrom didn't mention it," Alan told him. "Where's Morrison?"

Mason gestured toward the house. "Setting up a second listening device on the other side." And he pushed himself up to rest on his knees, dusting off his back side.

"I can understand why most of us are up here," Alan commented, "but why the head of the CIA himself? I should think he's got plenty of qualified field people—"

"He's got his reasons," said Mason laconically as he began to rearrange the several pieces of equipment hastily piled around the site. Alan moved to help him. He counted four automatic rifles, two shotguns, two radios, two tear-gas launchers, plus assorted boxes of ammunition and food supplies. "On your next trip," Mason told him, "have Ingstrom bring up two of the SWAT people, their best two snipers, and make sure they have food and water." He picked up a pair of binoculars and handed them to Alan. "Go up slow, with the glasses up."

Alan took the glasses, first checking their focus on a distant tree trunk and then slowly inching his way up. The exposed side of the house jumped into view.

"The best as we can tell," Mason said, "the area behind those bay windows is a main room. It has the best view, probably the living room. Note the massive chimney.

"Cathedral ceiling," Alan speculated, and he saw that the exterior of the house was stone, driftwood rock mixed in with pink and gray flagstone. "It's built like a fortress," he commented as he scanned beyond the bay windows, picking up the flying redwood deck running on down and around the other, blind side of the house. "Can't we get a plan of the house?" he asked.

"We're trying right now," Mason said. "But the place is so old."

"What about the last owner?" Alan asked. He was straining now, focusing the glasses back and forth along the side of the house, searching for some sign of movement.

"They're in Europe," Mason said.

Alan moved off to his left, working along the inner and more open grounds. "What's the smaller building?"

"Looks like a storage shed. Notice the chopping block. Also, around the front of the house, where you can see part of the driveway."

Alan swung the glasses slowly.

"See those bushes crowding the driveway?"

"Yeah."

"Those are manzanita bushes," Mason told him proudly.

"No pepper trees, though," Alan pointed out.

"No, not up here," Mason admitted.

Alan sat back down, letting the glasses hang loose around his neck. "Is the fence hot?"

"Negative. And we didn't expect it to be. An electric fence in this restricted fire area is illegal. Fawd is smarter than that. Ingstrom's boys found both trip wires and electric-eye surveillance just inside the fence. The perimeter is covered like a blanket."

"So, what do we do now?" Alan asked. He realized that his belly was turning over queasily.

"We wait while Morrison does his tricks. He's hoping to find a way to make the roof and get a line down the chimney." He looked sideways at Alan. "You've got to relax," he said understandingly, and he reached up trying futilely to smooth down his great mane of nearly white hair. "Between the mosquitoes, chiggers, and ticks, we'll all be lucky to get out of here alive anyway."

Alan felt encouraged by the older man's comment, a key to

his mood, which finally seemed to be on the upgrade.

Mason reached inside his shirt pocket to pull out a small, folded piece of paper. "While we've got a spare minute, I'll pass this message along from Bill Morrison. It's from the Israeli Ambassador's office in Washington in response to your inquiry about the return of the money. It states that Tel Aviv has no official record, or knowledge of any kind of agreement or transaction engaging either yours or Joshua's services. They also deny any knowledge of an operation described as Rahab." He casually folded the paper up and returned it to his pocket.

"You've got to be kidding," said Alan incredulously.

"That's their official position. However, Bill was advised, off the record, that if such an agreement had been reached, that you and Joshua certainly earned your pay."

Alan reached up to scratch the hairline above his left ear. "So what does that mean?"

Jerome Mason simply turned up his hands. "They refuse to take it back."

"Incredible," Alan stated. "Over forty thousand bucks—"

"Not incredible at all. Within the next few days Rahab will be spread all over the media. The investigative reporters are going to have a field day, exposing you and Joshua as hired conspirators, maybe even as outright Israeli spies. It will make interesting reading. Tel Aviv is simply taking the path of least exposure, minimizing both their direct involvement and that of Wolf Shertok." Mason pushed himself erect, staring curiously toward the house. "Why don't you break us out some coffee?" he said under his breath. "It looks like we're going to be stuck here for a while."

5:45 a.m.

The blackboard behind Jerome Mason's desk was again covered with a new set of scrawled options. Les Stalmeyer dropped his chalk into the channel, then wiped his hands on his shirt as he moved to sit down. Doctor Ewing Melbourne watched from his own chair, sensing the other man's discouragement, but all he could do was to continue clicking the pipe stem between his front teeth.

"So we can't blow up the place," Stalmeyer noted, the dejection heavy in his voice.

"Ingstrom suggested we deliver a thousand-pounder dead center—"

"Which is why Ingstrom is well placed where he is—in the

field," Stalmeyer said. "What about the option to flood the site with electronic signals, jamming all the known frequencies?"

"Still not foolproof," Melbourne argued. "He could get the signal out over an underground cable. They could easily have a remote booster."

"So," said Stalmeyer wearily, "we can't storm it by force, can't blow it up, and we can't jam it."

"Not as of this moment," Melbourne conceded.

"All right, then," Stalmeyer replied. "Let's bring in a fresh team, electronic and weapons people. Ingstrom built me a list yesterday of local people, and they're standing by. We've got some good brains out here on the coast. There's Litton, General Dynamics, Lockheed, plus the military."

"Let's set it for one o'clock," Melbourne suggested.

"Make it noon," said Stalmeyer. "I'm putting you in charge. Get with Bradshaw right now and start calling them in."

"You realize you're going to have to tell them the whole story."

Stalmeyer shook his head in the affirmative. "I don't see what else we can do."

"We can find the bomb itself."

Stalmeyer grunted derisively.

"Tell Morrison to look for a buried cable," Melbourne went on. "Get with the telephone company; they've got detection gear," and he paused briefly. "And, don't forget Kate Felton's thesis, that the human factors' end usually accounts for the more decisive action."

"You mean her extemporaneous factor theory—"

"She's played umpire on too many of these terrorist exercises. As she sees it, a planned situation exists, which only needs a catalyst, something to get it moving in an unplanned direction, which then requires impromptu decisions. So, we've got that to develop if we can. At any rate, we've got to keep trying, sir."

Stalmeyer came out of his chair with a renewed show of energy. "You're right, and I'm sorry I started going negative on you," and he strode off toward Ingstrom's desk and the mobile radio.

5:50 a.m.

The early sun angling in through the bay windows brought

light to the room, and Kabir opened his eyelids just enough to inspect the area. Anne Delemar was still in her chair next to the card table, but she was slumped over now, either asleep or dozing. From the sound of Fawd's departing footsteps, Kabir assumed he was in the kitchen, probably after another cup of coffee. Kabir had not been asleep at all, very much to the contrary. For the past few hours, he had been biding his time while pretending to rest, waiting and hoping for the break he desperately needed. His final plan had come quickly, once he had deduced the way to control the door to the computer room. He had neutralized the destruct timer under the staircase. That, plus the presence of Anne Delemar, whose attitude he had been carefully going over in his mind. Alone, he didn't stand a chance. He closed his eyes once again as he heard Fawd coming in from the kitchen.

He listened, then, tracking Fawd across the room.

Minutes passed, and he fought with himself to stay awake.

He heard the sound of Fawd's cup on the card table.

Again, Fawd moved across the room, but this time up the stairway.

Kabir considered his chances, and he opened his eyes more fully this time. He shifted his weight on the couch, flexing his forearm muscles. The sound of running water came to him, telling him that Fawd was in the bathroom at the head of the stairs.

A buzzer started ringing on the monitor console—
Bizzzzzt.

Kabir came upright, cursing under his breath.

Anne Delemar was also up, staring blankly across the room.

Fawd came down the stairs, walked briskly to the console and reached up to punch a light button. The buzzing stopped. Fawd studied the panel briefly. "It's the inside, lower trip," he said then.

"Number seven?" Kabir asked.

"Yes," Fawd answered, obviously annoyed.

"What does that mean?" Anne asked them.

"There's an animal path through that zone," Kabir explained. "It happens about once a day, especially early in the morning like this. A rabbit, probably," and he pushed himself off the couch. "I'll check it out."

"No," Fawd told him harshly. "You two stay here." He tied his robe more securely around his waist. Heading for the sliding glass door, he stopped to pick up the shotgun standing in the corner near the window. The gun was a single-shot 410 gauge, which they had been using to frighten the small game away from the grounds.

Outside the door, Fawd moved to his right, and was out of sight in a second.

Kabir felt his heart pounding as he jumped up, moving to sit down opposite Anne Delemar. "There is a way we can stop this," he blurted hurriedly, "but you've got to help me."

Anne stared at him in total disbelief.

"I'm telling you the truth—"

"He put you up to this."

Kabir wrung his hands helplessly. "Don't you see—he's gone crazy . . . talking about extending this for weeks, even months. Please, please," and he was pleading now, "we only have a few minutes."

Anne stood up, pushing away from the small table. She bit once on her lower lip. "All right; what do we do?"

"I can divert him for at least two, maybe three minutes."

"How?"

"Never mind," he said quickly, and he pushed her to the sliding glass door, glancing apprehensively over the grounds. "Down there, the shed—"

"The motorcycles?"

"Yes. Go there now, and quickly. Can you ride?"

"Of course."

He pushed her out the door, following behind a step. "Then get moving, get help!" He shoved her across the landing. "But you've got to get back here within four hours."

"What are you going to do?"

"The booster," he hissed under his breath. "I'll take down the last two circuits—" and he grimaced abruptly, shaking his head. "Never mind that; get moving, and he turned back through the sliding glass door.

With Anne on her way, Kabir ran to the console next to the fireplace. He had pulled a dime out of his pocket, which he used to lever the four quarter-turn fasteners securing an inspection panel. With the panel hanging loose, he reached inside to the exposed mechanical component section. Using his fingernail, he broke the contact arm away from one particular circuit breaker. He was turning down the last of the quarter turns when he realized that the nearby intercom speaker was humming, indicating an "on" station somewhere in the house.

He flattened himself against the flagstone wall, shivering cold, realizing that Fawd was in the house and had been listening over the intercom.

Which way will he come? Kabir wondered frantically, as he pushed away from the wall to bound up the stairs. It was both his guess and hope that Fawd would go after Anne first. His only chance now was to try to play it out.

Fawd Al-Shaer rounded the corner of the flying redwood deck. Anne Delemar had already made the shed. Tossing the shotgun down, he slipped inside the den and hurried to the gun cabinet, where he selected the small-bore 220 rifle, a varmint gun, with a variable power scope. Besides its four-thousand feet-per-second muzzle velocity, it was unique because its slug travelled practically flat for the first three hundred yards. It occurred to him as he vaulted back toward the door that the life of Anne Delemar could now be measured in seconds.

Jerome Mason was on his feet, exposing himself, the binoculars glued to his eyes. "It's the girl," he reported excitedly.

Alan Hunt jumped upright, straining to see.

"She's in the shed!" Mason exclaimed as he shifted his glasses back to the house. A figure came onto the flying deck, and Jerome Mason had the sinking sensation that the man holding the rifle was Fawd Al-Shaer.

Fawd simply leaned onto the forward rail of the deck, waiting patiently for Anne Delemar to come out of the shed.

Kabir hit the computer room on a dead run. He fell to the floor on his stomach, turned the safe combination off its half-lock position, and pulled the heavy lid open with a force he didn't know he possessed. Glancing over his shoulder he saw the metal door closing off the outside hallway light. He pushed himself to his haunches, letting his head hang between his knees as he gasped for breath. We're committed, he admitted to himself, and he stood up to move to the computer console. With what he had already done, it would take him less than one minute to jam the last two telephone circuits. Which gave Anne Delemar almost four hours to save his life in return.

Jerome Mason watched helplessly as Fawd pushed the rifle into his shoulder.

"Do something!" Alan Hunt shouted vehemently, his face screwed up into an agonized mask.

Jerome Mason was unable to sort it all out. It came to him that he could not just stand by and watch. What difference did it make, anyway, that Fawd knew he was surrounded. Reaching for the nearest automatic rifle, he punched the safety off, swung the weapon over his head, and squeezed the trigger at the same time.

Anne Delemar had come out of the shed.

Fawd flinched as he squeezed the trigger—distracted by the staccato sound of an automatic weapon hammering into his left ear.

The small-bore bullet streaked across the grounds, entering Anne Delemar's back slightly off center to the right. It hit her right clavicle, exploding, spinning her off the bike.

Alan Hunt crashed down through the manzanita with the force and determination of an angry bear.

Jerome Mason tried to give him cover, spraying the area above Fawd's head.

Fawd ducked back into the house.

Watching Alan vault the chain-link fence, Mason thought that it might be all over. Kate Felton's extemporaneous factor had just been pumped into the situation. It was now time for impromptu decisions. He turned to the radio and cranked it into life. Trying to hold the image of Fawd Al-Shaer in his mind as he waited for Ingstrom to acknowledge, he then remembered Ben Caplan's descriptive profile on this perhaps his own worst enemy. *The man is a cobra . . .*

The cobra was now back in his lair, and he knew his sanctuary was no longer a secret.

Finding the emergency door to the computer room closed, Fawd loped down the connecting hallway to the staircase. As he dashed down the carpeted stairs, he reminded himself that Kabir was consistently a predictable sort. Breathing hard, he pulled up before the wall-mounted console. There were several warning lights glowing on the monitor board, indicating breaches in the yard security, so he shut them down, thinking that he must take things in order. Kabir first. He flipped the toggle switch to release the door to the computer room. He was turning away when he noticed that the actuator signal button below the switch was still on red, reporting that the door was still closed. Flipping the switch several times, he finally slammed the intercom switch for the computer room, angrily shouting Kabir's name again and again.

No response.

Next he dashed up the stairs, hoping that the indicator light was out of order.

Anne Delemar was still conscious when Alan reached her.

He kicked the motorcycle away from her, bending down, asking her gently, "Where is it?" Her face was ashen, and she didn't seem to recognize him at first. As he moved her gently behind the cover of the shed, he saw the great crimson blotch on her right shoulder. He grabbed the pullover at her neck, and ripped it apart.

The wound in the front was huge, the size of a tennis ball, a throbbing mass of exposed flesh and bone.

Oh, no, he thought deliriously, please no—

"It's bad, isn't it?" she said weakly.

He shook his head no, trying to compose himself, thinking that she would bleed to death in five more minutes.

He was aware then that there was someone at his elbow, and he whirled to face the dark blue uniform, one of Morrison's men. He looked over the agent's shoulder to see another quartering in toward them, running low, an automatic weapon in his hands also.

"She needs help," Alan said helplessly.

"There's a medic with the SWAT team," the agent told him, and he put his weapon down to bend over Anne. "We need a compress," he told Alan, and he looked around briefly, finally picking up the plastic windscreen shield, apparently knocked off the helmet strapped to the rear of the motorcycle. "This will do fine," he said, and he went to work expertly, as though he knew what he was doing.

Anne reached up weakly, took hold of Alan's arm, pulling him toward her. He bent down, turning his ear to her mouth and listened briefly. He sat up then, seeing that the second agent was moving in to help.

"Get her out of here fast," Alan said haltingly, and he lurched off toward the house, clambering up the incline without regard for the path, his eyes fixed on and only seeing the sliding glass door.

Watching through his binoculars, Jerome Mason stood dumbfounded as Alan stormed the landing in front of the bay windows. The fool wasn't even armed! In the next instant Alan kicked his way through the sliding screen door, disappearing into the house. *He's trying to give Anne Delemar cover!*

Mason dropped the glasses to his chest.

Alan Hunt, a well-intentioned mongoose, was now in the snake's lair.

Mason turned thoughtfully to the radio, calling for Bill Morrison. The best he could do now was to try to give Alan some back-up, and he hoped that the young man in his rage would not forget that he was closer than anyone else to the Rahab trigger.

Walking more slowly and deliberately now, Fawd made his way back to the staircase. He still held the small-bore rifle in his right hand. At the top of the stairs he hesitated, taking the time to remove the actuator box from its belt clip, holding it in his left hand. He forced himself to take stock. They were out there now, desperate men perhaps, and a foolish sniper might be tempted to take him.

He elected not to start the program yet; there was a good chance that he could still salvage the situation. He still had the advantage. Both Anne Delemar and Kabir had tried their thing. Nothing had changed. He still controlled Rahab. He only had to convince Kabir to end his foolish rebellion; then all things would be back to normal. He started down the stairs, stopping after the third step. There was something wrong with the room.

The screen door was broken down.

Alan Hunt stepped out from behind the bottom of the staircase.

Fawd did not move. His left thumb was on the first button.

Alan showed his hands, palms up.

The eyes of Fawd Al-Shaer narrowed to suspicious slits.

"I'm alone," Alan said softly.

"You must be the one called Alan Hunt."

Alan nodded once, slowly.

"You are also insane," Fawd said icily.

"Along with the rest of the world," Alan said, "except, of course, for you."

Fawd allowed a shallow grin to pass across his face. "Don't waste your time trying to provoke me." He walked the rest of the way down the stairs, satisfied that Hunt was in fact alone and here on an idiot's mission. Keeping Hunt covered with the rifle, he checked out the rest of the room, finding it empty.

"You're kind of out of character, aren't you?" he offered as he pulled up on the higher vantage point of the fireplace mantel. "I mean, playing the role of the enraged lover," and he was smiling again. There was another warning light blinking on the monitor board, and he reached up with the back of his left hand to clear it off.

"I'm enjoying it," Alan admitted candidly. He too was using the time to survey the room. There was a door no more than two steps behind him. "I'd say you're even more out of character," he proposed then. For the present moment, conversation was his best and perhaps only recourse, especially if he could taunt Fawd into a mistake.

"How is that, my young friend?" Fawd said cordially.

"You're holding that silly little box, acting like you're god, and it won't even work."

Fawd grunted. "That's a poor bluff."

"Ask Kabir," Alan proposed. "He's cut your circuits."

"No, no," Fawd assured him, shaking his head. "Kabir is a fool but he is an even greater coward, and he fears me most of all."

In the computer room, Kabir had been listening to the conversation. While he could only guess at what had taken place outside, he presumed that the estate perimeter had been breached. Anne Delemar must've made it out, since Alan Hunt now knew that he had altered the trigger circuitry. He reached up calmly to lever the switch on his intercom line, and when he spoke, he enunciated his words carefully, "The man is correct, Fawd. You see, I bypassed the cable circuits minutes ago—"

Fawd jerked to his right, staring unbelievingly at the intercom speaker.

Locked in the computer room, Kabir slammed his fist into the wall. He quickly levered the switch again, and this time his voice was higher pitched, frantic, as he addressed himself to Alan Hunt, "Don't let him use the phone! Keep him away from the phone!" The actuator box was nothing more than a remote control box. Without it, Fawd could still dial the necessary three local numbers, in the proper sequence, from any telephone. Kabir slumped to the floor. Prior to cutting the last two circuits, he had reset the trigger timer. And he could still lead them to the bomb. It should turn out well for him, after all.

Fawd had been staring down at the box in his hand. He finally pushed the first button, then the second—it failed to light. He released the second button expectantly, waiting—

Alan took one measured step toward the door, then turned to blast his way into what he discovered was the kitchen, which he crossed on a dead run, hitting the back outside door with his shoulder. The dutch door collapsed, and he sprawled onto the flagstone paving of the adjacent walkway.

By the time he got his rifle turned, Fawd saw that he was too late. Chasing Hunt would only run him into the waiting arms of those on the north side of the house. He figured he would more wisely work his way back into control. Clipping the actuator back to his waist, he moved to the phone located on the end table next to the couch. He lined up the three phone numbers in his mind and started dialing the first.

Alan circled the house on the north side, where he found Bill Morrison with two men near the driveway.

"The telephone wires!" Alan yelled breathlessly, and he pointed up to the corner of the house. "Shoot them out!" he screamed.

"You mean knock them down," Morrison said uncertainly.

"Blow them down!" Alan yelled wildly. "He's going to trigger the bomb over the phone!"

The three men instantly raised their automatic weapons, and in the ensuing burst of gunfire Alan watched the entire corner of the house explode. The remnants of the telephone lines fell limply to the driveway.

Fawd heard the gunfire, and he was not surprised to find the phone dead before he could finish the second number. He wasted several seconds cursing Alan Hunt. Still calm, he moved to the base of the staircase and depressed the paneling with his knee. A section of the panel slipped open on a piano hinge, revealing a standard one-hour timer. He closed his eyes briefly, estimating the time he would need, before setting the timer on five minutes. About to close the panel, he hesitated. Kabir would never trap himself in the computer room, knowing the house could be blown out from under him. Fawd grabbed the timer frame, working the assembly out of its socket. Rotating the base upward, he saw that one of the two wires was not attached. Clever, clever, Fawd had to admit to himself. But not clever enough, my predictable friend. Smiling to himself, he wrapped the stripped end of the loose wire around its post, securing it with the knurled lock nut. He punched the timer back into place, resetting it to an even five minutes.

Kabir pushed himself to his feet. He had considered that the circumstances still might not see him out of the room within his allotted four hours. Fawd, with all his skill and luck, could easily orchestrate a standoff. Moving listlessly and without feeling, he walked slowly to the blackboard, one of the more essential items comprising a project manager's private office. He picked up an eraser and began to clear away the carefully scrawled computations. There was no address for the garage that he could recall; the old building was simply the only one left on what remained of the street. Rahab's nest. The garage on Pepper Tree Lane. He lifted his arm, feeling its weight. He paused for a second, before starting to print in bold letters what he now considered a far more appropriate message, *MOKSHA*! He dropped the chalk in its channel, turning away toward the floor safe and its small vials with black screw caps.

Fawd was pushing through the sliding glass door when he realized that he actually had the lever to force Kabir to repair the trigger circuitry. Of course, the idiot would do anything once he knew the plastic in the basement was now armed! Turning back toward the fireplace control panel, Fawd figured he only had to inform Kabir, neutralize the staircase timer, and allow Kabir a limited time to comply.

Back to ground zero.

He had one foot on the mantel, reaching up with his right hand, when the panel literally exploded before him—

He ducked to his left, closing his eyes against the shower of debris.

The short burst of gunfire had been from his right, and he spun away to his left, opening his eyes to see Alan Hunt poised in the kitchen doorway, an automatic rifle still in his shoulder. The weapon was pointed at his chest.

The two men stared at each other.

It dawned on Fawd that Alan Hunt dared not kill him, that the burst was only a warning. "Go ahead and shoot," Fawd taunted him. "Then you can try to find Rahab by yourself!" He could see enough out of the corner of his eye to verify that the intercom controls were totally disabled—the Kabir option had just been frustrated by a sheer stroke of luck.

There were about three minutes left on the staircase timer.

Fawd angrily jerked the trigger on the 220.

Alan Hunt ducked back into the kitchen as the slug smashed through the adjacent door jamb. The door swung closed. Fawd quickly pumped another round through the door before slipping through the sliding glass door. Then he turned on the landing, firing a third round through the kitchen door, hoping to keep Alan Hunt pinned in the kitchen just a little longer. He discarded the now unneeded rifle before starting quickly down the path. Out in the open now, he pulled the actuator box off his belt, held it out in front of him as he hurried down the path toward the shed. Those on the edge of the perimeter didn't yet know that Fawd Al-Shaer was really vulnerable.

The twenty pounds of plastic explosive in the basement would give him the needed diversion. With a normal share of luck, he could make the safe house in Sierra Madre, where there was a phone which would work.

Alan Hunt pushed warily into the living room, not surprised to find it empty. Bill Morrison, with one man behind him, followed when Alan motioned an all clear.

"He may be outside," Alan said as he started toward the sliding glass door. "You two hit the upstairs, and watch out for Kabir."

The two men started up the stairs, holding their weapons at the ready.

On the outside landing, Alan saw Fawd pushing off on a motorcycle, heading south. Alan put down his weapon, exchanging it for the 220 rifle. Watching Fawd carefully, he levered a round into the chamber. The shot would be an easy one, and he raised the rifle to his right shoulder, thinking calmly that he must try to wing the man only.

He lined up the crosshairs on Fawd's left thigh.

A string of automatic fire ripped the driftwood rock above his head.

Alan ducked involuntarily.

A second burst laced the stone again, and he saw that one of Morrison's men was standing off to the right of the shed, his weapon now aimed at Alan's chest. The agent motioned for Alan to drop the rifle.

He doesn't know! Alan thought helplessly. The man was only doing his job, protecting Fawd Al-Shaer. Alan obediently dropped the rifle. He vaulted the landing, hitting the decline on a dead run. By the time he reached the shed, Fawd was at least a hundred yards away, gaining in speed. Another one of Morrison's men stood about ten yards off to the left, watching, but obviously not knowing what to do. Alan stumbled into the shed, snatched at the one remaining motorcycle. There wasn't time to try to explain.

Jerome Mason was befuddled at the strange turn of events.

Bill Morrison had just reported that Fawd apparently no longer had his hand on the trigger.

And there he went now, down the hill, with Alan Hunt in

hot pursuit. He was reaching to alert the standby helicopter when the explosion hit.

The entire center of the house was blown skyward in an enormous eruption of debris and smoke; the shock wave was immediate and awesome, knocking Mason flat on his back, stunning him. He dazedly rolled to his stomach, trying to cover his head as the ground around him was peppered with flying rocks and bits of mortar. He was hit by something, just above his right ear, and he lapsed into unconsciousness.

The fragmentary reports reaching Les Stalmeyer were jumbled and confused, giving him an altogether uncertain picture of the action taking place on Mount Wilson.

Anne Delemar had been seriously wounded, by whom and for what reason nobody knew.

Jerome Mason had also been injured, unconscious at last report.

The estate house had been blown up, totally destroyed.

Bill Morrison and several of his men were unaccounted for.

Burt Ingstrom had finally lost his cool and was near hysteria, having allowed a fire fighting team to breach perimeter security to contain the minor brush fire ignited by the explosion.

The SWAT commander was moving in, under his own cognizance.

And, to top it all off, Fawd himself was thought to have escaped.

The situation had gone totally to pot.

There was no effective leader left on Mount Wilson.

Les Stalmeyer hurried out of the CP office, on his way to the nearby helicopter pad. He stopped for a second outside the hangar door, glancing east, out across the sprawling city of Los Angeles. At least, he thought gratefully, we're still here.

The upper part of the descent was the more difficult, the ridge lines harsh and implacable, and Fawd took his time, manipulating the machine under him with a calm and certain confidence. His first advantage was that he knew the various links between the down-falling fire trails. Topping a ridge now, he braked down on the decomposed granite, turning to look back over his shoulder. Alan Hunt had gone down at the explosion, and, with any luck, either he or his machine had come out of the fall disabled. Fawd cranked the throttle, watching the higher ground, expertly tracking the terrain in selected segments.

Higher up, the smoke from the explosion had mushroomed out, starting to drift lazily eastward. So, he thought, Kabir had finally made it out.

Movement from above caught his eye.

The swiftly moving bike and its rider cleared a crest about two hundred yards away. Fawd swore under his breath once again. The man was a devil, he thought angrily as he watched the machine drop out of sight. Then, before he could turn to start away, the pursuing motorcycle jumped another crest and was close enough for Fawd to see Alan Hunt high off his seat, the front wheel up.

Fawd slammed his machine in gear, fishtailing away off the fire trail.

His advantage, too, was in the strength of his forearms and wrists.

Having recovered from his fall, Alan had cleared his mind of any thought except to stay on the machine. A spill in this terrain and it would all be over for sure. The bike under him was of a far more powerful and exotic breed than the dirt bikes he and Joshua had used around the ranch. But the terrain was similar, and he concentrated now, getting more used to the machine with each passing second. Another crest loomed up ahead, and he hit the throttle, powering over the ridge.

Fawd's dust was less than a hundred yards ahead now.

It was still cool on the slope of the mountain, and the rising sun slanted in brutally from the east, sharp and contrasting from the bluish-purple of the western horizon. Les Stalmeyer held up his right hand to shade his eyes as he squinted down at the more gentle foothills now passing under the helicopter. They had just passed the familiar landmark of the Santa Anita racetrack. He felt his stomach bottom out as the chopper began to strain for a higher altitude.

He used the next couple of minutes to call Burt Ingstrom, advising him of his expected ETA.

The pilot jabbed him with his elbow, pointing down, off to their right.

Les Stalmeyer picked out the two motorcycles. He grabbed the gyro glasses, focusing in on the area. Two riders, moving seemingly in slow motion, the pace deceptive from his height. The bikes moved in and out of the long shadows, their dust trails lingering in the still air. He ordered the pilot to drop down. In another minute he identified the trailing rider as Alan Hunt.

He realized then that the front rider had to be Fawd Al-Shaer!

Alan was within fifty yards of the front bike now, and he felt a new sense of hope because he could virtually follow directly in Fawd's tracks while the other man had to make the trail selection. He shifted his weight farther forward while at the same time cranking the throttle up a quarter turn.

Fawd fought the temptation to look over his shoulder.

He increased speed, forced now to concentrate on the ground jumping up at him. His grip was still strong, but he felt the strain in his thighs as he risked another glance at the helicopter holding above them.

The fire trail was a short dog leg, left then right, and Fawd miscalculated the dropping distance between the two sharp turns. He made it through the left turn a little too much on the high side, so that as he shifted to his right, he overshot. As he went airborne, he struggled to right the machine, seeing only blackness below him.

He skidded along the edge of the escarpment on his right side, letting the bike go finally, thrusting his hands out in front in the typical self-protecting gesture of a rider going down at high speed. He bottomed heavily on his stomach. The white box was ripped loose from his waist.

The motorcycle launched off into midair.

Fawd felt himself going over the edge of the adjacent cliff. He grasped out with his hands, clawing at the underbrush.

Alan also lost control as he hit the dog leg. Seeing that Fawd had gone down, he tried to brake, locking his wheels, which put him into a bumpy slide. He pushed off the bike quickly, tumbling away to his right, trying to keep himself on the more even ground of the fire trail.

Les Stalmeyer watched like a man hypnotized. Fawd had disappeared over the edge of a cliff, while Alan Hunt was sprawled in the middle of the nearby trail. Stalmeyer came out of his own shock and turned to the pilot. "Find a place to put this thing down," he told him, hearing the break in his own voice.

Alan Hunt rolled to his feet. His legs were like cooked spaghetti, and he weaved uncertainly, trying to determine if and where he might be hurt. He took a tentative step, pulling his elbows in. He cried out then, recoiling from the stabbing pain in his right rib cage. He wanted to breathe hard but couldn't, gasping instead in the now settling dust. He staggered off the trail to his left, moving around his own machine, following the path ripped out of the underbrush. At the edge of the cliff he knelt carefully to look over the edge, reaching up to shade his eyes against the angular sun. His breath stopped in his throat.

Fawd was about twelve feet down the face of the cliff.

The white box was caught in the crook of an exposed cedar root.

Fawd was hanging free at the end of the three-foot chain, his body turning slowly. His right hand still gripped the chain just above his right ear.

Before he turned away, Alan noticed that both of Fawd's hands were a bloody mess, suggesting he must have fought with the chain before it had finally strangled him to death.

Epilogue

The Navy Department sedan dropped off the freeway at Del Mar Heights Road. As they crossed over the freeway, heading west toward the coast, Joshua Bain shifted self-consciously in his seat. He suspected he still smelled of stale alcohol and old sardines. He turned his window down another notch, hoping to ventilate the car. It was getting dark outside, and the cool air felt good on his face.

"Fielding would want to be here," he suggested.

Les Stalmeyer opened his eyes. Seated next to Joshua in the rear seat, he leaned his head forward and reached up to rub his eyes. "He'd only complicate things; besides, we have his statement."

Joshua supposed the Attorney General was right, or, at least it was within the realm of his office to be right when he wanted to be. Joshua followed his companion's cue and relaxed back into his seat, closing his own eyes. The day's casualties had finally been sorted out. The dead included Bill Morrison, along with two of his men, making the CIA the heaviest loser. Also the man known as Kabir. And, finally, the corpse of Fawd Al-Shaer, whose body lay unclaimed in the county morgue in the City of Los Angeles, California.

Jerome Mason would make it.

So would Anne Delemar, and Joshua Bain felt especially better at that thought, as no doubt did his friend, Alan Hunt, who had come down off the mountain with nothing more than a cracked rib.

Ben Caplan had been right in favoring the mongoose.

Rahab was in the process of being disarmed by a team directed by Ewing Melbourne, the gentlest and most deserving of scientists. Joshua assumed the Doctor would use the most simple method, avoiding, hopefully, his tendency to procrastinate. Joshua supposed he should introduce Melbourne to Edwin Fielding, who could give the sometimes reluctant scientist a crash course on how to economically use one's time.

Rahab had been located quickly by the telephone company, following the discovery of an automatic dialing device buried not far from the destroyed mountain hideout. A most fortuitous discovery, in the words of Les Stalmeyer, who had pointed out that had the dialing device been in the house itself, they probably would've had to evacuate the city.

Fortuitous, as Joshua recalled, was just a fancy word for luck.

"What will happen to the Delemar woman?" he asked, looking up to see they had turned left on the old coast highway.

"Not much, if anything," Stalmeyer conceded dryly, suggesting, too, that his mind was preoccupied elsewhere.

So, Joshua thought, it looked like Rancho Canaan was going to have a couple of convalescents around for a while. He was smiling to himself as the car braked down. They had stopped on a side street near the ocean. Joshua noted the curb number for the house across the street; it was odd and one higher than the address of the Del Mar estate belonging to Wolf Shertok. They were parked behind a dark blue sedan with two men in the front seat. One of the men got out, walked back to the car. Les Stalmeyer rolled down his window and flashed his ID.

"Are the Fieldings still inside?" Stalmeyer asked.

"Yes, sir. They are all still inside."

"Wait for us here," Stalmeyer told him. He then gestured to their driver, who moved the car around the sedan to pull into the long curving driveway fronting the house.

At the front door, Wolf Shertok greeted the two men without apparent surprise. He was dressed in tennis shorts and a short-sleeved shirt open at the neck, with a pair of leather sandals on his bare feet.

Joshua quickly introduced the Attorney General, and Wolf Shertok, with his usual flawless self-control, merely shook his hand and invited them in.

"We'd like to see the Fieldings, please," Stalmeyer said, still holding his position near the front door. "Would you please ask them to come here now."

"Of course," Shertok said pleasantly. "You caught us having dinner."

"I'm sorry," Stalmeyer apologized. "But it is very urgent."

Shertok hesitated for a moment. "They are my guests; can you please explain to me—"

"In due time, yes," Stalmeyer said curtly.

Joshua watched suspiciously as the professor moved away down the hallway. "I don't like it," he said under his breath.

"He's got one minute," Stalmeyer said.

Shertok returned in less than the allotted time, with the Fielding family following behind. He stood aside then, allowing them to pass. Joshua took the extended hand of Edwin Fielding and pulled him out onto the front porch. Martha Fielding and her son followed behind.

"What's wrong, Joshua?" the older Fielding inquired puzzledly.

Joshua still didn't answer, leading them quickly to the waiting Navy sedan.

With the three of them settled in the back seat, he finally spoke, "This car will take you home. Stanley is there now, waiting, and he is just fine," and he turned away, anxious to be back in the house, satisfied that his coded message to Jerome Mason had been complied with, that the fact of Stanley Fielding's apprehension had been kept away from this house.

Shertok escorted them down a hallway, out onto the patio, where they sat down at a metal table near the swimming pool. Joshua recalled that the western horizon looked the same as it had the evening Ben Caplan had been killed. The setting thus seemed to be even more appropriate.

"What is it, gentlemen?" Shertok asked as he took his chair. "Are you here officially, or what . . . "

"That hasn't been decided yet," Stalmeyer said. "But, to start with, we'll go on the assumption that we're here off the record."

"Fair enough," said Shertok. "So, what's happening? I understand from my sources that you've had a good day of it."

Joshua Bain had during the day reviewed Wolf Shertok's past options many times, especially the older man's responses to those options, and he finally realized that he had lost all respect for Professor Wolf Shertok, that he now held him in complete contempt. "It's what *has* happened," Joshua said coldly, "that brings us here. You see, old man, we took Stanley Fielding into custody earlier today, and, he has told us everything, right down to the last ugly little detail." He noticed that the Professor was unmoved at the revelation.

"Aha," Shertok exclaimed. "I suspect that your Mister Fielding is in trouble, and it appears he is trying to implicate others in an effort to clear himself."

"Horse manure," said Joshua.

"Tell him," said Stalmeyer.

"It's very simple, appallingly so," said Joshua. "Even from the very beginning, where it all started." He had to compose himself before going on. "When Fielding was contacted by Fawd, who was posing as an Israeli agent, he at first went along with the ploy. As he explained it, it was the opportunity to help Israel. Fawd dazzled him all right, but after only a few days Fielding began to have second thoughts. He was confused, needed help badly. And, who better to turn to at such a time than the renowned Professor Wolf Shertok. Of course, since you're a kind of resident for Ha Mossad, you immediately contacted Tel Aviv to confirm the Armatrex program. Naturally, Tel Aviv gave you a negative. Rightly deciding Fawd was a fraud, you then developed the plan to switch the plutonium for the lower grade uranium. You were able to persuade Fielding to help; but, you knew Tel Aviv would wisely turn the plan down. After all, stealing plutonium from the United States, no matter how vital the material, would in no way be worth the long-range consequences, especially if the plot were fully uncovered. That would be an outright disaster—"

Shertok laughed shortly, raising his hand in a placating gesture. "You're not making sense in accusing me; you've just pointed out yourself that Tel Aviv would turn down such a scheme."

"Not Tel Aviv," Joshua pressed on, "but you, personally, my fine feathered Professor. You figured the way. Not only could you thwart a hated enemy agent and expose him in due time, but, you could also pick up the plutonium in the process. Ironically enough, your plan at that point in time could be considered understandable, certainly justified for one in your position. Finding out later that the agent was Fawd Al-Shaer must've come as pure frosting on the cake."

"What good would the plutonium do me?" Shertok snapped, his demeanor hardening.

Joshua laughed then. "That was the least of your problems. After a respectable length of time, the plutonium would turn up on the black market, Buenos Aires, Hong Kong, wherever, and there's little doubt that a man of your ability could find a way to work it into Israel without implicating yourself." He paused reflectively. "The terrible tragedy is that at an early point you could have pulled the string on Fawd, and none of this would have happened. But, you wanted more, how you must've wanted more . . . "

"A fairy tale," Shertok proposed. "What about the dead man in Mexico City? We all agreed that was Fawd's doing."

"Oh, yes," Joshua seemed to agree, "Fawd was involved in the exchange. But, it was *his* man who was killed and cremated. And, that was the one instance when you really put one over on Fawd." Joshua turned to Stalmeyer. "Prior to going to Mexico City, Fielding began to suspect that no matter which side he was working on, he would have to pay with his life. He was the incriminating link, the only outside witness. And, of course, he correctly deduced that he had to be eliminated. As he explained to me on the boat, Shertok prompted him to cooperate with one of his men when they arrived in Mexico City. The apparent plan was to take Fawd's man, who was assigned by Fawd to escort and kill Fielding, and force him to reveal that part of Fawd's plan, which they did." Joshua turned to look at Wolf Shertok. "Your man worked him over with a blow torch, and when that didn't work, he was soaked down with gasoline—"

"I'm not interested in horror stories," Shertok told him.

"Neither was Fielding," Joshua went on, "and that little exercise made up his mind for good. At any rate, once they got Fawd's man to spill his guts, the rest was a snap for your agent. They stripped Fawd's man of his escape papers, the phoney passport, and so on, then planted his body in the fake auto accident after your man killed him. It was in the confusion of wrecking the automobile, which took place late at night, that Fielding took his chance to escape. With Fielding gone, and on your orders, your man simply carried out the rest of the plan, flying on to Israel under the passport originally supplied by Fawd. The Mexican authorities routinely notified Fawd, using the papers found in the wrecked car. Fawd just as routinely had the body cremated, thinking it was Fielding."

"If that were true," said Shertok accusingly, "then Fawd would've known something was wrong when his man failed to show after passing through Israel."

"Not at all a problem," Joshua suggested. "The fact that his man failed to report at whatever his assigned destination was after landing at Tel Aviv was of little or no consequence to Fawd. Lower echelon Arab agents are picked up in Israel every day, without fanfare, as you are very well aware, Professor, which is precisely why it didn't matter to you either. Or, the man could simply have defected. It wouldn't have mattered to Fawd, anyway, since the critical part of his plan had gone off perfectly."

There was a following silence, broken finally by Les Stalmeyer, "Where is the plutonium, Professor?"

"I don't know what you're talking about," Shertok said bluntly. "I have enough of a legal background to know you have absolutely nothing against me, aside from the word of another man, an admitted thief. It takes two, remember."

Joshua Bain pushed to his feet to glare down at Wolf Shertok. "You're not only without a conscience; you've lost your soul as well. Like right now, at this moment, I can see this whole tragic mess reduced down to just Wolf Shertok versus Fawd Al-Shaer. Just the two of you. You were really the ones in control. You've been the big decision makers, the prime movers. And for how long? Half your lives? You've been at each other's throats. While the rest of us, we're just along for the ride, trying our best to survive your escapades. When one of us expires, like Ben Caplan, just order up a replacement. Right, old man?"

"You don't understand."

"You'd better believe I don't understand!"

"We're in a war, remember."

"Nuts!" Joshua snapped. "Ben Caplan was a real soldier, one who could justify himself right up to the very end. You and men like Fawd, on the other hand, use the cause to cover your own private little hate campaign."

"Easy talk for an assimilationist," said Shertok.

Joshua shook his head wearily, before replying slowly, "Address that kind of criticism to Moses, who started out as the greatest assimilationist of them all—"

"That borders on blasphemy—"

"Words wisely spoken," Joshua seemed to concede before adding, "from the mouth of one expert in blasphemy. Your hate runs deep enough to include God—"

"Now look, you two," Stalmeyer interjected.

Joshua waved him aside, continuing to glare at Shertok. "Stay out of this," he warned Stalmeyer. "This is between us two, a pair of Jews whose credentials are up for grabs—"

"Speak for yourself," growled Shertok.

"Gladly," said Joshua. "Ever since you were notified that Fielding had escaped, you've been after him to shut him up, which, to you, meant killing him, and, at any cost. You convicted yourself on this point when you had Ben Caplan murdered—"

"You have no right," Shertok exclaimed, and he came to his feet.

"I have every right!" Joshua exploded. "Not only did you kill Ben, but you also threw in the life of one of your own people. I remind you that the present scoreboard against the Jews reads the Arabs zero, Shertok two! And don't jazz me about one man's word against another," Joshua went on witheringly. "One of the ambush team survived, maybe more, and at least he is still alive and around to talk, which he'll gladly do when he discovers he helped to kill one of his own." Joshua looked aside then. "The irony of Ben's death is that we avoided telling you the truth about the Fielding meeting simply as a matter of procedure," and he looked searchingly into the eyes of Wolf Shertok. "In other words, Professor, you blew Ben up because he went by the book. How does that grab you, old man?"

Shertok looked away.

"Look at me, old man!" Joshua raged then, and he bent forward to deliberately spit on the deck next to Shertok's feet. "I remember the time I first met you, and your very words, that Fawd Al-Shaer was a beast diseased with hate, a ruthless killer. How are you any different?" Joshua felt his self-control slipping away, but he didn't care anymore. There was a metal chair between him and the Professor; Joshua kicked it aside, taking a threatening step closer to the old man.

"That's enough," Stalmeyer said, and he came to his feet.

"No it isn't," Joshua snapped. "As soon as I can I'm boarding a plane for Tel Aviv, where immediately upon my arrival I'm going to hold a press conference. Fielding's statement is the first item I'll make public, along with whatever else

I can turn up. I'm sure Israeli intelligence will be interested in the ambush team you sicced on Ben Caplan. I've a hunch the ambush team was the original kidnap squad you put together to take Fawd prior to the MUF. I'm also sure Tel Aviv will still have your original inquiry on file regarding the plutonium. Along with a record of the funds you've expended recently. Then there's the private detective you hired to follow the Fielding family. Plus, your agent who passed through Tel Aviv, if you haven't already disposed of him too."

Wolf Shertok was standing stock still, slowly shaking his head no.

"Ha Mossad will give me another Ben Caplan," Joshua went on. "Maybe a couple of Ben Caplans, because they are justifiably fussy about their own dirty laundry, and together we'll nail you. Do you fully understand, Shertok, that we're going to get you, no matter how long it takes?"

Shertok was now looking out over the swimming pool, on to a distant point along the ocean's darkening horizon. "I will admit to nothing," he said slowly then. "I can only say that Stanley Fielding called me and asked for help."

"When?" demanded Joshua.

"A couple of days ago. Wednesday, I think."

"You're lying," Joshua insisted. "He was on the open sea and had been for nearly a week."

Shertok continued to stare out into nothingness, refusing to look at either of them. "Regardless, the man said he was Stanley Fielding and that he knew where a certain shipment of nuclear material was hidden, probably stolen," he said. "I intended to report the call, but I haven't had the chance to check it out yet."

Joshua drew a disbelieving breath through his nose.

"Go on," Stalmeyer said gently.

"I have the address written down inside," said Shertok. "It's in the den safe." He turned toward the house. "If you'll please excuse me, I'll get it for you."

Joshua started to follow, but Stalmeyer held him back.

"We've got what we came for," Stalmeyer said quietly.

Joshua Bain watched suspiciously as the preoccupied Wolf Shertok moved across the patio toward an open sliding glass door. "Do you really think he's going to give it to you? It's direct evidence to convict him of a dozen crimes."

Stalmeyer followed his line of sight.

Shertok moved sideways through the door, then turning,

he pulled the door closed. Without looking up, he threw the lock closed.

"You just might be right," Stalmeyer exclaimed under his breath, and he broke away, striding out toward the hallway door.

Joshua turned to stare out across the black surface of the ocean, knowing that Wolf Shertok had no place to go now, and that he probably had locked the door out of habit, security conscious to the end.

Feeling let down, he finally thought after a moment that none of it was really worth it—a running, continuing waste. Men like Fawd Al-Shaer and Wolf Shertok left nothing in their wake but destruction and grief and there was no way to reach them, ultimately, except to deal with them on their own terms.

And, what justice was there now for Benjamin Caplan, the gentle yet strong right hand?

He shut his eyes, trying to close off the tears . . .

Barrump!

Joshua flinched.

A muffled pistol shot, flat and heavy—fired inside, behind a closed door.

Joshua reached inside his right trouser pocket, palming the Viper into his hand.

Deal with them on their own terms—

He reached the den via the connecting hallway, turning cautiously into the room. The Viper was in his right hand. Les Stalmeyer was standing near the center of the small room, looking down at the body of Wolf Shertok. Joshua replaced the Viper in its holster as he stared impassively at the remains of the man thought by many to be a giant, perhaps a deserved position in the beginning, in time past.

Joshua looked up to see an open wall safe as Stalmeyer turned to face him.

"The pistol was in the safe," Stalmeyer said slowly. "He just put the barrel in his mouth." He raised his hands in a gesture of bewilderment.

"Will you take care of it?" Joshua asked, his voice without feeling as he turned toward the door.

"Yes, I'll take care of it. Why, where are you going?"

"I don't know."

A few seconds later, he passed listlessly through the front door. It was fully dark outside now as he walked slowly along the driveway, trying to measure his feelings. He found himself drained empty inside; there was no more disappointment, to be sure, but no triumph either, just a void . . . and he realized the special irony of suicide, for it was at once both the most difficult and yet the simplest of all ways out.

Ockham's razor, applied arterially.

A great sorrow pushed into the void. And he felt his breath choking in his throat. *Oh, God!* he implored then, *when will it ever end?*

Joshua pulled up on the driveway apron coming off the street. Still unable to compose himself, he stood still for a while before moving on toward the waiting sedan parked down the curb. He could only resolve one fact for sure, that he was no longer the same man he had been just a week ago. While he could not break out and identify them, there were the deeper feelings now tugging at him, perhaps a new consciousness, which in time he would come to understand.

Behind him, two brick pilasters straddled the entrance to the driveway, and each one was capped with a brass plate facing the street. The nearer plate, to his right, was engraved with the six-pointed Star of David. He turned to pass the opposite one, and he once again came to a standstill as he strained in the poor light to make out the single inscribed word, which finally came into focus: *Shalom.*

Joshua Bain stared at the raised burnished letters, thinking that they formed a truly beautiful and eloquent word, one whose sound even suggested a sublimity of expression. Yet, it was in fact only a work of art in sound and appearance, for it actually was otherwise meaningless to the people who had created it, a people who had never known peace.

It was not a word to be—

It was a crying out, a plea.

The brass plaque stood like a grave marker.

An ironic post mortem for one Wolf Shertok, who two thousand years ago might have been a high priest of a similar kind and who also might have had the same bronze plate on the gate to his garden.

Moving away, Joshua sensed a new curiosity. There was simply the why of it all. *Shalom.* . . . Such a popular word used so often by so many. *Shalom.* Like the cipher zero, meaning nothing by itself, empty and passive, yet still flagged as a national standard.

A cover perhaps, but for what?

Shalom.

Only a dream.

Why?